## "FAST CARS AND FAST WOMEN. THAT YOUR SPEED?"

"Throw in buckin' broncs and bulls, and you pretty well sum up my lifestyle until a few months ago," Maverick admitted. "What about you?"

"Evidently at one time I liked a fast cowboy, didn't I?" Bridget sassed.

"Being a mother doesn't have to mean you give up your whole personality. It should just mean that you put your child first and the good times second."

"Does being a father mean the same thing?" she asked.

"Yes, ma'am, it does." He pointed over toward the baby. "Can I read her the bedtime story tonight?"

"Sure," she said.

Bridget plopped down on the sofa and listened while Maverick did the voices of the animals in the book. There was something so sweet about seeing a big, old rough cowboy with a baby in his arms, taking time after reading each page to point out the animals and other items in the book. It was like there were two Maverick Callahans. One was that wild, carefree man she'd met in Ireland, and the other was a kind, gentle soul.

But which one was the real Maverick?

# High Praise for Carolyn Brown

"Sizzling romance between believable characters is the mainstay of this whimsical novel, which is enhanced by plenty of romantic yearning."

—*Publishers Weekly*

## COWBOY HONOR

"The slow-simmering romance between Claire and Levi is enhanced by the kind supporting characters and the simple pleasures of ranch life in a story that's sure to please fans of cowboy romances."

—*Publishers Weekly*

"Friendship, family, love, and trust abound in *Cowboy Honor*."

—Fresh Fiction

## COWBOY BOLD

"Lighthearted banter, heart-tugging emotion, and a good-natured Sooner/Longhorn football rivalry make this a delightful romance and terrific launch for the new series."

—*Library Journal*

"*Cowboy Bold* is the start of a new and amazing series by an author that really knows how to hook her readers with sexy cowboys, strong women, and a bunch of humor...Everything about this book is a roaring good time."

—Harlequin Junkie, Top Pick

"Everything you could ever ask for in a cowboy romance."

—The Genre Minx

# Christmas with a Cowboy

# Also by Carolyn Brown

## *The Longhorn Canyon Series*

*Cowboy Bold*
*Cowboy Honor*
*Cowboy Brave*
*Cowboy Rebel*

## *The Happy, Texas Series*

*Toughest Cowboy in Texas*
*Long, Tall Cowboy Christmas*
*Luckiest Cowboy of All*

## *The Lucky Penny Ranch Series*

*Wild Cowboy Ways*
*Hot Cowboy Nights*
*Merry Cowboy Christmas*
*Wicked Cowboy Charm*

# *Christmas with a Cowboy*

## A Longhorn Canyon Novel

## Carolyn Brown

**FOREVER**

New York   Boston

Copyright © 2019 by Carolyn Brown
*Rocky Mountain Cowboy Christmas* copyright © 2018 by Sara Richardson

Cover photography by Rob Lang. Cover design by Elizabeth Turner Stokes.
Cover copyright © 2019 by Hachette Book Group, Inc.

Forever
Hachette Book Group
1290 Avenue of the Americas, New York, NY 10104
read-forever.com
twitter.com/readforeverpub

First Edition: September 2019

Forever is an imprint of Grand Central Publishing. The Forever name and logo are trademarks of Hachette Book Group, Inc.

The publisher is not responsible for websites (or their content) that are not owned by the publisher.

The Hachette Speakers Bureau provides a wide range of authors for speaking events. To find out more, go to www.hachettespeakersbureau.com or call (866) 376-6591.

ISBNs: 978-1-5387-4874-9 (mass market), 978-1-5387-4872-5 (ebook)

Printed in the United States of America

OPM

10 9 8 7 6 5 4 3 2 1

*In memory of my Irish ancestors,*
*Especially Martha Cummins, my*
*great-great-great-great-great-grandmother.*
*We tie her wedding ring into the girls'*
*bouquets in our family for something old.*

Dear Readers,

Mama told me that I came from Irish ancestors and that my great-great-great-great-great-grandmother, Miz Martha Cummins, came over to the United States from Ireland. Mama kept Grandma Martha's wedding ring in her little cedar jewelry box, and it's been passed down to me. It's nothing fancy, just a little band that her groom made for her out of a nickel, but in our family we tie it into the girls' wedding bouquets for their "something old."

According to my DNA test, Mama was right, so it was a real treat to get to know Bridget, since she comes from County Cork, Ireland. Of course, Maverick has Irish ancestors too, so that made it doubly fun to write. I fell in love with Maverick in *Cowboy Rebel*, and throwing him into a situation with Bridget was so much fun. Hopefully all of you will enjoy reading it as much as I did writing it—there's always a little magic in the air when I'm writing a Christmas book.

Like always it takes a team to pull a book together from one of my ideas, and I've got an amazing one at Grand Central. I couldn't ask for a better editor than Leah Hultenschmidt. She's walked through muddy waters with me on several books, helping me get the tone and emotions just right from the time we go brainstorming to finished product. I owe her big Texas-size hugs for that right along with the rest of my team: Estelle and Monisha in marketing, Elizabeth for my gorgeous covers, Raylan and Bob and Gina in sales, Melanie and Luria in production, and Cristina to help keep everything on the rails. Y'all are all fantabulous (I know that's a word because spell check didn't try to turn it into something else), and I appreciate each and every one of you!

Thank you to my agent, Erin Niumata, and my agency, Folio Management, for everything they do for me. My undying gratitude to my husband, Mr. B, who is simply the best. And huge thanks to all my readers for all the times they've told a neighbor or a friend about one of my books, written a review, or sent me a note of encouragement. I love you all!

You'll be reading this book in the fall and winter, so grab a cup of hot chocolate and one of Granny's quilts. Snuggle up and enjoy the story!

Until next time,
*Carolyn Brown*

# Christmas with a Cowboy

# Chapter One

The minute Maverick Callahan pushed through the door of the pub in Ireland he zeroed in on a tall blonde playing darts. He threw a little extra swagger in his step as he walked past her and settled onto a barstool. When he caught her eye, he tipped his hat toward her and then removed it, laid it on the bar's polished wooden surface, and raked his fingers through his dark hair. When she finished her game, he'd ask her to dance.

"Jameson or Guinness?"

His focus shifted from the blond woman to the bartender, a redhead with a voice like honey. "I was thinking more of a shot of Jack Daniel's."

"You're in an Irish pub, not a honky-tonk, cowboy," she said with a sparkle in her green eyes.

Oh man, he'd always had a weakness for redheads. "Well, then I guess you'd better give me a pint of what you suggested since y'all ain't got good Tennessee whiskey."

"Ooooh, now those are fightin' words." She did a cute little head shake, and the dim light above the bar caught the sparkles of Christmas tree earrings. "And speaking of fightin' words, Denise McKay's husband will have a few if he sees you eyein' his wife like that." She nodded toward the tall blonde playing darts.

"Why are you telling me this?" He almost reached out to touch the tiny shamrock topping the tree on her earrings.

"Just trying to help you keep out of trouble," she answered. "Something tells me you have a way of findin' it pretty fast."

With a toss of her hair, she went to the other end of the bar to draw the beer up in a tall mug. He glanced around the place. Some of it was the same as the Rusty Spur honky-tonk in his home state of Texas—stools in front of a long bar, mirror behind the bar with shelves of liquor, beer mugs and shot glasses at the ready. But where the places in Texas had signed pictures of bull and bronc riders on the walls, along with old beer signs, the Shamrock Pub had dartboards and pictures of the rolling hills of Ireland hanging on the walls.

The cute little bartender set a pint of foaming Guinness on the bar in front of him. "Where'd you come from, cowboy?"

"Texas, darlin'," he said. "What's your name?"

"Bridget." She smiled.

"Bridget what?"

"Just Bridget, cowboy," she said. "What's your name?"

"Maverick," he answered.

"Maverick what?"

"Just Maverick." He gave her a dose of her own medicine.

"Well, then, just Maverick, welcome to Ireland. What

brings you to our little town of Skibbereen?" She tucked a strand of red hair into her ponytail.

"My grandmother wanted to visit an old friend, and I didn't want her to travel alone. Plus, it gave me a chance to visit some distant cousins I've always heard about but never met," he answered. "It's been such a great trip, I'll be sad to leave tomorrow." What Maverick didn't tell her was that nothing he'd seen yet compared to the sight of her. Whether she was laughing with another customer, pulling a pint, or wiping down the bar—he was hyperaware of her every move, inexplicably drawn to her smile and sparkling eyes.

And she didn't exactly seem immune to his charm. Every time she caught a break, she was down at his end of the bar, chatting about anything and everything until he suddenly realized it was closing time.

As Maverick shrugged into his coat, he gave one last longing look at Bridget on the other side of the bar. Had he been home, he would've asked her out in a heartbeat. But he could tell Bridget wasn't exactly a one-night-stand kind of woman. And he'd be leaving in the morning. Reluctantly, he turned and strode out the door to make the cold, lonely walk back to his hotel.

The whole scene was surreal that night. Holiday decorations threw multicolored lights everywhere he looked. He stopped to stare at a huge Christmas tree that had been set up in the middle of the main street. It reminded him of those earrings Bridget was wearing and that his grandmother would be fussing at him and his brother, Paxton, to help her get her tree up as soon as they got home. A few snowflakes drifted from the skies and frosted the pine branches. He looked up, and sure enough right there on the top of the tree was a shamrock ornament.

"Skibbereen goes all out for Christmas." He knew her voice within a split second. He whipped around, and there was Bridget. Her red hair was now covered with a dark green cap, and she was bundled up in a black coat. She barely came up to his shoulder, and her hands were shoved down into her pockets.

"I feel like I'm in a Hallmark movie," he joked. "But it's so beautiful and peaceful."

"I just love Christmas," Bridget said. "We hardly ever get snow, though. So it's a special night indeed." Her eyes were shining as she tilted her head to look up to him. "There are some moments you just never forget."

It took all the willpower he possessed not to cup her face and kiss her right there in the softly falling snow. "Can I see you home safely?" he asked.

"Oh, that's all right. I'm just across the street here." She gestured down the road.

"Well, what a coincidence. That's my hotel there." He nodded toward where she'd pointed. "They usually have tea or coffee twenty-four hours a day if you want to join me for a cup in the lobby."

"I usually do have a cuppa to wind down before bed," she said. "Sure, I'd be happy to join you."

Maverick held out his arm to her, relishing the feeling of her sliding close to his body as they crossed the street together and entered the hotel.

With their steaming beverages, they sat down on either end of the worn sofa in the lobby and talked until the sun peeked through the windows, its rays making the snow coating the trees and grass shine like diamonds.

"I've got scones, jam, and a coffeepot in my flat next door. Would you be hungry?" she asked.

"Starving." He smiled.

* * *

Bridget might not have known Maverick long, but she felt like she already knew him well. He loved his family, especially his grandmother. He loved the land and described Texas with such great detail, it seemed like she'd taken a trip there herself. He took his coffee black and his bacon almost burned. In her heart, she knew he could be trusted, and sweet Jesus, he was a sexy cowboy. What would it hurt to spend a little more time with him? He'd said he would be leaving that afternoon to catch a plane back to Texas with his grandmother. Besides, she liked to listen to his deep southern drawl.

She led the way up the stairs of her building to the second floor and went to room 212. She tried not to fumble with her key as she unlocked the door. It's just breakfast, she reminded herself.

As soon as they entered her flat, it felt like Maverick's big frame took up the whole kitchen. She immediately busied herself with starting a pot of coffee and tried not to think about how close they were to her bedroom. Thank goodness she'd picked up her laundry and made the bed before her shift at the bar!

As she got out a container of scones she'd made the day before, Maverick plucked two mugs from her little shelf. They didn't even need words—they just moved around each other effortlessly, like they'd been doing the dance their whole lives.

When he reached for the first scone their hands got tangled up together. And after that everything moved in slow motion. Somehow things went from his big hand over her small one, to a kiss, and then more kisses. Then she realized where the make-out session could be headed, and she took two steps back.

"I'm sorry," he said. "I should be going."

"No, please stay." She could feel the blush heating her cheeks. "It's just...I'm not..."

"I know, sweetheart." His eyes were so kind, so understanding. "I get it. I just wish we could have met sooner."

"Me too." Bridget sighed. "Truly, though, please sit and have a scone with me. I'd hate to send you away hungry."

"I'd like that too." Maverick pulled out a chair and sank into it, stretching his longs legs out right as she turned to get more coffee. Next thing she knew, she had tripped over his feet and landed in his lap. His arms instinctively drew her close to steady her. When she got her bearings and looked up into his dark green eyes, she didn't even fight the pesky voice in her head telling her another kiss was a bad idea. She just put a hand on each side of his face and drew his lips down to hers.

Several hours later, Bridget awoke to find Maverick propped up on an elbow beside her, smiling into her eyes. She was glad that the sheet covered her because she was more than a little embarrassed. She'd never had a one-night stand—or, in this case a one-morning stand—in her life. What happened now?

Maverick reached out to twirl a bit of her long hair in his fingers. "So soft. Like silk."

Bridget knew she could fall in love with that voice. That she could fall in love with everything he'd made her feel in their short time together. She also knew falling in love with him would be a disaster.

"I have to be going," she said abruptly. "The first bus leaves in fifteen minutes, and Nana will be expecting me for church this morning. God only knows that I'll be needing to send up extra prayers this week."

"Just, Bridget, I will never forget this night." Maverick

rolled over to the other side of the bed. "You're so beautiful there with the sunlight coming through the window to light up your red hair." He snatched up his phone and snapped a quick photo. "You don't mind, do you?" he asked.

"No," she said softly. "I'll never forget you either. But it's best if we just part ways now." She scooted off the edge of the bed and frantically started pulling on any clothes she could find. Why, oh why, hadn't fate given them more time? "We never did get around to scones and jam. I'll just leave them for you. Safe travels back to your Texas."

"Can I get your number?" he asked. "Or email or something?"

"I don't think that's a good idea," she said as she waved goodbye and slipped out the door.

The bus pulled up just as she made it to the stop. She glanced up at her kitchen window, hoping for one last glance of Maverick, but there was no cowboy looking down at the street. While other passengers boarded, Bridget stared at the big Christmas tree. This was the season of magic and miracles. She'd just spent a magical night, and she decided that she wasn't going to let guilt cloud her memory. She thought about Maverick all the way to her nana's house. But as soon as she walked in the door, there was no more time for daydreaming. Nana immediately started fussing that they'd be late if she didn't hurry.

"My friend Iris just left. I was so hoping you'd be home in time to meet her," Nana said.

"Sorry," Bridget said. "The bus was a little late." As her grandmother finished gathering her things for church, Bridget took a deep breath. She swore she could still smell Maverick's shaving lotion in her hair. She wondered how long it might take to fade. And she wondered how long it would take the memories of their very special night together to fade too.

# Chapter Two

*One Year Later*

Maverick sang a whole string of Christmas songs along with the radio's country music station as he drove past the exit to Tulia, Texas, and kept driving north, past Happy and Amarillo, until he hit the exit to Daisy. For the first time in six months, he was going home.

He was singing "Jingle Bells" as he drove down Main Street and waved at the folks he knew. The fire trucks were putting up decorations on all the light poles down Main Street, and the store windows were decorated. Just when he thought things couldn't get any better, it started to snow. Now that was setting the scene right for him to be home for the holidays.

The next song was "Christmas Cookies." Maverick wiggled his shoulders and kept time with his thumbs on the steering wheel as he headed east toward his grandmother's ranch. The lyrics talked about eating Christmas cookies all year long because it took fifteen minutes for them to cook, and that left time for kissin' and huggin'. Maverick loved the Christmas holiday, almost as much as he liked the kissin' and huggin' business.

"Well, maybe it's a toss-up." He remembered where he'd been last year at this time. Anytime he saw a red-haired woman who came up to just his shoulder, he thought of Bridget and wondered where they might be if fate had put them together earlier. "Don't get all melancholy wantin' for something that you weren't meant to have," he told himself and turned up the radio when Blake Shelton started singing "I'll be Home for Christmas."

He swayed from side to side as he made a turn into the lane leading up to Granny's house, and picked up where Blake left off as he parked the truck in the yard and hurried inside the house.

"Is that you, Mav?" his grandmother yelled from the living room.

"It's me, Mam," he called back. "I mean Granny." When he and Paxton had been little kids they'd called her Mam, because when she got bossy with Grandpa, he'd say, "Yes, ma'am." She'd insisted that they call her Granny, but Mam still came out occasionally.

He kept singing and two-stepped with an imaginary partner from the foyer to the living room. "Merry Christmas!" He tossed his cowboy hat up on the steer horns hanging above the fireplace mantel and crossed the room to hug her.

Iris giggled. "Silly boy, it's not Christmas yet. I don't even have my tree up."

"You would have had it up a couple of weeks ago if you hadn't played fast and loose with a pear tree," he said as he removed his coat and tossed it on a recliner. "And now you're laid up with a busted hip."

"No, I'm not," Granny declared. "It's a brand-new hip. My body just has to get used to the damn thing." She pointed a finger at him. "So don't you be givin' me no sass about it. I didn't call on you to come help me for a month or two to listen to you bitch at me."

"Yes, ma'am." He sat down on the other end of the sofa from her. "Now tell me what's going on. When you called yesterday, you just said that Buster had to leave and you needed help. You do know that me or Paxton or even both of us could have come and stayed with you in the hospital."

"I didn't need a babysitter then, and I don't"—she paused—"want one now. But the doctor said if I don't have help in the house, then he'd make me go to a nursing home until I got on my feet again."

"Whatever you need, Granny," Maverick said. "I'm here for you. All you have to do is tell me. Like I was singing, 'I'll be home for Christmas.'"

"Yes, you are," Granny told him. "You've got your old room, but I put my new housekeeper and cook in the guest room. You remember my friend Virgie, who I went to visit last Christmas? You met her that first day before you went off to visit other parts of Ireland."

"Yep." Maverick remembered a short, round lady who'd insisted that he have a snack before he caught a bus up to Skibbereen. She'd had a thick Irish accent, and two long gray braids wrapped around her head.

"Well, she died a couple of weeks ago. When I heard her granddaughter didn't have a home and would be alone for the holidays, I invited her to come here and help me until after the first of the year. I'd hate for Virgie's only living relative to spend Christmas all by herself, without any family.

She arrived three days ago, just when the doctor released me from the hospital," Granny explained. "She's off at the grocery store right now, but she'll be home by the time you get settled in and get the evening chores done."

"I'll bring in my stuff and get right out to the barn. You want or need anything before I go? Coffee, a glass of tea, or a beer, or maybe a little two-steppin' around the livin' room to loosen that new hip up?" Maverick stood and stretched the kinks from a five-hour drive from his neck.

"You just give me time to get off this damned medicine, and I'll drink you under the table, and wear you out on the dance floor." Granny laughed out loud. "Now, get on out of here and get the cows fed."

"Your new housekeeper know anything about cookin'?" He sniffed the air. "Is that a pot roast I smell?"

"She knows enough to keep your body and soul together." Granny picked up her cane and shook it at him. "If you ain't out of this house in ten minutes, I'll use this to get out to my truck and do the chores myself."

"I'm on my way." He grinned and hummed "Jingle Bells" on his way out of the room, singing all the way out to the barn and to the cows as he tossed hay out to them. Being home for Christmas, even under these circumstances, was great. He couldn't wait to see all his old drinking, two-stepping buddies at his favorite honky-tonk next Saturday night.

* * *

Bridget kept glancing at the pictures on the dining room wall of the two cowboys riding bulls as she slid some rolls into the oven. Had she known that Maverick Callahan was Iris's grandson, she would have thought twice before accepting the invitation to come to Texas for the holidays. Thank God Iris told her he was all the way on the other side of the state helping friends get a newer ranch up and running. She wouldn't even have to see him while she was there. She wasn't sure her heart would recover if she had to say goodbye again.

She was on her way to the living room to check on Iris when the back door opened and brought a gust of cold wind across the kitchen. A voice that she thought she'd never hear again, and one that she couldn't forget, was singing something about rockin' around a Christmas tree. She froze right there in the middle of the kitchen floor—he wasn't supposed to be there. Her heart fluttered and then raced ahead with a full head of steam. Maverick was there—right there in front of her—and all the memories of that night flooded back to her mind.

Maverick stopped in the doorway, blinked several times.

"Bridget?" he said.

"Maverick." She breathed. "I had no idea you were going to be here."

His long strides had him across the room in a heartbeat. But as much as she longed to sink in his open arms, Bridget extended her palm in a "stop" gesture. His chest hit her hand and she almost groaned aloud at the solid muscle she could feel even through his coat.

"What are you doing here? It's so good to—" he started.

"We can't do this," she cut in. "Things have changed."

"Are you"—he grabbed her hand and held it—"Granny's helper? Was it your grandmother she was staying with in Ireland?"

She jerked her hand free. "Small world after all, isn't it? But things aren't the same as they were a year ago."

His expression changed as he processed what she was

saying. "Are you engaged or…" He shook his head. "No, Granny said that you were all alone?"

"Not really alone," she hedged.

Lord have mercy! She glanced down at her hand, hot from the heat that fired it up when she touched his chest. She wanted to hug him and tell him how often she'd thought about that night, but he couldn't be burdened with her life— not now, not the way things had turned out. Iris told her that both her grandsons were on the wild side. They liked to work hard all week and party on the weekends. Bridget had different priorities now. She couldn't start something with Maverick that had no future.

* * *

Maverick was totally confused. If Bridget was alone in the world, why was she so standoffish, and what had changed so much in only a year? He certainly hadn't turned into a different person.

A noise across the foyer and down the hallway caught his attention. Was that a baby crying out?

"Laela is awake," Bridget muttered and brushed past him on her way out of the kitchen.

Maverick trailed along behind her. When he got to the room, he was stunned to see a baby girl sitting up in a crib. She had dark hair and big green eyes exactly like his, and she was staring right into his face. She cocked her head to one side and then the other and then stuck out her lower lip and began to whimper.

"It's all right, lassie," Bridget crooned as she took her out of the crib. "I'd like you to meet Maverick. He'd be Miz Iris's grandson. He'll be here for a while, and you'll be get- tin' to know him better in a few days."

Maverick looked from Bridget to the baby and back again. He felt like his veins were filled with ice water. Was that his baby? It couldn't be, or could it? Even though they'd used protection, it wasn't always foolproof. If this little girl was a Callahan, he'd do right by the child for sure, but so many questions swirled through his mind that he couldn't catch one of them to find answers to. "Why didn't you find a way to tell me about her?"

"Oh!" Bridget suddenly realized what he was thinking. "She's not yours, or for that matter even mine, biologically. Remember the dark-haired bartender who worked with me at the pub?"

Maverick's heart slowed down a little. "Just barely." He kept staring at the baby, who had his eyes.

"Laela is her daughter. She and her boyfriend were killed in an automobile accident when the baby was only a few weeks old. I'm her godmother, so she became mine."

"Wow," he muttered, still in shock.

"Believe me, I didn't have any idea that my nana's best friend was your grandmother, not until I saw your picture on the mantel the morning after I arrived. I lost my nana, and Iris offered me this job for a few weeks." Bridget headed for the kitchen with Laela on her hip.

"Hey," Iris called from the living room. "I see you two have met. Is supper about ready?"

"Yes, in about five minutes," Bridget called out and then turned back to whisper to him, "I didn't tell her that I knew you from last year. I didn't figure I'd ever see you again, not even here. After all, Texas is a pretty big place."

"We'll talk later about all this," Maverick said and turned to go into the living room. "I'll come help you, Granny."

"So what do you think of Bridget?" Iris managed to get to her feet on her own and get a handle on her walker.

"She seems like she knows how to cook, but a baby in the house?" He frowned.

"Laela is delightful." Iris pushed her walker out into the foyer. "Too bad you and Paxton haven't given me great-grandchildren."

"Granny, we've talked about this." He helped guide the walker around the corner of the door. "When Paxton and I get ready, we'll settle down."

"Yeah, right, but the question is, will I still be alive to hold my great-grands?" Iris fussed.

"Of course, you will," Maverick assured her. "You'll still be drinkin' me under the table and two-steppin' when you're a hundred."

"Bullshit!" Iris said as she eased down into a kitchen chair.

Maverick continued to think about Bridget—how could he not, when she was right there in front of him all through supper—and their night together. Sometimes he doubted that it had ever happened. If it hadn't been for the picture on his phone, he would have thought that he had dreamt that amazing night not long before Christmas in Ireland the previous year. Holy smokin' hell! She'd sure enough been right when she said that things had changed. She'd lost her best friend in a car accident and then her grandmother and become an instant mother all in one year. He couldn't imagine having to go through all that in only twelve months.

His grandmother and Bridget kept up a lively conversation all during the meal about Bridget's grandmother, Virgie, and Ireland. Maverick could have sat there all evening just listening to the Irish lilt to Bridget's voice, but when supper was over Iris needed his help to maneuver her walker back to the living room.

"You didn't talk much," Iris said when she was sitting in

her recliner. "You don't like Bridget and the baby stealing your time with me?"

"No, it was just a surprise," Maverick answered.

"You'll get used to having them around. Now go on in there and help her with the cleanup," Iris said. "The quicker you get it done, the quicker I can watch the baby play. She makes me happy, and laughter will make me heal faster."

Shaking his head, Maverick started back to the kitchen but stopped in the foyer. He slapped his palm against his forehead. Now that the shock had worn off, he realized that he would be spending the better part of a month in the same house with Bridget. If that one night was any indication of what a relationship with her would be like, then he had a second chance. He'd weigh the pros and cons of a second chance later.

He stepped into the kitchen, picked up the two toys that Laela had thrown on the floor, and put them back on the high chair tray. "Bridget, I'm real sorry that you lost your friend and your grandmother both in such a short time." He took a deep breath before continuing. "I can't begin to imagine losing Granny and Paxton."

"Paxton is your brother," she said.

"Yes, but he's also my best friend." Maverick rolled up the sleeves of his chambray work shirt, and picked up a towel to dry the pots and pans as she got them washed.

"I wish Iris would have told me that you were coming." Bridget handed him the lid to the roasting pan. "I might have been a little more braced for the shock."

"It would have been nice if she'd told me that she'd hired you. I thought she was using home health care."

"Well, what now?" Bridget said. "Like I said before I'm not the same girl I was back then."

"Did you ever think about me?" he asked.

"Of course I did." She frowned. "I wished that I'd gotten your full name, maybe a phone number, or an address, but then I'd remind myself that would have been silly. Our paths would never cross again, and the chances that I'd be in Texas were slim to none and you'd probably never be back in Ireland."

"Same here." He leaned against the cabinet and locked eyes with her. His way. "But here we are, so what now? I still see that sassy, beautiful bartender when I look at you."

She picked Laela up from the high chair. "And I still see the sexiest cowboy in the world, but that don't mean much, since we were only those two people for one night."

"I guess we've got a month to figure out just who we are now." Maverick grinned.

* * *

Bridget fell backward on the bed and covered her eyes with her hand. There was something magical in that night last year. No one had ever made her feel like she had in his arms. She'd tried to convince herself that she was just one in a long line of women that he'd had a one-night stand with, but she still couldn't get him out of her mind.

Laela's whimpers brought her back to reality. Bridget jumped up so fast she got a head rush, before she realized the baby was just fussing in her sleep.

"Bridget, darlin', could you come here?" Iris's voice came down the hallway from the living room.

Bridget hurried out of the room and bumped right into Maverick.

"I'm so sorry," she stammered, "I didn't know you were in the hall, and she called for me."

"I just heard her say something," Maverick said and

then raised his voice and said, "We're on the way, Granny."

"Shhh..." Bridget frowned. "I just got Laela to sleep."

"Yes, ma'am." Maverick stepped aside to let her go first.

Bridget hustled up the hallway, across the foyer, and into the living room, with Maverick right behind her.

"Why are you here?" Iris looked up at Maverick. "I called for Bridget."

"I didn't hear a name," Maverick said. "So we're both here. What can we do for you?"

"I'm tired." Iris grimaced when she got to her feet. "I'm going to bed early, and I need Bridget to bring a bottle of water and maybe some cookies to my bedside table."

"Let me help you." Maverick held the walker steady.

She slapped his hands. "I have to do a few things for myself. I'm just not able to push this damned walker and carry water at the same time."

"They sure didn't take out any of your bossiness with that old broken hip, did they?" Maverick asked.

"I'm not bossy," Iris argued.

"The day you stop being bossy is the day that St. Peter calls you home." Maverick chuckled.

She shot a dirty look his way and then smiled. "I have to be bossy with wild grandsons like the good Lord gave me. But now, I can rest easy and heal now that you're here. Bridget and I could've run this place and just been fine if Buster hadn't had to take a couple of months off."

"Or if you hadn't taken it upon yourself to climb up in that pear tree." Maverick fussed at her. "What were you thinkin'? And why didn't you let me and Pax know about your accident until you'd already had the surgery and come home?"

Iris crossed her arms over her chest. "Stop fussin' at me.

I'm not helpless. I'm just laid up for a few weeks until this damned hip heals. And when it does, I'll kick you all the way back to Sunset with it."

"That's my granny." He chuckled. "Full of spit and vinegar."

Bridget giggled. "You remind me so much of my nana."

"Virgie and I grew up together." Iris's face registered pain with every step. "It's only natural that we'd be alike in our old age."

"Old, my Irish arse," Bridget said. "Nana didn't go down without a fight, and neither will you."

"Amen to that." Maverick winked at Bridget. "Since you two ladies have everything under control, I'm going back to my room."

Bridget got a bottle of water from the refrigerator and then arranged several cookies on a plate. By the time she got down the hall and into Iris's room, Iris was unsnapping her cotton duster.

"I hate these damn things. I want to get better so I can wear my jeans and shirts. Damned old nightgowns and robes are for old people in nursing homes, not for ranchin' women," she fussed.

"It'll only be for a few weeks. We get the staples out Monday, and then it'll all be downhill healin' after that," Bridget assured her.

"I hope so, darlin' girl." Iris threw the robe over the handles of her walker, and slowly turned around.

Bridget set the water and cookies on the nightstand, and then flipped the covers back before Iris could ease down on the bed. Taking care of Iris wasn't so different from what she'd done with her nana the last several days of her life. It had to be frustrating to be active and then boom, be an invalid.

"What'd you think of Mav?" Iris asked as she got her legs swung up onto the bed.

"He's even more handsome than his photograph." Bridget pulled the covers over Iris.

*And just as sexy as he was in Ireland*, she thought.

"Going to have trouble living in the same house with him?" Iris pressed.

"Of course not," Bridget answered.

*And that's a lie*, the pesky voice in her head said. Just a simple wink sent your heart into flutters.

"Good," Iris said as she picked up the remote and turned on the television in her room. "I wish me and Virgie had introduced you two while we were in Ireland, but you were off on a holiday for the first bit we were there, and then Mav was exploring the country. We often talked on the phone about how y'all would have gotten along if you'd ever met. Her granddaughter and my grandson—oh, well, it is what it is—and we can't change the past. Good night, Bridget, and thank you for everything you do."

"My pleasure, ma'am." Bridget headed for the door. "Thanks should be to you for giving me a job and takin' me and the baby in for the holidays. Sleep tight."

Iris picked up another remote and raised the head of her bed. "Buyin' this bed must've been an omen. It sure comes in handy now."

"Yes, ma'am." Bridget eased the door shut behind her, checked on Laela, and went to the living room to tidy up a bit before she went to bed.

"This is just another change in the past year of my topsy-turvy life," she muttered as she fluffed pillows and folded the quilt Iris used through the day.

A little burst of heat shot through her insides as she thought of the night she'd spent with Maverick. The very next day

Deidre had found out that the baby she was carrying would be a girl. She'd already picked out a name and asked Bridget if she'd be Laela's godmother when she was born. Of course she would. Bridget figured her biggest duties would be birthday parties, christenings, and the other events in Laela's life.

Bridget had been there when the baby was born. Other than Laela's parents, Deidre and Jimmy, Bridget had held her first and lost her heart and soul to the baby right then and there.

"I got me a first-rate set of settlin' down and baby fever," she said as she carried a couple of empty water bottles to the kitchen.

The memories kept coming as she made herself a cup of tea and sat down at the table. Bridget was babysitting her two-month-old goddaughter when she got the news that Deidre and Jimmy had both been killed in an automobile accident. Both of them had been raised in foster care and had no living family, so Bridget became an instant mother.

"Thank God for Nana," Bridget muttered.

Virgie O'Malley had insisted that she could take care of the baby while Bridget worked, and had even gotten her a job in a bakery right there in Skibbereen so she could be home at night. Bridget hated the work and missed the pub, but she didn't have a choice in what she did, now that she had Laela.

A teardrop fell from her cheek into her cup of tea. What she really missed was being around all her friends who frequented the pub and Deidre, who usually worked with her. She still missed that life, and she'd never have it again.

The next memory that popped up was when Nana told her that the doctor said she had only six weeks, at the most, to live. Bridget had thought then, just like she did that evening, sitting in a kitchen thousands of miles from

Skibbereen, that her world had turned completely upside down. Her nana was her stability. She'd lived with her since before she was even in school. How could she go on without Nana? Bridget remembered that feeling of total helplessness as she watched Nana's health get worse and worse. There was absolutely nothing, not one bloody thing that she could do, other than make her nana comfortable.

When Nana couldn't care for Laela anymore, and needed help doing even the little things, Bridget quit her job and used up the last of her savings for doctor bills, food, rent, and finally for a funeral. Two weeks later, the food was getting low, and the rent was coming due, and that's the day that Iris called with her offer. It seemed like a godsend.

She laid her head on the table and let fresh tears flow freely for Deidre, Jimmy, and her nana.

* * *

Maverick figured that the scratching noise he heard was Granny's dog, Ducky, and if he didn't let him in, he'd set up a pitiful howl. He pulled on a T-shirt and a pair of pajama pants, tiptoed down the hallway, across the foyer, and opened the door. The short-legged, little mutt of a dog dashed into the house, lost traction when he slid into the kitchen, and hit his hip, but he didn't even yelp.

Maverick followed him and was surprised to find Bridget, her head on the table and sobs wracking her shoulders. He pulled up a chair beside her and sat down. "Are you all right?" he asked.

She shook her head, but didn't look up at him. He grabbed a paper napkin from the holder in the middle of the table, lifted her chin with his hand, and dried the tears. "Can I help?"

"Not unless you can undo the past year." She took the napkin from him and blew her nose. "I'm sorry. I shouldn't be weeping. I should be giving thanks that I have a job and food and a place for me and Laela to live."

He slipped an arm around her shoulders and drew her close to his side. "You probably haven't even had time to mourn your grandmother, and you've been through too much for one year, so if you feel like cryin', just wail away."

"Thank you. Just when I think I'm all done with crying, the slightest little thing will set me off," she told him. "Is that the cat at the back door?"

Maverick could have wrung the cat's neck right then. He liked comforting Bridget and having his arm around her. "I'll let her in," he said.

"Ducky and Dolly"—Bridget carried her cup to the sink and rinsed it before putting it in the dishwasher—"are strange names for a dog and a cat. I've been meaning to ask Iris about that, but keep forgetting."

"Ducky because when he was a pup, he waddled like a duck," Maverick explained, "and Dolly because she sings like Dolly Parton when she's hungry, like right now."

A big yellow cat took her own sweet time in coming inside the house when he opened the door. She went straight to a bottom cabinet door and sat down.

"Yes, Madam Queen," Bridget said as she got out a can of cat foot, pulled the tab to open it, and put it on a plate. "She acts like she owns the place and Ducky is only allowed to visit." She set the cat's plate on the floor and turned to Maverick. "Did she have these animals before you left this ranch to work on another one?"

"Nope." Maverick shook his head. "She got them after Paxton left. She said it was too lonely in this big old house, and she needed something alive and breathing. She only intended to get a dog when she went to the rescue center down in Amarillo. When she saw Dolly, she fell in love with her as well as the short-legged mutt, so she got them both the same day."

Bridget smiled.

Maverick decided that Bridget needed laughter and happiness in her life if she was ever to get over all the sadness. Maybe that was his job—make her forget all the sorrow with fun and laughter.

* * *

Bridget's heart suddenly felt lighter than it had in weeks, and she felt as energized as if she'd just drunk a whole pint of Guinness. "I'm not ready for bed," she said, "so I'm going to make gingerbread. It should age for two to three weeks before Christmas, so this is the perfect time to make it."

"I'll help if you tell me what to do," Maverick offered.

Bridget bit back a giggle. Nana would turn over in her grave for bloody sure if she ever found a man in her kitchen. Bridget had been the only one she'd ever let into the tiny kitchen in their flat in Skibbereen, and even then, she had to do just what Nana said.

"You can get the flour, sugar, and molasses from the pantry," she told him as she got down the biggest mixing bowl she could find in the cabinet.

"What's going on in here?" Iris pushed her walker into the room. "I couldn't sleep. What are you making?"

"Nana's gingerbread," Bridget answered. "It has to sit for a while before it's really good."

"Did we wake you?" Maverick carried the flour and sugar bins from the walk-in pantry.

"No, I never went to sleep. Don't know what I was

thinkin' anyway. I never go to bed before eleven." Iris parked her walker and sat down at the table. "Virgie must've got that recipe from her mother. I remember eating those Christmas ginger squares when we were kids. Haven't had them since I left Ireland."

"Well, Merry Christmas to you, then." Bridget smiled. "We'll have plenty to last all the way until New Year's."

"That depends on whether you hide some of them. Paxton and Maverick each have a sweet tooth that never gets enough." Iris laughed. "Maybe you could make one batch tonight and another in a week."

"That's the only way we'll have them until after Christmas," Maverick agreed.

"Well, gingerbread squares will surely remind me of my Christmases in Skibbereen," Iris said. "Time goes by so fast when you look back on it. Just yesterday, Virgie and I were running over the green fields of Ireland. Leaving your grandmother to come to America was even tougher than telling my parents goodbye, but I loved my Texas cowboy so much that I was willing to do it."

"Was Nana already married when you left?" Bridget stirred the liquid ingredients into the bowl, and added flour. "It's time now to work more flour in with our hands. If you want to help, Maverick, then wash up."

"We got married in a double ceremony. She and her sweet Johnny. Me and my wild Texan," Iris answered. "And, honey, I'm having one of those as soon as they cool and you get the icing on them. They'll be better after a week or two, but tonight they'll take me back to my childhood days when Virgie's mama would let us have one before she stored them away."

"I've heard Nana's story about how she and Grandpa grew up next door to each other, but how did you ever meet a Texan?" Bridget sucked air when Maverick put his big hands into the bowl with hers. His arm on her shoulder had been comforting, but the touch of his fingers when they got tangled with hers sent shivers of desire down to the pit of her stomach.

"He came to Ireland to look at my poppa's cattle. The owner of the ranch where he was foreman sent him. Virgie and I went to a pub for a pint one evening." Iris grinned. "It was not a good first meeting. He and Paddy O'Riley were bowed up at each other like a couple of little fightin' roosters. Since Paddy was Virgie's cousin, we got between them. No, ma'am, it was not love at first sight between me and Thomas Callahan."

"But you worked it out, right?" Bridget said.

"Yes, we did." Iris smiled at the memory. "Johnny—that would be your grandfather—and Thomas became friends. My mother liked him because he had an Irish name. He came from good Irish blood, but he was third-generation Texan, and she didn't like that. She didn't want me to leave Ireland, but I loved my sweet Thomas, even if he did have a lot a swagger."

Bridget remembered the way that Maverick had strutted into the pub last year. He'd for sure had enough swagger for ten men. And to think if she hadn't told him that little white lie about Denise McKay being married, he might have left the bar with her that night, and Bridget wouldn't have ended up having the most amazing night of her life.

"I hate having to sit here and not be able to help." Iris groaned.

"You might remember how much you hate it when you want to climb up in the top of a tree and trim it," Bridget told her.

"Hey, now!" Iris pointed her finger at Bridget. "Don't

you and Maverick gang up on me. When I get this damned hip healed up, I'll climb any tree I want to."

Maverick caught Bridget's eye and winked. "And we'll be right here to take care of her when she's moanin' about breaking that other hip, won't we?"

"Don't be askin' me a thing like that, Maverick," Bridget answered. "After the way my past has gone, I don't make plans past tomorrow."

# Chapter Three

Bridget was getting out the ingredients to make biscuits when Iris pushed her walker into the kitchen that morning. Laela was pushing around some Cheerios and singing to herself in a high chair Bridget had found out in the barn and cleaned up.

"Is our sweet baby girl rested and ready for some food?" Iris asked the baby.

"Good mornin'." Maverick came in through the kitchen door. "Chores are all done, but, Granny, this place needs a ton of work. Why haven't you called me and Paxton to come help get it done?"

"Well, I haven't been out to check on things in a while," Iris said. "And the last thing I'd want to do is hurt Buster's feelings. He's worked here a long time."

"I'm glad he's taking some time off. He deserves it. But he's gonna need some help with tearing out fences and puttin' up new, and it's not safe for him gettin' on the top of the barn to repair the leaks." He went straight to the sink after he'd hung up his coat and hat, and started washing up for breakfast. "We wouldn't want him to break his hip." He flashed Iris a pointed look.

"Now, you stop sassin' me, young man," Iris snapped.

Maverick laughed, and the sound sent a zing straight through Bridget's body. Just looking at him in those tight jeans, a shirt with the sleeves rolled up to his elbows, and scuffed-up cowboy boots, took her breath away. And when he smiled on top of all that...Lord, have mercy! Living with him wasn't going to be easy, but if she let her heart do the steering instead of her brain, leaving would be even harder.

"I'll have breakfast on the table in just a little while," Bridget said. "Can I pour you some coffee, Iris?"

"I'll do it." Maverick headed toward the coffeepot. "And I'll make the bacon and eggs," he offered. "You do know how to make biscuits, right?"

"Of course." Bridget shot a look his way.

"I'll watch the baby." Iris eased down into a chair. "Don't forget to put on some water for Laela's oatmeal."

Bridget had already figured out that biscuits were cousins to scones and had learned to make them from the recipe on the back side of the bag of flour. Iris said her first attempt was good and Laela liked small bites of them as well as scones, especially if she put a dot of strawberry jam on what she fed her.

What she hadn't figured on was the two of them bumping into each other, brushing hips or elbows—every single touch sent a heat wave through her body. She hadn't been out with a man in five months, not since Laela had come into her life.

"So what are we doin' after church today, ladies?" Maverick asked as he cracked eggs in a bowl.

Iris drew in a long breath. "I've been the Sunday school teacher for the six- to ten-year-old kids for years, but I don't think I can do it until this hip heals, so I called the preacher last night and told him that y'all will take over my class until after New Year's. And"—she got a wicked grin on her face—"you'll also be in charge of the Christmas events this year."

"Don't you go to the Catholic church?" Bridget asked.

"Used to when I was a kid, but not anymore. No problems with the church. It's just that my sweet husband wasn't Catholic, and way I figure it is that God ain't in the church. He's in your heart. The church is for fellowship," Iris said. "Now did you hear me about how y'all are in charge of the Christmas program?"

"Are you serious?" Maverick's deep voice went all high and squeaky.

Bridget overflowed the measuring cup with milk. "I've never..." She realized what she'd done, grabbed a towel, and began to clean it up.

"Don't matter if you've never done it before. You'll be fine. Besides, I've taken care of it alone for years. And surely you two can manage to do what one old woman who doesn't have enough sense to stay out of a pear tree can do alone."

"You have notes, yes?" Bridget asked.

"Yes, I do. Today you'll teach them the lesson from my book for the first half hour. The next half hour, you will practice the carols that they'll be singing in the Christmas program," Iris said.

That didn't seem so terribly tough, Bridget thought. She could do that by herself. Maverick didn't even need to help.

"Then on Friday and Saturday evening, y'all will work with Alana and her dad to get the props all cleaned up and ready to use," Iris went on.

Maverick actually groaned.

"It won't hurt you to stay out of the honky-tonk for one month," Iris told him. "It won't fall into bankruptcy without the dollars you spend there."

"But what about you?" Bridget asked. "I need to stay home with you in case you need my help."

"I can certainly manage for the hour or so you'll be gone. And some of my church ladies have promised to stop by."

"When did you tell the preacher all about this?" Maverick asked.

"I got to worryin' about it last night so I called him while y'all were in here startin' up that gingerbread. I told him not to worry, that Maverick was here, and he's good with carpentry work, and that Bridget would help."

Bridget slid the biscuits in the oven. "Are you going to survive without your weekend pub dates?" she whispered as she put a pan of water on the stove to make oatmeal for Laela.

"The honky-tonks will still be there after Christmas." He sighed. "And maybe God won't get real upset with me over drinkin' a few extra shots if I've already done my penance at church through the month."

"I don't reckon God gives out hall passes to the honky-tonk for goin' to church for a whole month," Iris said.

Bridget giggled. "I've never heard it put like that."

"It's the truth," Iris said. "And speakin' of Christmas, my tree isn't up yet. Broke my hip before I could get it decorated right after Thanksgiving," Iris said. "We're goin' to get that done this afternoon right after church services."

Maverick piled the bacon onto a plate. "I hope your tree doesn't smell like mice. That cat of yours is so lazy that she wouldn't open her eyes if a mouse curled up under her belly."

"Don't be talkin' about Dolly like that," Iris told him. "Just cook the bacon and eggs, and…" She stopped and touched her chin with her forefinger. "That reminds me, you will need to take cookies to the nursing home next Saturday. The kids will practice their Christmas carols there, then they'll pass out Christmas cookies to the old folks. It's tradition."

"We'd love to decorate the tree and bake cookies," Bridget said. "This will be Laela's first tree. I can't wait to see her eyes when it's lit up for the first time."

"All right then," Iris said. "I'm going to get my notes and put them on the dining room table on the way back so you'll have them."

"I can do that for you," Bridget said.

"I need to walk a little. Doctor said that sitting too long isn't good. I'll be right back."

Bridget thought about the previous Christmas when she'd helped her nana decorate the Christmas tree. They always put it up on the first Saturday in December and took it down the day after Christmas. Nana had bustled around that day, telling Bridget where to hang the ornaments and teasing her about settling down. *One year could sure change everything*, she thought.

"I miss Nana this morning. Last year, I helped *her* decorate for the holidays." Bridget sighed. "Are you all right with all this church stuff?" she asked Maverick.

"I'm pretty brave, but I don't argue with Granny." He grinned. "I just hope that God don't send a lightning bolt down between the church rafters to strike me dead. Who would have ever thought Maverick Callahan would be teaching Sunday school?"

"I'll be the one dodging all that lightning right along with you," she said.

* * *

Bridget paid more attention to her surroundings on the way to church that morning than she had the two times when she'd driven to the grocery store in Daisy. On those days, she'd had Laela with her and had been trying to be very careful—driving on the opposite side of the road from what she was used to was a bit nerve-wracking. The flat land that reached out to touch the sky on the far horizon, the cattle and more cattle but no sheep and very few houses were so different from her Ireland.

The heater in the truck blew the scent of Maverick's shaving lotion to the backseat, and that brought on a visual of tangled legs and crumpled sheets in her flat. The shirt he'd worn that night was identical to the one he had on now, and if it was the same shirt, she could visualize the streaks of lightning shooting down into the Sunday school room. She couldn't help but smile when she thought that God wouldn't take too kindly to him teaching kids about the Bible in the same shirt that he'd worn for a one-night stand.

"And here we are," Iris said from the front seat.

The church looked to be about the same size as the one that Nana dragged her to every Sunday, but this one was white and the one in Ireland was a little stone church. Maverick parked as close to the front door as he could, left the truck engine running, and hurried around to help Iris. Bridget got out of the truck and was busy with Laela when she heard a groan. She whipped around to see Maverick holding Iris under her arms while the walker slowly rolled away. Running to grab it, Bridget came close to falling when her high-heeled boot slipped on a plastic candy wrapper in the gravel parking lot.

"What happened?" Bridget asked as she pushed the walker back to the truck.

"Damned slick-soled shoes. I should've worn my rubber boots even if they do look like crap with this dress. Thank goodness Mav was here to catch me," Iris said.

"You sure you're up for this, Granny?" Maverick had a worried expression. "The pews have cushions, but an hour is a long time to sit."

"Of course, I'm sure!" Iris exclaimed. "It was just a little slip. Now, give me that walker and let's get going."

He kept a hold on her arm until she was on the sidewalk, and then he turned her loose. "If you'll keep a hand on her arm, I'll park the truck and bring the baby inside with me."

"Don't forget Laela's diaper bag and that small tote with her toys," Bridget said.

Maverick nodded. "After Sunday school is over, maybe we should sit on the back pew during church so we can get her out quietly if she gets tired."

"Bullshit!" Iris said. "I'm sitting on the pew where I always sit. Second from the front on the right. If you don't stop babying me, I'll send you back to Sunset."

"Granny, I was talking about Laela getting fussy, not you," Maverick said.

"Hmmph," Iris grunted and pushed the walker into the church and down the center aisle.

Bridget had just gotten her seated, her walker folded and propped against the wall beside her, and started out the door when Iris called out, "Your Sunday school room is down the hall, first door on the right."

"Where would I be finding the nursery?" Bridget asked.

"Last door on the left," Iris answered.

She met Maverick coming down the hallway with the diaper bag and the tote slung over one shoulder and the baby in his arms. With all Laela's dark hair, folks might think that the baby did, indeed, belong to him. Bridget took her from him so he could untangle himself from the baggage and said, "The nursery is this way."

"I'm glad you thought to ask," Maverick whispered. "I had no idea where it was or where we're supposed to go for the class we're teaching."

"Why are you whispering?" she asked.

"I'm hoping that maybe God won't realize what I'm doing until it's too late to zap me," he answered.

She used her free hand to air-slap him on the arm. "You weren't this funny in Ireland."

"No one asked me to teach a Sunday school class over there," he said.

"Ohhh," a sweet little gray-haired lady said, "Iris called this morning and said we'd have a baby in the nursery today. She's beautiful, Maverick. How'd you get a child to look so much like you?"

"Luck, I guess," he answered.

Bridget raised an eyebrow at him.

"But she's Bridget's adopted daughter, and doesn't biologically belong to either of us," he said.

"Well, her daddy must've been tall, dark, and handsome. By the way, I'm Dorothy, and I keep the nursery. Today it's just me and this pretty little girl, so I get to spoil her for a couple of hours." She held out her arms, and Laela went right to her.

"Her name is Laela, and here's her things," Bridget said.

"I used to keep Maverick when he was a baby, you know," Dorothy said. "Always flirting with the ladies, that one." She laughed. "Y'all go on now. You've got a Sunday school class to teach."

They left the room and noticed several children going into the room before they even arrived. When they got there, Maverick held the door for her, and she pulled the lesson book from her purse.

"Hello," Maverick said. "Since we're new here today, I thought maybe we'd all introduce ourselves."

"I'm Randy," the smallest of the seven little kids said. "Where's Miz Iris? We had the preacher for two weeks, and he didn't bring us cookies."

"I'm Lily Rose," a little blond-haired girl said, "and this other girl in our room is Katy. She's my best friend."

"Darius," said a little guy who was evidently of mixed race with his jet-black curly hair and green eyes. "This here"—he pointed beside him—"is Elijah. He's my brother but he's kinda shy, and don't talk much, but he can sure sing."

"I'm Slade," the next little boy said. "I'm ten years old, and I get to go to the next class next year when I'm eleven. I read our lesson about forgivin' others, but I ain't forgivin' Bubba Joe Thorn for sayin' that Elijah is slow. He's smart enough to keep his mouth shut 'lessen he has something to say."

"I'm C-C-Colton, and I'm s-s-seven…" a little guy stammered, "…sometimes I stutter, but I c-c-can sing real g-g-good."

"Well, thank you all for that." Maverick nodded. "This is Bridget, and I'm Maverick. Miz Iris is my granny, and we'll be taking over this classroom until she gets well."

Bridget opened her study booklet to the right page. "We're supposed to read verses in the Bible today about forgiveness, and then talk about them for a little while before we practice our songs for the Christmas play." She read a verse from Matthew and then asked what the kids thought about that.

"Well." Lily Rose sighed. "I guess I can forgive Lisa for not comin' today. She was supposed to bring back my Barbie doll clothes that she borrowed last Sunday, but I bet she ain't here because she still wants to keep them." She stopped for a breath. "But I'll forgive her if she brings them back next Sunday."

"You ain't from Texas, are you?" Slade asked. "You talk like them people from England on the television."

"I'm from Ireland, a little place called Skibbereen," Bridget told him.

Bridget shivered when Randy, the youngest child in the room, shoved a finger up his nose. She rushed over to the desk, grabbed a tissue, and handed it to him.

Katy rolled her big brown eyes. "Rannn-dee! You don't pick your nose in church. God don't like boogers."

Randy cleaned his finger on the tissue. "God put them in my nose, so why don't he like them?"

Katy put her hands in a prayer pose and said, "I forgive him, God, because he's just a little kid."

Maverick chuckled under his breath, and reached for the book. "The next verse is in Luke and it says that if we don't forgive then we won't be forgiven. What do you think that means?"

"It means that if I don't tell Darius that I'm not going to whoop him all over the playground for sayin' that my mama is crazy, then Jesus won't forgive me, right?" Slade asked.

"That's right," Maverick said.

"Anyone else?" Bridget asked. This wasn't as tough as she'd imagined it would be—it was actually kind of fun, but she wondered why Darius had said that Slade's mama was crazy.

The thirty minutes went fast with all the kids wanting to express their opinions. Even Elijah opened up a little toward the end of the lesson when he said, "I forgive Bubba. He's just a bully."

"All right, I guess it's time for us to practice singing,"

Bridget said. "It looks like we'll be singing three songs at the Christmas program. The first one is 'Up on the Housetop.'"

"I like that one." Elijah grinned and started the group off with the first lines.

He really could sing, and he'd probably be the one who carried the whole group at the program, but what amazed Bridget even more than the child, was Maverick's deep voice singing with the children.

They sang two more songs and then it was time to march them into the church. Elijah tucked his hand into Bridget's and said, "I like the way you talk, and you sing pretty."

"Well, thank you." She smiled.

"How about me?" Maverick whispered from her other side.

"You have a beautiful singing voice," Bridget told him. "Did you sing in the choir when you lived here?"

Maverick chuckled. "I didn't even sing in the bars unless I'd had a lot, and I mean a lot, to drink."

The minute they were in the sanctuary, the kids all scattered to find their parents. Bridget scanned the church for Iris and found her sitting on the second pew. Holy crap on a cracker! Bridget always sat on the back pew, not right up front so the preacher could look her right in the eye, but she slid into the pew beside Iris. "I thought we were sitting close to the back in case I need to go get Laela."

"She'll be fine, and this is where I always sit," Iris said.

Maverick made his way down the pew to sit beside Bridget. When latecomers arrived, he had to move closer and closer until his shoulder was pressed against hers. Bridget decided that the lightning bolts were invisible but still just as hot as they shot down between them, firing up every desire in her body.

She tried to listen to the sermon. But the preacher mentioned something about teenagers, and her mind wandered back to when she and Deidre were in their teens—the first time they'd gone to a pub together, the special little place in the middle of a stand of trees where they'd thrown down one of Nana's old quilts and had lain side by side and shared their deepest secrets—and were just starting to find their way in the world.

About halfway through the sermon, someone tapped Bridget on the shoulder. That jerked her back into the real world, and she looked up at Dorothy, with Laela in her arms. "She's really fussy, so I thought maybe I'd better bring her on in here to you."

Laela reached for her, and Bridget took the baby from Dorothy.

"Thank you," Bridget said. "She usually has a nap in the middle of the morning, and she can be pretty clingy at that time."

"You're welcome. Maybe next week, she'll let me rock her," Dorthy whispered and sat down in the pew behind them. Laela fidgeted and whined, fighting sleep. Bridget tried giving her toys, but she just threw them on the floor.

Maverick startled her when he reached for Laela, but instead of arguing with him, she mouthed, "Thank you."

Instantly, the baby lay her little head on Maverick's shoulder, sighed, and closed her eyes. He rocked gently from side to side with her until she was sound asleep. There was something about a big man like Maverick holding a baby that showed a softer side to him than any other man Bridget had ever known. Nana had said that if kids and dogs liked a person, then they were probably good people. But if kids shied away and dogs wanted to bite them, then a smart person would run the other way.

She was startled out of reverie a second time when the

preacher asked for Orville Jackson to deliver the benediction. Bridget bowed her head and gave a simple prayer giving thanks that she'd made it through the Sunday school lesson, and that she was finally getting some space away from Maverick, who'd practically turned her into a pile of ashes during the service with all the electricity between them.

People began to stand and stir about when the last amen had been said, but Laela didn't open her eyes. "I'll carry her out for you. No need to wake her until it's absolutely necessary," Maverick whispered as he picked up the diaper bag with his free hand and put it on his shoulder.

He moved out into the center aisle. Bridget followed him and got Iris's walker ready. Using the pew to steady her steps, Iris slowly took a couple of steps.

"Well, Iris O'Malley," said a thin-voiced lady with a gray bun on top of her head. "It's right good to see you in church this morning."

Iris turned to see who was talking to her. "Hello, Maudie. It's good to be here."

As she was turning back around, her hand slipped on the pew. Bridget grabbed for her. Using his free hand, Maverick tried to catch her, but they both failed. Iris was on the floor, her legs under the pew, her head in the aisle, and her face an ashen color.

"Call an ambulance," she groaned. "I think I might have messed up my hip, again."

Several people already had their phones out poking in numbers. One brought a pillow and put it under her head. Iris's neighbor, Alana, dropped down on her knees right next to Iris and asked, "What happened?"

"I fell right on my hip, and it hurts like holy hell, and I'm not even going to apologize for sayin' that in church," Iris said, bluntly.

"Do you have pain anywhere but your hip?" Alana asked.

"No, but it's hurtin' like a real bitch," Iris said through clenched teeth.

Bridget noticed a blood spot on Iris's skirt and knelt beside her. "I think you've busted loose one of the staples." She could hear the sirens of an ambulance fast approaching.

"Feels like more than one," Iris moaned.

The paramedics rushed in and everyone moved back to let them through. In minutes they had Iris on a gurney. As they were taking her out, she grabbed Bridget's hand. "I want you to go with me in the ambulance."

"Go on," Maverick said. "Laela and I'll be right behind you. It's only three blocks to the hospital."

Iris hung on to Bridget's hand the whole way to the ambulance, and took it again when they were inside. "I should've listened to my doctor. He wanted me to go to the six weeks of rehab, but I was stubborn. I wanted to be at home, and I thought of you in Ireland with no job and that baby to take care of, so I called and you were willing to help me. This hurts like a son of a bitch. But you have to promise me that you'll stay at the ranch. Mav needs someone to help him out while I'm in the hospital."

The ambulance stopped and the two paramedics jumped out and swung open the door, ready to take her into the emergency room. Iris stared right into Bridget's eyes without blinking. "I won't let them take me out of this thing until you give me your word."

"I promise," Bridget said.

They were rolling her through the doors when Maverick and the preacher both rushed in behind them.

"You can all wait right here. Someone will come and get you when the doctor has taken a look," one of the paramedics said, and they pushed Iris through the waiting room and straight back into the ER area.

Shortly after they all took a seat on the hard, plastic chairs in the waiting room, Laela began to fuss. Bridget dug around in her diaper bag for a bottle and then took the baby from Maverick. Laela hadn't even drunk a third of the milk when a doctor came out.

"Maverick." He stuck out his hand. "Been a while. Seems like the last time I saw you it was to set your wrist after a bull riding event."

"Yep, about three years ago. How is Granny?" he asked.

"She's torn a couple of the staples out, and several are infected," he answered. "If she'd been at the rehab center where I wanted her to go, we'd have already known about this. We're admitting her for a couple or three days, and I'm going to try to talk her into going to the rehab center. But we all know Iris. She has a mind of her own. She would like to see you before we start patching her up and getting her into a room."

Maverick got the diaper bag. Bridget carried Laela. The preacher followed behind them as they paraded through the doors and into a curtained cubicle where Iris was lying on a bed.

"Iris, did they give you something for the pain?" Bridget asked as she took Iris's hand in hers.

"Don't worry about a thing, Granny," Maverick said. "We'll take care of the ranch, and we'll bring anything you want to you. All you have to do is call."

"They've given me a shot for the pain, and it's helping," Iris said, "and Mav, you know how to run a ranch. So I'm not worried about that."

"The doctor said it's only going to be two or three days," Maverick said.

"And then he wants me to go to the rehab center," Iris told him. "I was too stubborn to do it the first time, but I don't want to go through this again. I made up my mind. I'm going straight from here to the rehab center."

"I think that's a good idea, Granny."

Bridget nodded. "Like Maverick said, we'll take care of everything and have Christmas all ready for you as soon as you come back."

"Good. I expect y'all will get my tree up and decorated this afternoon. I want pictures of every step. Go on, now. The doctor has to get me patched up, and that pain shot is making me feel like I've had too much Jack Daniel's. Besides, Laela needs to be home."

Bridget's mind ran in circles as she and Maverick walked side by side to the truck. "She made me promise that I wouldn't leave, but now that she doesn't need me..."

"I can keep things going on the ranch by myself, but she made us agree to help out with the Christmas stuff at church, so you'd better stick around." Maverick took Laela from her and set the baby in her car seat. "You'd better strap her in. I couldn't figure out all that stuff, so I just used the regular truck belt. It was only three blocks, and we had an ambulance leading the way."

"It's all right." Bridget got all the straps fastened. "So how are you with us living together in the same house?"

"I'm fine with it. How about you?" He looked down into her green eyes.

Her heart pounded, and her pulse raced. She hadn't felt like that since—she tried to remember when she'd been so drawn to a man—not since Maverick had swaggered into the Shamrock Pub and flirted with her. She felt like she was sinking into his eyes as she whispered, "I gave her my word. Can we come into town and visit her often?"

"Every day if she'll let us." Maverick opened the passenger door, put his hands on Bridget's waist, and lifted her into the passenger seat. "I noticed that you had to struggle to get up into the seat when we left the ranch."

He'd slipped his arms around her from the back that night in Ireland, and his hands on her waist had affected her now the same way it had then. She wished that she could whip around like she had at that time, wrap her arms around his neck, and kiss him. But a year changes lives, and God only knew what all those months had really done to her and Maverick.

"You said you gave Granny your word about stayin'? Was that why she wanted you in the ambulance?" Maverick asked when he was behind the steering wheel. "She sure changed her mind about rehab in a hurry."

"I have no idea if that's why she wanted me to ride with her, but she was so insistent that I promised. Why didn't she listen to the doctor and go to rehab from the beginning?" Bridget asked.

"Paxton and I both tried to talk her into it, but as she said, she was just too stubborn then."

Maverick started the engine, backed out of the parking space, and headed toward what Bridget assumed was the ranch. She'd gotten so turned around in the ambulance that she didn't know where she was.

"We told her back then that we'd come take care of the ranch," Maverick went on. "But like I said, she's stubborn and independent. She told us that she'd have a lady here the day she went home, and our neighbor, Alana, had volunteered to stay with her until you arrived."

"There was no one there but Iris when I got there, and she was sleeping on the sofa," Bridget said.

Maverick chuckled. "She didn't say that she'd taken

Alana up on the offer, so technically she didn't lie to me, but I'd bet my hat and boots that she stretched the truth."

"Sounds like my nana." Bridget smiled. "They must've been cut from the same bolt of Irish plaid."

"You're probably right." He turned east out of town and she began to recognize some of the sites she'd seen on the way to church that morning. "Do you always go to church in Ireland?"

"Nana insisted." Bridget nodded. "It didn't matter if I'd worked until two the night before, she would ring me up at nine and tell me to get dressed for church. She always said that working in a pub, I had one foot on a banana peel and the other one dangling over the flames of hell, and the only way I wouldn't slip and fall right into the fire was to go to church on Sunday morning. But I've got to admit, my mind wandered this morning."

"Mine too. I heard the part about God having a plan for us all, and then I kind of blocked a lot of the rest out. What were you thinking about instead of listening?" he asked.

"My best friend Deidre and the fun we had when we were kids," she answered. "I really, really miss her. We were both only children and were more like sisters than simply friends. She lived with Nana's friend who fostered a child at a time."

"Why didn't that friend want to take in Laela?" Maverick asked.

"She died two years ago, leaving Deidre with no family, not even a foster mother. All she had was me and Nana, and Jimmy. He'd been raised in Dublin in a foster home, and they met at the pub." She paused. "What were you thinking about?" she asked.

"I was wondering"—he shrugged—"what God has planned for me."

"Well, I can tell you what we've got planned for the rest of today. We're going to have Sunday dinner, and then put up Iris's tree. And we're sending pictures to her cell phone to prove it." Before coming to Texas, Bridget had only met Iris once and that was when she was a little girl, but Nana had talked about her a lot, especially in those last days. Knowing as much as she did about her grandmother's best friend had helped her make the decision to leave Ireland, but getting to know Iris better the past few days had taught her that anyone would have to be bat shit crazy to cross the old girl.

Maverick chuckled, and for a minute she thought he could read her mind. "What's so funny?"

"Granny's fall kept me from having to answer questions about why I showed up in church with a baby in my arms, and it kept you from having to try to remember all the people's names that she would have introduced you to." Maverick parked in front of the house. "I'll get the baby if you'll grab the diaper bag."

Just like at church, he held Laela in one arm and carried the diaper bag with the other. "You sure look pretty today in your orange dress, and so does your mama in her green one." He talked to the baby, but Bridget could hear him as she walked away from the truck. "Ireland green is her color with all that gorgeous red hair."

"Thank you, but flattery doesn't get you any points," Bridget threw over her shoulder.

*It did at one time.* That niggling voice in the back of her head said loudly.

*But a year has passed, and I'm not that the same girl as I was back then*, she argued.

"Laela just now told me that she likes to be complimented," Maverick said from behind her.

She unlocked the door with the key that Iris had given her the first day she was in Texas and went inside. "And she told me that she's got on a soggy nappy, and that she's hungry."

Bridget took the baby from him. "I'll change her and then check on the roast in the oven. Wait for me in the living room."

"Does Laela have to eat that nasty stuff in jars?" Maverick removed his coat and hat, hung them both on the hall tree, and followed her into her bedroom.

"No, Laela hates it. She eats whatever I do," Bridget answered.

"Is that all right? I thought all babies had to eat baby food."

"She has oatmeal for breakfast, and I smash her vegetables and fruits. So far, I haven't given her meats. The doctor says she shouldn't have that until she had the proper number of teeth to chew it." Bridget laid her in the crib to remove her coat and hat and then changed her diaper.

Maverick reached down and picked Laela up. "Come on, pretty girl. Let's go see if the pot roast has burned."

Bridget threw her coat and scarf on the bed and followed him to the kitchen. The aroma of onions, potatoes, carrots, and beef filled the room. She took the pan from the oven and set the lid aside. "This would be a nice lamb or maybe a pork roast in Ireland."

"We eat more beef in Texas, especially since we raise it right here," he said.

Laela started to squirm and lean toward the high chair. "Guess she's telling me it's time to eat," Maverick said. "I like babies and little kids, but to tell the truth, I'm not too smart about all that goes on behind the scenes. I've never changed a diaper or fed a baby. Mostly, I just get to play with them a while and give them back to their mamas."

"I had to learn pretty fast." Bridget got down the plates to set the table. "But I'd say that liking the wee ones is a good start."

*And speaking of starts, is it possible for us to start again?* Bridget wondered.

# Chapter Four

Right after dinner, Laela started rubbing her eyes and fussing. She'd had a big morning with no nap other than the short one she'd taken in church. Maverick tried to appease her with a toy or two, but she tossed them to the floor.

"Did I do something wrong?" he asked. "This morning she wanted me to hold her."

"Nap time," Bridget said. "I was hoping she'd stay awake for the tree decorating."

"Why don't you go on and get her to sleep? I'll take care of the cleanup here, and then go get all the Christmas decorations hauled up here from the barn," Maverick offered.

"That would be great. She can have a little rest while we do most of the tree, then she'll be all fresh for when we turn on the lights." Bridget smiled as she got the baby from the high chair. "It amazed me that Iris had a crib here. She said that she borrowed them from the church."

"She's got contacts everywhere," Maverick said.

"Well, it was a welcome sight to see that crib. I thought I might have to sleep with Laela." Bridget headed out of the room with the baby in her arms. Just when she thought she couldn't take another change or problem, this had popped right up. She wasn't sure how much more she could stand. Now she had days of living in a house alone with Maverick, who'd no doubt go right back to his wild, freewheeling days as soon as Iris came home permanently. She had to hold herself at a distance or she'd go home to Ireland with a broken heart, and that on top of everything else might just break more than her heart.

She stopped by the bathroom and washed Laela's hands and face and then went on to the bedroom, where she sat down in the rocking chair. The baby's little eyes fluttered shut. Dark lashes like her mama's fanned out on her plump little cheeks, and with a long sigh, she was asleep. Bridget continued to rock her for several minutes until she gave a familiar little sigh that said she was truly sound asleep. Until that moment, if Bridget tried to put her in the crib, her eyes would pop wide open and her chin would begin to quiver.

"Sleep, little darlin'," Bridget whispered. "And when you awake, we've got a big surprise for you. I wish your mama could see your eyes when you look upon your first Christmas tree."

Bridget kept the tears at bay when she thought of all that Deidre would never get to experience with Laela. Life wasn't fair to take her and her fiancé away at such a young age, but Bridget vowed that she'd do her best to tell Laela all about her mother and keep her memory alive.

"Is she asleep?" Maverick whispered from right outside the door.

How a man that tall could sneak up on her like that was

a total mystery. Bridget nodded and stood. She laid Laela in the crib and put her favorite teddy bear close to her.

"I'm done in the kitchen and going out to the barn for the Christmas stuff," he whispered.

"What should I do to get the living room ready?" She made sure when she passed by him that she didn't touch him. Maybe if she starved the electricity between them, it would simply die.

He followed right behind her, close enough that she got a whiff of his shaving lotion, but she was determined not to let his charm or that delicious smell deter her from her decision to steer clear of him. "If you could move that little table and the lamp"—he pointed toward the big picture window that looked out over the front yard—"over to that corner. Granny likes the tree in front of the window. I'll be back in a few minutes."

"I'll have things ready for you." She started toward the table but stopped midway and watched him swagger out to his truck. "Stop it! I can't change some things, but this one I can, and I will," she scolded herself in her Irish tongue.

He brought in more than a dozen boxes later, including one with a picture of a tree on the front. He'd barely gotten it off his shoulders when his phone rang. He fished it out of his hip pocket, answered it, and then said, "Yes, ma'am. You are now on speaker with me and Bridget here in the living room with all the Christmas stuff around us."

"I want the tree up and the place all pretty even though I won't be there. And I want y'all to go to the Rockin' B Christmas party next Sunday evening. It's not that much of a drive, and you can be home in time for supper," she said.

"Are you bossin' us from your hospital bed?" Maverick asked.

"If you want to call it that, then go ahead. Way I see it is that I'm directin' you. I called to tell you that I'm in a room. I'm hooked up to an IV, and the doctor says that since I've agreed to go to the rehab center that he'll let me go tomorrow evening. Don't come see me tomorrow. I'll be trying to get adjusted. You can come on Tuesday and Thursday this week, but I might call on the other days during the visiting hour. Other than that, they'll have us in therapy sessions," Iris said.

"Granny, we will be there to see you every day," Maverick said.

"No, you won't. You've got work to do, Christmas to take care of, and a party to get ready for a week from today. If you come any other day than what I just said, there'll be hell to pay," she threatened.

"Granny—" Maverick started.

"I'm getting sleepy now," Iris interrupted before he could finish. "You heard me. I will see you both on Tuesday and bring Laela. Bye now," she said.

She ended the call before either of them could say a word.

"I guess we've got our walking orders." Maverick put the phone back in his pocket. "I swear, she'll still be bossin' me when she's in her grave." He clamped a hand over his mouth. "I'm so sorry. That was insensitive of me to say something like that when your grandmother has just passed away."

"But it'd be the truth." Bridget nodded. "Nana still bosses me from the grave. She just pops into my head at the craziest moments. Sometimes I think she's right behind me."

"My grandpa does that," Maverick admitted.

"It's the way we cope with losing them."

\* \* \*

Maverick could feel Bridget's vulnerability in that moment. Her eyes were brimming with tears that she wouldn't allow to flow down her cheeks, and her face was a study in absolute sadness. She'd had so much happen in such a short time, and now there was still yet another change. He'd like to have a second chance with her, but not at the expense of breaking her.

*Are you ready to be a father?* His grandpa's voice was loud and clear in his head.

Maverick couldn't answer the question. He liked holding Laela, but he could always give her back to Bridget when she got fussy or needed a diaper change. To take on that responsibility full-time—he wasn't so sure that he was ready for that. Why did life have to be so damned complicated, anyway?

Bridget opened the first box and pulled out a gold garland. "Does this go up first or the lights?"

"Lights first." Maverick opened a second box. "And then the garland. Did you help your grandmother put up a tree?"

Bridget opened the box with the lights. "Every year, but we usually bought a real tree. It wasn't very big, though. I kept a lot of the ornaments."

"Where are they?" Maverick asked.

"A friend, Sean, let me store five boxes in his spare room until I get back to Ireland. Nana rented her place, and we had to get everything out the day before we flew to Texas. I had no place to store the furniture so I sold or gave it all away. All I kept was pictures, ornaments, and things that reminded me of Nana," she answered.

Another thing that had been piled on top of all her other sorrows—Maverick was a big, tough cowboy, and when he thought of losing Paxton, and then Granny, and then the ranch, and only having five boxes to pack his memories in, and then after all that, flying halfway around the world to a new place—it's a wonder she wasn't crazy as a rabid raccoon. Maverick sure didn't want to be her breaking point.

"Did you live close to your grandmother your whole life?" Maverick carried the box to the window and strung the lights on the inside of the frame.

"Not my whole life. Nana had lived in the same house since before I was born, though. I went to live with her when I was four. My mother decided to run away to Egypt with another man and leave me with my father, who was in the Irish Army," she answered. "How about you? Where did you grow up?"

"Right here until I graduated from high school." Maverick continued to string lights as he talked. "Then I went to work on the Rockin' B Ranch. You'll see the place when we go there for the Christmas party next Sunday. Granny is a distant cousin to the lady who owns the spread. Then when Paxton graduated two years later, he came to work with me. We wanted to stay right here, but Granny said it would be good experience for us to work for someone else and learn all we could about big ranchin'. Buster has been the foreman here for as long as I can remember. They've always hired several high school kids to help out through the summer."

"Seems like you would have known most of the ranching business by staying right here," she said.

"Maybe so, but Granny has her reasons, and truth is, I wanted to go." He carefully got another foot of lights around the edge of the window. "So why didn't your father keep you with him?"

"He was gone away on deployment too often. He was killed in one of those missions when I was sixteen, and then it was just Nana and me. And now it's just me and Laela," she said. "What about you? Did your father live here on the ranch in this house?"

"My dad and mother lived in town. Mama hated anything to do with the ranch, and she worked in Amarillo in a bank. Dad worked here on the ranch with Granny and Grandpa, so he'd bring us with him and Granny would take care of us. Then he died when I was just five and Paxton was three. Mama didn't like the idea of driving out here every morning, so she let us stay here all week. Six months after Daddy died, she remarried, moved to California, and signed us over to our grandparents. Grandpa was the father figure in my life."

"Do you see your mother often?" she asked as she unwrapped ornaments and laid them on the coffee table.

Maverick shook his head. "We went for a week in the summers a couple of times. She sent us Christmas cards with money in them a few times. She retired last year and moved to the Bahamas with her fourth husband. We hear from her on our birthdays every couple of years."

"We've got a lot in common, only my dad came home to see me and Nana every chance he got, and I had him until I was sixteen," she said.

Maverick ran the light cord to the floor and plugged it in.

"Ohhhh!" Bridget's full mouth made a perfect little circle.

Maverick wanted to kiss those lips, but he took a step back instead of forward. "So you like the lights, I guess?"

"Christmas is my favorite time of year. I love all the decorations and the cooking and"—her eyes stayed glued on the window—"shopping, and especially being with family. Deidre, Nana, and I always had Christmas dinner together."

"Have you gotten to go Christmas shopping?" Maverick

thought maybe seeing the mall in Amarillo all decorated for Christmas might cheer her up.

"No, and I do need to buy a few things for Laela," she said.

"I'll be glad to take you," Maverick said.

"Thank you, but our weekends are pretty well taken up with the church program," she reminded him.

"We'll go one evening during the week." He strung the garland around the lights.

She stood back and watched every move. "That reminds me of the Shamrock. Denny, my boss there, and his wife used to fix the windows like that for Christmas."

"I remember." He smiled.

Her voice let him know that she was homesick already. At the end of the month, she'd be more than ready to get on a plane and go back to Ireland where her roots were. He was insane to think about a second chance with her. The place for her to heal and find closure was in a little village south of Skibbereen, not in Daisy, Texas.

"Thinking of Christmas makes me want to start baking biscuits, or cookies as you call them here in Texas, or maybe scones to take to Iris the days we can visit her." Bridget got a faraway look in her eyes and then sighed. "Nana and I made shortbread cookies and breads for her friends when they were ailing. And then on Christmas we made her famous almond pound cakes and took them around to all the neighbors."

"If you haven't discovered it already, Granny has a terrible sweet tooth. Dessert is her favorite part of any meal." Maverick chuckled. "We should make our cookies for the nursing home tomorrow evening. We could take some of them to the rehab center for Granny on Tuesday." Maverick finished the last bit of garland, then took a few steps back to eyeball his work. "Time for a picture. Stand right there to the side of the window and smile. Granny wants to see photos of everything as it happens."

Maverick took several pictures and then handed Bridget the phone and let her choose her favorite one. While she was flipping through them, she came upon the photo Maverick had taken just as she was about to get out of bed, the sun streaming through the window and lighting her red hair on fire.

He reached for the phone and smiled at the picture.

"I should have at least gotten your last name," she said.

He nodded. "I asked for your phone number, remember? But..." He shrugged.

"But," she butted in, "we weren't ever going to see each other again, and a clean break after that night seemed to be the right thing to do, right?"

"Right," he said.

"I pick this one." She held up the phone, displaying a photo they'd just taken. "If you look close, you can see a reflection of you taking the picture in that mirror behind me. That way Iris gets us both."

"Let's take a selfie of both of us in front of the window with the lights all around us." He joined her in front of the window, stooped slightly so he could get their faces together, and put his cheek next to hers. The sparks were definitely there when his skin touched hers. He held the phone out as far as he could and snapped two pictures before he straightened up.

"What do you think?" he asked as he showed them to her.

"They're both good. Could you send them to my phone too?" she asked. "I'd like to send them to my friend who's keeping my things."

"Sure will." He handed her his phone. "Program your number in there. Sean is your friend, right?"

She put her number into the phone and gave it back. "That's right. He offered to let me rent the spare bedroom in his flat until I could get on my feet, but then Iris called with her invitation. He was a couple of years behind me in high school, and then we worked at the bakery together in Skibbereen before I had to quit. He made me promise to send pictures."

"I'll send everything that we take and you can decide what you want to send him." Maverick opened the box with the tree and began to sort through the limbs, laying them in piles.

"What are you doing?" she asked.

"Sortin' by color. Red ones are longer and go at the bottom," he answered. "I guess you didn't have to do this, since you bought a live tree."

She shook her head. "We only had a three-foot tree that took about thirty minutes to decorate."

"We have a tradition in this house," he said. "The youngest person in the house on the day we decorate gets to put the star on the tree. So if Laela isn't awake, we'll have to wait for her to wake up to put the crowning touch on the top."

"And just how is a wee babe going to reach to the top of a seven-foot tree?" Bridget asked.

"I'll hold her up there and help her." Maverick reached to the top of the tree. "See, no problem."

"She'll have the star in her mouth as soon as you hand it to her, and cry when you take it from her. You better rethink this, cowboy," she said.

A wide grin covered his face, and his eyes twinkled. "Darlin', what I'll do is put the star on the tree, then hold her up beside it for you to take a picture. I'll bet that she reaches out for it. The picture will look like she actually put it there."

"What would we be bettin'?" she asked.

"Whatever you want to bet is fine with me," he told her.

"Then we'll bet on a kiss on the cheek as friends, under this mistletoe." She held up a ball of artificial mistletoe tied with a red ribbon.

"Just as friends?" He got the tall tree set up and ready for the branches.

"We really should be friends, since we have to live in the same house, bake cookies together, and share the Christmas program. If Laela touches the star, I owe you a kiss. If she doesn't, you owe me one, but don't be thinkin' that a kiss on the cheek will be giving me a case of the round heels," she told him.

"Round heels?" He raised an eyebrow.

"Surely you've heard that. Round heels means that you kiss me, and I fall backward into the bed and pull you down with me," she explained. "Now where do we hang this?"

"It always goes right above the door from the foyer into the dining room." He took it from her hand and hung it on a small gold hook.

Maverick had never had a friend that was a girl. As her friend maybe he could help her find some kind of closure for all the sorrows in her heart. He was willing to give it a try, but that would probably rule out any of those second chance ideas.

* * *

"A perfect place for it." She smiled and then began pushing the color-coded branches into the right places.

When they were all in place, Maverick went around the tree a dozen times, tweaking the branches here and there before he was satisfied with it. She woulda never guessed that a Texas cowboy could be so fussy about things.

"Granny will throw a shoe and leave the hospital if it's not right," he explained. "Now for a picture. Stand right there on the left side, and do this." He posed, hand out toward the tree, like he was showing it off for a television commercial. Bridget snapped two pictures with her phone before he could move.

"Now she can have one of you," Bridget said.

"But you look like a model. I'm just a rough old cowboy," he argued.

"But you're her old cowboy grandson, and she'll cherish the picture. I'm sending it to her right now," Bridget told him. "Now the lights, right?"

"Yep, I'll wrap them around my arms and you can place them. We'll start at the top and work our way down," he said.

Bridget found out really quickly how often skin brushed against skin during the time it took to decorate a tree. By the time they were finished with the lights, ornaments, and garland, it felt like the temperature in the room had risen at least fifteen degrees.

As if on cue, Laela awoke and started jabbering just as they'd hung the last ornament. Bridget started toward the bedroom with Maverick so close behind her that she could feel his breath on her neck. She almost wished that a case of round heels would jump right off the walls and onto her feet.

"Hey, baby girl," he said.

Laela reached up toward him.

"Oh, no you don't." Bridget took her out of the crib. "You belong to me until we get you a clean nappy, and then we'll take you to see the lovely tree and all the decorations. It's so pretty, love. But you can't try to climb it."

The baby squirmed and wiggled the whole time Bridget tried to change her, and then jabbered and pointed toward the floor.

"Does she want down to crawl around and play?" Maverick asked.

"I think she's looking for Ducky and Dolly," she said.

"Well, if she wants the cat and dog to come inside and share the moment, then I'll go call them," Maverick said. "But wait until I get there to take her in the living room. I want a picture of her face when she sees everything."

"You're spoiling her," Bridget said.

"Little girls are supposed to be spoiled."

He left the room. Bridget heard him call the dog and then the cat. Both animals bounded into the room and jumped onto the bed. Laela held out her hand. Ducky licked it, and Dolly rubbed against her shoulder.

"All right, pretty girl, you've got your animals now, so let's be going to see the pretty living room." Bridget picked her up.

Ducky and Dolly hopped off the bed and followed them to the living room, where Maverick waited, ready to take a picture.

"What do you think, lassie?" she said, facing Laela toward the tree.

Laela's little mouth made a cute little round circle and her big green eyes popped wide open. Then she reached for Maverick.

"I think she's afraid of it," Bridget said. "Or else she wants to play with your phone. Don't let her do that. She chews on everything."

"No, she wants me to let her put the star on it." Maverick took her in his arms and carried her right up to the tree. She reached out and touched a bright red ornament, then pulled her hand back and said some things that Bridget was sure that God didn't even understand.

Bridget got her phone ready to take the picture when Maverick held her up to the top of the tree. With his free hand, Maverick picked the star up and set it right on top of the tree. Then he lifted the baby up, and as if she knew what to do, Laela wrapped her little hands around it.

Bridget got half a dozen pictures before the baby let go and started to squirm. Maverick put her on the floor, and she crawled a distance away and sat up. She cocked her head, as if trying to decide what to do with the new thing in the living room.

"Don't move her," Maverick said. "I can get really good pictures from the floor." He got down on his hands and knees, and started snapping pictures with the other. Laela's eyes glittered at the sight. She pointed and jabbered at the dog and cat, then at the tree, as if she was telling them to look at the big, beautiful thing.

"Look at her, Bridget. Her eyes are big as saucers. She likes it. Granny is going to love these pictures." Maverick was so excited that he dropped his phone.

"Sean will love them, too." Bridget snapped several before Laela finally crawled away to chase Dolly around the coffee table.

Maverick rolled up on his feet. "I believe you owe me a kiss."

"But I didn't say when you could collect." She grinned.

"Hey, now!" he protested as he took several steps toward her.

"No, you have to wait until we're under the mistletoe," she teased.

He was close enough that she could see the little gold flecks in his green eyes, and then he backed away. "I'm going to go get a beer. You want one?"

"Yes, please." She sat down on the sofa and sent pictures to Sean.

Maverick brought back two beers and handed one to her. Then he sat down on the floor beside Laela in front of the

Christmas tree. She crawled up in his lap and reached for a bright red ornament hanging on a low branch of the tree. He took it off and let her hold it. When she grew tired of it, he put it back and got another one for her to touch. He had a baby in his lap, and a beer on the coffee table behind him, each representing a very different lifestyle. *Which would he choose if he had to give one up to have the other?* Bridget wondered.

# Chapter Five

Bridget was busy doing laundry on Monday morning when Maverick came back to the house unexpectedly. She could tell from his expression that he was excited. "We've got a new baby calf in the barn. Laela needs to see it. Can we put some warm clothes on her and take her out there?"

"I'll get her stroller and get her bundled up," Bridget said. "Why's the calf in the barn? Don't they stay with their mamas?"

"Most of the time, but this is a first-time mother, and she's rejected him. That means I'll have to try to put him on another heifer that has a new calf and see if she'll take him as her own."

Laela wasn't the only one excited to get a breath of fresh air that morning. Bridget could hardly wait to take a nice little hike out to the barn. Ducky met them at the front door and followed them around the house. Dolly was sleeping in the sun on the back porch, but she awoke at the clacking sound of the baby stroller wheels on rough ground and ran along with Ducky just ahead of them.

"Looks like we've got us a parade." Bridget zipped her fleece-lined coat up to her neck. "This wind is drier than what we have in Ireland. Even inland, we get a little of the ocean salt in the wind. Where will we go to do Christmas shopping?"

"Up to Amarillo. That would be the city that you flew into," Maverick explained.

"That's a lot of distance. It took us thirty minutes to get here in the car that Iris sent for us. Is there not a closer place?" Bridget shaded her eyes from the sun with the back of her hand.

He shook his head. "When you leave Daisy, there's nothing but ranchland from here to Amarillo."

"Holy Mother of God!" Bridget gasped. "Just how big is Texas?"

"Pretty big," he said. "Eight hundred miles wide from east to west and almost that many miles from north to south. I looked it up on the flight home from Ireland. Texas is about eight times the size of your country."

Bridget just shook her head. "That's hard to take in. Iris said this ranch is really quite small, but it's bigger than the whole village where I lived. Is that the barn up ahead of us? I've seen it in the distance from the kitchen window, but it looks so different from our barns in Ireland."

"That's one of the barns. There's another one on the back of the property where we store most of the hay for the winter months," he answered.

Laela giggled and reached out for Ducky every time he hung back and got close enough to the stroller. She really got excited when Dolly hopped right up in her lap. She pulled the cat's ears and tail, but Dolly only purred the louder. Finally, Laela buried her little hands down into the cat's fur and used her like a muff.

"I believe they like each other," Maverick said.

"Do you think that the animals liked baby Jesus like this?" Bridget asked.

"Probably so," Maverick answered. "There's just something magical about the whole Christmas holiday. I wish Granny was here to see the way Laela loved the tree and the way she's acting this morning."

"Deidre loved Christmas. Maybe she passed that on down to Laela," Bridget said.

"Grandpa did, too," Maverick said. "He passed a lot more than just his love for the holidays down to us boys, though."

"Like what?" Bridget asked.

"Love for the land, how to take care of cattle, and how to treat a woman are just a few of the things," he said.

"I'd have liked to have met him," she said. "He sounds a lot like my dad."

"He would have loved having a baby to share with us today." Maverick kicked a rock out of the way of the stroller wheels.

"Us?" She shot him a sideways look.

"She's ours today. She belongs to you on paper, but she's on my ranch, so that makes her part mine," he said.

"I will remember that next time she needs her nappy changed," Bridget said.

"That part is yours. My part is getting to let her hold the ornaments from the tree and tell her stories." His biceps strained the seams of his jacket when he slid the barn door open. She shouldn't have been surprised. He'd picked her up that night in her flat in Ireland like she wasn't anything more than a feather pillow, and he had twirled her around until they were both dizzy.

Maverick waited until she'd pushed the stroller into the barn, and then knelt so he and the baby were eye to eye. "Welcome to the barn on the Callahan Ranch, princess."

Ducky reared up on Maverick's jean-clad knee and licked him across the face, but Dolly just opened one eye and then closed it.

"So? Do you like Texas?" he asked the baby, but he'd changed his focus and was looking up at Bridget. A picture of him propped up on an elbow in her bed flashed through her mind. His green eyes had bored into hers that morning just like they were doing now.

"We're impressed," she said, feeling every bit of the heat from his gaze going from her toes to the top of her head. "It's a bit warmer in here than it is outside. Maybe I should remove my jacket."

Maverick stood up and helped her with her coat and then hung it over the back of the stroller handles. "The new calf is this way. Want me to push the stroller for you?"

"Thank you." She handed it off to him. "We're not used to traveling over such rough ground when we go for our strolls."

He led them to the first of five stalls and opened the door. The little black calf was lying in a bed of straw, but his head popped up when he realized someone was there.

Dolly jumped out of the stroller and went to rub around the new calf's shoulders. Ducky sniffed him from tail to nose and then walked away. Laela wiggled and tried so hard to free herself that Maverick finally picked her up and set her down beside the calf.

"Would you look at that?" Maverick whispered when the baby laid her head on the black fur and the calf didn't seem to mind. "She's definitely special, Bridget. Granny used to say that the angels give some babies a little extra love in their hearts. It sounds crazy but…"

"Nana said the same thing. It's an Irish thing, not a crazy one," Bridget told him.

* * *

Maverick leaned his elbows on the top rail. "I'm glad you told Granny you would stay on until she gets out of rehab. Sharing times like this with you is priceless."

"Me too," Bridget said. "These are special moments for me too, Maverick. They're like healing balm to my heart."

Maverick didn't want the moment to end. If they stayed in that little bubble of time, maybe her heart would magically be whole again. If he could have one Christmas miracle that year, he'd give it to her so that she wouldn't be sad anymore.

Laela left the calf, crawled over to the side of the stall, and pulled herself up on the open gate. Holding on with one hand, she reached the other up to Maverick.

"You ready to go for another ride back to the house, are you?" he asked.

"We really should. There's things I should be getting done," Bridget answered.

He put the baby into the stroller and kissed her on the forehead. "Sure you don't want me to push or maybe carry her to the house? She might be tired of sitting in that thing."

"She's fine," Bridget said. "You have things to do, and I won't get lost in that short distance. See you at noon, and thanks for the outing. The new calf is beautiful."

He took his arm from around her and whistled. Ducky came running from somewhere inside the barn with Dolly right behind him. He waited until both animals were outside the barn and dashing on ahead of Bridget before he closed the door.

Once in the tack room, he grabbed a broom and swept the floor. Then he began to clean off the worktable. When that was done, he'd have a place to set things from the dusty, dirty shelves. He'd barely gotten the table cleared when he thought he heard the squeak of the barn doors being pulled open. He listened intently but there was no other sound, so he went back to work.

"Hey, Maverick," Alana said as she pushed into the tack room. "Bridget said I could find you in here."

Alana was a tall blonde who lived on the spread next door. She'd ridden the school bus with Paxton and Maverick when they were kids, and now she helped her dad run their ranch. With her looks and ability to do anything she set her mind to do, she intimidated the hell out of most men.

"Hello," Maverick said. "Welcome to the messiest tack room in the world."

"I've offered to help Iris many times, but you know how independent she is," Alana said. "I came over to see if you could use some help with anything this next week. Iris called to thank me for helping her at the church and tell me her plans. She said I could visit her on Fridays at the rehab center, and to bring chocolate."

"Sounds just like her, giving everyone their orders." Maverick chuckled. "Thanks for the offer, but I think Bridget and I can handle it for a month."

Alana started for the door and then turned back. "We've been neighbors and friends our whole lives. I think that gives me the right to get all up in your business. Is that baby yours?" she asked bluntly.

Maverick shook his head. "No, she is not."

"Then what's the story? Why's Bridget here?" Alana asked. "Iris could have hired anyone, or hell's bells, I would have come over and stayed with her for a few weeks."

"Bridget is the granddaughter of Granny's childhood friend who died a few weeks ago. Maybe you'd forgotten that Granny is from Ireland? Anyway, Bridget needed a job and a place to live, so Granny called her and asked her to come to Texas. It was a way to help out her old friend one more time," Maverick explained.

"Where's Bridget's husband?" Alana asked.

"No husband, and the baby doesn't belong... well, she does now..." He went on to explain about Deidre.

"That's a lot of sorrow to pile on one person," Alana said.

"I know," Maverick agreed.

"Thanks for telling me. Can I tell Daddy? We've been wondering how all this fit together and why she didn't call on us for help."

"It's not a secret." Maverick went back to work.

"And you've only known her a couple of days?" Alana pressed for more.

"That part is a secret." He grinned.

"Fair enough." Alana crossed the room and wrapped her arms around him. "Didn't know if I should be hugging you anymore if you were in a relationship, but now I guess it's all right."

"You can hug me anytime you want, darlin'. We're friends." He kissed her on the forehead without bending. She had always been the tallest kid in his brother's class until they were sophomores, and Paxton finally grew enough to be two inches taller than she was.

"Thanks for that, and if you change your mind about help, just holler at me," she said.

Maverick draped an arm around her shoulders and walked her out to her truck. "I think between me and Bridget, we can manage, but thanks for the offer."

"All you have to do is call if you change your mind," she

said. "And, Maverick, be careful. Bridget is cute and that accent is adorable, but you're like a brother to me, and I'd hate to see you with a broken heart when she goes back to Ireland," Alana warned.

"You're giving me romantic advice?" he asked.

They stepped out of the barn, and she wrapped her arms around him. "Honey, I'm the best person in the world to give you advice."

"Why's that?" He hugged her back.

"Because I'm a woman, and we're smarter than men when it comes to things of the heart." She stepped back. "Tell Pax that I asked about him." She got into her truck and started the engine.

"Will do," he said with a wave.

He went back to the messy tack room and sat down on the barstool beside the work bench. What had changed Granny's mind about him coming back to West Texas to help her out? She had something up her sleeve for sure. It couldn't be that she wanted him to be with Bridget. She had no idea about that night in Ireland—hell, he still didn't even know Bridget's last name. Granny had been trying to get either him or Pax interested in Alana for years, but to Maverick, kissing her would be like kissing his younger sister.

On the other hand, kissing Bridget again... Now, that idea sent a tingle down his backbone.

# Chapter Six

Bridget hurried through removing Laela's coat and hat and got her situated on a pallet with her toys on the kitchen floor. Then she alternated between watching the baby play and looking out the window above the sink. She wished for a pair of binoculars so she could better see all the way to the barn. Alana, who'd been first to get to Iris when she fell in the church, was out there with Maverick.

She'd driven up in a fancy, bright red pickup and asked where she could find him. Bridget had directed her to the barn and then almost jogged back to the house. Now, she wondered if Maverick and Alana had something going, either in the past or the present, and a jealous streak shot through her heart.

It wasn't long until Alana and Maverick came out of the barn, arm in arm. Then she hugged him for a long time before she got into her truck. He waved and went back inside.

"I wonder..." Bridget muttered as she watched the

vehicle drive right past the house, "if Iris caught the vibes between me and Maverick. Maybe she wants to squash anything between us by matchmaking with him and Alana."

*Why would she do that?* Nana whispered in her ear.

"Because if something came of this attraction, then he might go to Ireland with me, and she shouldn't want that," Bridget muttered.

The phone rang and she rushed to the living room to answer it, but got there just in time to hear a woman's voice on the message machine. "This is Retta. I'm callin' to check on your grandmother and to tell you that you need to come home. You've spoiled Annie to the sound of your voice, and she won't go to sleep without you. Miss you and hope everything is going well."

"Jesus, Mary and Joseph!" Bridget threw herself back on the sofa. How many women did this cowboy have?

Laela crawled from the kitchen to the living room and pulled herself up on the sofa. Bridget picked her up and held her close. "He's still the wild cowboy I met in Ireland, lassie. But I'm not that free-spirited party girl, and I sure wouldn't have spent the night with him if I'd known he had a girl back home about to have his baby."

The phone rang again, and the only name that came up on the caller ID was *Emily*. Bridget let it go to voice mail and hoped that it was a neighbor asking about Iris.

"Maverick, honey, this is Emily. Is Iris in the rehab center yet? I'd like to send her some flowers. And the ultrasound yesterday didn't let us know if the baby is a boy or a girl. Maybe next month we'll find out. Know you've got your hands full, but call me."

Sweet angels in heaven! He had a baby to one woman, had another one pregnant, and a third one had just visited him in the barn! And he'd been flirting with her!

"He's got a harem." Bridget groaned. "But, by damn, I won't be a part of it. I'll do my job here and go home to Ireland where I belong."

Nana had always told her that work helped relieve a troubled mind, so she took Laela back to the kitchen and put her on the floor with her tote bag full of toys. Bridget whipped up a batch of shortbread cookies with a touch of lemon. She'd put back some of them for the trip to the nursing home on Saturday, would take some to Iris tomorrow, and then put a dozen or so into the cookie jar. While those were baking she made a lovely apple and pear pie from the fruit Iris had canned last summer. After that, she put a nice little chicken pasty in the oven for the noon meal. It had baked and was cooling on the top of the stove when Maverick came in the back door. He hung up his work coat and went straight to the sink to wash up for dinner.

"Where's our pretty baby girl?" he asked as he lathered up his hands and forearms.

Bridget wanted to say that his daughter was wherever Retta lived, but she couldn't force the words out of her mouth. By then Laela had crawled over to him and pulled herself up on his leg. He dried his hands, picked her up, and twirled her around until she was giggling.

"Nothing like the sound of a baby's laughter," he said.

"So you like babies, do you?" Bridget asked as she took the meat pie to the table.

"Love 'em. Always have," he answered. "But no one has made me ready to settle down yet."

*Then why did you have a baby with one woman and get another one pregnant?* she thought. It was on the tip of her tongue to ask how many babies he intended to have along the way while he looked for the right one. Or maybe if he ever intended to let his legitimate kids know the illegitimate ones.

"Did Granny call you? I thought for sure she'd already be transferred to rehab, and she said she'd let me know when that happened." He sat down at the table with Laela in his lap.

Oh, he was a slick one all right—changing the subject from babies to his grandmother. "No, haven't heard. I thought I'd call and check on her right after we eat."

* * *

Something wasn't right.

Maverick could feel it in his bones as well as in his heart. Out in the barn, they'd been like a couple as they watched Laela with the animals. Now, the whole house felt like the A/C had been turned on right there in December.

*Alana!* It hit him like a brick wall—could Bridget be jealous? Had she seen him with Alana earlier at the barn? She would have no idea that their neighbor was like a younger sister.

Not quite sure how to thaw Bridget out, he talked to the baby instead. "How did you spend your morning, Miz Laela? Did you help make pies, or did you just keep Ducky and Dolly chased out of the kitchen?"

He thought that Bridget might answer, but she kept her silence, so he tried a different approach. "Did your mommy make cookies? I thought I smelled something lemony when I came inside the house."

Still no answer from Bridget. "Well, I had a visitor," he said. "Our neighbor Alana, who's been like a little sister to me for years, came over to offer her help if we need her."

"I don't need any help, but if you do, she can help you." Bridget's tone had more than a little ice in it. She put a pie in the middle of the table and set about getting cranberry sauce and sliced cheese from the refrigerator.

"I don't think she was talking about the house," he said. "You're doing a fine job with it."

*Don't be tryin' to butter me up, boy-o,* she thought. *I'm not having a baby for you. You've already got one and one on the way, and no telling how many more older ones.*

"She was thinking more about the ranch," Maverick went on. "I had no idea it had gotten in such bad repair, but then, Buster is almost as old as Granny, and between them, they were hardly keeping up, not doing much maintenance. The cattle look great, but the tack room hasn't been cleaned in years. And don't get me started on the fences, but Alana has her own place to help take care of, so I'd only call on her if I couldn't get something done any other way."

Bridget nodded, but she still didn't make eye contact with him. "If you'll put Laela in her high chair, I'll get dinner on the table."

"Sure thing." Dammit, anyway! He'd thought this morning that having her and the baby in the house for a whole month would be right nice. But now he wondered if he would survive the chill.

He opened his mouth to explain further that he and Paxton had grown up with Alana and she was like a sister to him, but he clamped it shut. His grandpa had told him that the first thing to do when you found yourself in a hole was to simply stop digging. Seemed to him like fitting advice at the moment.

Bridget put the pie in the middle of the table and sat down beside the baby. "Iris always says grace before we eat."

Maverick bowed his head and said a simple prayer, then cocked his head sideways at the pie. "We're having dessert first?"

"It's a meat pie. We have biscuits or an apple/pear pie

with whipped cream for dessert." She handed him a spoon. "Dip into it."

He put two big scoops on his plate. "Chicken pot pie." He took the first bite. "Very good, but what is the baby going to eat?"

"I pick out the chicken, and just give her the vegetables and sauce. She loves it," Bridget answered.

The rest of the meal was eaten in awkward quietness. The only time they spoke at all was to talk to Laela, and that wasn't very often. When they'd finished, Bridget brought a pie and a bowl of freshly whipped cream to the table.

"If you'd rather have biscuits—I mean, cookies—or maybe take some to the barn with you this afternoon for a snack, they're right there." She pointed toward the counter.

"Enough," Maverick said. "Why are you so mad at me?"

"Figure it out for yourself," she said, tersely.

He pushed back his chair, stood up, and went straight to the utility room to put on his coat. Settling his hat on his head, he returned to the kitchen, picked up the whole container of cookies, tucked them under his arm, and headed out the back door.

How could he figure anything out when he had no idea what had set her off? Hell, he didn't even know she had a temper until today. He worked until dark, and when he closed the door to the tack room, there wasn't a speck of dust or a cobweb in sight. The old wood floor was spick-and-span clean, and every piece of trash or bucket of dried-up paint had been thrown in the back of his truck to be taken to the dump ground the next day.

The feeling in the house was still pretty chilly when he got there that evening. Laela eased the tension a little when she crawled over to him and raised her arms for him to take her.

"She's never met a stranger," Bridget said. "Deidre took her to work at the bakery with her every day when she quit working at the pub. The owner said those few months before Deidre died were the best he'd ever had at his shop. The baby drew the people in, and they bought all their bread and supplies while they were there."

Well, well—Bridget was talking to him again. That was a step in the right direction.

"I think she's going to be a cowgirl when she grows up. She likes my hat."

"She's going to be whatever she wants to be, but I doubt that it will be a cowgirl," Bridget told him. "We've already eaten. Leftovers are on the stove, and your sweet tea is in the refrigerator. We'll be in the living room." She removed the cowboy hat from Laela's head, and stood on tiptoe to place it back on Maverick's head.

"I'll take her in there. I thought we were making cookies this evening," he said.

"I made cookies all afternoon. There's plenty, so we can take some to Iris, and to the nursing home on Saturday, plus feed you through the week," she said.

"I was looking forward to making them tonight. That song about Christmas cookies has been on my mind all day," he said.

"What song?" Bridget asked.

He brought up the song by George Strait, took Laela out of the high chair, and two-stepped around the kitchen with her. The lyrics said that every time she put another batch in the oven that there was fifteen minutes for kissing and loving.

"Grandpa used to dance around the floor with Granny when this song played. They had an old cassette player and he loved George Strait," he said when the song ended. "Granny will be eighty right after the first of the year, and

Buster isn't much younger. I wouldn't be surprised if he stays with his daughter and doesn't come back to Daisy." He carried the baby to the living room and set her on the floor.

"And what happens if Buster doesn't come back?" Bridget asked.

Maverick sighed. "Then it'll be time for either me or Paxton to step up and come back to help her."

"How do you feel about that?" Bridget sat down on the floor in front of the baby.

"I always figured Granny would eventually sell the place so she'd have the money to really retire"—he hesitated—"and I hoped I'd have the money to buy the place. I've always wanted something of my own."

"Why wouldn't she just pass the place down to you?" she asked.

"I wouldn't expect her to do that," Maverick said. "She and Grandpa worked to build this place, and it can be a profitable business again with some hard work. It's her retirement fund, so to speak. Besides, I've been raised to make my own way in the world, not depend on handouts."

"If you have your own ranch, you won't have time for going to the pub so much, either," she reminded him. "Iris told me that a ranch is a twenty-four-hour-a-day job, and that it pretty much owns you, rather than you owning it."

"The Baker brothers I've been helping out on the Longhorn Canyon ranch and me and Paxton"—he stammered, trying to find the words—"we do kind of have a wild reputation, and I realized that owning a ranch would mean giving up part of my previous lifestyle, but it doesn't mean that I'd be dead. I could still go to the honky-tonk and do some two-steppin' once in a while."

"That'd be havin' your cake and eating it too, now wouldn't it?" she asked.

"Everyone needs a little kissin' and lovin' like the song says," he told her. "And I usually find it at a honky-tonk, so if that means I'll be havin' my cake and eating it too, then I'll enjoy every minute of it," he said as he disappeared back to the kitchen to heat up his supper.

* * *

*Well, you can bloody well think twice if you think you'll be kissin' and lovin' on me for fifteen minutes while the cookies bake, not when you've got a harem out there waiting for you.* Bridget closed her eyes and shook her head. She would run too, if she were in his shoes. Even if Alana was just a friend, Maverick still had Retta and Emily—one with a baby who wanted him to rock her to sleep and one with another baby on the way.

She heard the ring tone of his cell phone and the deep, low tones of conversation, and wondered which of his women he was talking to. Was it a different one from the two on the answering machine? Her imagination went wild, thinking about that, until he finally returned to the living room.

"Granny called." He kicked off his boots and sat down on the floor with Bridget and the baby. "She said y'all talked earlier this afternoon. She's already lookin' forward to those cookies, and she's getting acquainted with the other folks at rehab."

"She told me that the place is really nice. She has her own room, and she eats in the dining room with the other folks. She says that there's about ten of them right now, but some will go home in a few days," Bridget said.

"She says she's already made a friend. It's some lady from down around Happy who's living in an assisted place in Amarillo. Who knows if she'll stay, or not? She may make it through tomorrow and decide she's had enough or she might stay the whole time. You never know about her," he said.

"Happy?" Bridget asked.

"I don't know," Maverick said. "Are you?"

"I mean is there really a village called Happy?" She didn't mean to look into his eyes, but their gazes locked and she couldn't look away.

"Yep," he said without blinking. "Just fifteen minutes north of here, but we call them towns, not villages."

"Ten minutes"—she finally looked away—"if I was driving."

A broad smile covered his face. "So you like to drive fast?"

"Sean won't let me drive his car anymore. He says that I scare the bejesus out of him, but"—one shoulder raised slightly—"if a car will go a hundred and ninety kilometers per an hour, then why only hold it back to one hundred twelve?"

"You are preachin' to the choir." His grin got even bigger. "Did you drive that fast with Laela in the car?"

"Of course not." She shot a dirty look his way. "Fast cars and fast women. That your speed?"

"Throw in buckin' broncs and bulls, and you pretty well sum up my lifestyle until a few months ago," he admitted. "What about you? You like anything other than fast cars?"

One of her eyebrows shot straight up. "Evidently at one time I liked a fast cowboy, didn't I?"

She thought he might say something about mothers and their responsibility, but instead, he said, "Being a mother doesn't have to mean you give up your whole personality. It should just mean that you put your child first, and the good times second."

"Does being a father mean the same thing?" she asked.

"Yes, ma'am, it does."

*Then why aren't you home with your baby, or at least with Emily while she waits on the birth of her child?*

He pointed toward the baby. "She's rubbing her little eyes. I think she's ready for a bath and bed. Can I read her the bedtime story tonight?"

Bridget suddenly felt like she hadn't done her job. She'd been so busy trying to keep body and soul together, that she hadn't even thought about starting to read to Laela every night. Besides, wasn't seven months kind of young for a child to be entertained with a book?

"Sure," she said, unwilling to admit her failure.

She drew a bath for the baby and tested it with her hand to see if it was too warm. Then she laid out a towel and washcloth on the ladder-back chair beside the tub, but even with all that preparation, she didn't feel like she was doing enough— not when she hadn't been reading Laela a bedtime story.

The baby loved water and was usually fussy when Bridget took her out of the bath, but that night she was grouchy all through it. She threw her toys over the side and tried to crawl out before Bridget could even get her hair washed. Not until she was finally wrapped in a towel did she eventually smile.

"You are a spoiled lass, for sure," Bridget said as she put a gown and a nappy on her. "You don't even know what reading a bedtime story is, and yet you're having a bit of a fit for it."

Once she had Laela's hair dried and brushed, she carried her to the living room and handed her off to Maverick, who was sitting in a recliner. He popped the leg rest up and reached for a children's book on the table beside him.

"Where did that come from?" Bridget asked.

"Granny has a whole bookcase full of them in the fourth

bedroom. Tonight we'll be reading *The Mitten*, a story about a big snowstorm and animals. There's lots of pictures to entertain this princess," he said.

Bridget plopped down on the sofa and listened while Maverick did the voices of the animals in the book. He really was good with children, she thought, and should have a dozen, but not with as many women.

Still, there was something so sweet about seeing a big, old rough cowboy with a baby in his arms, taking time after reading each page to point out the animals and other items in the book. It was like there were two Maverick Callahans. One was that wild, carefree man she'd met in Ireland, and the other was a kind, gentle soul. When he finished the last page, Laela leaned her little head onto his chest and closed her eyes.

"I think she's asleep," he whispered.

"Not quite yet," Bridget said. "You'll know when she's really sound asleep."

"How?" he mouthed.

"Just wait a minute or two. You'll feel her sigh, and that'll be when she's really asleep," she told him.

Still feeling guilty about not reading to Laela, she promised herself that when she got back to Ireland, she'd read Irish books to Laela. She should hear the stories that Nana had read to Bridget in her native language.

"I hadn't thought to start reading to her," she said.

"Never too young for books," Maverick said. "That's straight from Granny. She read to us every night. I don't know who liked Harry Potter more. Us or her. There it is—that sigh you talked about. Can I take her to the crib?"

"Sure," Bridget said.

She might not approve of his lifestyle, and they might not even be able to be friends, but she had to admit, he was damn good with kids!

# Chapter Seven

When Bridget walked into Iris's room she thought that Iris's color was fantastic compared to what it had been when they went to church on Sunday. Evidently the medicine they were giving her for the infection had kicked in and started to work. Iris was sitting in a lift chair and motioned them over. "Give me that baby. I've missed her. What's in the bag?"

"Shortbread cookies and scones that'd still be warm. I made fresh strawberry preserves this morning to go on them," Bridget said as Maverick put the baby in Iris's lap.

"I'll give Laela some Granny sugar and then get right into them. The food here is good, but scones remind me of Ireland and my childhood," Iris said. "My new friend Wanda is coming down here to meet y'all. Mav, you sit right here." She pointed to the folding chair on her right. "And this one is for you, Bridget." She nodded toward the one on her left.

When Iris kissed her on both of her chubby, little cheeks,

Laela laughed out loud, so she did it again. "Did you see that big Christmas tree in the lobby? It's not as pretty as the one at home, is it?" Iris was one of the few who didn't talk in a "baby voice" to Laela. "Mav sent me pictures of you putting the star on the tree. Until you get a baby brother or sister, that can be your job every year."

Bridget bit back a smart-ass reply about Laela not getting a sibling, and that she'd be taking her baby home in a few weeks. Maybe next year Maverick could bring Retta's baby, Annie, or Emily's baby to put the star on the tree.

"Knock. Knock." A husky voice floated into the room before a lady with lavender hair pushed her walker inside. "I'm Wanda Jackson, but I'm not that famous country singer from years ago. I can't carry a tune in a galvanized milk bucket. Iris invited me to come into her room and meet y'all."

"Take this precious child and let us get into the scones." Iris lifted the baby up to Maverick. "Wanda, this is my grandson Mav, and this is Bridget and the baby is Laela. All y'all, this is my new friend."

"It's nice to meet you, Miz Wanda." Maverick flashed a brilliant smile.

"It's a pleasure," Bridget said. "Did you break a hip too?"

"No, honey, I had to get my knee replaced for the second time. I wore the hell out of the one they put in fifteen years ago. The doctor argued with me about having another surgery, since I'm seventy-five, but I told him he'd replace it or I'd beat him to death with my cane." She laughed. "You ain't from around here, are you? Is that a British accent?"

"Irish," Bridget said. "I'm only here for a few weeks to help Iris."

"Well, that's right sweet of you. That baby is beautiful. She's going to grow up to be a handful."

Bridget laughed, but it was forced. She hadn't thought of Laela's teenage years until that moment. There would come a time when she'd be as ornery as Bridget and Deidre had been, and Bridget didn't look forward to those days one bit.

Iris dug into the bag they had brought and took out the containers. "And we have scones and fresh-made strawberry preserves. You forgot to bring us plates and silverware. Maverick, go right down that hallway, all the way to the end." Iris talked with her hands. "The last door on the left is the dining room. Ask the lady in there for a couple of paper plates and some plastic spoons. You might get us some napkins too."

"Yes, ma'am." Maverick stood up, handed the baby off to Bridget, and held Wanda's walker while she sat down in the chair he'd vacated.

He'd barely gotten out of the room when Iris turned to Bridget. "What's going on at home? Talk fast. As fast as he walks, he'll be back soon."

"Everything is fine," Bridget said.

"No, it's not. The temperature dropped twenty degrees in here when y'all came in. You're fighting or at least arguing, and I want to know why." Iris removed the lids from the two containers and handed the cookies to Wanda.

She selected one and bit into it. "This is so good, and you're such a sweetheart to share with me, Iris."

"You are welcome. Everyone needs friends and family," Iris told her, then focused her stare on Bridget again. "Time to 'fess up."

Bridget couldn't tell Iris that her precious grandson had knocked up at least two other women, so she put all the blame on another one. "Alana came to see Maverick. He says that she's like a sister, but she's so beautiful."

"Don't ever let anyone intimidate you, my child," Iris scolded her gently. "If Alana was going to get involved with a Callahan, it would be Paxton, not Maverick. He's the one who's always had a thing for her and wouldn't ask her out because he was afraid of rejection. On the way home from Ireland, I caught Maverick looking at a woman's picture on his phone. That lady looked a lot like you. Did y'all meet over there?"

Bridget couldn't lie to Iris. For one thing, she'd been too good to her. For another, the woman would see right through it. "We met at the pub where I worked the last night he was in Ireland, but I didn't even know his last name until I saw pictures of him at your house."

"I thought so, and so did your grandmother. Virgie said something happened right before I left, and you weren't the same," Iris said. "I think there was a flame there between y'all even if you didn't spend much time together, and you need to see if it has any fire left in it or you'll always wonder why you didn't. That's my advice, and your nana would tell you the same thing. You think about that. I hear Mav coming back, now."

"Yes, ma'am." Bridget had no choice but to spend time with Maverick, but she couldn't say that there was no chance in bloody hell that there was fire left between them, without spilling the beans about Maverick's women. Retta's and Emily's voices on the answering machine had been like pouring water on any spark that might be there. "And thank you for the advice, but"—she hesitated—"another thing is that I'm going through a little depression. At first I was in denial when Nana told me she only had weeks to live. Then when she was gone, I was angry at God for taking her. Now, I'm just kind of numb." She wiped a tear away.

Wanda patted her on her arm. "Honey, I know just how

you feel. I had four children and lost every one of them. My oldest two died in the Gulf War, my daughter with cancer, and my baby boy in a car accident. A mother should never have to bury her children. It's an unnatural grief, but, honey, happy memories help heal all the pain and soon just the sweet things are what you'll remember."

Iris laid a hand on her shoulder. "I miss Virgie too. We wrote to each other every month, and these past few years, when it got to where it wasn't so expensive to call, we talked once a week. I knew her well and she wouldn't want you to be sad like this. Virgie was a fun, upbeat person."

Maverick brought in the plates, napkins, and a couple of individually wrapped envelopes of cutlery. "Here you go, ladies." He handed them to Iris and turned to Bridget. "Are you all right? Have you been crying?"

"We're talking about her grandmother and how her death is just now hitting Bridget." Iris split two scones in half and put them on her plate, then passed the open container over to Wanda. Then she turned her focus back to Bridget. "Your nana was so worried about you, trying to raise a baby by yourself. But she was proud of you. She told me so right before she passed away."

Tears rolled down Bridget's cheeks and dropped onto her shirt. "I just wish I'd had more time with her, and Laela could've grown up with her like I did."

"So do we all, but the good Lord saw different," Iris said. "Now I'm going to have a scone, and we're going to talk about something else. Have y'all been making cookies for Saturday?"

"Yes, we have." Bridget dried her eyes and managed a smile.

*But he's had enough of that loving stuff with his other women while his cookies baked*, Bridget thought.

"That little Elijah sure has a pretty voice for a little kid, don't he?" Iris asked.

"Yes, ma'am, he does, and the others sound pretty good too. They should be ready for the Christmas program for sure," Maverick said.

"They miss you," Bridget said.

"Take cookies every Sunday," Iris said. "They love treats. Did they do good on their Sunday school lesson?"

"Lily Rose fussed at Randy for picking his nose." Bridget laughed.

"That's not a new thing." Iris bit into a scone. "Man, these things take me back to when I was a little girl, runnin' around with Virgie. Them was the days."

"I ain't never been to Ireland, but I'd be willing to pay for the plane tickets for us both if I could have these every day," Wanda said.

Bridget wondered how these two elderly women could strike up such a solid friendship in only a day and a half. Was it easier to be so trusting when a person got older? One thing for sure, Iris was going to go up in smoke when she found out about Retta and Emily.

"I stayed with Virgie when I visited Ireland last year. If we were ever to come back, would you tell us what hotels are good?" Iris asked.

"You two are welcome to stay with me. Just give me time to find a place."

"That's so sweet." Wanda sighed. "Family is special, Iris. Don't you ever take them for granted."

"Trust me, honey, I don't." Iris looked up at Maverick.

He'd propped a hip on the arm of her lift chair and smiled at her. Bridget wondered how he could hide so much from his grandmother, the very person who'd been so good to him. She could have never hidden things from Nana. Maybe

Maverick hadn't told Iris about her great-grandchild and the one on the way for the same reason. He didn't want her to be disappointed in him.

Iris poked her on the arm. "Where's your mind, child? You're staring off into space like you're lookin' at a ghost."

"I'm sorry," Bridget said. "Just woolgathering."

"Laela is squirmin' like a worm in hot ashes. Put her down so she can explore. Me and Wanda want to watch her play," Iris said.

Bridget set the baby on the floor, and she immediately headed straight for the door. Quicker than a bolt of lightning, Maverick was on his feet. He closed the door before she reached it and sat down on the floor in front of it. Laela giggled and crawled up in his lap.

"Ain't that sweet," Wanda said.

Bridget wondered if the baby named Annie loved him like Laela did, if he read her bedtime stories, and if he'd make some excuse to be gone on Christmas Day to be with her. When it was exactly four o'clock, Iris pointed at the clock. "Wanda and I've got to go to thirty minutes of therapy now, and then we have supper in the dining hall."

"That's our cue, princess. We need to go home and do evening chores anyway." Maverick got to his feet. He bent to hug his grandmother and then gathered Laela up into his arms.

Bridget slung the diaper bag over her shoulder. Last year at this time, she would have been picking up her purse to go to a pub for a pint. She would have had a little money, a small makeup kit, and a hairbrush in the purse, not diapers, small stuffed animals, and wet wipes. A phone call could sure turn a life around. That's how she'd found out about Deidre's death. One minute she was playing darts in the pub and the next she got a phone call—Deidre was dead.

* * *

Maverick got the baby situated in the car seat, and then handed Bridget the truck keys. "When Granny called this afternoon, she told me to give the keys to her truck to you. I guess this one is yours until she comes home."

She shook her head. "You drive. I'll only use it when it's absolutely necessary."

"Thanks. I really don't like being a passenger," he said.

"Especially when I told you that I like to go fast, right?"

"Well, there is that." He helped her inside and then rounded the back end of the vehicle to the driver's side. "And there's a baby in the backseat."

"Do you think I would ever, ever do anything to harm my child?" Her eyes flashed pure anger toward him.

"Hey, I was teasing," he said.

"Don't." She raised a hand. "Just don't."

He started the engine and backed out of the parking lot. "You need to work on getting that bee out of your under britches. Would going by the ice cream store help?"

"Just drive us back to the ranch. We've got ice cream there," she told him.

*Women! Can't live with them and Granny would kill me if I threw her out on the side of the road for being so damned stubborn.*

She kept her eyes on whatever was going past the side window at fifty miles an hour, and he focused on the road. Laela talked to herself and the small teddy bear that she favored.

Too bad that grown-ups couldn't act like children—they just went with the flow and didn't let things bother them. He turned off the highway and down a farm road to the lane that took them back to the ranch. He'd barely gotten the engine turned off before Bridget bailed out of the truck, swung open the back door, and took Laela out of her car seat. She flipped the diaper bag over her shoulder and stormed up on the porch.

Maverick unlocked the door for her, and followed her inside. He went straight for the refrigerator, and got out a beer. Bridget had already gotten both her and Laela's coats off and hung on the hooks on the coat tree in the foyer. He took his time removing his coat and hat, and then carried the beer to the living room.

He plopped down on the end of the sofa and took a long drink. When he set the bottle down on the end table, he noticed the red light flickering on the phone showing that there were three messages.

He started to hit the play button when he realized that he hadn't offered to get Bridget a beer. Sure, he didn't like her coldness, but that was no reason for him to be hateful. "Want a beer or a glass of sweet tea?"

"No, I'll make myself a cup of hot tea later, but thanks," she said.

With a shrug, he hit the button and listened to the digital voice say, "You have two old messages."

The first one that played was from Retta and the second from Emily. He tipped up the beer for another drink.

"Well?" Bridget popped her hands onto her hips. "What have you got to say for yourself? How can you just sit there and not say a word?"

"Annie likes me. All babies do. Emily doesn't know if she's having a girl or a boy. What's there to say? I've already talked to them both since those calls were made."

She wanted to slap him hard enough to rock his jaw. How dare he talk about those two unsuspecting women like that! They probably loved him, and little Annie no doubt missed her daddy.

It took him a minute to realize what had happened. The two older calls had been made the day before, and Bridget had heard them. She had no idea who Retta and Emily were, so what if she thought those babies were his? After the way both he and Bridget had been so impulsive in Ireland, he didn't blame her, but it was funny. He chuckled, then laughed, and then roared, his laughter bouncing off the walls.

"You think it's funny to deceive your grandmother like that?" she asked.

Then he remembered the timing mentioned on the machine. The two old messages would have come in about same time Alana was in the barn with him. Bridget must think he was quite the ladies' man to be seeing Alana, have a baby on the way, and one already born.

"Why didn't you just ask me about all this yesterday?" he asked.

"Why didn't you tell me about it in Ireland? I wouldn't have fallen in bed with you if I'd known you were married or engaged or whatever you Yanks do when you have a harem," she smarted off.

"I wouldn't know, darlin'. I've never been able to get into even one serious relationship. Sit down here beside me and let me explain about Retta and Emily," he said.

"I'd rather stand." She glared at him.

"Have it your way. Retta is married to Cade Maguire, and Emily is married to his brother, Justin. They own the ranch next to the one that the Baker brothers, Tag and Hud, bought last summer. Pax and I moved there to help them get it up and running. It's kind of an extended family between Canyon Creek with the Bakers and Longhorn Canyon with Maguires, since Emily is Tag and Hud's older sister," he explained.

"Oh. My. God." She sank down on the sofa beside him. "I'm sorry."

He reached across the distance separating them and laid a hand on her shoulder. "Apology accepted. If I'd been in your shoes, I might have thought the same thing after that wild night we had in Ireland. We really don't know each other, Bridget, but I've never forgotten that night. There was something between us that I'd never felt before, and it's still there. So what do you say? Can we start all over and get to know each other?"

She placed her hand over his. "Hello, I'm Bridget O'Malley. I used to be a party girl, and I did a few things I'm not real proud of. Like one night I gave in to the impulse to go to bed with a stranger, and I did it. Now he probably thinks I have round heels."

Maverick pulled his hand free from hers and stuck it out. "Pleased to meet you, Miz O'Malley. At least now I know your last name. It's very Irish. I'm Maverick Callahan. I used to be more of a party cowboy than I am now, and sometimes I miss the excitement of those days. How about you?"

She shook his hand and then dropped it. "Oh, yes, I do. I really do, but Laela needs me, and there's a certain satisfaction about being a parent."

"Could I buy you a cup of coffee this evening? Or maybe a cup of tea? I imagine we'll have to make it at home, but I'd like to get to know you better," he said.

Bridget looked down at the baby, who'd pulled herself up to the sofa and then lost her balance and plopped down on her bottom. "Laela's bedtime is seven thirty, and I don't have a sitter, but I might let you make me a cup of tea."

"I make a mean peanut butter and jelly sandwich, and we could watch a movie right here in the living room," he suggested.

"That might be doable," she agreed with a nod. "But be warned. I don't usually give out kisses on first dates."

"Then, darlin'"—his grin was downright wickedly sexy—"I must be real special."

"You might have been when I met you in a pub. But this is now and we've just met in your grandmother's living room. Life changes everyone," she said.

"Amen to that," he said.

# Chapter Eight

Supper was ready and waiting, and it was past time for Maverick to come inside. Dark clouds covered the sky and a hard north wind shook the tree limbs. Bridget stood in the kitchen window, watching the last few diehard leaves from the pecan tree right outside the window let go, and the wind whipped them around as they tried to reach the ground. A calf bawled in the distance as if he was telling his mama he was afraid of storms. Lightning zipped across the sky. The thunder that followed brought Laela crawling across the floor so fast that the baby was almost a blur.

Bridget picked her up and held her close to her chest. "It's just the Irishman dumping the potatoes, lassie. Nothing to be afraid of. We're in the house, and we're safe."

A movement in her peripheral vision caused her to look out the window again, and there was Ducky, running hell for leather straight to the house. She opened the back door, and he and Dolly both dashed inside and headed for the living room. Laela began to wiggle and whine to get down, so Bridget carried her into the room. The baby pointed at the Christmas tree and jabbered something that only seven-month-old babies could see, and crawled over to it the minute that Bridget put her on the floor.

"Look but don't touch," Bridget told her.

Laela crawled from the tree to where Ducky was hiding from the thunder and seemed to give him a lecture in her baby language. Then she lay down beside Dolly and rubbed her ears. Bridget raced back to the kitchen window, but there was no Maverick in sight. She couldn't leave Laela alone in there with the cat and dog. Sure, they were good animals, but even a good pet could only take so much abuse before it snapped and retaliated.

She'd gone as far as the sofa when her phone pinged. She took it from her hip pocket and sat down. A text from Sean: Are you coming home soon? I might have a renter for my room if you don't want it.

She typed: It'll be at least a month. Don't hold it for me.

She got one back immediately: I'll interview the guy then. Miss you, luv.

She sent back a heart emoji and put the phone back in her pocket. Those words, *miss you,* were one of those little things that put tears in her eyes. The house phone rang right beside her, startling her so badly that she was on her feet before she even realized it.

"Callahan residence." She wiped her cheeks with her shirtsleeve.

"Have you been cryin'?" Iris asked.

"Just a little," Bridget admitted. "This ugly weather doesn't help my mood very much."

"It's teatime in Ireland," Iris said. "Make yourself a

cup. The warmth will help a lot. What did you make for supper?"

"Clam chowder and hot rolls, but Maverick isn't back from chores yet," she answered.

Laela left the cat and crawled over to Bridget. She flashed one of those baby smiles that melted Bridget's heart.

"I hear the baby. She's tryin' so hard to talk already. She's goin' to be a bright one," Iris said. "What I called for is to tell you that now I'm here in rehab, I'm enjoyin' it, but I need you to bring me some more clothes. I'm tired of runnin' around in hospital gowns and no under britches. I'll be in therapy all morning tomorrow, so you can just put the suitcase on my bed. Bring about a week's worth of bras, too."

"I can do that. Need anything else?"

Iris laughed and then said, "Wanda says to bring us a couple of really good-lookin' cowboys. If they look like Sam Elliott, she'll leave her entire estate to you."

"You ladies are quite the pair." Bridget smiled. "I should've thought to bring you some of your own things before now."

"Didn't know if I'd really stay until me and Wanda struck up a friendship. Oh, and stop on the way and get a big bag of those little chocolates. I'd tell you to sneak us in a bottle of wine, but that's against the rules." Iris giggled again. "Wanda says that we don't want to sit in the time-out chair."

"I'll be there in the morning. Call or text me if you think of anything else." Bridget heard the back door slam. Laela cocked her head to one side and took off in one of those fast crawls toward the sound.

"Will do. Bye now," Iris said.

Bridget hung up the phone and went straight to the kitchen. Maverick had hung up his coat and hat and was kicking his boots off at the back door. "Honey, I'm home," he called out.

With a smile on her face, she asked, "How was your day?"

"It's kind of fun to play house, ain't it?" He grinned.

"Playing house and really sharing a home are two different things," she replied. "Looks like it's going to start raining any minute."

"It's nasty out there, but I'll take rain over snow and ice any day of the week. It was a bad day for a heifer to deliver a calf. I put them in the barn, but the new mama didn't want to go, so it took me a while to persuade her." He picked the baby up and held her close. "I washed up out in the tack room so don't think I'm holding her with dirty hands."

"That's good, not about the cow but that you washed up. What's going on with the little baby calf you had out there in the stall?" She stirred the pot of clam chowder with a long wooden spoon.

"One of our other cows took him right on and is raising him with her little bull calf. You'd think they were twins," he answered.

"That's good," Bridget said, but she wondered what it would have been like if she and Deidre could have raised their children together. "Supper is ready to put on the table. Since you've already washed up, you can put the baby in the high chair while I bring it over from the stove." She set the basket of hot rolls beside the chowder. "It's a good day for soup."

"Any day is a good one for clam chowder." He bowed his head and waited for her to get seated before he said a short prayer.

When he'd said, "Amen," Bridget pinched off a tiny bit of the bread and blew on it until it was cool enough to put in Laela's mouth. "I got a text from Sean. He's got a chance to rent out his spare room. I don't want to stand in the way of him making money, so I told him to rent it if he can. I should have enough from this job to get a small flat for me and Laela when we get home."

* * *

"Tell me about Sean," Maverick said as he dipped soup for her first and then for himself.

"He's just a friend—maybe like Alana is to you—we grew up in the same little village that's only maybe a fourth as big as Skibbereen. Everyone knew everyone, so we were friends, but not like me and Deidre," she said.

"What does he look like?" Maverick asked.

Bridget pushed back her chair, went to the living room, and came back with her phone. She flipped through her pictures until she found one of the three of them and held it out for Maverick to see. "He's the blond in the middle. He's what you Yanks call a player. Women have always flocked to him like flies on honey."

Maverick couldn't help but think that he and Sean had a lot in common, even if they didn't look a thing alike. They both had chased and caught a lot of skirts. He wondered if Sean ever wished that he hadn't been quite so wild.

"He's cut his hair now, and grown a bit of a mustache." Bridget looked at the picture with longing in her eyes. "And he's the best pub dart contestant in our whole village." She put the phone on the table. "Even though he's a couple of years younger than me, Nana pushed me toward a relationship with him, but it would be like kissing my brother." She shivered. "I can't imagine it."

"Kind of like me kissing Alana," he whispered.

"Probably so. But Sean and I know each other so well, we might have made decent roommates."

"You've given this a lot of thought, haven't you?" he asked.

"Yes, I have, but then I have to think about it. Laela and I will have to rent something, and in our little village there aren't a lot of flats available. I'm all she has, so I'm always thinking about what she'll need. Wanda said something at the center about when she's a teenager. I have to think of her future as well as the present." She tried to give Laela another bite but the baby shook her head. "Guess she's done." Bridget took her out of the high chair and washed her hands and face.

"Speaking of the future, who's going to be Laela's guardian if something should happen to you?" Maverick pushed back from the table and carried his bowl and plate to the sink.

"Never thought of that." Her beautiful eyes widened. "That's downright scary. Deidre went to the lawyer before Laela was even born, and here I've had her for months and didn't think to do the same. What happens if I don't?"

"I don't know about laws in Ireland, but here, I'd guess that Laela would go into foster care, since she has no relatives to take her." Maverick felt bad that he'd even brought up the subject.

"I'll see a lawyer as soon as I get home, but I'm not sure who would take her. I've got a distant cousin, Danny O'Rourke, who might agree, but I'd have to talk to him and his wife," Bridget said.

Laela talked to her stuffed animals and pointed at the Christmas tree. Maverick envied the hell out of Danny at that moment.

# Chapter Nine

Bridget had been in Iris's bedroom many times, and she'd been in the little private bathroom to clean it a couple of times. But for her to go in there with the purpose of going through her things—that felt downright awkward. Getting the suitcase out of the closet wasn't so bad, but there were *some* things that were private, even if they were granny knickers and white bras.

"All right, it's got to be done." She talked to Laela, who was following right behind Dolly as the cat sniffed every single corner. Bridget pulled open a drawer and started packing the things that Iris had asked for. "It's a good thing that she's getting help, but we miss her, don't we?"

Laela flipped around to sit on her butt and grabbed the cat by the ear.

"I guess that means you and the cat both miss her, right?" Bridget finished packing and zipped the suitcase. "I'll pull this up to the living room, and then we'll get you changed.

I'm still a little bit worried about driving, what with it being on the opposite side of the road and such a big vehicle, but we've survived it twice to go to the store, so we can do it again." She set the suitcase on the floor and popped up the handle so she could pull it.

Bridget parked the suitcase, and Laela reached up for her as if she'd understood exactly what had been said while the thing was being packed. "Maybe we'll stop for ice cream on the way home."

*Home?*

Bridget couldn't believe she'd said that word out loud. *Home* was Ireland. It wasn't on a ranch where she had a temporary job. It felt like she'd disgraced her homeland by even saying such a thing.

It didn't take long to get Laela changed into a cute little pink corduroy outfit and wrestle her into a coat. The hat had to be tied under her chin because she kept taking it off, throwing it, and giggling.

"You think that's funny, do you?" Bridget gathered her up in her arms and kissed her a dozen times on her chubby little cheeks. Laela squealed with laughter and tried to wiggle out of her embrace.

"Now that's a sight right there," Maverick said from the bedroom doorway.

Bridget turned to face him. "You snuck up on us."

Laela reached out for him, and Maverick took her into his arms. "Don't you and your mama look pretty today? Pink is a good color for a princess, and green always looks good on your mama."

"Thank you." Bridget set about putting on her coat. "You gave me a start there. You usually holler at the back door."

"I didn't mean to startle you," Maverick said. "I heard the baby giggling and just followed the sweet sound. I'm on my way into town for a load of feed. Do you want me to take that stuff to Granny?"

"No, I want to do it, and besides, I'd like to stop by the food store for some things we need," she answered.

"If you have any trouble, you can call me. I should be going." He started down the hall with the baby still in his arms.

Bridget grabbed Laela's bag and followed him. "I kind of promised her ice cream."

"It would be fun to show her off in the feed store and lumberyeard." Maverick picked up the suitcase in the foyer with his free hand. "But you got to deliver what you promise. That's straight from Granny's mouth."

Bridget opened the door for him. "I heard the same thing from Nana. Guess we were raised a lot alike, even if there was a lot of water separating us."

He carried the baby to the truck and got her all situated. "Look at that. I got all those straps done up right without help."

"You get the gold star today," Bridget teased.

Maverick leaned against the fender. "I'll trade it for that kiss you owe me."

She gazed up into his eyes. "It'll take more to get that kiss than just learning to buckle all the straps on Laela's car seat. See you at noon." She whipped around and rounded the front of the truck, leaving him standing there.

"Do I have to be the knight in shining armor that rides up on a white horse and saves the damsel in distress?" he drawled as he headed to his own vehicle.

"I don't need a white horse, and I've never been a woman who needs saving." She raised her voice and deliberately waited for him to leave before she started the engine. No way would she drive with him following right behind her. If she made an error or two, she for sure didn't want him to see.

"Lassie, girl." She glanced up into the rearview at Laela. "If all that jabbering you do reaches God's ears, you might say a prayer for us. They say the third time is the charm, so I expect we'll do fine, but a prayer wouldn't hurt—especially from a little angel like you."

Laela gave her a big grin that showed off four of her front teeth.

"I'll take that as a sign your angel powers are in fine form today," Bridget said.

Starting the engine was no different from doing so in Sean's car, but the truck was so different from his tiny little vehicle. She took a deep breath, put the truck in reverse, and hit the gas a little too hard. The truck slipped on the slick grass and wove all over the yard before she got it under control.

*You ready for that knight on a white horse?* that pesky voice in her head asked.

"Not yet," she said as she changed gears and slowly drove down the lane toward the road. She drove ten miles below the speed limit, and she parked out at the edge of the rehab lot where there were lots of spaces. She took the suitcase from the backseat and rolled it across the concrete to the other side of the truck. Then she got Laela out of her seat and slung her on a hip, reached for the handle of the suitcase, and remembered she had left the keys in the truck.

"Thank goodness I didn't lock myself out," she muttered. "We're going to conquer this beast of a truck, darlin' girl." She tucked the keys into her hip pocket and rolled the suitcase toward the center. A cold north wind whipped her long, red hair around in her face, and there was a hint of rain in the gray skies. She pushed the button for the doors to open automatically and was surprised to see Iris sitting in the lobby.

"I thought you might be here about this time." Iris patted the place beside her on the sofa. "I wanted to see Laela's face light up when she saw the decorations in here. Turn her loose and let her check out things. My therapy got pushed up half an hour, so I've got maybe fifteen more minutes. Are you catchin' on to drivin' here in Texas?"

Bridget sat down and put Laela on the floor. "Pretty good."

"It's like the time change between here and Ireland. It takes a while to adjust, but you'll get the hang of it, and then it'll feel all wrong when you go home." Iris pointed at Laela. "Ain't that cute. She touches the ornaments on the tree so gentle-like, but she don't pull at them."

"Maverick sits on the floor with her, and they discuss the ornaments," Bridget said. "Sometimes I think they have their own language."

"He's always been good with kids. You'd think that as wild as he's been..." Iris sighed.

Bridget's eyes popped wide open.

"Honey, I may be old but I'm not blind or deaf," Iris said. "I can see and hear just fine, and I know both my grandsons better than anyone else. What I was going to say before you looked so surprised, is that as wild as he's been, there could be several children out there with his pretty eyes."

"I thought there were," Bridget admitted and went on to tell Iris the story of the misunderstanding about the messages from Retta and Emily.

That brought out a burst of laughter. "That's priceless. I have to share it with Wanda. She'll get such a kick out of it."

"Dammit!" Bridget slapped her knee. "I was so intent on

getting here that I forgot to bring chocolates. Maverick is in town for feed. I'll call him and have him bring them by."

"I already talked to Mav. He should be getting here any minute. I figured I'd share one with Wanda and hide the others for myself." She pointed toward the window. "There he is now."

"Are you ready to go home, put on some George Jones, and two-step with me?" Maverick handed off two bags of chocolates to Iris.

"Thank you for these," Iris said. "I will be ready to dance when I get through with all this rehab crap. I almost called you to come get me this morning, but I ain't a quitter. When I start a job I finish it, even if I don't like it."

"That's what you always told me and Pax," Maverick said. "I couldn't get a big bag like you wanted, so I brought two smaller ones." Then he focused on Bridget. "Did you have any trouble getting here?"

"It was my third time driving the truck. I'll get used to it before long." No way was she admitting that she was just now calming down from the ten-minute drive. "Just to be on the safe side, I parked out a ways, so I could back out easier."

Laela left her place in front of the tree, crawled across the floor, and pulled herself up on Maverick's leg. He picked her up, twirled her around a couple of times until she giggled, and then handed her to Bridget.

"I should be going," he said. "See you at home."

"Dinner will be on the table at noon." She stood up and took the baby from Maverick. "We should be going too."

"Mav, y'all can go. Bridget, you can stay a little longer. The aide will come for me when it's my turn in the therapy room." Iris gave orders as usual.

Bridget sat down again. Iris was her boss. If she wanted

her to stay, then that's what she'd do. Besides, it would give Maverick time to be gone before she had to back that truck out again.

Iris sighed. "I wish Laela was my great-grandchild and that you weren't going back to Ireland."

"I'd be honored if you'd be her grandmother," Bridget said. "And anytime you come to Ireland, I'll have room for you."

"Virgie mentioned that you had a good friend named Sean. Are you going to marry him?" Iris asked.

These Texans had kind hearts, but they sure were nosy. "Sean is just my friend. I'm not interested in marrying him. Besides, he's quite a ladies' man. The day that he gets married, there'll probably be mourning all over Ireland. Women wearing black because the great Sean Cleary was no longer a bachelor."

"A lot can happen between now and Christmas." Iris nodded to her left. "There's my good-lookin' aide to help me down the hall to rehab. You can put my suitcase on my bed. I'll unpack it this afternoon. Put the candy on my nightstand. I'll share with Wanda, but be sure to bring me another one to hide." She winked at Bridget. "I have a sweet tooth almost as big as the state of Texas."

"Miz Iris, are you ready for your walk down the aisle with me?" The aide was a slightly overweight, dark-haired man with wire-rim glasses.

"Last time I walked down the aisle with a Texan, he stole my heart," Iris teased as she held out her hand for him to help her.

"I promise I won't break your heart." He put the walker in front of Iris. "But if I were thirty years younger, I might try to break this pretty redhead's heart."

Iris snorted. "Try forty years younger, Will. I know how old you are."

"Can't get nothing past you, Iris Callahan." He chuckled. "Now, let's get this Cadillac of a walker rollin'."

"Give me a minute to say goodbye to my family," Iris told him and made introductions. "This is Bridget, my surrogate granddaughter, and my great-granddaughter, Laela."

"Pleasure to meet you," Bridget said.

"Same to you," Will said.

"Y'all be careful going home now," Iris said. "Hold the baby down over here so I can give her a kiss."

Bridget did just what Iris said. "We'll see you tomorrow afternoon. If you think of anything else you want, just give me a call."

Iris nodded but she was focused on the baby. "Bye-bye, my sweet girl."

Bridget tucked the candy she had brought into the outer pocket of the suitcase and rolled it into Iris's room. After putting the candy on the nightstand and the suitcase on the bed, she and Laela went back outside. She'd barely gotten into the car when sleet started to bounce off the windshield.

"Maybe in this weather, we'll just go home and eat our ice cream there," she said as she got Laela all tucked into the car seat. "The roads could get pretty slick in a hurry if this gets any more serious. But we do have to stop at the food store for milk and bread, and a few things. We'll just have to hurry."

When she reached the supermarket, she parked at the outer edge of the lot just like she'd done at the rehab center. She didn't bother getting Laela's bag but tucked Laela close to her chest and braced herself against the sleet and wind. She rushed across the lot, into the store, and was suddenly bewildered by the size of the place.

She was used to buying bread and pastries in one shop, meat in another, and the stores in Ireland weren't a lot bigger than her grandmother's little house. To her, this place was a monster with its tall displays. Thank goodness there were signs above each aisle or she would have been hours just looking for the items she needed.

She rounded up what she had to have, charged it to the ranch, and was back in the truck in a half hour. She'd just started the engine when her phone rang. It took a minute to undo her seat belt and get it out of her pocket.

"Hello, Sean. You'd never believe the store I just came out of," she said.

"So everything really *is* bigger in Texas?" He chuckled.

"Don't know about everything, but that was one massive store. Breads, cheeses, dairy, meat, and even canned goods all under one roof."

"Is the cowboy with you?" he asked.

"No, and I've been driving myself to town. I think I'm starting to get the hang of it. Iris needed some things and I'm telling you—it was kind of scary, driving on the other side of the road in a big pickup truck," she said.

"I liked the pictures you posted. I miss you, girl. The new woman at work is slow and surly," he said. "I can hear a little of that Texas drawl already. You changing your mind about coming back to Ireland?"

"Of course not, but speaking of accents, it's sure good to hear yours today. I miss that most of all." She turned the engine off and unfastened her seat belt.

"What? Hearing some good old Irish, or do you miss working with me?" he teased.

"Both," she answered.

"I've got a confession." Sean's voice sounded strained.

"I'm not your priest, darlin'," she said.

"But I've got to get this off my chest. It's been eatin' at my heart for a few days." She could imagine him frowning with his eyebrows drawn down. "You remember when you told me to go ahead and rent out my spare room?"

"Yes," Bridget answered.

"Well, I did, and now those boxes you left are sitting in my bedroom. They take up a lot of room, luv." Some of his words were in Irish, some in English.

"And you don't want your bedroom all junked up when you bring your ladies home, do you?" she asked.

"That'd be the honest-to-God truth, right there. I can't keep them forever, so..."

"I'll be home in no more than six weeks to get them out of your way," she said.

"I'm holdin' you to it," Sean said. "But there's this other thing. I kind of told your nana that I'd take care of you. I believe that she thought I meant as in marriage, and I let her believe I meant that so she could die easy. I hope she didn't say anything like that to you."

"She didn't, and darlin', you're more like a little brother to me than a boyfriend," she said.

"Thank God!" He cleared his throat. "I didn't want you to come home with that on your mind. It will be years before I find a woman and settle down."

"And when you do, all the women in Ireland will be sad," she teased.

"I hope so." He laughed. "I kind of thought maybe you had a thing for me at one time."

"I love you, Sean, but like I said, only as a friend."

"Praise the Lord!"

She could imagine him crossing himself, and then kissing his fingertips and blowing a kiss toward heaven.

"I have worried over this call for days. I love you, Bridget, but you and Deidre were like big sisters to me. I'm so glad we've got it settled," he said.

"When you do fall in love, don't get in a hurry. Let things go slow so you can be sure if it's really love." She shivered and glanced back at Laela, who was busy chewing on her teddy bear's ear.

"This comin' from the girl who went to bed with a Yank the night she met him without even knowing his last name. I would have loved to have been a fly on the wall when you figured out he was Iris Callahan's grandson," Sean argued.

"It's comin' from a woman who's already walked a mile in a pair of shoes that hurt her feet. Be careful and don't rush into anything. Maverick and I are barely friends, so don't go getting your knickers in a bunch," she said.

"Got to go, and, honey, I'm not wearing knickers so they can't get in a bunch." Sean laughed. "I'm taking a woman named Kelly for a picnic tomorrow down to the edge of the river. It's my day off."

"In the winter?" Bridget gasped. There was no way in hell that she would consent to a picnic in the weather she was looking at right then.

"Cold weather means snuggling up under the quilt in my car." He chuckled.

"You need to burn that quilt," Bridget told him.

"My sister gave me a brand-new one. I'll retire the old one on the day I get married, but that will be years from now," he said. "I'll call again in a few days."

"I'll look forward to it," Bridget told him and ended the call. She looked over at Laela and said, "Let's go home now. I mean to the ranch. Jesus, what's the matter with me? A person can't have two home countries any more than they can ride two horses with one arse."

She drove even slower, now that the roads were getting a bit slick. There was no problem with getting home in time to make dinner for Maverick, even at the speed she was driving. She'd put a beef stew into the slow cooker early that morning, and there was a rising of bread on the countertop. In one hour, she could easily have a meal on the table, so it wasn't necessary to go fast. She'd left the main road and was traveling on the farm road when a deer ran out in front of her. She stomped on the brakes, swerved to the right, and missed the animal, but she went into a spin and wound up with the truck nose down in a ditch. No matter how hard she tried to back out of it, the wheels just kept spinning.

"Well, bloody hell!" she fumed as she took out her phone and called Maverick.

# Chapter Ten

Maverick had just unloaded the first bag of feed from the back of his truck when his phone rang. He saw that it was Bridget and answered with, "Knight-in-shining-armor service. What can I help you with?"

"If you'll bring that white horse you talked about and a rope, you can pull this truck out of a ditch. I had to swerve to miss hitting a deer," she said.

His heart almost jumped out of his chest. "Are you hurt? Is the baby all right?"

"We're fine," she answered. "I hit the brakes and the truck wound up in this bloody ditch. You'll find us at the end of the lane leading up to the ranch."

"I'll be there in a few minutes with the tractor. We can pull the truck out easier with it." Maverick ended the call and ran to fire up the tractor. Paxton had done something like that in high school to avoid hitting a dog. While he was swerving all over the road two wheels had dropped into the ditch, and his truck was just about upside down. He'd driven the truck with a smashed fender until he had saved enough money to get it fixed.

Bridget had gotten out of the vehicle and was standing beside it. The cold wind whipped her hair across her face and it was evident by her expression that she was really pissed.

Maverick hopped down out of the tractor and yelled, "Knight-in-shining-armor truck towing is here to rescue you."

"I don't want to hear it." She shot a dirty look his way.

He'd seen her happy and sad, but damn, she was the cutest ever when she was thoroughly pissed. "But darlin', if I don't identify myself, how will you know that I'm the person you called to help you."

"Do you want a burned dinner?" she threatened.

"No, ma'am." He shook his head. "Seriously, are you and Laela really all right? No bumps, no bruises."

"Just my pride," she admitted. "And Laela giggled the whole time like she was on a carnival ride. I'd slowed down to make the turn and did a couple of loops on the slick road, then went nose down in the ditch. I hope I didn't hurt the truck."

"It doesn't look like there's even a dent. There's mud on the back fenders, but a little water will take care of that in no time. The important thing is that *you and Laela* aren't hurt," he said. "Just get back in the truck while I hook up a chain and pull the truck out. You want me to drive you to the house then? I can always walk back down here and get the tractor after we have dinner."

"You get me out of here, and I'll drive to the house," she protested.

He took a step back. "Get-back-on-the-horse philosophy, huh?"

"Something like that," she told him.

"When I honk, put it in reverse and give it a little gas," Maverick told Bridget. "Not too much. Just ease it out slow and let the tractor do most of the work."

She did exactly what he told her to do, and in only a few minutes, the truck was back on the road. He jumped out of the tractor and found only mud and grass stuck to the front bumper. Other than that, it looked fine.

He knocked on the window, and she fumbled around until she found the button to roll it down. Laela was rubbing her little eyes in the backseat, and Bridget's knuckles were white from gripping the steering wheel so tightly.

"Sit still while I get the chain undone. I'll honk when you can start toward the house, and I'll follow along behind you," he said.

"Thank you," she said.

"Reckon this will get me that kiss you owe me?" he teased.

"Maybe." She smiled as the window went up.

He whistled Blake Shelton's "Honey Bee" all the way to the tractor. The whole ordeal must have scared her more than she was ready to admit because she drove up the lane at less than five miles an hour. Maverick parked the tractor right beside the truck. While she got the baby out, he gathered up the bags of groceries in the floor of the backseat and carried them inside the house.

Bridget had set the baby on the floor, but she was whining and clinging to her mama's leg. Maverick scooped her up into his arms and patted her on the back.

"What's the matter with the baby girl?"

Bridget threw a bibbed apron over her head, wrapped the strings round her waist, and tied them in the front, just like she'd done at the pub. "All of the above," she answered for the baby. "She didn't get her nap and she didn't get her mid-morning bottle of milk, so she's tired and hungry. After we eat, I'll try to get her down for a little afternoon nap to make up for it."

"What can I do to help hurry things up?" Maverick asked.

"Holding her is a big help." Bridget removed the lid from the slow cooker, and the delicious aroma of beef stew filled the kitchen. She filled a big crock bowl with it and set it in the middle of the table. Then she brought a loaf of homemade bread from the pantry and a round of sharp cheddar from the refrigerator. She cut thick slices of the bread and put them into a basket, then stuck a knife in the top of the cheese so they could serve themselves.

"That all looks good. What's for dessert?" Maverick asked. "Not that I care if we have dessert with every meal, but if we don't, then I think you should at least give me a sweet kiss."

"Dream on, cowboy," she said. "There is a nice banana pudding in the refrigerator. I made it this morning before I went to the rehab center."

\* \* \*

Cooking. Cleaning. Ranching. Taking care of a baby. Doing whatever Iris wanted her to do. *Was this all there was to life?* Bridget wondered. Now that she was a mother, did she never get to do anything exciting again?

"I was thinking…" Maverick danced around the floor with the baby.

"I remember when that kind of got us into…" she started.

He grabbed her by the waist with his free arm, pulled

her to his side, and sang Josh Turner's "Your Man" as he danced her and Laela around the room. The baby squealed with laughter, and Bridget couldn't wipe the smile off her face. Maverick was such a fun-loving person, and even if they never got past the flirting and friendship stage, he was opening up a whole new adventure for her.

*Maybe I'll stay in Texas and get a job here*, she thought, then shook her head. *That's the craziest notion I've ever had. Who'd be there to take care of Nana's and Deidre's graves? Ireland is my home and always will be.*

"What were you going to say when my thinking kind of got us into trouble?" He spun her one more time, brought her around to face him, and brushed a kiss across her lips. "That's not the kiss you owe me."

"No, it's not. When you get that one, steam will come out your ears," she said.

"Like in Ireland?" His gaze bored into hers.

"Yes, cowboy, like in Ireland," she said as she broke free and went to the refrigerator for ice.

Laela wiggled her head and shoulders for more. Maverick began to sing "The Drunk Scotsman."

"Good God in heaven!" Bridget jerked the tea towel from the countertop and snapped it at his butt. "That is no song to be singing to my baby girl. Where'd you learn that song anyway?"

"From my grandpa." Maverick laughed.

"So if your grandpa was Irish, why would he sing a Scottish song?" Bridget asked.

"He said it used to make Granny madder'n a wet hen after a tornado when he sang it, so when they had a fight, he'd sing it until she got in a good mood. She always argued that she wasn't in a good mood, but that she pretended to be just so he would shut up."

"I used to play that song on the jukebox at the pub when things got boring." She smiled at some of the memories of those wild nights. "I don't intend to tell Laela those stories, though."

"Or the one about the night a cowboy came into your pub and…"

She put a finger over his lips. "That's enough about that."

Bridget dipped out some of the potatoes and carrots to cool for Laela, and then bowed her head. Maverick said grace and then ladled up stew in Bridget's bowl before filling his own.

Maverick dug into his food, and Bridget fed Laela in between bites. She couldn't get that silly notion about staying in Texas out of her mind. Maverick had said that Iris had contacts everywhere. Could Iris help her find a job and recommend a good baysitter? Was such a thing even a possibility? Or had the thought come to her because she'd been excited when Maverick had danced her around the kitchen floor? Was she just yearning for the past days of fun? Questions and more questions, but none of them had answers.

*Everyone has to grow up someday. Excitement is just found in different ways*. Those had been her grandmother's words. Two years ago Nana had told Bridget that it was time for her to settle down. "You and Deidre have had your fun. If you don't start a family soon, you'll be raising kids when you have gray hair."

"But where's the excitement in being married? It's the same thing every day," Bridget had said. "I'm not ready to give up my good times."

*Today, I think I understand what you were talking about, Nana.*

# Chapter Eleven

Maverick had just nailed the last piece of sheet metal on the barn roof and climbed down the ladder to the ground. He pulled off his work gloves and shoved them into his hip pocket, and checked the time on his phone. He had thirty minutes to get cleaned up and make it to the rehab center or Granny would be fussing at them for being late. He hit the door in a run, spoke to Bridget and Laela as he passed by them, and went straight to the bathroom. He took the quickest shower he'd ever taken, ran a razor over his face, and slapped on some shaving lotion. His jeans needed to be ironed, but he didn't have time to do that. He grabbed his coat on the way out the bedroom door and was putting it on when he reached the foyer.

Bridget pointed at the clock above the hall tree. "She doesn't like for folks to be late."

"Don't I know it?" Maverick picked up the diaper bag with one hand and opened the door with the other. "You should have had to grow up in this house. I thought for sure the devil would pop up out of the earth and drag me straight to hell if I was ever late to anything, church or even just dinner."

Bridget nodded knowingly. "Nana used to fuss about one of her friends who was always late to everything. She'd say that Birdie was going to be late to her own funeral. I wonder where that saying came from. I mean, how can someone be late to their own funeral?"

Maverick settled the baby into her car seat and then helped Bridget into the truck. "Well, if they are, maybe St. Peter won't let them through the pearly gates."

"That sounds like something Iris and Nana would threaten us with, for sure." Bridget nodded.

They made it to the rehab center with a minute to spare. Iris was so happy to see them and the baby that she didn't even point to the clock.

"Don't you look all pretty?" Bridget smiled.

"I won't gripe about these damned housecoats anymore, not after wearing hospital gowns that leave your whole backside naked," Iris told her. "Give me that baby, and y'all sit down so we can visit. Tell me what all happened today."

"I slid into a ditch on the way home from our last visit," Bridget said.

"Were you or this baby hurt?" Iris began to check Laela for cuts or bruises.

"No, and the pickup is fine," Maverick said. "I rescued her and the truck just needs a good washing. She went into the ditch at the same place Pax did when he was in high school."

"Oh, Lawd!" Iris put her hands over her eyes. "You two boys like to have put me in the grave more than once."

Maverick remembered being scared out of his mind when

Paxton came walking into the house that night. He looked like he'd been mud wrestling. The memory was funny now, but that night he thought that Paxton might have to spend a few days out in the tack room until Granny cooled down.

"And your grandson sang 'The Drunk Scotsman' to Laela," Bridget tattled.

"Don't throw me under the bus to save your skin." Maverick chuckled. "That ain't no way to treat me after I dragged you out of that ditch and then danced around in the kitchen with you so you'd feel better."

Bridget's emerald-green eyes twinkled, reminding Maverick of the way they looked when he first met her in the pub. He'd dance with her more often if that's what it took to put a little sparkle back in her eyes.

Iris shook her finger at him. "Mav Callahan, I should take a switch to your arse. That's not a fit song for a lady's ears, much less for a baby's. If your grandpa was here, I'd give him a solid piece of my mind for ever teaching you boys that rowdy song."

Maverick shot a dirty look toward Bridget. "Tattletale."

She stuck her tongue out at him. "That's a horrible song."

"Don't you two start fighting," Iris scolded. "I've been waiting all day for this visit. And besides, y'all know that I will find out everything anyway, so you might just as well tell me when something happens."

Maverick just smiled. There was one thing she didn't know, and he damn sure had no intentions of telling her about his last night in Ireland.

\* \* \*

It wasn't quite time for them to leave when Bridget noticed that Iris was having a hard time keeping her eyes open. Poor old darling was used to having her naps at home, and here they probably kept her in therapy most of the day.

Laela began to fret, and not even Maverick could make her happy.

"We should be going. Laela has been off her schedule all day," Bridget said.

"Twice a week isn't enough." Iris yawned. "Next week you can come see me on Monday, Wednesday, and Friday. I'll want to hear all about how the Christmas program is coming along."

Bridget loved Christmas and everything about it, so she didn't mind doing anything. "Just to be straight," she said, "we've got Friday night at the church doing props this week, and Saturday we go to the nursing home here in town, and back to the church that evening."

"Yep, you got it, and then to the Rockin' B Ranch Christmas party after church on Sunday," Iris said. "And you need to be sure to have plenty of Christmas cookies on hand. Alana will be helping on Friday and Saturday at the church, and she always brings snacks, so you can take cookies." Bridget's head was starting to spin with all the details.

"Yes, ma'am." Maverick stood, and then bent to kiss his grandmother on the cheek. "You still happy bein' here?"

"Why wouldn't I be? They're taking care of me real good. I have a new friend. She would have come to see y'all, but she was worn plumb out after that last therapy session and needed a nap. The food ain't bad, and you're takin' care of things for me at the ranch," Iris said. "Now, y'all run along, and maybe I'll catch forty winks before they come get me for supper."

Bridget took the baby from Maverick and let Iris kiss her. "We'll be back on Monday, then?"

Iris nodded. "And you'll have plenty to tell me about

the whole weekend. Take pictures so I can see what you've done." She pushed the remote button on her chair to lay it back. "We'll talk before then." She closed her eyes.

When they reached the lobby, Maverick chuckled. "I can hear her snoring already. I vote that we have an early supper at the little diner down on Main Street. It will be dark soon after we eat, and we can drive around town and let Laela see all the pretty Christmas lights."

"That sounds like fun," Bridget said. "I haven't got to see much of town. Just from the ranch to the grocery store and to the rehab center."

"There's not a lot to see right here, but maybe one day we'll take a drive down to the canyon and see it," Maverick said.

"You mean your ranch that's five hours from here?" She couldn't imagine Laela being happy with a drive that long, not even if there were Christmas lights everywhere.

"That's Canyon Creek, and it's out in Sunset, Texas," he explained. "The canyon I'm talking about is the Palo Duro Canyon, not far from here."

"I'd like that," Bridget said. "So, is this village about the size of Skibbereen?"

"Possibly, but it's spread out a little more," he answered.

"Well then, my white knight, let's see it before we go home." She smiled.

There was that word, *home*, again, and this time she'd said it out loud. Was she really beginning to think that the ranch was home? Perhaps it was because it was a house that was available for her and Laela, and she didn't have even a flat back in Ireland.

Maverick made a couple of turns, drove a few blocks, and parked in front of a small café on Main Street. Texas towns were laid out so differently from small Irish villages, and there was no public transportation in towns the size of Daisy. No wonder everyone had a car or a truck.

The café wasn't so different from an Irish one. There were booths on one side and tables and chairs down the middle. The waitress, a cute little lady in tight jeans and T-shirt advertising the place of business, told them to sit anywhere. Then she looked up and her eyes got big, and her smile got even bigger.

"Well, I didn't recognize you with a baby in your arms, Maverick." The waitress picked up a high chair and followed them to a booth. "When did all this happen?"

"Mary Jane, meet Bridget O'Malley. Bridget, this is an old friend, Mary Jane. And this little beauty"—he put the baby in the high chair—"is Laela. Bridget came to help Granny out while she's laid up with that hip. I'm here for the same reason."

Bridget didn't need a road map of the state of Texas to know that Mary Jane was right in the middle of Flirtsville. The expression on her face said that she was relieved to know that Maverick wasn't a father or in a relationship. Bridget pasted on a fake smile and nodded. "Pleased to meet you."

"Likewise. Love your accent. Is that British?"

"Ireland, County Cork." The Irish words that were running through Bridget's mind would have fried the hair right off St. Peter's head.

Mary Jane turned back to Maverick. "Will we see you at the Wild Cowboy Saloon tomorrow night?"

"No, Granny volunteered me to work on Friday and Saturday nights at the church. We have to help get the Christmas program ready." Maverick hung his black hat on the horseshoe tacked to a post at the end of the booth. Then he sat down.

Of course, any wild cowboy would have rather been at the Wild Cowboy Saloon than at church working on things for a Christmas program. Bloody damn hell, Bridget would rather be with him, if the truth was told, but Iris made out her paychecks, so she'd do what Iris said.

"Things don't get to rockin' real good until after nine, so come on over after the church stuff. I'll save you a dance." She winked. "What can I get y'all to drink?"

"Sweet tea, please." Maverick picked up the menu.

"Coke." Forget about saying *please* to the woman.

*You're bein' rude.* Her nana's voice popped into her head.

Bridget ignored her nana's voice.

"Be back in a minute." Mary Jane laid a possessive hand on Maverick's shoulder and whispered, "I might save you more than a dance." She headed back toward the kitchen, with an extra swing in her hips.

Damn it! Bridget couldn't deny the jealous streak blasting its way through her heart.

"Old girlfriend?" Bridget could feel the chill in her own voice.

"Old wannabe, maybe," he replied. "She's one of those round-heel gals you talked about. I'm not interested."

"So you like the chase as well as the reward at the end?" she asked.

"Never thought of it, but I suppose you could be right." He looked over the menu. "What about you? You like to be sweet-talked and romanced?"

Before she could answer, Mary Jane brought their drinks and whipped an order pad from her apron pocket. "Y'all ready to order?"

"Chicken fried steak for me." Maverick handed her his menu.

"Same as what he ordered, and one extra order of mashed potatoes with gravy," Bridget said.

"That's easy." Mary Jane tucked a strand of jet-black hair up under her ponytail, and bent to whisper something in Maverick's ear before she left with the order.

Maverick's face turned slightly pink—an almost blush.

Bridget barely restrained the impulse to stick out her foot to trip Mary Jane.

"Sorry about that," he said.

"Does every woman's knickers crawl down toward her ankles when she's around you?" she muttered.

"She's actually one of Paxton's old girlfriends," he explained in a low voice. "When things didn't work out between them, she let it be known all over Daisy that she would do whatever it took to get back at him. I guess I'm *whatever it takes*."

"No wonder you moved to another part of this state. You needed new pastures." Forget that crazy idea of living in Texas. She'd be locked up in a jail cell and poor little Laela would be an orphan if she had to put up with all the Mary Janes in the state.

"Did you ever need to move?" He finally made eye contact with her.

"No, I did not." She took a cracker from a container on the table and put it on the high chair tray. "I'm not a saint. I've had a few relationships, none of which lasted very long, but I haven't completely depleted the pasture in my small village. I was born in Ireland and I'll die in Ireland."

The café started to fill up, and by the time Mary Jane brought their food, she was too busy to flirt with Maverick. That was a good thing, because Bridget was ready to scratch her brown eyes out. Only a real bitch would plot brothers against each other.

Laela loved the potatoes and green beans, but what she really liked was the ice cream that was served at the end of the meal.

"Guess she's got a sweet tooth like Granny," Maverick said as he fed her small bites.

"Deidre loved ice cream too. I'd buy a pastry if we had money, but she always, always wanted ice cream," Bridget said.

Maverick scraped the last bite out of the cup for Laela. "That's all of it, sweet baby girl."

Bridget wiped the baby's face, and then slid out of the booth. She slung her purse over her shoulder and picked Laela up from the high chair. Maverick took the ticket to the front counter, paid the bill, and then took the baby from her. "I'll take her out to the truck and get her settled."

"You think about what I said," Mary Jane called from a table she was cleaning.

"Do I even want to know what she whispered to you?" Bridget asked.

"Probably not, but I'll tell you anyway. She said if I'd come to the Wild Cowboy Saloon tonight that she'd save me the last dance," he told her.

"Does that mean something?"

"The girl that a cowboy dances last with is usually the one that takes him home with her for the night," he said, honestly.

"And I'm sure you'd read the Bible and get ready for Sunday school class, right?" Bridget smarted off.

Bridget pointed out the sunset there on the horizon. "Those swirling colors remind me of the icing on the Easter cupcakes at the bakery in our village. Sometimes Nana would buy three of them the day before the holiday—one for me, one for Sean, and one for Deidre. We liked them better than the eggs and chocolate bunnies in our baskets.

Maybe we should make Christmas cupcakes to take to Sunday school for our class."

"The kids would probably love them even more than cookies." Maverick drove slowly up and down the streets, showing off the decorations. "Our sunset will soon be gone. I missed them Texas sunsets when I was in Ireland. The ones over in the middle of the state aren't as pretty as these," Maverick said. "The ones over there are gorgeous but they're never as big as what we get here."

"Well, it *is* Texas." She smiled.

"Yep, it is," he agreed.

"Look, Laela." Bridget undid her seat belt and turned around so she could see Laela's face.

The baby laid her little hand on the window like she was trying to touch the pretty multicolored lights.

"Her eyes are sparkling. I don't think she's going to fall asleep on the way home with all this excitement." Bridget pointed to another house. "Oh, look at that. How do they do that?"

"There's a machine in the yard that rotates and makes it look like snowflakes on the house," he explained.

"I wish it would snow so much that we could build a big snowman. We've only had enough once to build one since I've been old enough to remember. Deidre and I rolled up all the snow in Nana's yard and our neighbors' yards to make one about two feet tall," she said.

"We've had snow, but nothing major in years. It would take magic to grant that wish." Maverick drove slowly through street after street.

"I thought Texas promised magic and miracles," Bridget said.

Maverick laid a hand on her shoulder. "I'll get in touch with the highest Texas authorities and see what I can do."

"That just might get you that kiss you've been whining about."

He gave her shoulder a gentle squeeze. "Cowboys don't whine, but, honey, if it snows that much, I'll gladly collect that kiss."

# Chapter Twelve

Bridget sent Sean a text and several pictures the next morning as soon as Maverick was out of the house. She was surprised when she didn't hear anything back until almost five o'clock that evening.

She answered Sean's call with, "Did you get the pictures?"

"It's almost midnight here, love. I got the pictures, but"—he paused—"well, I was at Kelly's place, and we were...anyway, you understand."

"Oh, I understand all too well," Bridget said.

"I think she's the one," he answered. "I'm almost ready to burn the famous quilt."

"Are you going to tell her about all the women you've been with on that quilt?" Bridget asked.

"Bloody hell, no!" He yelled so loud that she had to hold the phone out from her ear. "And you are going to give me your promise that you will not do some god-awful thing and tell her, or even hint at it."

Bridget rolled her eyes toward the ceiling. "Save the ceremonial burning until I get home, and we'll do it together. You bring the gas masks, and I'll get a bottle of wine for the party."

He chuckled. "You're like the sister I never had."

"Yes, I'm that for sure." She smiled at the very idea of Sean ever settling down.

"We even talked about kids," Sean said. "This morning, she told me that she loves the little buggers and wants to have at least five or six."

Hearing Sean's thick Irish accent was like a breath of fresh air to Bridget. She was glad that she had a friend left in her home state that she could talk to, even if it was bantering about his women.

"If you're getting all serious, maybe I should be lookin' around for someone too," she teased.

"Not that cowboy." Sean's tone turned serious.

"Why not?" she asked.

"Because he's not one of us, Bridget." His voice was loud enough that she had to hold the phone out from her ear again.

"Maverick is at least a quarter Irish," she said.

"He wasn't raised here. He doesn't know our ways," Sean said flatly.

"He's a good man," she told him.

"We are fighting for naught, love." He simmered down. "Kelly is probably not the one, and your cowboy isn't the right man for you. So let's make up before I have to go to bed. It's past me bedtime."

"Yeah, right," Bridget said. "I've seen you party until two and known that you took a woman home to rumple the bedsheets for another couple of hours, and then go to work at seven. But good night."

"Good night or maybe I should say good evenin', since it's only five o'clock in your Texas." He ended the call before she could answer.

"My Texas," she muttered.

Laela had been crawling across the floor toward the tree, but when she heard Bridget's voice, she stopped and flipped herself into a sitting position.

"Sean's being a bit of a jackass about Maverick. It is a good thing I'm not there," Bridget said. "Meals don't take long. Iris isn't here to need things done for her. Maybe I should be getting out my knitting to be making scarves for Christmas presents."

Laela smiled up at her and jabbered something in baby language.

"Is that English or Irish? I don't recognize either one," she said.

"I think it might be Texas hillbilly," Maverick said from the doorway. "I can't imagine you with knitting needles."

"I had no choice but to learn," she told him. "One day Nana came home from the meat market. I was sitting on the stoop with nothing to do. I told her that I was bored. She sat down beside me and said that was too bad, because that meant she got to pick out my husband. When I asked her why, she told me that boring people got bored. That meant I'd have to marry a stupid man who didn't care if his wife was boring."

Maverick's laughter echoed off the walls. Laela chased after Dolly, who'd come inside with Maverick. "I don't think that little girl will ever get bored."

"Oh, yes, she will. When she's a teenager and her nails are polished, her hair has been fixed three times that day, and all her friends are away from home, she will get bored," Bridget told him.

"Not if she lives on a ranch. There's always something to do here. She could ride four-wheelers through mud puddles, help gather up cattle to be worked, feed new baby calves, all kinds of things," he said.

"Da-da-da-da," Laela said.

"Did you hear that? She called me Daddy." Maverick beamed.

"The books I've read on child care say that most babies say that first, but that they really don't know what they are saying," she told him.

"I don't believe it. You called me Daddy, didn't you, princess?" Maverick smothered her face with kisses. "This is the best Christmas present ever."

Bridget was stunned. Didn't he realize that a baby, no matter who was the mother, would blow the bloody hell out of his lifestyle?

He sat down on the sofa and picked up a book to read to Laela. She pointed to the big red apple on the first page and jabbered.

"*A* is for apple," Maverick said.

"Da-da-da," she said.

"See there." Bridget laughed. "Now the apple is her daddy."

"You don't understand baby talk. She's saying that Daddy is supposed to turn the page to show her that *B* is for bear," he argued.

Bridget heard a scratching at the front door and headed out of the room to let Ducky into the house. She shivered against the blast of cold wind that blew in with him. She was about to close the door when Dolly came across the porch in a big yellow blur and raced into the foyer so fast that she had to jump over Ducky.

The dog and cat went straight to the rocking chair and

curled up beside it. Laela looked even smaller in Maverick's big strong arms. Every time he turned the page of the book, she pointed and said, "da-da-da," and he beamed. With the tree in the background, all decked out with ornaments and lights, the scene looked like something on a Christmas card.

She tiptoed across the room and put one of Iris's vinyl records on the turntable. Maverick looked up from the book and raised an eyebrow.

"I thought we would get in the mood for going to the church tonight with a little music," she said.

George Strait started singing "Santa Claus Is Coming to Town," and Laela began to weave back and forth in Maverick's arms.

"We bought Granny a CD player, but she'd rather listen to her music on vinyls," Maverick said.

"Nana was the same way. I left a box of her records with Sean." Bridget frowned. If that new woman of his gave her things away because they were taking up too much room she was in for a fight.

Reba McEntire was next on the record with "Let It Snow."

\* \* \*

*Coming home to a woman and a baby after a hard day's work, a Christmas tree with twinkling lights, and music filling the house—this is the good life,* Maverick thought.

*No, it's not,* the voice in his head yelled loudly. *The good life is doing what you love and being free as a bird.*

"If you'll put Laela in her high chair, we can have a sandwich for supper, and I'll heat Laela up some leftover pie," Bridget said. "I'm surprised that I've gotten used to calling it supper rather than dinner so fast."

"Texas grows on you." Maverick laid the book to the side and stood to his feet with Laela still in his arms. "Come on, princess, I'll get you all situated on your throne."

Once she was safe in the chair, he cut pieces of leftover ham into the right thickness for sandwiches. Bridget sliced the rest of a loaf of homemade bread, and then brought out cheese and olives.

When it was on the table, Laela began pounding on the tray of her high chair. Maverick tucked her hand into his, bowed his head, and said a simple prayer. He thought about all the times when he was alone at the cabin and had dived right into his food without even saying a silent thanks to God. He could almost feel Granny glaring at him.

Bridget sniffled and was dabbing her eyes with a napkin when he raised his head. "Are you all right?" he asked.

"It's the little things that bring back a memory of my nana. She used to hold Laela's hand when she said grace," Bridget said. "It was sweet of you to do that."

Maverick reached around the high chair separating them and patted her on the shoulder. "It's bittersweet, but a good memory. Hold on to those."

\* \* \*

If someone had told Bridget a year ago that she would be on her way to a church in Texas to help get the props ready for the Christmas program, she would have ordered them a straitjacket. Yet, there she was, watching the countryside go by at sixty miles an hour with a baby in the backseat of the truck, and with a sexy cowboy at the wheel.

"Do you realize that it was one year ago today that you came into the pub where I worked?"

"I didn't remember the exact day, but I knew it was about

this time of year because Granny and I were home in plenty of time for her to get things ready for Christmas. What did you do after I left?" he asked.

"I went home on the bus," she answered. "Nana fussed at me, saying we were going to be late for church, but we weren't. Then I slept all afternoon. What did *you* do?"

"I stared at your picture on the long plane ride home and wished that I'd met you the first day I was in Ireland instead of the last day. I would've tried to call, but I didn't even know your last name." Maverick parked the truck at the back of the church, turned off the engine, and turned to face her. "I like having you here, Bridget."

"I like being here." She smiled as she unfastened her seat belt. "But not even God can move Ireland next door to Texas. This is your place. Mine is in Ireland."

"I'll pray real hard that he works on that between now and Christmas." Maverick slung his door open.

"I'm not sure *that* prayer will get past the church ceiling, but you can try. We'd better go on inside if we're going to get anything done tonight."

"I'd rather take you to the Wild Cowboy Saloon and dance with you all evening." He grinned.

"Last I checked babies weren't welcome in those places." She opened her door and slid out of the seat. "Besides, would you want to be telling Iris that we didn't get the props ready?" she asked.

"Party pooper." He got out of the truck. "I'll take the baby. You get the diaper bag."

"Maybe so, but we aren't those same two fly-by-impulse people that we were last year in Ireland." She picked up the diaper bag and started across the parking lot. She reached for the knob, and the door flew open before she could get a hand on it.

Even in her jeans with holes in the knees and a paint-stained chambray shirt, Alana looked like she had just stepped out of a photo shoot for a magazine. "I thought I heard slamming doors. Come on in." She motioned them inside. "We've got the curtains out to hang tonight." She talked as she led them down a long hallway with Sunday school rooms on either side. At the end, she turned left and went into a fairly large storage room. On one side was a closet with burgundy choir robes hanging all pressed and at the ready. The rest of the room looked like a Christmas store had blown up in there. What it needed was some severe organization, and all they had was two weeks.

*A bit like your life right now, isn't it?* that niggling voice in her head whispered.

*Yes, it is.* Bridget didn't even argue. After the holidays, not one thing about her future had been sorted out. Not a place to live, a job, or a babysitter for Laela.

"Okay, there's the sewing machine. We've got a couple of curtains that need mending." Alana pointed at a table. "If you can run it, I'll gladly take care of Laela. I like kids. I hate sewing."

"I can sew a straight seam, but don't ask me to do anything real fancy." Bridget looked around at the dusty floor and all the things that could fall on the baby.

"Don't worry." Alana held out her hands, and the baby went right to her. "When Iris said you were going to help, I brought a playpen in here from the nursery. I even put a few toys in it to entertain her."

"Well, hello, everyone." A tall cowboy with blond hair and brown eyes came through the open door.

"This is Ryan Daniels." Alana made introductions. "I roped him into helping for a couple of hours tonight."

"Small price to pay." Ryan's smile deepened his dimples.

"Afterward I get to take her to the honky-tonk and dance with her until they close the joint down."

"Or maybe until midnight. I've got a field to plow tomorrow morning," Alana said.

"Well, we'll take any help we can get," Maverick said. "How about the two of us go get the rods set in place for these curtains?"

Bridget sat down at the table and picked up one of the long blue panels. She found the first rip, stitched it, and then reinforced the hem that was coming out. Alana brought out a scrub bucket full of water and started washing the dust from a six-foot wooden cutout of Santa Claus.

"How're things working out without Iris at the ranch?" Alana asked.

"Just fine." Bridget laid the curtain aside and picked up the next one.

"I met Ryan at the Wild Cowboy last weekend, and he asked me for a date. I don't usually date the guys I meet there," Alana said.

"You don't have to explain to me." The memory of Bridget's night with Maverick rushed a little heat though her body.

"But I want to," Alana said. "He seemed like a nice guy, and he's taller than me"—she smiled—"so I decided to test him."

"Looks like he's passing." Bridget wondered if she should test Maverick.

"I believe he just might be. He'll have to jump through a few more hoops before I'm ready to introduce him to Daddy, but so far so good." Alana finished washing the top half of Santa.

Bridget would have liked to have the privilege of introducing Maverick to her father or to her nana, or even to

Sean, but that wasn't going to happen. She remembered the day that Deidre told her that she was going out with Jimmy. Bridget hadn't been a bit surprised, since they'd been flirting for months. She tried to think what Deidre would say if she'd told her that she was dating a Texas cowboy, but it was so far-fetched that she couldn't even imagine it.

"Maverick likes you a lot," Alana said.

Bridget hit the foot pedal too hard and almost ran the needle right through her thumb. Could Alana read her mind? Did her face look different when she was thinking about Maverick?

"What makes you say that?" Bridget stammered, and laid her hands in her lap.

"I'm pretty much like a sister to him." Alana pulled out a chair and sat down. "I know him pretty damn well. There's something different about him, and I think it's you."

"Maybe it's just that he's back home on his own land," Bridget suggested. "Or that he likes the holidays."

"I've seen him on the Callahan Ranch and at Christmas," Alana said. "This is a different Maverick than I've ever seen. I don't think he even realizes it, but he will."

"We've only been around each other a short while." Bridget chose her words carefully.

"Long while. Short while," Alana said. "Y'all have got something going, and if you don't act on it, you're both crazy."

"What if it's just a case of lust, not love? How do you tell the difference?" Bridget asked.

"I've partied with him," Alana said. "I've seen his lust in his eyes. He's different, now. He's happy, and it shows. He was sad when he came home from Ireland a year ago, but then he moved across the state. I thought that might help, but anytime I called or talked to him, the sound of sadness was still there. It's gone now, and the only thing that's different in his life is you and Laela." Alana stood up and went back to cleaning Santa Claus.

"Ireland is my home. Texas is his," Bridget whispered. "There's no bridge between the two."

"But there could be a bridge between two hearts. Ever heard that old song 'Love Can Build a Bridge'?" Alana asked.

"No, I haven't ever heard it," Bridget admitted.

Alana pulled her phone from her hip pocket, found the song, and played it.

Laela pulled up on the side of the playpen and wiggled her whole body to the music.

"See, even a baby likes it." Alana grinned.

"It's a beautiful song. Thank you for playing it for me," Bridget said. "Can I help you wash the rest of the props, now that I'm done mending curtains?"

"Don't go tryin' to change the subject," Alana said. "Listen to the lyrics. When it says that everything begins with you and me, just put your name and Maverick's in there."

"Maybe so," Bridget agreed. "Time will tell."

"Don't break his heart, or I'll have to hurt you," Alana cautioned.

Bridget didn't know the woman well enough to know if she was teasing or not, but just in case she wasn't, she said, "You better pack a dinner, because it will take all day."

Alana took a few steps forward, wrapped Bridget up in a hug, and said, "You are exactly what Maverick needs in his life."

"Why would you say that?" Bridget asked.

Alana stepped back and sat down in a chair beside the playpen. "You're sweet and kind, but you hold your own. He's sown wild oats, but down deep he's not as self-confident as the tough cowboy everyone thinks he is. He doesn't think he can have a relationship because he doesn't have anything to offer."

"That is a bit of horse crap," Bridget said. "Why would he think that?"

"It's a long story, but he's..." Alana stopped and cocked her head to one side. "They're coming back in here. We'll talk later."

Oh, yes, they would, Bridget vowed. Maverick damn sure didn't seem like he was lacking in self-confidence to her—not one tiny bit—so she'd like to know why Alana would say such a thing.

# Chapter Thirteen

The next morning, Bridget was still thinking about what Alana had said about Maverick. In her eyes, he had always been way out there beyond confident—even a little cocky. She had done all her chores that Saturday morning, talked to Iris on the phone twice already, and told her about what they'd accomplished at the church the night before. Dozens of cookies were wrapped on colorful disposable plates and stacked in boxes to give to the nursing home patients. Everything was ready, and she'd just made herself a cup of tea when her phone rang.

"Hello, Sean. What's on your agenda this Saturday night? Darts at the pub?" she asked.

"I haven't been to the pub since we talked last," he said.

Sweet Jesus and all the angels in heaven! What was that woman's name—Katy, Karen? Kelly! That was it. She must've really gotten her hooks in him if he wasn't going to the pub every night to play darts and flirt with the lasses. "Have you been sick?" Bridget asked.

"Never better, luv." He chuckled. "What are you doin' tonight? Going to a Texas honky-tonk? Sleeping with a cowboy?"

"I asked first," she reminded him.

"Kelly and I are in a good place in our relationship," he said. "But she just might be the one."

He'd only known the woman a week at the most. Was he out of his mind?

"Are you still there?" Sean asked.

"I'm here." She put the phone on speaker and fixed a midmorning bottle for Laela.

"Did you just put me on speaker? Who is there in the room with you?" Sean asked.

"Yes, you're on speaker. I'm making a bottle for Laela and she's in the kitchen with me. So is Ducky and Dolly, but one is a dog and the other is a cat, so you can talk freely," she said.

"Good," Sean said. "Where's the cowboy?"

"Out at the barn or mending fence," she answered. "He mentioned both this morning. This afternoon we're taking the eight kids in our Sunday school class to a nursing home to sing for the elderly."

"They must be hard-pressed for Sunday school teachers." He chuckled.

"It's only for a few weeks until Iris gets back on her feet and takes it over again," she explained. "And it's not funny."

"It kinda is," Sean said. "I can almost see myself teaching Sunday school if Kelly and I move in together after the first of the year—"

"What?" she squealed when she butted in. "You'll only have known her a few weeks. That's not long enough to be askin' her to live with you."

"And that, luv, is my business, not yours," he said with

an edge to his voice. "I was about to say that I'm ready to settle down, and I really like this girl"—his tone softened—"and that if we do make that decision, her flat will be up for rent. It'd be a right nice place for you and Laela when you come home."

Evidently every dark cloud did have a silver lining, just like Nana said. "That sounds great, but think about all you'll be givin' up if you have a woman living with you all the time. She won't make your breakfast and then go home. You won't be flirting or maybe not even going to the pub every night."

*That would be just as much for Maverick to give up,* she thought the minute that she said the words.

"Don't go off half-cocked, luv," he told her. "We haven't even talked about that yet, but I can see it could happen and wanted to tell you about her flat. But by then, you might be living with a cowboy and not even need a place for you and Laela."

"I will not be living with him," Bridget argued.

"Listen to me, Bridget," Sean said in a stern tone. "I thought there was plenty of time for me to settle down to married life. Then Deidre passed on before she was even thirty and it jarred me to the ends of my soul and back. We are not guaranteed to live so long that someday we sit on a porch and watch great-grandchildren play in the yard. We could be snatched away tomorrow like she was. I want a wife and children before I die. I do not want to leave this earth with no one to—"

"You cannot marry the first girl who comes along," she butted in, "for that reason."

"I'm not arguing with you," he said. "I'm hanging up now before we say words that we can't take back, and we aren't friends anymore." The call ended.

She stomped her foot, but that didn't make enough noise, so she opened and slammed a cabinet door. Bridget felt horrible when Laela stuck out her lower lip and began to whimper.

"I'm so sorry, sweet baby." Bridget gathered her up in her arms, picked up her bottle, and carried her to the living room. She'd just settled down into a rocking chair when she heard the front door open.

"Anybody home?" Alana called out.

"In the living room." Bridget raised her voice.

Laela spit out her bottle and stared at the door. When Alana arrived, she held up her arms. Alana removed her coat and cowboy hat and tossed them at a nearby recliner, then took the baby. "What's the matter, darlin'? Were you ex-pectin' Maverick?"

"She thinks it'll be him every time the door opens," Bridget said. "Want a glass of tea or something to drink?"

"No, I'm good." Alana sat down on the floor and handed Laela a toy giraffe. "Look at that. She's smilin' so I'm for-given for not bein' her favorite person."

"She likes most everybody," Bridget replied, "but I have to admit, she does love Maverick."

"We didn't get to finish our conversation about him last night, so I thought I'd come over while Maverick is out working," Alana said.

"How did things go with Ryan?" she asked.

"It was a one-date thing. He's divorced, has three kids all under the age of six, and lives with his mama so she can help out with the children. I'm not ready for that," Alana said.

"But he seemed like a nice guy," Bridget argued.

"He is," Alana nodded, "and he's a great dancer and won-derful kisser, but why start something that has no finish?

I don't want a self-made family, and I don't want a man who'll leave his kids at home and go bar hopping, either. So that's over. But what I came to talk to you about isn't Ryan."

"Okay…" Bridget said. "But we're both supposed to be at the church tonight. You might've told me then."

"Not with Maverick and my dad there," she went on. "You should stay in Texas. I'll give you a job on my ranch when Iris comes home and takes the reins back. You can help out in the house like you do here. I'll pay you very well, and you won't even have to shell out your money for a babysitter. I talked to my dad about it, and he thought it was a wonderful idea."

"Why would you do that?" Bridget asked.

"Because it will give you and Maverick more time to get to really know each other, and"—she shrugged—"because we can use the help. A live-in housekeeper and cook is almost impossible to find, and I hate that kind of work. I'd rather be outside plowing fields, working cattle, building fence—anything but being cooped up inside the house. And besides, Maverick has always been one of my best friends, and he will be heartbroken if you go back to Ireland. He might not even know it right now, but he will be, and I don't want to see him like that."

"Thank you." Bridget was breathless at the idea of the possibility of a job that perfect for her and Laela. "I'll think about it, but, Alana, I'm replaceable. Maverick knows how to pick up women, and with his looks he won't ever be alone. I imagine that he'll be in the pub, or Wild Cowboy as you call it, the weekend after Iris is back home, and he'll have no trouble picking up a woman to keep his bed warm."

"Maybe so, but that kind of woman isn't the kind that you form a permanent relationship with." Alana sighed.

"You and Maverick have chemistry. Someday I hope to find someone that makes my eyes sparkle like he does yours. And Laela loves him, so that's a plus."

"She loves him now, but she won't remember him a month if we go back to Ireland," Bridget argued.

"Then y'all have to recognize the vibes between you and get to building on them, because the way I see it, you need to stay in Texas." Alana got to her feet and sat down on the sofa. "Want to hear my theory about Maverick?"

"Yes, tell me your theory." Bridget nodded.

"He's lived in the shadow of the superwealthy Baker brothers his whole life. Iris is a distant cousin to Tag and Hud's grandmother, so they were back and forth between this little spread and that huge one down south of us. Don't get me wrong, Tag and Hud are good men, and they'd never deliberately lord it over Maverick and Paxton."

"So even though they lived on this lovely ranch, they were like the country cousins?" Bridget asked.

"That's right," Alana went on. "The Baker brothers wanted to buy a ranch on the other side of the state, and their folks gave them part of their inheritance to do it. It's twice as big as this place. They needed help to get it up and running, so Maverick and Paxton agreed to go out there as foremen for the place."

With just that much explanation, Bridget was beginning to understand Maverick a little better. "Are Maverick and his brother ever planning to come back to this area? Like maybe when the Bakers get their place in shape."

"Iris has always said that she didn't want them to feel like they have to help her. She sent them to work on the big spread so they'd be out on their own. She's just waitin' for them to get the wild oats out of their systems and settle down before she hands this place over to them." Alana stood up. "I'll take you up on something to drink now if you've got some tea made up."

"Then let's go to the kitchen. I can brew a pot in just a few minutes." Bridget led the way with Laela crawling behind them and Dolly coming along behind the baby.

"I want five or six of those." Alana nodded at the baby. "Iris and my dad thought Maverick and I'd have at least two by now. Trouble is, there was no chemistry between us—not ever. Now, it could be different with Paxton. I could work up a little heat for him, but he goes for the short, busty little brunettes. A tall, gangly blonde isn't nearly frilly enough for him."

"I understand." Bridget went to the stove and put on a pan of water to boil. "My grandmother had it all planned that I would marry my friend Sean. I love him. I really do, but more as a little brother."

"We need those breathless moments that make a woman's life complete, don't we?" Alana glanced at the cookie jar. "Mind if I get into the cookies?"

"Not a bit," Bridget said. "This can be our midmorning tea."

"We just call it a snack." Alana opened the jar and put several cookies on a plate. "Should I put the baby in the high chair?"

"Yes, please." Bridget's mind was whipping around so fast, thinking about what Alana had said about breathless moments and the offer of a job right there on the next ranch over, that she almost forgot to take the lid off the teapot before she poured the hot water into it.

"Well, damn it to bloody hell," she swore as she grabbed a tea towel to mop up the water on the cabinet. "You'll be wanting to take back that offer to work for you if I can't even get the water into the teapot."

"Not damn likely. You could even burn the biscuits occasionally, and I wouldn't gripe." Alana put the baby in the chair and then got a wet washcloth to wipe her hands and face. "You do realize that Maverick won't always be just a foreman on somebody else's ranch, don't you?"

"I wouldn't care if he was. If anything should ever come of this crazy situation, all I would want would be his heart. It would not matter to me if I had to work to help support us." Bridget refilled the pan with water to boil and got down two cups.

"My thoughts exactly," Alana said. "I'd rather live in a one-room cabin on the Red River with lots of passion than live in a lukewarm relationship in a mansion on a hill."

Looking at Alana, Bridget realized she was as different from Deidre as night and day, but talking to her was easy— like it had been with Deidre. She had never thought she would find a friend like that again.

* * *

That first part of Saturday morning went fine for Maverick. He had gotten a lot done right up until the middle of the morning. Then things took a turn for the worse. If things could go wrong, they did. Even things that seemed there was no way on God's great green Earth that could possibly go wrong, they managed to find a way to do it somehow. Maverick hit his thumb with a hammer and had to drill a small hole in the nail to ease the pressure of the blood building up under it. On his way to the house for dinner the wind blew his favorite old work hat into a mud puddle and then rolled it on over into a fresh pile of cow manure. It was old and just about worn-out, but he liked that hat. Then Granny's prize bull got out on the road at the backside of the ranch. When he tried to get the sorry bastard back into the pasture, the animal charged him and knocked him into a ditch filled with icy cold water left over from the recent rain.

When he had finally gotten the bull back into the pasture and shored up the fence, it was well past noon. Maverick was cold, wet, hungry, and tired. All he wanted was a hot shower. He damn sure wasn't looking forward to going to a nursing home with a bunch of kids and passing out cookies to the elderly.

He walked into the house to a woman at her wits' end with a bawling baby, the smell of something burning on the stove, and the house phone ringing. He grabbed the extension hanging on the utility room wall, and said, "Hello."

"What in the hell is going on?" Iris asked. "I haven't been able to reach anybody all day."

"Chaos," Maverick said. "It's been one of those days. I'm wet, cold, and in bad need of a shower. Talk to Bridget." He handed the phone off to Bridget and headed straight for the bathroom.

The last thing he heard before he closed the door was Bridget explaining that Laela had been throwing a fit for half an hour, the battery in her phone needed charging, and she had no idea what was wrong with Maverick.

He stood under the shower long after he'd lathered up and rinsed the soap from his body. The hot water beating down on his shoulders felt good after that roll in the dirty ditch water. When he'd finally gotten out of the shower, dried off, and dressed in clean jeans and a soft T-shirt, he could still hear the baby whining. He took time to put a clean Band-Aid on his thumb, and wished that he didn't have to load cookies into the truck for the singing that afternoon.

When he finally made it to the living room, Laela was sitting on the floor in front of the Christmas tree. She took one look at him, slapped the lowest ornament, and sent it rolling across the floor. Dolly chased after it and batted it around the floor like a ball.

"Looks like she's punishing me for being late," Maverick said.

Bridget popped her hands on her hips. "You could have called. Your dinner is on the stove. You'll have to heat it up in the microwave and eat fast. We only have an hour before we've got to be at the nursing home for our rehearsal with the children."

"I might have called if my phone had been workin'. I fell in a ditch with a foot of cold water in the bottom. If I can't get my phone dried out, I'll have to buy a new one." Maverick told her about his horrible afternoon.

"Well, you'd best go eat while I get Laela ready to go, and then we'll have to get the cookies all loaded up," she told him.

She disappeared from the room, and he ate his food standing up at the kitchen counter, washed it down with a glass of sweet tea, and then loaded all the boxes of cookies into the backseat of the truck. As he was going back into the house, Dolly got under his feet and tripped him up. He threw out his hands to keep from falling and hit the glass window in the door so hard that it broke.

"What have you done?" Bridget asked.

"Damn cat," he muttered. "I'll put a plastic garbage bag over it until we can get home and fix it."

"Are you hurt?" she asked.

"My best pair of gloves is cut up and ruined, but I'm fine," he grumbled.

"Thank God you had them on," she said on her way out to the truck. "Laela and I'll be waiting for you."

He mumbled the whole time he duct-taped a black bag over the window to keep the cold out, and was still cussin' hammers and cats when he got into the truck. Surely nothing else would go wrong.

"What's happened to your thumb?" Bridget asked before he could even get the truck engine started.

"I had an argument with a hammer and it won," he said. "Tell me about your day." Maybe listening to her would put him in a better mood.

"Alana came over and offered me a job after Iris comes home and heals up. She says I'd be doing the same thing over there that I do now, and I can keep Laela with me rather than sending her off to a sitter," she said.

*Well, that was just grand.* He grimaced. He thought Alana was his friend and there she was stealing Bridget.

"And Sean called," Bridget went on to say, "and if his girlfriend, Kelly, moves in with him, then her flat will be up for rent. I could possibly get my job back at the bakery. Deidre worked there"—Bridget reminded him—"and the owner let her bring Laela to work with her, so there's that. What would you do?"

"It's your choice, not mine," he snapped at her.

"I'd be asking for your advice, but if you're going to be a jackass, then I don't even want it." She crossed her arms over her chest and stared out the side window. "I'll be making my own decisions and not bothering you with them anymore."

The trip from ranch to nursing home was only a five-minute drive, and by the time he'd parked not far from the door, he was sorry he'd snapped at her. If he hadn't been tired, maybe it wouldn't have rubbed him wrong.

But it did.

"Right now I don't even want to hear about Sean," he said.

"What bee has gotten into your knickers?" Bridget asked him.

"It's been a bad day." He opened his door.

"Those come along," she told him when he got around to her side, "but did you ever think that it might be a test to teach you a lesson?"

"Oh, yeah," he growled. "Like how to hit my thumb with a hammer, or put my hands through the door window."

"Well, you can sure enough get over this mood in the same knickers that you got into it, but it better be soon," she told him.

"Are you threatening me?" He stacked three boxes on his shoulder and started across the lot.

"No, I'd just be stating facts, but if you drop those cookies, it could be a threat," she told him as she got Laela out of the car seat and slung the diaper bag over her shoulder.

Seven mothers trying to keep control of their kids met them at the door. They turned the kids over to Bridget and escaped for the next hour. Maverick wished he could go with them rather than staying in a place with old people and rowdy kids, but Iris would have his hide—and besides, it wasn't anyone's fault but his own that he was in a grumpy mood. Truth be told, most of it was brought on from thinking about Bridget going back to Ireland as he worked that morning, and then she'd talked to her friend and to Alana.

"Right this way," a lady in pink scrubs said. "You can practice for fifteen minutes in the recreation room. When we get the patients in the lobby, we'll come and get you. If you need a piano player, we've got an orderly who does an amazing job."

"That would be nice," Bridget said.

Maverick set the cookies down on a table and heaved a sigh of relief. The way his day had been going, it was a wonder he hadn't dropped them and then fallen backward on the boxes.

# Chapter Fourteen

"All right, kids," Bridget said over the top of their excitement. "Let's do a quick run-through of 'Santa Claus Is Coming to Town.'"

"Can I hold the baby while we sing?" Lily Rose asked.

"I'm bigger than you so I should get to hold her," Katy argued.

"I don't even like babies, but if we're going by who's biggest, then I get to hold her," Slade said.

"I'll hold Laela, and…" She shot a look toward Maverick. "Maverick is going to sing with you. Elijah can start the songs, but Maverick will be singing along with you."

"You're bein' a bit bossy today," he whispered.

"Singin' is good for the soul. Maybe you'll be in a better mood when you leave," she said out of the corner of her mouth, and then raised her voice. "Elijah, you can begin."

The little boy tipped up his chin and started singing. Lily Rose, Lisa, and Katy were downright theatrical, shaking their fingers at the boys during the songs, and doing choreography through the whole song.

"When did you three figure that out?" Bridget smiled.

"We been workin' on it since Sunday," Lily Rose said. "Anybody can sing, but we're performers."

"Yes, you are," Bridget told them. "Your audience is going to love you."

The lady in pink knocked on the door and nodded at Bridget. The kids filed out behind her, one by one, with Maverick bringing up the rear. *Men!* Bridget thought. *They always talk about women being moody, but an annoyed woman couldn't hold a candle to a pissy man.*

"Oh, look at that precious baby." One little lady on the front row of chairs reached out to touch Laela's arm as they passed by. "How old is she?"

"Seven months." Bridget stopped and sat down beside the woman.

"And these cute little kids." An old guy poked his friend sitting next to him. "I hear they brought homemade cookies for after their singing."

Maverick waited for someone to step up behind the microphone to introduce them. When no one did, Bridget pointed and nodded at him.

"What?" He frowned.

"Say something. It's time," she mouthed.

He took the microphone from the stand and tapped on it. There was plenty of sound coming from it, so he held it out a little. "Merry Christmas, everyone! Are all y'all ready for Santa Claus?"

That brought on applause. While the old folks were clapping, an orderly rushed into the room and sat down behind the piano.

"Looks like we're ready to sing," Maverick said. "We're

the Sunday school class from the Daisy Community Church, so give the kids a little more love before we start."

Another round of applause echoed down the halls. When it died down, Maverick leaned down and whispered all three songs into the piano man's ear. He nodded and ran his fingers down the keyboard in Floyd Cramer style and then hit the first notes for "Santa Claus Is Coming to Town."

Maverick sang with the kids through all three songs, and by the end a wide smile covered his face, and he even lost a few words when he chuckled at the girls' antics. When they finished and took a bow, Bridget followed the kids back to the recreation room, where they began to tear into the boxes of treats.

"Whoa!" Maverick came in right behind them. "Let's be organized about this, guys. Each of you take a plate in each hand. Start on the front row and work your way back. Make sure every one of the grannies and grandpas gets a plateful, and tell them—"

"Merry Christmas!" Randy shouted. "That's what Mama told me to say, and to be nice."

"That's right," Bridget said. "Walk, don't run in the hall." Then she turned to Maverick. "I'll go up front with them and manage things from that end."

He nodded. "I'll be up as soon as the last cookies leave out of here."

By the time the cookies were passed out, the mothers were trickling back into the lobby. Bridget was right in there among them, talking to the elderly, discussing kids and recipes. Maverick stood to the side, and checked the time on his phone. When they'd been there more than an hour, Bridget caught his eye and nodded. She said a few words to the little lady who'd complimented her on Laela, and began to get Laela bundled up.

"Wasn't that just the cutest thing ever?" she said when they were outside. "The kids did great to have only that one practice last week. I bet the program at church is going to be smashing."

She was still talking about the program while she buckled Laela in her seat. Maverick had started around the truck when Randy came running across the parking lot. For a minute Bridget thought the child was going to hug him. Then she noticed how green the little guy was around the mouth and knew what was about to happen. She opened her mouth to yell at him but she wasn't fast enough.

The little guy leaned over at the waist and upchucked all over Maverick's jeans and boots. The north wind picked up the scent and brought it right to her nose.

"Sorry." Randy looked up sheepishly, "Mama told me to run to the grass. I didn't make it."

Randy's mother came around the end of the truck apologizing. "We were in the car when he started to gag. I didn't want it in the car. I'm so sorry. I'll feel just horrible if he's got a bug and gave it to those sweet old folks. I probably shouldn't have let him come today because he was complaining with a stomachache at breakfast, but he pitched a fit, and he'd learned all his songs." She picked him up and carried him back to her car, patting his back all the way.

"I hope it's just a stomachache and nothing serious," Bridget said, but she wanted to scream that she should never bring a child with any possibility of sickness to the nursing home.

"I apologize again." She got him into the car and drove away.

Bridget rustled around in the diaper bag and found a package of baby wipes and a plastic bag that she put soiled diapers inside. She carried them over to Maverick and handed them to him. "That'll help get it cleaned up until we can get home."

He did what he could, but nothing could take the stench from his jeans or his boots. "I'm so sorry that you and Laela have to smell this," he apologized when he got into the truck."

"It's not your fault. Randy's mother shouldn't have let him come if there was any possibility that he was sick." She didn't care how cold it was—if it wouldn't have given Laela a chill, she would have rolled down her window.

"But you got to admit, he was sure enjoyin' himself, and he was so good with those old folks." Maverick cracked the window beside him. "This is worse than skunk. Maybe this will blow some of it outside."

He drove fast, and in minutes they were home. He rolled the window back up, jumped out of the truck, and yelled over his shoulder, "I'll see you on the other side of a shower."

Bridget nodded and got the baby out of the backseat, carried her and the diaper bag inside, and went straight to the bedroom. She took Laela's afternoon bottle from the bag and sat down in the rocking chair with her. In seconds, the tired little girl was sleeping soundly. Bridget laid her in the crib and hurried to the kitchen. She slipped a bibbed apron over her head and was busy tying the strings when Maverick appeared in the doorway. He wore a pair of clean jeans, a chambray work shirt, and white socks. Water droplets hung to his hair like dew on a rose, and he smelled heavenly— like soap and a woodsy shaving lotion.

"Much better," she said.

"More cookies?" he asked as she got a beer from the refrigerator.

"And cupcakes for tomorrow's Sunday school class." She stood on tiptoe trying to reach the big mixing bowls.

Maverick came up behind her and brought two bowls down from the top shelf. He was close enough that she could almost hear the electricity between them crackling. All she would have to do was flip around and remain on her tiptoes—and she did owe him that kiss, but forget that business of a kiss on the cheek, she wanted a real kiss. But he'd been like an old ram with a toothache all day, and in this mood, he might reject her. She waited until he put the bowls on the counter and had taken a step back to say anything.

"You've been in a snit today. Want to talk about what's really bothering you?" she asked.

"Nope," he muttered. "What good would it do?"

"It would get it off your chest." She laid a hand on her heart. "In here."

"Men don't get all emotional about their feelings," he said.

"They do if they want to get over a pissy mood," she told him.

"Let's just make cookies and muffins," he said as he brought up the song about Christmas cookies and played it on his phone. "Maybe this will get us both out of our moods."

"I'm not in a funk," she declared, "and when you get ready to talk to me about what's really eatin' on you, we might talk about those fifteen minutes of kissin' and lovin', but until then forget it."

"You want me to sing about the Scotsman?" he asked.

She couldn't keep the smile off her face. "I do not!"

"Okay, then, let's make Christmas cookies." He grinned, but the antsy feeling in his chest was still there. He took her by the hand and spun her around in a swing dance move. They'd survived somewhat of an argument. That was a good sign, wasn't it? But it would be a better one if he'd open up and tell her what was really troubling him.

While the first batch of cookies baked, Maverick went to the living room and put on a stack of vinyl records, all playing Christmas songs by country artists, going all the way back to Hank Snow and Hank Williams. Bridget had heard many of the songs, but the artists were new to her.

"What can I do to help now?" he asked.

"Get out the mixer and whip up the icing," she told him as she used cookie cutters to make Christmas trees, bells, and Santa Clauses from the dough she had rolled out on the countertop.

He followed her directions and soon had a big bowl of white icing made up. "Now what?" he asked.

"Now you put about half a cup full of that"—she pointed to smaller bowls on the table—"and drop a little food coloring in each one—blue, red, green, and yellow—so we can decorate the cookies as they cool."

Before she could tell him to only use a drop at a time, he'd smeared a bit of icing on her lower lip. When she looked up from the cookie sheet, he had a wicked grin on his face.

"Oops, my hand slipped when I was removing the beaters from the mixer. Let me get that for you." He leaned over and his lips were on hers.

The taste of almond-flavored icing blended with the delicious woodsy scent of his shaving lotion, and sent her senses reeling. Her knees went weak and her breath came in short bursts as one kiss led to another, and still yet another. The only thing that stopped her from ripping off his shirt and leading him to the bedroom was the loud timer reminding her that another batch of cookies should be taken out of the oven.

"Damned timer, anyway," he muttered.

"Or maybe good timer," she panted as she grabbed a hot

pad and opened the oven door. "We could've burned the house down if we'd have let that go on much longer."

"By the cookies or what would have happened right here on the kitchen floor?" He grinned.

"Both," she answered.

* * *

Bridget thought about their short make-out session all the way to the church that evening. If five minutes could turn her whole body into a quivering mass of emotions, she wasn't sure she could stand fifteen minutes like the silly Christmas song mentioned.

The back door to the church was unlocked, so she and Maverick went straight back to the prop room, where Alana and her dad were already cleaning the next couple of cutouts.

"Hello, I'm Matt Cleary, Alana's dad. I'd shake with you but"—he held up wet hands—"and Alana has talked all day about Laela. I've seen y'all in church but didn't get to speak to you in the crowd."

"We brought cookies and cupcakes for snacks." Maverick set a plate on one of the tables beside a small plate of pumpkin bread. "The Christmas trees are the best because I made them."

Matt peeled off a couple of paper towels, dried his hands, and then picked up a green tree and bit into it. "I love iced sugar cookies, and this is pretty good for a tough old cowboy's makin'. Get yourself a piece of Alana's pumpkin bread, and we'll take Mr. Santa Claus up to the sanctuary and get him positioned behind the curtain."

When the guys left, Alana took Laela from Bridget and sat down in a chair with her, but the baby instantly began to squirm and lean toward the playpen full of toys. "I guess she's telling us to get busy. Dad says we should get the sleigh ready tonight so the guys can get it positioned next weekend. It's the biggest prop we have, and it's probably going to need some touch-up painting done when we get it washed down."

Bridget picked up a washcloth and started at the end of the sleigh where Matt had left off. Matt was an inch or two taller than Alana, had silver streaks in his dark hair, and big brown eyes.

"I see where you got your height," Bridget said.

"Didn't have a chance of being little and cute like you." Alana nodded. "Mama was almost six feet tall too."

"I always wished I could be tall and have blond hair," Bridget admitted.

"We all want what we can't have, don't we?" Alana smiled as she went to work cleaning the other end of the sleigh. "Have you thought about my job offer?"

"Yes, but it's a big decision," Bridget said.

"No rush," Alana said. "We don't even need an answer until after Christmas."

"Thank you," Bridget said.

The guys came back when they still had a bit of sleigh left to wash, and Matt entertained Laela by picking up the toys she threw out of the playpen and tossing them back in for her to throw out again. Maverick ate a few more slices of pumpkin bread and two more cookies. When it was time for them to leave, Bridget and Alana traded plates. Bridget had the leftover pumpkin bread, and Alana took home the rest of the cookies.

"See you tomorrow in church," Alana said. "I'm off to the Wild Cowboy for a couple of hours."

"Tell anyone I know hello for me," Maverick said.

Bridget thought she heard wistfulness in his voice. "Do you miss that life?"

"Yes," he admitted.

"Don't let me and this baby hold you back from what you want to do."

"I'm not," he said.

His tone said something altogether different, though.

"So Sean has a girlfriend?" He changed the subject.

"Yes, but I don't think she's right for him." She told him how her friend was feeling old because of what happened to Deidre. "He wants to settle down, but he's not ready."

"How do you know that?" Maverick asked. "You're thousands of miles away."

"Sean is a player"—she hesitated—"different woman every weekend, and sometimes every night. He has this quilt that he keeps in the trunk of his car. The tales it could tell would curl your toenails. He's not ready, and I know it in my heart. A commitment is more than picnics by the river and tumbling in the sheets."

\* \* \*

Maverick realized she'd probably just described him as well as Sean. Both of them needed to sow their wild oats before they were truly ready to settle down. He wondered if Sean liked coming home to a woman in the house but still yearned for the chase. Maverick loved flirting with Bridget, and those kitchen kisses had practically set him on fire, but was he ready to settle down with one woman for the rest of his life? He was still on the fence about that.

"Sean reminds me of you," she said. "He wants his cake to look all pretty on the table, but he wants to eat it too. I can tell you're itching to go have some fun."

"I'm fine," he said, but she was right, he did want to get away from Christmas props and kids, and think about the future. Even when Buster came back, the two old folks couldn't keep up with all the maintenance on the ranch. It was time for him to come home and help Granny. But living with family again would be a big change. Over at Canyon Creek no one asked him where he was going or how late he'd be staying out. Tag and Hud didn't care as long as he worked hard and completed his jobs.

"You don't sound fine. You sound angry," she said.

Why didn't she just leave it alone? If all women were like that—wanting to talk about emotions and analyze his every word—then those one-night stands were beginning to look better by the second.

"I said I'm good." He parked the truck and helped take the baby inside like usual. She carried in the diaper bag and the pumpkin bread, dropped the bag in the foyer, and went straight to the kitchen.

It was definitely time to start singing about the drunk Scotsman, but she took the baby from him, and headed to her bedroom.

"Good night," he said.

"I hope you get up in a better mood tomorrow," she said.

"You too," he said.

She didn't even answer him but kept walking.

"I'm going for a drive," he said as he got to his feet. "We both need to cool off. Maybe while I'm gone, you can think about *us* rather than Sean."

"I might not be here when you get back," she threw over her shoulder as her bedroom door slammed.

"That's your choice." Maverick walked out the door and got back into his truck. *That was a stupid fight.* Iris's voice was clear in his head. *You've got to go at this with a carrot instead of a stick. Bridget is struggling just like you with all these emotions.*

He didn't even bother to argue with his grandmother but drove straight to the honky-tonk. The parking lot was already full at eight o'clock that Saturday night. He went straight for his favorite barstool, removed his hat, and laid it on the counter.

"What can I get you?" asked Sally from behind the bar.

"A double shot of Jack, neat," he answered.

"Haven't seen you in here in months! What've you been up to?" She poured a generous double into a glass and set it on a paper coaster.

"Been out near Bowie with the Baker brothers on their ranch. Came back for a short while to help my grandmother out." He took the first sip and felt the warmth of it go all the way to his belly.

She topped off his glass when he set it down. "That's on the house because you look like you lost your best friend."

"We had an argument, all right," he admitted. "Thank you."

"Want to talk about it?" She propped both elbows on the bar, giving him a good view of a lot of cleavage.

"Nope, he don't, and put whatever he's drinkin' on my tab tonight." Alana got him by the arm.

"Wait a minute," Maverick growled. "I'm not leaving my drink behind." He picked it up and followed Alana to a table.

"You can drink all you want, but you'll not be going home with a woman tonight, my friend. If you want to dance, I'm right here. Now tell me what's wrong," she said.

"I don't know what in the hell I want," he admitted.

"Well, you better decide because the best thing to ever come across your path is living with you on the Callahan Ranch," she said. "Tell me what happened."

"I don't want to talk about it," he said. "I just want to sit here and enjoy a few drinks."

Two of his old drinking buddies dragged chairs across the wooden floor and joined him. "Haven't seen you in months," Lane said.

"Heard you'd been back at your granny's place." Will raised a glass. "Here's to good drinks, good times, and wild women."

"To it all." Maverick threw back his drink and slammed the glass on the table. "It's been a day I'd like to forget."

"Has that Irish woman I heard y'all got out at the ranch been givin' you fits?" Will Jackson asked. "If so, then we should do some tequila shots. It's purely for medicinal purposes if your heart is hurtin'."

"Medicinal, my ass." Lane Freeman chuckled. "Just because you're a preacher's son and say you're drinkin' for the medicinal value in the liquor, it don't mean we are. Alana, get us four shot glasses and a bottle of Patrón. By the time we get the bottle finished, we'll have Maverick right as rain."

"Hell." Will chuckled. "We might even send him home with Sally. They say the girls all get prettier at closing time."

"Get your own drinks," Alana said. "I'm not your bartender." She waved at a couple of women coming into the bar and leaned down to whisper in Maverick's ear. "I'm keepin' my eye on you."

Will pushed back his chair and wove his way through the line dancers and the drunks to the bar, and brought back a full bottle of tequila. "Before you get plastered, I promise that I won't let you go home with Sally, even if I have to throw you in the bed of your truck to sleep it off until morning." He poured three shots and passed them around.

Maverick threw back another shot and held out his glass for a refill.

\* \* \*

The next morning he awoke stretched out on the sofa. He was still dressed but he had a raging hangover and his boots were gone. Ducky was curled up so close to his face that the doggy breath gagged him. He pushed the critter to the side, sat up too fast, and held his head in his hands. "Where are my boots, and how'd you get in here?" The dog's tail thumped against the floor and sounded like someone pounding on a bass drum. "Did you eat my boots?"

The cat made a leap from the recliner to his lap, and the jar when she landed made his head hurt even worse. He needed aspirin and hot coffee, but he didn't want to stand up to go get either.

"Last night was downright stupid of me." He set Dolly to the side. She hopped down, and with her tail held high, went to the door.

"You want outside?" he asked.

As if the dog understood what he said, he ran to the door and barked. "Hush, dammit! You'll wake the baby and Bridget, and I'm too hungover to fight with her anymore."

With his hands still on his head, he stood up and let the animals outside. Then he padded barefoot to the kitchen, made a pot of coffee, and chewed up two aspirin. He checked his phone and found two messages. One was from Alana: How you holdin' up this mornin'? Will drove your truck home, and then I took him home.

The other was from Bridget about midnight: You are a bloody jackass, and I don't like you right now.

"Well, darlin', I still love you," he said. "But I'm in no shape to argue."

\* \* \*

Bridget slept poorly and awoke to the sound of Ducky barking. She hadn't let him in the night before, so what was he doing in the house?

"Maverick!" she whispered. She was out of the bed in one jump and stormed down the hallway in her bare feet without even stopping to put on slippers. The hardwood floor was so cold she felt like she was walking on a layer of ice, but she didn't care.

"There had better not be a woman in his bed this morning, or I'm packing my things and calling a car to take me to the airport," she muttered as she threw open his bedroom door without even knocking.

The bed hadn't even been slept in, but she heard a rattling in the kitchen, so she spun around and muttered on the way across the foyer. "You are a lucky duck this morning, cowboy, because if there'd been a woman in your bedroom, I would've been on the first flight back to Dublin."

She found him with one hand on his head and the other trying to pour a mug of coffee. "Well, what do you have to say for yourself?"

"I've got a hangover. I'm going to go do chores, and then I'm going to sleep it off," he answered.

"The hell you are." Her hands went to her hips. "You are going to go do your chores, come back and eat breakfast, and then we're going to church. You need to pray for your sins."

"You can pray for me." He groaned. "I need sleep."

"You should have thought of that before you got drunk. Put on your boots and coat and go feed the cattle. I'll have a cure ready for the hangover when you get back." She put her hands on his chest and shoved him toward the door. "And if you'll remember, we have that ranch party to go to after church."

"Can't I even have a cup of coffee first?" he asked.

"No, you may not. If you want to get over this thing, you have to do things in the right order. Now get out. I've got things to do before we go to church," she said.

"You're downright mean," he muttered as he shoved his arms into his old work coat.

"And you smell like you fell into a barrel of liquor," she said. "Go before I change my mind about giving you my special cure."

He jerked on his boots, grabbed a hat, and said, "I don't need your damned old cure. I just need coffee and sleep."

"Well, you are not getting either," she told him.

He groaned and muttered through the morning chores and shielded his aching eyes from the bright sun when it rose up over the eastern horizon. He vowed if he never saw another bottle of Patrón or Jim Beam, it would be too soon.

When he got back to the house, he kicked off his boots at the back door, hung up his coat, and moaned all the way to the table. He didn't even look at Bridget but sat down beside Laela and said, "Baby girl, don't ever get drunk. The after-effects are hell."

Bridget threw a couple of pieces of bacon in a cast iron skillet, and the smell gagged him even worse than the doggy breath had done. While that cooked she handed him a banana and a bottle of some kind of orange drink.

"You've got to be kiddin' me," he growled.

"The orange stuff has electrolytes in it. It's probably not as good as what I can buy in Ireland, but it's what I give Laela. The banana has potassium. Get after them. When you get them down, I'll have the bacon and fried eggs ready," she told him. "And Maverick, this is the one and only time I will help you get over a hangover, so either remember the order of things, or suffer next time."

"You really are mean," he said.

"I am stating facts. Take it or leave it—makes no difference to me," she said. "I do not abide men who get drunk because they're angry."

"Not even your precious Sean?" he asked.

"Not even Sean. If he gets drunk because he is having a good time, that's one thing, but to go off in a fit of anger is a different thing. Grown-ups don't go off in a fit and get drunk. They talk things out," she said.

More of that talk crap—how could he tell her what he was battling when he couldn't make up his mind about a damn thing? He thought for sure he'd throw the banana and that awful-tasting orange drink up, but it went down fairly smoothly.

She set the plate of bacon and eggs in front of him. "Eat that and then you can have some coffee. By the time you take a shower and we get to church, you'll feel better. And, Maverick, I'm struggling with decisions too, but I'm willing to talk about them."

She took Laela from the high chair. "Finish your food. We'll be ready to go by the time you are. Meet you in the living room." She carried the baby toward the bedroom.

"I don't even know where to begin to put what's in my heart into words," he whispered.

# Chapter Fifteen

Maverick was amazed at how much better he felt when he'd had a shower. Maybe Bridget did have a magic hangover cure. He whistled the tune to "All I Want for Christmas Is You" while he ran his electric razor over his face. He splashed on aftershave and opened the bathroom door a crack to peek out. The coast was clear, so with nothing more than a towel around his waist, he hurried to his bedroom.

He pulled the cleaner's plastic from a pair of jeans and a white pearl snap shirt, and got dressed. As he was combing his hair he noticed something shiny in the reflection of the mirror above the dresser. He laid the brush down and picked up the tiny Christmas tree earring that he'd brought with him from Ireland. He wondered if Bridget even remembered that she'd lost it on that unforgettable night back in Ireland. For nearly a year it was all he had of her, but now she was here in the flesh, and to tell the truth, it scared the beje- sus out of him. What if he talked her into staying in Texas, and then she was miserable? What if they got married—surprisingly enough the idea didn't give him hives—and in a few months she hated him for not being able to send her back to Ireland for visits?

Granny had come to Texas and made a life here. He kissed the little shamrock at the top of the earring and put it back on the dresser. "I'm not sure I'd know what to do with your heart either, darlin', not the way things are, but if you'd trust me, I'd do my best to make you the queen of mine."

* * *

Bridget got the baby dressed first and put her in the crib. She flipped through the few dresses she'd brought from Ireland and finally pulled out the same outfit she'd worn to her grandmother's funeral—a little emerald-green velvet dress that skimmed her knees. She'd only brought one good pair of shoes with her—black high heels, so they would have to do. Iris had told her a couple of days ago that they would go straight from church to the ranch party. According to her, there would be a big buffet of barbecue and all kinds of desserts.

She twisted her red hair up on top of her head and held it there with a clasp that had belonged to Nana's mother. Then she opened a small pouch of jewelry—the only really good piece was a vintage ruby pendant on a fine gold chain that had also belonged to the great-grandmother that Bridget had never met. She fastened it around her neck and turned to face Laela.

"What do you think, lassie? The necklace really doesn't go with the green dress, but red and green are Christmas colors, so I think I'll wear it anyway. It doesn't matter what I look like anyway. You will steal the whole show today in your pretty dress." She turned back to look at her reflection in the mirror and then picked up a single earring—a tiny Christmas tree with a shamrock at the top rather than a star. "I wonder where the other one got to?"

As she looked at it a shiver danced down her spine. The Texas flag had one star on it, like what was on the Christmas tree in the living room. The Irish were known for their shamrocks like the one Nana always put on the top of her tree. Which one would her nana tell her to decorate with next year—shamrock or star?

She took Laela from the crib, picked up the well-stocked diaper bag, and opened the bedroom door to find Maverick leaning against the doorjamb.

"You scared the hell out of me," she gasped.

"I was just about to knock and ask if you needed any help." His eyes started at her feet and traveled to her hair and then back down to her eyes. "You look gorgeous. That's the color of the sweater you wore that night in Ireland."

"Thank you," she said. "You look pretty fine yourself."

She was frozen in place. She wanted to take a step forward, but she was afraid to blink for fear he'd disappear, then she remembered the argument they'd had. The way he'd stormed out and gone to a pub, come home drunk, slept on the sofa, and gotten up grouchy.

"We should be going. It's a sin to be late to church, and we've got to teach Sunday school before that." She pushed past him.

When they reached the foyer, he put on his fleece-lined suede jacket and settled his black hat on his head. Bridget was almost ashamed of her coat. It was so plain compared to her fancy little dress, but it was what she had, so it would have to do.

"Beautiful," Maverick said.

She whipped around to see who he was talking about, and their eyes met. Time stood still, and the world stopped turning, but only for a second. Laela squirmed and wanted down, so he stood up with her and the moment was gone.

"Are we okay?" he asked on the way to his truck. "Or are we still arguing?"

"An argument is something where a resolution can be reached if both parties are willing to compromise. So since you won't talk, I guess we are." She opened the truck door, and together they got the baby into her car seat.

"That's a lot of big words for a plain old rancher like me to understand." Maverick closed that door and opened the one for her. He slipped his hands around her waist and lifted her up into the seat. "Those shoes would make it hard for you to get into the truck."

"Thank you." She waited for him to get into his seat before she said, "And I will be hearing no more of that crap about you being a plain old rancher. You are smart, sweet, and kind, and you understood what I said perfectly."

He laughed. "You've got my number. I can't even play the underdog with you, can I?"

"No, you can't," she said.

They made it to Sunday school, and afterward headed on into the church to the pew where Iris had previously sat. The people were still milling around, finding seats and trying to get settled, when Alana slid in beside Bridget.

"How did you ever get Maverick to come to church? I know he's got a helluva hangover," Alana whispered.

"You were there?"

Alana nodded. "I made sure that he didn't drive home drunk. For your information, he didn't even look at another woman the whole evening. I'm surprised that he was able to get out of bed this mornin'."

"I gave him my hangover cure, and it was good enough for him to have to come teach Sunday school this morning," Bridget said out of the side of her mouth. "But I'm praying that the singin' will be real loud this morning to teach him even a bigger lesson."

Alana stifled a giggle.

The preacher stepped up behind the pulpit and the noise level went from a good eight to a one in about a second. "I want to thank Alana, Matt, Bridget, and Maverick for getting the curtains all mended and up for next week's program. I understand that the props will be set in this weekend and we'll be ready for the program to be presented on Sunday. I also need to thank all the Sunday school teachers, including Bridget and Maverick, who are stepping in for Miz Iris, for working all month on their classes for the upcoming presentation. I understand that the Sunday school class who went to the nursing home yesterday was a big success, and that the teenage group will be going to the rehab center this afternoon. We're all right proud of our youth. Now I'll turn this over to our choir director and we'll have a couple of congregational songs before the sermon."

All through the singing and the service, Bridget worried about whether she might be overdressed. Alana wore a denim skirt, a red sweater, and cowboy boots that morning. If that's what she planned to wear to the party that afternoon, then Bridget really should go back to the house and change into something less formal.

Finally, after what seemed like two hours instead of thirty minutes, the preacher called on someone to give the benediction. When the final amen was said, Bridget asked Alana, "Are you wearing what you have on to the ranch party?"

"Nope, I've got a cute little red satin cocktail dress, but, honey, it was cut way too low to wear to church," Alana answered.

Bridget heaved a sigh of relief. "I was afraid I was over-dressed."

"You look great. I'm going to run by the house and change. I'll be there as soon as I can. I hear Emily is coming, so you'll want to meet her for sure. You'll love her. See you in a little while. I'm going to sneak out the back door." Alana waved as she hurried over to the far end of the pew and disappeared behind the curtains that had been hung for the program.

* * *

Maverick had told her she was gorgeous, but when they arrived at the huge ranch house, just walking into the foyer intimidated her. Nana always told her to hold her head up and not let anyone make her think less of herself, so she tried but wasn't so sure she could pull it off. She and Maverick were standing in a foyer as big as her entire flat over in Ireland. There was a curved staircase on either side that led up to a second floor. A huge credenza decorated for Christmas with a large mirror above it was situated between the two staircases. A sitting area on the other side had a small settee and two matching deep red velvet chairs. It was like a rich and famous house featured in a magazine.

Suddenly, Bridget fully understood exactly what Alana was talking about. This was where Tag and Hud had grown up, and even though they were Maverick's good friends, she could see where he would feel like the country cousin. A lady appeared from the end of the area, took their coats, and disappeared down a long hallway with them.

*So many people!*

That's all Bridget could think when she and Maverick reached the living room.

"I'll have to be careful to not let you out of my sight tonight," Maverick said. "Every bachelor in this place will want to run away with someone as gorgeous as you are."

"Oh, stop it." She sighed. "I'm plain compared to other ranch women. Look at them in their fancy dresses."

"Darlin', you'd look good in a feed sack dress tied up around your tiny waist with a piece of rope," Maverick said.

Alana took her by the arm before he could say anything else. "Come with me. Emily is dying to meet you."

"What if Laela..." she started.

"Laela and I are fine," Maverick assured her. "I'll just take her around and show her off a little."

"Are you sure?" Bridget asked. "I could take her with me."

"I'm positive. We may get us a plate of food and find a corner. Don't worry. I won't feed her anything that you wouldn't," he said.

Alana slung an arm around her shoulders and led her through the dining room, where caterers were serving barbecue with all the sides. "We'll eat later. Right now let's get out of this crowd. It's always like this for about an hour, and then it'll thin out. I grew up with these parties, but all these people still make me claustrophobic."

"I didn't think anything would make you nervous. You always look so poised and classy," Bridget said as she weaved among the people.

"Well, thank you, ma'am, but I never felt like that in my life. I was always the tallest kid in class, and it took a long time for me to get comfortable in my skin." Alana went past the open door into the kitchen and rapped on the next one.

"Y'all come on in," a voice called out.

They went into an office. A desk was set so that whoever

was working could look out a glass wall over a flower garden. It would be beautiful in the spring, but right then the only things growing in it were a few pansies.

"Hello, Bridget. I'm Emily." A tall pregnant woman stood up and stuck out her hand.

Bridget shook hands with her. "Pleased to meet you."

"Where's the baby that Iris has told me all about?" Emily asked.

"Maverick is showing her around right now," Bridget answered. "I hear that you have a wee babe coming into your family."

*Lord, please don't ever let her and Retta know what I thought about them and Maverick*, she sent up a silent prayer.

Emily laid a hand on her stomach. "Yes, and Justin and I are so happy about it. God, I hate these big parties, but my grandmother insists that I come every year."

"You really don't like this kind of thing?" Bridget asked, amazed that a woman who grew up in this house wouldn't love to dress up and go to parties.

"It's a ranchin' wife's job," Alana said. "And if you're the daughter of a rancher, you have responsibilities too."

"I don't want to talk about parties." Emily grinned. "I want to hear about you and Maverick. I need some good juicy details to take back to Sunset with me."

Bridget felt the blush start on her neck and travel all the way to her cheeks. "We're friends—at least I think we are— we argued last night and he went to the pub—no that would be the honky-tonk here in Texas—and he got drunk off his arse."

"Well, that's a good sign." Emily was beautiful, but when she smiled the whole room lit up.

"How in the bloody hell could it be a good sign?" Bridget asked.

"It means that he feels something for you, and he's fightin' it. Men are like that. I have three brothers, and I saw Tag act the same way this past summer," Emily said.

Maverick poked his head in the door. "The baby won't eat for me. Emily!" He came on in the office and crossed the room to hug her. "I've been trying to find you, so I could show off Laela to you."

"You know how I hate crowds." She hugged him and the baby together. "Now step back and let me look at this child. Oh, I hope I get one that looks like her."

"You might. Justin has dark hair." Maverick smiled.

Emily let out a long sigh and swept the tail of her long green dress to the side. "I'd rather stay in here and talk to you girls all afternoon, but Granny will have my hide tacked to the smokehouse door if I'm not social. Bridget, we've got to get better acquainted. I'll give you a call when I get back to Sunset."

"I'd love that," Bridget told her.

Alana followed her. "I'm going to get out there and see if I can find a good-lookin' cowboy who likes big girls."

"You're not big, honey." Emily slung her arm around Alana's shoulder. "I'm the plus-size girl. You're just tall."

They slipped out the door, and Maverick's grin got bigger and bigger until finally he chuckled. "Looks like you girls were having a good time. Did you tell her that you thought she was having my baby?"

"I did not! And don't you dare tell that either. I would be mortified," Bridget said.

"I'm going to leave the baby in here with you." Maverick put her on the floor. "I'll go get y'all a plate fixed and bring it in here. She's hungry, but with so many people around to get her attention, she won't eat. What do you want?"

"Just fix it, and I'll eat it," she said.

"All right then. Be back in a minute." He smiled.

He'd barely gotten the door closed when her phone rang. She fished it out of her tiny purse and said, "Hello, Sean."

"I sure wish you were home." He sighed.

"What's happened?" She sat down in one of the two wingback chairs.

"Kelly and I had a fight. She might not be the one after all," Sean said.

"Are you going to try to make up with her?" She kept an eye on Laela. The baby was peeking around the corners like she was looking for Dolly.

"I've heard that make-up sex is good, but I don't think so. She got really jealous over Sally O'Ryan and me playin' darts at the pub," Sean said. "And while we were fighting, she said that if we were going to ever move in together, then I had to cut off ties with you. I'm not so sure that I could ever live with a woman that jealous. So there goes the possibility of you renting her flat."

"Never mind about that," Bridget said. "The flat isn't as important as you not making a big mistake."

"That's what I thought," he said. "But I miss havin' you at the bakery to talk things through with me."

"And I wish Maverick would talk things through with me," she said.

"It's probably a Texas thing—cowboy tough and all that." He chuckled. "I've got to go, luv. I'm at the pub, and if I win this next round of darts, I go home a little richer. Maybe I'll use it to buy you a Christmas present"— he paused—"if you come home."

"If?" she asked.

"Darlin' girl, you have to like that cowboy a lot if you want him to talk to you." Sean chuckled again. "Bye now."

The call ended, and Maverick brought in food. "You okay? You look like you could cry."

"Sean called. He and Kelly broke up, and hearing my native tongue makes me homesick," she answered. "And to tell the truth, all these people and this place kind of intimidate me."

"I didn't think anything could ever scare you," he said. "I thought you could look a wild bull in the face and spit in his eye."

"I put on a good front," she admitted.

"Eat and then we'll mingle for a few minutes, then we'll leave," he said. "It's going to be past time for the baby's afternoon nap anyway."

Bridget nodded and said, "Thank you. I guess I'm a little like Emily. I'm not cut out for all these big parties."

"Me, either," he admitted. "I can fake my way through them, but I'd rather be home, spending my Sunday afternoon with you and the baby." He grinned.

"And your Saturday nights throwin' back so many drinks that you can't make it all the way to your bed?" she asked.

"That may be the last time that happens," he said. "I also figured out that I don't like the aftereffects of a night like that, and besides, all I thought about the whole evening was you. Would you consider stayin' just a little longer if you're able to change the return date on your plane ticket?" he asked.

She didn't have a place to live when she did go back, so she and Laela would have to stay in a hotel until she could find a flat. She had no job to make money, and what Iris had agreed to pay her wouldn't last forever. She thought about what he'd asked as she fed the baby several bites of potato salad and bread.

"If Iris wants me to stay on until she can get wholly back on her feet, I would be willing to stay another month or two." That would give her more money, and it would be springtime when she returned instead of winter. "How about you? Will you stay and help your grandmother longer?"

"It'll take until spring just to get things in decent order around the ranch. Shall we seal the deal with that kiss you still owe me?"

"I'm not sealing anything until we see what Iris has to say," she told him. "I think this lassie is full, and she needs a nap. Let's go get the mingling over with and go home."

She caught herself right after she said the word, but this time it didn't seem so bad. If Iris wanted her to stay on a while longer, it would be home for a few months.

# Chapter Sixteen

The trip to the store to buy sugar and flour wouldn't take more than twenty minutes, and that was there and back. Bridget didn't need the diaper bag, and there were a couple of stuffed toys still in the truck, so she tucked a nappy and a bottle in her purse. She put her coat on, and then got the baby into hers, and since there was a cold wind rattling the tree limbs, she bundled a fleecy blanket around Laela.

The baby whimpered when the blanket covered her head, but Bridget assured her that it would only be there for a little while. She turned the lock on the knob to lock the door and hurried out to the truck. She reached for her purse to get out the truck keys and it wasn't hanging on her shoulder. She retraced her footsteps across the yard, but no purse, nor was it on the porch. She distinctly remembered locking the door from the inside and closing it, but she turned the knob and tried to open it anyway—it didn't budge.

"Bloody hell!" she swore under her breath as she reached

into the hip pocket of her jeans for her phone, and it wasn't there. "I put it in my purse," she moaned. "We'll just have to go around the house and come in the back door. Maverick never locks it when he leaves in the morning."

Carrying a squirming baby and walking fast did not work so well. Bridget was huffing when she got to the back door, only to find it locked that morning too. Sunlight reflected off the barn out there in the distance, but she didn't see a truck parked out front.

"It looks like we may be spending some time in the barn. I guess if it was good enough for the baby Jesus, we'll manage until someone finds us. I'd trade a knight in shining armor on a white horse for a shepherd in a pickup truck this morning," she muttered as she flipped the cover over Laela's face. The baby promptly threw the cover off her head, but when the north wind whipped across her tender little face, she buried it in Bridget's shoulder. "I'll do the best I can." Bridget huffed as she lengthened her stride. "What I wouldn't give for your stroller right now can't be measured in money."

The barn seemed to get farther away instead of closer. When she was about a third of the way there, she sat down on an old limb to catch her breath. Heavy air and gray skies held the promise of rain—or maybe even snow. She only rested for a moment and then trudged on. "We can't get wet or we'll freeze," she told Laela. "And I will never lock a door again until I make sure I have my keys and phone."

They were almost to the barn when the first raindrops hit her in the face. She took a deep breath and started to jog. Seconds after she'd slipped inside the barn, the rain sounded like bullets hitting the tin roof. "We made it, lassie. We may be cold but we are not wet to the skin."

A light from the back corner dimly lit the way to the tack room. But when she turned the knob, she found that it was also locked. That's when she remembered there was a heat lamp clamped to the stall where the baby calf had been. With her fingers crossed, she headed that way, and shouted, "*Slán abhaile!*" when she saw that it was still there.

She plugged it in and sent up a silent prayer of thanks for the tarp that had been left on one side of the stall. It was still bitter cold when she opened the gate and sat down on the straw-covered floor, but she could already feel a little warmth from the light.

"We'll be fine until Maverick comes and finds us." She wasn't sure if she was talking to the baby or to herself, but the thought brought a little comfort.

Ducky slipped under the gate and licked Bridget across the face. Then Dolly climbed the side of the stall and jumped down to join the party. Laela squirmed out from under the blanket and off Bridget's lap. Dolly stretched out beside her and started to purr.

"No shepherds or knights, but we have got animals. Dolly's fur will keep your hands warm, baby girl," Bridget said. Laela dug her little fist down into Dolly's soft fur and talked baby gibberish to the cat and the dog.

"I wonder if they can understand baby language." Bridget smiled.

\* \* \*

Maverick's shoulders ached from pounding fence posts in all morning. When the first raindrops fell, he finished stringing wire to the post he'd just replaced, threw his tools into the bed of his truck, and drove to the house. It was too early for dinner, but he couldn't build fence in pouring-down rain.

The storm had gotten serious by the time he parked close to the back porch. He held his hat to keep the wind from blowing it halfway to New Mexico. He dashed to the back door, grabbed the back doorknob, found the door locked. That was unusual, since no one locked doors unless they were leaving the house. He fished his keys from his pocket. The moment he was inside, he could feel that something wasn't right. There were no baby noises and no good aromas from cooking food. Maybe Bridget had fallen asleep with the baby when she was putting her down for her morning nap.

He kicked off his boots and hung up his coat and hat. Then he tiptoed to the foyer and down the hall to Bridget's bedroom. The door hung wide open. The bed had been made, and the crib was empty. He went to the living room, and no one was there, not even Ducky sleeping on one end of the sofa and Dolly curled up next to his belly.

"They must've gone into town." His voice seemed to echo from the walls.

He went to the window and saw Granny's truck parked where Bridget had left it the last time she drove. He jerked his phone from his pocket and called Bridget's number. When he realized that the tune "Too Ra Loo Ra Loo Ral" he was hearing was real, and not just in his head, his blood ran cold. That was her phone, and it was somewhere in the house. Following the sound, he found her purse sitting on a chair in the foyer.

He rushed to the front door and found it locked. It only took a split second for him to realize that she'd locked herself out of the house, and out of the truck. There was only one place she would have gone, since she had no way of getting in touch with him—the barn.

He was still stomping his foot down into his last boot when he stepped out onto the porch. The rain beat down on his head because he had forgotten his hat, but he ran to the truck, started the engine, and gave it so much gas that he slung mud all over the porch. When he got to the barn, he jumped out, swung open the big door, and pulled the vehicle inside. If she and Laela hadn't gotten to the barn before the rain started, they were probably wet to the skin and freezing cold. He turned off the engine and noticed a light coming from the nearest stall.

"Bridget," he yelled as he started to run that way. "Are you in here?"

Before he reached the stall he could hear Bridget singing the Irish version of "Silent Night" in her native tongue. He found her with Laela and Dolly in her lap and Ducky hugged up beside her.

"Shhh…" She put a finger to her lips and whispered, "I just got her down for her morning nap. She missed her bottle, but she was a good little lassie."

Maverick opened the gate and eased down beside her. "We'll hide a key outside as soon as we get home. This will never happen again."

Bridget nudged him with her shoulder. "I knew my knight in shining cowboy hat would come rescue us. I'm just glad we got here before the rain got serious."

Big, tough cowboys don't cry, but he had to swallow hard more than once to get past the lump in his throat. Her red hair and green eyes looked ethereal in the light thrown from the little lamp clamped to the top of the stall.

"Where is your hat? Your hair's all wet and you're shivering," she said.

"I was in such a hurry, I forgot to get it," he answered. "How long have you been in here?"

"An hour at the most," she answered. "Ducky and Dolly entertained Laela until she got sleepy, and the lamp kept us fairly warm."

"Let's get y'all back to the house," he said. "Shift her over to me, and I'll carry her to the truck. It's parked inside the barn." He reached for the baby.

"But it's still raining. What about Ducky and Dolly?" She tucked the blanket around Laela and handed her to him.

"They live in the barn part of the time. Dolly hates to get wet, and neither of them ride well, so we'll leave them here." He stood up with the baby in his arms, unplugged the light, and slipped his free arm around Bridget's shoulders. "I bet you were worn-out from carrying this little girl all the way out here."

"I offered to trade my knight in for a shepherd in a truck." She smiled up at him.

"So now I'm a shepherd?" he asked.

"No, silly, you're a cowboy. You raise cattle. Shepherds raise sheep. But when I was trudging out here I knew that you'd come find us eventually," she said.

* * *

He got the baby into her car seat and then whipped off his coat to wrap around Bridget's legs, then rushed around the truck to get inside and poke the buttons to turn on the seat warmers. "You've got to be chilled to the bone."

"Thank you. I didn't realize how wet my pants legs got," she said. "With all this rain, do you think we'll be able to go see Iris this afternoon?"

"Honey, we wouldn't dare miss seeing her over a little rain. We might have to build a boat, but we will get there." He chuckled. "Not even God wants to piss off Granny." He started the truck engine and backed out of the barn, then got out and shut the doors, leaving them open just slightly so Ducky and Dolly could leave when they wanted.

"Does the wind ever stop blowing in Texas?" she asked.

"There's not much to slow it down but barbed wire fences and a few dead trees," he answered as he drove to the house and parked as close to the back door as possible. "I'll get the baby inside and then come back and take you in."

She pushed herself out of the door and ran toward the porch. "I can get there on my own. We have wind off the ocean in Ireland, but it's nothing like this." She shivered as she hung up her coat. "I liked those seat warmers in the truck. Sean's little car doesn't do that. I'll have to tell him about them next time we talk."

"Have he and Kelly gotten over their fight?" Maverick asked.

"I have no idea. What I really miss is being able to talk to him every day about the little things in life. I couldn't have made it past this last year if he hadn't offered me a job in the bakery. He's been my therapist, and he says I've been his."

"That's friendship," Maverick said.

"Yes, it is." She gave him a knowing look.

* * *

As if the rain was on Iris's schedule, it stopped an hour before it was time to get ready to go to the rehab center. Together, Maverick and Bridget bundled the baby up and took her back out to the truck. Water stood in the ditches, and there were puddles in low spots on the road.

"When you were a kid, did you ever stomp in the puddles on the way home from school?" Bridget asked.

"I rode the bus home until I was sixteen and got my driver's license," Maverick said. "But I got in my fair share of stomping in them from the end of the lane to the house." He snagged a parking place not far from the door. "Granny threw a fit if we came in all muddy. She used to tell us that someday we were going to have to do our own laundry, and she'd be willing to bet we didn't get dirty just having a good time. Did you and Deidre run through the puddles together over in Ireland?"

She slung open the truck door. "We did, and it was so much fun. She was the smart and pretty one. I'm the friend who listens to problems and tries to fix things. It's kind of like that with Sean too. As you saw by his picture, he's a pretty boy."

Maverick stopped what he was doing and laid his hands on her shoulders. "You are smart. You are pretty, and you definitely have a sense of humor. Don't ever let anyone, not even your friends, tell you otherwise."

"Thank you for that," she said. "But—"

He put his forefinger over her lips. "There are no buts, just facts. Now let's get inside and go see Granny." He carried Laela into the lobby, where Iris was waiting. She immediately got up from the sofa and motioned for them to follow her down the hall to her room.

"Close the door," she said. "We need to talk."

Maverick did what she asked, and Iris sat down in her lift chair and picked up the remote. When she was comfortable, she reached out for the baby. "I need to get some lovin' off this precious child first."

"You're scaring me," Bridget said. "Are you sick like Nana was?"

"Don't worry. I'm not dyin'." Iris hugged Laela and kissed her on the forehead. "She's had enough of this. Put her on the floor now, and let her play."

"What are we going to talk about?" Maverick sat down in one of the two folding chairs.

Bridget took the other chair. "Do you need for me to leave?"

"Hell, no!" Iris raised her voice. "I'll just spit it out. Buster ain't comin' back. He called me and said that he was in town getting his things together. Then he came by this morning to say goodbye. We both cried, but it's for the best. He's seventy-five years old, and he's needed to retire for ten years."

"I'll be glad to stay on as long as you need me," Maverick said. "It's been good to be home. I didn't know how much I missed it until I got back."

"I was hopin' you'd say that." Iris looked straight at Bridget.

"I will extend my stay if you want me to," Bridget said.

"Good." Iris nodded. "I need you both on the ranch."

"How long?" Bridget asked.

"We'll talk about that later. I just needed to hear that things would be taken care of for right now. Now let's talk about the big ranch party. Did you meet Emily? She's a sweetheart, isn't she? She came to see me last night after the party was over and brought me a plate of barbecue, and that pretty poinsettia over there." She pointed to a huge red plant on the dresser. "It spruces things up in here."

"You want me to get a little Christmas tree for your room?" Bridget asked.

"I thought about that, but I'll only be in here until Christmas Eve. Then, me and Wanda are springing this joint. I've invited her to the ranch for the day, since she don't have family. I've been shopping online. Boxes will begin to arrive in the next few days. Just put them in the spare bedroom. I'll be there in time to wrap them for Christmas morning," she said. "There's a huge box of leftover Christmas paper in the closet in that room. If y'all need to use it for your presents, that's fine."

"I'll be sure the boxes are moved to the dining room,

and the room is ready for Wanda before you get there," Bridget said.

*  *  *

Maverick could have kissed Bridget right there in front of his grandmother and even God. She hadn't hesitated a single moment about staying on longer than Christmas, and extra work with another elderly woman didn't faze her.

"Now that we've got the ranch business settled," Iris said, "I want to thank you both for agreeing to this. I was frantic when Buster called me. I can't run that place by myself. It's goin' downhill with me and Buster both workin' as hard as our old bodies will let us. So it's a relief to know that worry is over. Since it is, I want Bridget to go down to room twenty-two and help Wanda come up here. She's been a little unsteady today even with her walker."

"I could do that," Maverick offered.

"I want Bridget to do it." Iris turned to face him. "You can tell me about what all you've gotten done. I know you've been working hard, and I want details."

"Room twenty-two." Bridget repeated the number and started to pick the baby up, but Iris shook her head. "We can watch Laela. You can't hold her and help Wanda too." When she was out of the room, Iris turned to Maverick. "Well?"

"I started in the tack room, and then I walked the fence line. It'll take until spring to make the repairs that need doin'." He took a sniff of the air. "You smell that?"

"Laela's diaper needs changing."

"Can't we wait until Bridget gets back?" Maverick could build a fence, hang drywall, or put a roof on a barn. Hell, he could build a barn from the ground up and round up cattle on a four-wheeler or a horse, but he'd never changed a diaper before.

"Surely you're not afraid of a diaper if you can run a ranch," Iris told him. "I'll walk you through this first one. After that, you're on your own. Get the changing pad out of the diaper bag and put it on the bed."

Maverick followed his grandmother's instructions and then laid Laela on the pad. She immediately flipped over and took off crawling toward the pillow on the bed. He got a hold on her before she got very far and situated her on the pad again.

"Now you unsnap the legs of her britches," Iris told him. "You might do well to give her a toy to keep her entertained."

Maverick handed the baby her favorite stuffed giraffe.

"Now pull up her britches to about waist level and pull the tabs holding the diaper on her body," Iris said.

"Holy shit!" he exclaimed.

"I wouldn't call it holy since we're not in church, but it is definitely shit. I could smell it all the way across the room. Now, get the wet wipes and get her all cleaned up. From where I'm sittin', it looks like about a ten-wipe job. When you're done, tuck them all inside the diaper, roll it up, and use the tabs to close it," Iris said. "Bridget keeps little bag things in the outside pocket to put those in. You can tie it off and put it in the trash can over there once you have gotten a fresh diaper on her."

Maverick had never had a good gag reflex, but he managed to get through the procedure with only watering eyes and a twitching nose.

"Last step," Iris said. "Take a diaper from the bag, open it up, and reverse the process."

Before he could get Laela's clean diaper from the bag,

the baby had flipped over a second time, and with her little romper flopping along behind her, she was about to crawl right off the edge of the bed when Maverick caught her.

"You got a live wire there." Iris laughed. "Paxton was like that. I learned to hold him down with one hand and change him with the other one."

"When do they get potty trained?" Maverick finally got the job done.

Iris laughed. "When I was a young mother, we figured about a year or eighteen months. Nowadays, they wait until they're a little older."

Laela twisted around, sat on her butt in the middle of the bed, and held up her little arms for Maverick to hold her. He picked her up, and then she wanted back on the floor. He set her down and she began emptying the diaper bag, tossing diapers to the side. Finally, she found another stuffed animal and hugged it tightly. Maverick put everything back and zipped the top, then took the bag with the dirty diaper to the trash can.

"Looks like you've got a daughter—whether you fathered her or not," Iris said. "I also wanted to talk to you about Bridget going back to Ireland. I can see that you've got a thing for her, and you need to use the time you've got to show her how you feel."

"I can't force her to stay here," Maverick answered.

"No, you can't," Iris said. "But you can love her so much that she'd be as miserable as you are if she leaves."

"I don't want her to be unhappy." That was the truth, but he still wasn't sure about all this commitment stuff. After that horrible hangover he was sure he didn't want to be drunk anymore, though.

"I don't know what happened in Ireland, and you don't have to tell me, but I'm not blind or deaf. I know you saw her there because I saw that picture on your phone. You can't live in the past, and people change in a year, but you could start new and build something even better," Iris said.

Maverick couldn't believe his granny had known all along. But at the same time, he wasn't a bit surprised Mam knew everything. "I hope so," he whispered and nodded toward the door. "I hear them coming."

Wanda pushed her walker into the room. "That sweet baby gets prettier every time I see her. I could just take her home with me when I get out of this joint, and love those little chubby cheeks every day."

Bridget came in behind Wanda. "You folks already spoil her."

Maverick got up from his chair and gave it to the lady with the walker.

Iris poked a button on her chair and a voice asked if she needed help. "This is Iris Callahan, and we need another chair in here."

"Be there in just a minute," the voice answered.

"I changed a diaper," Maverick bragged.

"I'll give you a little gold star for your cowboy hat tomorrow." Bridget grinned.

"I'll wear it with pride. It was a messy diaper too."

"Oh, yeah?" Bridget clapped her hands. "That earns you two shiny stars."

Iris laughed so hard that she snorted, and then Wanda got tickled and passed gas. That brought on more giggles between them. Finally, Iris pointed at a tissue box on her bedside table and Bridget handed it to her.

Iris wiped her eyes and passed the box over to Wanda. "Getting old is a bitch except when you can laugh so hard that you snort or fart, and don't even care."

"Amen," Wanda said as she wiped her eyes. "I wish we

could just move in here together. I haven't had a friend like you in years."

Maverick winked at Bridget, but his thoughts were a lot like Wanda's. She and Iris had formed a friendship, and the old gal was going to be lost without her new friend. If Bridget went back to Ireland, his life was going to be empty. He'd bought a little time by getting her to agree to stay a few more weeks, or maybe even until spring. Even though the idea still scared him more than a little bit, what he wanted was a lifetime.

# Chapter Seventeen

Maverick had been watching Bridget, not the clock, so he was surprised when Wanda said that she had to get back to her room.

"Got my last little therapy session coming up in half an hour," she said.

"I'll walk back with you," Bridget said.

"Thanks again for letting me come to your room and visit with the kids." Wanda got to her feet and put both hands on her walker. "Watching that baby girl play is better than any show on television, and it soothes the soul."

"Does, don't it?" Iris smiled. "See you at the supper table. I hear we're having fried chicken tonight."

"I'm sure it won't be anything like what either one of us could make, but I'm lookin' forward to it. Bye now." Wanda pushed out into the hallway with Bridget right behind her.

Maverick waited until they were out of hearing before

he said, "What did Grandpa do to make you want to leave Ireland and move here?" Maverick asked.

Iris smiled so sweetly that Maverick could almost see her going back in time. "It wasn't anything big or what you might think is romantic. One night we danced until the pub closed, and when we went home, we were sitting on the front porch swing. He picked up my feet, put them in his lap, unbuckled my shoes, and gave me a foot massage. He had brought me a bouquet of wildflowers tied with a purple ribbon the day before, because he knew that I loved that color. Those sweet moments were what let me know what kind of man he was, and I was willing to leave everything to have more of them."

"Don't hardly seem like enough," Maverick said.

"Before you go further, you need to ask yourself. Do you love Bridget or Laela?"

"Can it be both?" Maverick asked.

"Yep, it can, but it better be Bridget first. Laela will grow up and leave home. Then it'll be you and Bridget, so you better love her the most," Iris answered.

"I think I loved Bridget from the moment I met her," Maverick admitted. "I wonder if it was hard for Grandpa to say those three words *I love you*. I just can't get them to come out of my mouth."

Iris patted him on the knee. "Thomas's voice shook the first he said them to me. But it got easier with time. Those were the very last words he said to me, just before he took his last breath. His voice didn't quiver a bit then. Don't go letting a good thing slip out of your fingers because you were too afraid to spit out the words."

"I'll try, but the time has to be right," Maverick said.

Bridget came through the door, talking and gathering up Laela's toys at the same time. "That Wanda is a sweetheart.

She reminds me so much of Nana. I'm not surprised that you struck up such a friendship, Iris. She's so looking forward to coming to the ranch for Christmas. I should put candy in the room where she will be staying, and pretty flowers in a vase. I saw some roses at the food store, or maybe daisies would be better."

"She'll love anything that you do for her," Iris said.

Maverick got the baby ready to take out in the cold weather and gave his grandmother a kiss on the forehead, but on the way to the truck his mind kept circling around to what she'd told him about his grandfather. Evidently, he'd gotten a healthy dose of Thomas Callahan's DNA, because just the thought of saying those three magic words to a woman left him tongue-tied.

"Want to get supper in town since we're already here?" he asked.

"Two nights in one week?" Bridget raised an eyebrow. "Iris will think I am falling down on my job."

"I was thinking maybe we'd hit the pizza buffet before we go home. I'll still have time for evening feeding before it gets too dark," he said.

"Sounds great to me. Laela and I love pizza. Is this a date?" she asked.

"Depends on whether there's a good-night kiss when I walk you to your bedroom door." He hoped that smile on her face meant she was looking forward to that kiss.

He got everyone settled into the truck and drove them to the restaurant. The waitress showed them to one of the last booths in the place. The place was packed and noisy, but to Maverick it was a special time. He felt like he was sitting there with his little family, and he liked the feeling.

\* \* \*

The skies were still gray and the air held the threat of snow when they got home that evening. Maverick slipped into a pair of coveralls and headed straight back out to do his chores. "Okay, Grandpa," he muttered, "what kind of advice would you give me about doing the right thing to make Bridget want to stay in Texas?"

*Romance.* His grandfather's voice was loud in his head. *Women like to be noticed and not taken for granted. I'm not talking about hot kisses and romps between the sheets.*

Sweet-talking and romps between the sheets were about the extent of Maverick's romancing abilities. Grandpa had given Granny a foot massage and brought her wildflowers. The massage he could do, but it was the dead of winter in Texas. It would be months yet before wildflowers were in bloom. Maverick did have one thing available right in his hip pocket that his grandpa hadn't had—technology. When he got back to the tack room he pulled out his smart phone and typed in: romantic things to do for your girlfriend. An article with nineteen items came up immediately. The little narrative at the beginning of the list was exactly what Iris had told him. Big romantic gestures were okay, but women liked the little things so much better.

The first suggestion was to cook something for her. "I wonder if she likes omelets," Maverick asked himself.

The next one was about calling or texting her spontaneously.

"Better work on that one." He'd never remember all of the things listed so he brought down a pencil and an old yellowed notebook from the first shelf above the worktable. It was the same notebook that his grandfather had used to keep track of how many bales of hay he'd used and how many were left. It seemed fitting somehow. He could mark off what he'd tried, like Grandpa had marked off the hay bales.

Another suggestion was: *Go back to the basics. Take her on a date.* He could do that. Only if he was being truthful, the basics for them started in Bridget's flat.

*Complimenting her when she has changed something about her appearance, like her hair, or when she's wearing a new dress shows her that you're paying attention to her. And don't just tell her about her looks. Compliment her on her accomplishments, also.*

When he finished reading and jotting down notes on all nineteen items, he had three pages covered on the notepad. The one that he decided to start on that very night was handwriting her a letter. It turned out to be more difficult than he thought, and he tore up three pages. Then he decided to simply begin and let it flow straight from his heart.

*Dear Bridget,*

*You said that we should talk to each other. Talking about my feelings and hopes isn't easy for me. I've actually been afraid to talk about them, because for one thing it seemed useless, and another it seemed a bit sissy. But you said that you and Sean talked about everything while you were working with him. I get tongue-tied when I try to say anything out loud to you, but if Sean can talk to you about emotions and feelings, then I should be able to at least write them down.*

*I grew up with a mother who didn't want me, and my father died when I was young. A therapist would probably say that was the beginning of my wild ways, and maybe he would be right. But that's no excuse because Granny and Grandpa were amazing parents. Grandpa knew that I needed to spread my wings, so he was the one who talked Granny into letting me work on another ranch.*

*I'm writing a history lesson, not my feelings. A sure sign that I'm skirting around the issue...*

*All right, here goes. When I walked into your pub a year ago, and caught a glimpse of you behind the bar, my heart almost boomed right out of my chest. I thought love at first sight was a big crock of bull crap, but for the first time I felt something besides lust. It felt like Fate.*

When he stopped writing he had four pages, front and back, and he'd quite literally poured out his heart and soul. Written on paper that was probably a decade old, the letter sure didn't look very romantic to him. He looked around for an envelope but couldn't find one. He finally just folded it, tucked it into the inside pocket of his work coat, left the tack room, and drove back to the house.

He was already on the porch when he thought about what he had just done. Tough cowboys didn't write love letters. Bridget would think he was an idiot. She'd laugh in his face and catch the next flight back to Ireland rather than wait until after the holidays. The door opened and there was Bridget, in the same jeans and green sweater she'd worn when they'd gone to see Iris earlier in the evening.

"Hey, I thought I heard Ducky on the porch," she said. "I just put Laela down for the night. It was a little early, but she was fussing and rubbing her eyes."

Maverick slipped out of his coveralls and hung them on a hook, took a deep breath, and brought out the letter before he lost his courage. "Mail call."

She took the folded pages from his hand. "What is this? I just made a pot of fresh tea. We can have a cup and maybe a biscuit...I mean, a cookie."

"It's a letter. I didn't have an envelope." He couldn't look her in the eye.

"A real letter from you?" Her eyes widened in shock. "Why?"

"Because sometimes it's easier to write feelings than it is to say them." He poured two cups of hot tea and carried them to the living room. "I'm a rough old cowboy. I'm not eloquent like educated men. I stumble and stutter when it comes to a serious relationship, but dating is a new thing for me. You can read it when you have time."

Bridget followed right behind him, sat down on one end of the sofa, and handed him the television remote. "Find something to watch while I read your letter. I cannot believe you wrote to me. This is just the most romantic thing any man has ever done for me. No matter what it says, I will cherish it forever."

"You might want to read it before you say that." He set one cup of tea on the end table beside her and put his on the one at the other end of the sofa. Then he sat down and waited. He didn't turn on the television but rather watched her expressions as she read the letter. She'd make a great poker player, he thought, because her face revealed nothing.

When she finished reading, she picked up her cup of tea and took a sip. She lowered the letter to her lap and sat for several minutes, staring at the opposite wall, her expression still unreadable. Finally, she turned to face him. Her big green eyes were swimming in unshed tears. "That was beautiful. Words cannot tell you how much it means to me for you to pour out your feelings like this." She raised the pages and held them against her heart. "We have always had this physical attraction, but this"—she blinked back the tears—"this comes from your soul, and I love that you wrote it all down so I can read it over and over." She laid the letter on the coffee table and scooted down to his end of the sofa.

He draped an arm around her shoulders and pulled her even closer. "You don't think I'm stupid?"

"No, darlin', I think you are the sweetest, kindest man I've ever known." She shifted her position so she could sit in his lap.

He brought her lips to his in a searing kiss that made him realize that this was the real thing, and someday he'd say those words that were still stuck in his heart.

She wrapped her arms around his neck and pressed her body even closer to his. Everything in the world, including Ireland and Texas, all the sorrows from the past year, faded away. He and Bridget were alone, and nothing mattered but the two of them. His hands moved under her sweater to caress her back. She unbuttoned his shirt and splayed her fingers in the hair on his chest.

"You are killing me, Bridget," he moaned.

"Then I guess we'd better take this to the bedroom where I can resuscitate you," she said.

"Are you sure about this? It's taking a big step." Those were words he'd never said to another woman. When any woman in his past had said they should go to the bedroom, he hadn't argued.

She pushed her way off his lap and to her feet, and then she took his hand in hers. "It'll have to be your bedroom. The baby is asleep in mine."

Maverick stood to his feet, scooped her up like a bride, and carried her down the hallway, kissing her the whole way. When they were in his bedroom, he kicked the door shut with his foot, set her feet on the floor, and pulled her sweater up over her head. She tugged his shirt from his pants, unbuttoned it, and then unbuckled his belt. He removed her bra and pulled her close enough that her bare breasts were against his chest.

"I feel like I'm in a dream," he whispered in her ear.

"Me too, but if I am, don't wake me." She slid the zipper of his jeans down.

When they were both undressed, he picked her up and laid her on the bed and stretched out beside her. "You are so beautiful lying there with the setting sun on your hair. It reminds me of the sunrise in Ireland."

*Don't rush. Don't rush*, he kept telling himself. *Savor every moment.*

\* \* \*

"I like feeling you naked beside me," she panted minutes later. "But I want more than just that." She flipped a leg over him and stretched her naked body out on top of his. Her heart was still pounding and her pulse thumped in her ears.

"I want to take my time with you, sweetheart." He flipped her so that he was the one on top. His kisses started at her lips, continued down her belly and to her toes, and then started back up again. She thought she'd pass out from desire before he made it back to her lips.

"Bloody hell, darlin', take me now, or my heart is going to explode right out of my chest." She panted.

He pushed her hair back with his hands and cupped her cheeks, staring into her eyes. "You deserve so much more than I can offer."

"Honey, I don't care if we're in a hayloft or on the floor in the living room, I just want to feel like I did in Ireland," she told him. "And this is softer than the floor."

"You are so beautiful." He ran his hands down the sides of her body to the dip of her waist and to the flare of her hips.

She cupped his face in her hands. "You make me feel so special."

"I never thought I'd have this again." He entered her and they began to work together with a perfect rhythm. "Tell me what you like." His warm breath caressed her ear as he shifted from low into high gear again.

"You don't even have to ask. You already know. I like everything you do to me. Don't stop any of it." She swung her legs up and wrapped them around his body.

"Protection?" He groaned suddenly. "I forgot about that."

"It's okay. I'm on the pill."

"Thank God."

She latched on to his neck, left a huge hickey, and then she was falling over the edge into the sweet satisfaction of a climax so intense the world seemed to disappear—like the one she'd had that night with Maverick in Ireland.

"Maverick!" she called out and went limp.

He rolled to the side but kept her in his arms. In spite of the cold weather outside, they were both slick with sweat. Right then, he wished that he never had to leave his bedroom.

"That was amazing," he said between breaths.

"I know." She cuddled up closer to his side and closed her eyes. "And darlin', if you ever offer your heart to me, that's plenty enough for me. I don't need or want more than you."

# Chapter Eighteen

Bridget awoke the next morning with a smile on her face. Thinking she was still in Maverick's bed, she reached over to touch him, but he wasn't there. Laela's jabbering jerked her right back into reality. Had she been dreaming the night before or was it real?

She sat straight up in her bed and it all came back. The letter—she had to get it from the end table so she could put it with her priceless mementos. The kisses—she blushed. The sex—sweet angels in heaven, it was amazing. She fell back on her pillow and stared at the ceiling. How could she ever leave Texas after last night?

Laela jabbered and pointed to the floor.

"Ducky and Dolly aren't in the house yet, sweetheart. They're probably out in the barn, but it's time for us to go make breakfast." Bridget slung her legs over the side of the bed and stood up. It wasn't until the cool air hit her that she realized she was still naked. As if the baby cared, she covered her breasts with her hands and ran to the closet for a robe. She belted it in around her waist and glanced over at her reflection in the mirror above her dresser.

Her hair was standing up like she'd stuck her finger in an electrical socket. Puffy bags sagged under her eyes from not getting to sleep until the wee hours of the morning. "God, how could any man want this?"

She got dressed, then changed Laela, and was headed down the hall when she caught the smell of coffee and bacon. Then she heard whistling, and when she reached the kitchen, there was Maverick making breakfast.

"Good mornin'," he said.

"A fine morning to you too." She put Laela in the high chair. "This is a nice surprise."

"I woke up early and reached for you, but then I remembered that you left me sometime before daylight," he said. "I'm not much of a cook, but I do know how to make bacon and eggs and pancakes."

She crossed the room and slipped her arms around his waist and smiled into his eyes. "I thought I'd been dreaming when I woke up this morning." Just feeling him close to her brought images of tangled sheets and sweaty bodies to her mind.

"It was very real, darlin'." He brushed a soft kiss across her lips. "Breakfast is almost ready, so sit down and let *me* serve *you* for a change. I even made a pot of tea."

"I see that." She would rather have stood there all day in his embrace as have tea or breakfast, but he'd gone to the trouble to do something nice for her, so she moved away and took a seat at the table.

He poured a cup and set it before her. "You can sip on that while the eggs finish cooking. I didn't attempt to make biscuits, but I can do a real good job on toast."

Laela slapped the tray of the high chair and pointed toward the stove.

"Comin' right up, darlin' girl," Maverick said.

"Sometimes I wonder if you want me to stay in Texas so you won't have to say goodbye to Laela." Bridget sipped her tea. It was perfect—just strong enough without being bitter, and he had added the right amount of sugar.

"I can't even think of telling her goodbye," Maverick confessed. "Just the thought of it makes this big old cowboy want to cry." He brought a platter with scrambled eggs, bacon, and toast to the table. "But, Bridget, it will tear my heart and soul right out of my body if I have to say goodbye to you, and that's the truth."

A lump formed in Bridget's throat. Those were the most romantic words she'd ever heard from any man. He might not have said that he was in love with her, but he had sure given her hope that he would say those words someday. She tried to think of something to say, but nothing came to mind. He sat down and bowed his head. The words he'd said kept going through her mind so loudly that she didn't hear a word of his prayer.

"Thank you," Bridget whispered after he finished.

"For saying grace?" he asked.

"No, for what you said before that about saying goodbye to me," she answered.

"It's the truth. Don't matter if you put whipped cream on the top or spread cow manure on it, the truth can't be changed. It's the way I feel, Bridget." He passed the platter to her.

She filled her plate and passed the platter back. "Nana said that the experiences that don't kill us make us stronger."

Maverick loaded his plate and nodded. "If you leave me, I should be able to lift the farm tractor in one hand."

She giggled. "Now that's a picture I'll have in my mind all day."

His smile brightened the day even more. "As long as I'm in your mind, then I'm happy."

It could be a line he'd used hundreds of times on dozens of women, but it sure made her feel like a queen.

* * *

Bridget went about her chores that morning either singing or humming. Ducky had gone off with Maverick to take care of ranching business. Dolly opted to stay in the house, so Laela had a playmate. Still humming she felt her phone ping in her hip pocket. She pulled it out to see that she had two messages from Sean.

His first one said: We have to talk.

The second one said: I really need to talk to you. Call me.

She called right then, and it went straight to voice mail. Her mind immediately started going through *what ifs*. What if he and Kelly had made up and decided on a whim to get married?

She stopped to stare out the kitchen window and saw that it was snowing so hard that she couldn't even see the barn out there in the distance. While she waited for Sean to call or text, she brought up the weather for Daisy, Texas. If the forecast was right, they could get six to twelve inches before the next day. If that was the case, she was going to build a huge snowman and send pictures of it to Sean, with a caption that said: EVERYTHING IS BIGGER IN TEXAS.

Her phone finally rang and she answered it on the first ring. "You're in big trouble. I've been trying to call ever since your text came."

"I didn't send a text," Alana said.

"I'm so sorry," Bridget apologized. "Sean, my friend from Ireland, just sent a text to call him, and when I did, he didn't answer."

"Are you homesick?" Alana asked.

"No, wondering what's on his mind and watching it snow," Bridget replied.

"Iris just called and volunteered you and Maverick to help with my New Year's Eve party. You don't have to do it if you don't want to, but I'd appreciate it a lot," Alana said.

"We'd be glad to," Bridget said.

"Great. After this blizzard, we'll get together and get things lined up. Is that a beep on your phone? Do you need to take the call?"

"Yes," Bridget said. "It's probably Sean. If I don't take it, we'll be playing phone tag for hours."

"Talk to you later." Alana ended the call.

She tapped her phone to go to the caller and said, "Sean, where have you been?"

"This is Iris, and I just came from walking on the treadmill. Are you expecting a call from Sean?" Iris asked.

"I am, but he must be out somewhere. He probably has news about him and his woman," Bridget explained.

"Well, I'm calling to tell you kids that the weatherman says the roads are going to be horrible tomorrow, so don't try to come see me. If they're cleared off by Friday, I'll see you then. You can tell Maverick so I don't have to call him too. I've been thinkin' about some things that I can't wait to tell you about."

"What things?" Bridget asked.

"I want to tell you in person, not over the phone," Iris said. "I'm finally admitting that I'm getting old. And life is like a roll of toilet paper. The closer to the end you get, the faster it goes. Don't fiddle fart around with time. Enjoy every day so that you don't look back with regrets later on down the road," Iris said.

"Advice noted," Bridget said.

"That's good. We'll talk on Friday." Iris ended the call.

When Bridget's phone rang an hour later, she'd given up on Sean and figured it was Maverick. She picked it up off the kitchen counter and said, "Do you need a sled and a horse to get you to the house for dinner?"

"Not really, but that sounds like fun." Sean laughed.

Hearing his Irish brogue instead of Maverick's drawl shocked her, but she recovered enough to say, "It's snowing here. I thought you were Maverick calling me. It's been hours since I called you, and you didn't answer your phone."

There was a pause and then Sean said, "I sent the text, and then Kelly showed up, and we had us a long talk. I had to wait to call you back."

"When can I talk to her on the phone?" She fixed Laela a midmorning bottle as she talked.

"I'm afraid that's not going to happen."

She waited for several seconds for him to go on before she asked, "Are you still there?"

"Yes, I'm here, but Kelly and I are moving in together. She thinks she can get over her jealousy, and I can keep you as a friend, but we have to figure out something to do with those boxes in my bedroom." Another long pause. "There's just not enough room for her things with them there."

"I'll figure out what to do with them by the end of the week," she said. "I really do wish you the best, but I still think you'd be rushing things."

"Maybe so, but I want to give it a try," he said. "I'll look to hear from you soon. Maybe you could store them at the church, or maybe I should just send them to Texas."

"I'll be needing to think on it," she told him.

"Fair enough. Goodbye, luv," Sean said.

She wiped the tears with the back of her hand. She couldn't seem to stop the steady stream of tears that flowed down her cheeks, so she plucked a tissue from the box on the end table and let it all out, sobbing like she'd never wept before. She grieved for Deidre, for her grandmother, for herself, and even for Laela, who would never know firsthand what an amazing woman had given birth to her.

She was crying so hard that she didn't even hear Maverick come into the house, didn't even know he was there until he had gathered her into his arms. "Are you hurt? Did someone die?"

Laela crawled over to the sofa and reached up for him. He picked her up and put her on his lap, then put his arm back around Bridget.

"I'm scared. I'm a failure, and nothing is going right," she sobbed.

"But are you hurt?" he asked, again. "Laela looks to be fine. Did she fall or something?"

"We're both fine physically. My pride and my heart are broken." She got control of the weeping but not the sniffling. "Today should've been lovely after last night. I hate myself for crying. Don't look at me. My eyes are all red and puffy, and every freckle on my nose is shining."

Maverick tipped her chin up and kissed one eye then the other. It seemed as if he kissed every single freckle on her face and then he said, "You're an amazing woman, and your freckles are where the angels kissed you, sweetheart. Now tell me about your day."

"Sean says I have to make arrangements to get my things out of his flat," she sniffled.

"Are you serious?" Maverick growled. "Well, just tell

him to slap an address label on them and send them to the ranch. You're more than welcome here for as long as you want to stay."

"Now you'll think that I had to stay because I didn't have a choice, and you'll feel like..." She buried her face in his chest. "I want to slap the bloody hell out of Sean for letting a woman lead him around by the nose. And the way I'm behaving now, you're probably thinking you'd like to throw me out in the snow."

"Even though Texas might not be your first choice, I can sure live with it being your second." He put his free hand under her chin and raised it. "You've had more laid on you than even the strongest person could handle. You don't have to make decisions about anything right now, except how to put up with this old cowboy all afternoon. I've done all I can in the barn, and the weather is too bad to do much else."

Bridget leaned back and looked deeply into his eyes. "What happens if we have another fling, and this time, we figure out that one of us doesn't want..."

"We'll cross that bridge when we get to it," Maverick told her as he set Laela down so she could play.

"How did you get to be so smart?" she asked.

"Well, I met this woman in Ireland, and her smartness kind of rubbed off on me," he teased as he took his phone from his pocket, found a song, and started playing it. He stood up and pulled her into his arms.

* * *

Blake Shelton was singing "Honey Bee" when he set Laela down and took Bridget by the hand. As they danced, he sang along with the lyrics that said all he knew how to do was speak from his heart. By the time the song ended, she was smiling and Laela was keeping time by bobbing her head.

"Look at her," Maverick chuckled. "She's telling you that she likes country music and wants to stay in Texas."

"You always make me feel better—like everything is going to be all right," she said.

"And you make me feel like I'm ten feet tall and bullet-proof." He brought her lips to his with a long, passionate kiss. "Now it's time we talk about last night."

Laela crawled over to her and held up her arms. Bridget picked her up and the baby's stomach grumbled. "She's hungry. If you think last night was a mistake, then don't say it. I couldn't take that."

"Last night, darlin'," Maverick assured her, "was even more amazing than what we had in Ireland. Are you fixin' to tell me that you don't think it was?"

She shook her head. "Not at all. I hope it was the beginning of something wonderful. You are the most stable thing in my life right now."

He felt as if he were floating a foot off the floor. "Thank you. I'll do my best not to let you down. Now we really should feed the baby and get her down for her afternoon nap."

"I appreciate you saying that, and thank you for making me feel better," she said.

"I've got an idea," Maverick said. "After we eat, I'll rock her to sleep while you take a nice, warm bath. That might help soak away some of that tension."

"Thank you." She sighed. "That would be beyond wonderful."

\* \* \*

Bridget sank down in the tub and let the warm water ease all the stress from her muscles. Maybe she would just send money to Sean so he could ship her things to the ranch. She poured water over her hair and worked in the shampoo and rinsed. By then the water had gone lukewarm, so she pulled the plug and stood up.

The bathroom door opened and Maverick took a couple of steps into the room. Bridget stood there with wet hair and water sluicing over her body. She was cold on the outside but his eyes on her body turned her into a quivering mass of heat on the inside. He slipped his hands under her arms and picked her up like she weighed no more than a helium balloon. He set her on the floor and wrapped a big towel around her body, and then picked her up and carried her to the living room, where he laid her down on the sofa.

"I've said it before, but you are so beautiful. I could stand here and look at you for hours," he whispered.

"Thank you, but..." she started.

"Shhh..." He put a finger over her lips. "Let me take care of you." He disappeared out of the living room.

"Just be still. You've had a tough day. Let me do this for you." He returned and dropped down on his knees at the end of the sofa. First he towel dried her hair and then laid her red hair out like a sheet of silk. Then he worked all the tangles out with a comb, and flipped the switch on the dryer and began to work on it, a section at a time, massaging her scalp as he dried her hair.

It wasn't fair to compare Sean to a Texan, Bridget told herself, but there was no way she could keep from doing it, so she stopped trying. She couldn't imagine Sean ever doing something like this for her—or even for Kelly. He'd be too afraid his pub buddies would find out and tease him for it.

That was the last thought she had about Sean that day.

All she could think about was the burning desire Maverick created with nothing more than his fingertips. But then, from the very first time he'd touched her, she'd felt the same way. She groaned and then clamped a hand over her mouth.

"That feels wonderful. Oh. My. Goodness." She moaned when he finished drying her hair and started brushing it out. "This is so romantic and it's turning me on."

"Me too," he said.

"Darlin', you've got all those clothes to take off. All I have to do is stand up like this." She got to her feet. "And drop this towel." She did just that and then reached for the first button on his shirt.

"You are so damn beautiful that I'm afraid to touch you," he said.

"You better get over that fear, because if you don't make love to me soon, I'm going to take control of this situation." She took his hand and grabbed the quilt from the back of the sofa. "I like the way the lights on the tree look in your eyes." She spread the quilt out on the floor.

He picked her up and sat down with her in his lap, and then gently laid her out on the quilt. "I like the way the lights look on your whole body," he said as his lips met hers and the sweet passion of the night before started all over again.

# *Chapter Nineteen*

The sun was peeking through the window when Bridget opened her eyes the next morning. She moved a few inches and snuggled up to Maverick's back. "You were right. This bed is much softer than the floor, but there was something magical about making love by the Christmas tree."

He flipped over and brushed a soft morning kiss across her lips. "I love waking up with you in bed with me."

"Me too," she said as she wiggled out of his embrace. "But I hear Laela jabbering, so it's time to start the day." She threw back the covers and hurried across the hall.

Laela looked through the bars of her crib and smiled while Bridget got dressed. "After Maverick gets done with his work this morning, we're going to build a big snowman and take pictures of you with it. Do you like him enough to live with him forever if I should be taken like your mama was?" Bridget picked the baby up, changed her nappy, and got her dressed in a cute little pair of long pants and shirt.

"We have good friends here, but Sean may realize that he's being henpecked and call us with an apology for his sorry-ass behavior." She giggled. "That sounded more Texan than Irish." She carried the baby to the kitchen, and Maverick immediately took her.

"Good mornin', princess. Did you dream that Santa brought you a pony for Christmas?"

"No, she did not." Bridget got out a cast iron skillet for the bacon.

"Mama doesn't know what you dreamed about, but you can tell me," Maverick teased.

Laela laid her head on his chest.

"That's what I thought too. You don't want to go back to Ireland, do you? You want to live here in Texas with me, right?"

"Of course she does," Bridget said right behind him. "You spoil her. Everyone here does."

Maverick's grin was downright impish. "I don't know how you're going to get her little Shetland pony over there. It won't fit in your suitcases, and I'm sure Sean won't let it live in his living room if you do figure out a way."

"Don't you dare." Bridget poured two cups of coffee and started the bacon frying.

"Too late," he teased. "And there's also a kitten and a puppy. Real ones, not stuffed toys. She says she wants a black and white kitten and a yellow dog."

"Don't joke with me, Maverick. It would be cruel to give those things to her when she'll have to leave them behind someday." Bridget slapped him on the arm.

Maverick grabbed her hand and kissed her palm. "I guess getting you a four-wheeler to use when you help me round up cattle is out of the question then too? You'll miss getting your hair brushed out or making love under the Christmas tree when you're in Ireland. If you stay here, we'll just leave it up all year to light up our sex life."

She wrestled her hand away from him. "That's cheating."

"All's fair in love and war," he told her. "Seriously, if and when you do go back to Ireland, I'm going to miss you and this baby so much."

"I know." She nodded. "After only one night together last year, I missed you. From what you've said, you weren't much better than me."

"I can't imagine life without you and Laela. The loneliness and sadness without y'all will be unbearable. I'm just enjoying every single moment right now like it will be my last one with you and this precious little girl."

"I've agreed to stay longer," she said.

"I know, but one more month, one more year or even a couple of years, the thought that you will be leaving and going back to Ireland, or even to work for Alana, is right there in my mind. I want to know that you are here forever," he said.

Bridget fidgeted with her hands—clasping them together and then opening them and rubbing her palms on the legs of her jeans. "Ireland is all I've ever known. I can't imagine not living there. How can a person's heart want two things?"

"My grandpa used to tell me that you can't ride two horses with one ass. You have to choose," he told her.

She giggled. "That's a pretty good saying."

"I thought of it all the way home from Ireland," he said.

"Think you'd ever want to live over there?" she whispered.

"I don't reckon there's many opportunities for an old cowhand in your world. I saw a lot of sheep over there, but not any cattle. I know about as much about sheep as I do about ballroom dancing," Maverick told her.

"I guess we've got us one of those conundrums, don't we?" she said.

"Guess so, but we've got a while to figure it out."

She nodded. "I guess we do, at that. Like you said, I'm going to enjoy every day I have with you. I'm looking forward to spending Christmas with a cowboy."

"Not just any cowboy, but *your* cowboy," he said.

* * *

Bridget had just laid Laela down for her short morning nap when her phone pinged with a text from Sean: Can we talk?

She sent one back: What are you doing up at two o'clock in the morning?

His next text said: Can't sleep. Can we talk tomorrow?

She typed: Sure. Give me a call when you have time.

She waited a few minutes, but nothing else came. Any other time, it wouldn't have mattered what time of day or night it was. If Sean or Deidre had called her or sent a text, she would have been right there, on the spot, ready to fix their problems.

*But dammit!* She thought. *I can't even fix my own feelings before I can help you this time.*

When she made it to the kitchen, Maverick was just coming in the back door. He pulled off his coveralls, his hat, and his gloves.

"Want a cup of hot chocolate? I'm making one for me. Laela should be up from her nap soon."

"Love some chocolate. I've been looking forward to playing in the snow all morning with y'all, so I'm glad she'll be up soon." He stopped on the way to the living room to kiss Bridget on the cheek. "Granny called this morning. She said for us not to come if the roads are bad, but I think we can make it in my truck. It's not that far. If you don't want to get the baby..."

She held up a hand to stop him. "Of course Laela and I

want to go. Iris said she wanted to talk to us about something important. I'm sure it's on her mind, so we should do our best to go see her." She couldn't imagine Sean driving in snow to see his grandmother, or wading in it up to the tops of his boots to take care of cattle, either.

Maverick started humming a song, pulled her to his chest, and two-stepped with her toward the living room. It felt oh, so right to be dancing with him, even if it was in the house and not in a pub.

"What are you humming?" she asked.

"It's an old song called 'Look at Us.' It says that a hundred years from now, everyone will look back and wonder how on earth an old Texas cowboy and a royal queen from Ireland ever made it work out," he said.

"You are full of crap. It doesn't say that. What does it really say?"

He tipped up her chin, and said, "It says that we're an example of how true love should be."

"Are we?" she asked as he backed her up.

"That depends on whether we work at it, or walk away from it," he said softly.

* * *

When Laela woke up, it was near noon, so they had dinner. Then Maverick helped get her bundled up and took Laela's high chair out into the front yard and set it down in the snow. When Bridget brought her outside she looked like an overstuffed pink bear, but she didn't seem to mind when Bridget put her into the high chair. She giggled when Maverick piled snow on the tray.

"She likes it." Bridget had already begun to roll snow into a ball.

"She likes Texas, period." Maverick kept one eye on the baby playing with the snow and the other on Bridget while he rolled a huge base for the snowman. "I'm surprised that you aren't making snow angels. Didn't y'all ever do that in Ireland?

"When we had enough snow, we did," she answered. "But that only happened twice in my lifetime. It gets really cold over there, but we don't get this kind of snow. I can't wait to put pictures on my Facebook page so Sean and everyone can see."

If someone else knew about her predicament, wouldn't they offer to give her a room until she could find a place? Like one of her nana's friends, or maybe even the preacher at the church where Nana had gone faithfully her whole life. He wanted to ask, but he kept his mouth shut. He didn't want her to leave, and that might put ideas into her mind.

"We should make a family of snow angels when we get this done. We'll line them up in a row. Me, then you, and then the baby." He stood back and looked at the huge snowball sitting before him. "I think we're ready to get yours set up on this one for his middle part."

She stood back and looked at what she'd rolled up. "Do you think we can lift it?"

Maverick picked it up, set it on top of the bottom, and only groaned once. "It's going to take days for this thing to melt. I'll make his head if you'll go get us a carrot and something for eyes."

"Can we use that old hat that the wind blew in the mud puddle? And maybe some leftover Christmas bows for the buttons on his belly? I've got an old scarf to tie around his neck." She trudged through the knee-deep snow to the porch.

"Yes on the hat and the Christmas bows," he called out as he started rolling a third ball for the snowman's head.

Laela had gotten bored with her pile of snow and had started to fuss. He hurried and set the head on the top of the snowman. Then he took her out of the high chair and carried her with him to the low-hanging limbs on the pecan tree. "Do you think this one will make a good arm?"

She giggled and reached for it.

"All right then, we'll break it off and try to find another one like it. Can't have a lopsided snowman." Maverick snapped a couple of similar limbs from the tree and stuck them in the sides of the six-foot snowman.

"I got the rest of what we need," Bridget called from the porch.

Together they wrapped a red-and-green plaid scarf around his neck, gave him a nose and some fancy bow buttons, and then she handed him two small chocolate cookies for his eyes. "I couldn't find any buttons or bits of coal so this will have to do."

The final touch was Maverick's cowboy hat, and then Bridget stood back in awe and clapped her gloved hands together. "He's just like I always imagined as a child. Stand over there beside him with Laela in your arms and let me take some pictures. This is like a dream come true. This snow is a great present. Merry Christmas to me!"

Maverick couldn't take credit for the snow, but he had helped build the snowman, and that had made a dream come true. To him, that was a pretty awesome feather in his hat.

Bridget took several pictures with her phone and then handed it to Maverick. "My turn, now. Let me have Laela, and you take some of us so everyone will know how big this Mr. Frosty really is. They don't know how tall you are, so they might think I'm exaggerating when I tell them this thing is at least six feet tall."

Maverick snapped several with her phone and then half

a dozen more with his own. "You ready to make our snow angel family now?"

"Yes," she answered. "You go first, then I'll do mine, and we'll help Laela make hers."

He carefully got down on his knees, then flipped around so that he was lying flat, and stretched his arms straight out. When he finished moving them up and down to make the wings of his angel, he got up very carefully so he wouldn't ruin any part of the outline he had made. As if she knew what was happening, Laela reached for him. When Bridget finished, one of her wings was touching his.

"Let's put her between us, under our wings," Bridget suggested.

Maverick laid the baby in the snow. He got a hold of one of her little arms and Bridget picked up the other one. They moved them up and down to make her fat, little wings. She giggled all the time and kept turning her head to sneak licks of the snow. When they were done, Maverick scooped her up and started for the porch.

But before entering the house, he took one look back at the impressions they'd made. One of the baby's wings just barely touched his side, and the other one, Bridget's. Their wings served as a shelter, and they really did look like a family.

\* \* \*

When it came time to go back out in the snow and load up the truck for the visit to Iris, the baby quickly tried to wiggle free of Maverick's arms.

Bridget giggled. "You are going to have to tell her no this time. I know it really hurts you to do that, but you cannot let her play in the snow."

"You are so right." He nodded. "I can't even think about

when she's a teenager and wants something she shouldn't have. I'm not sure I'll be able to tell her no then either."

"You can start practicing today." Bridget opened the back door to the truck so he could get Laela into her seat. While she was setting the diaper bag on the floor, she realized that she had all but said Maverick would have some say-so in Laela's raising when the girl was a teenager.

She hadn't decided to put his name on the papers giving him guardianship of the baby, and she still wasn't planning to stay in Texas forever—like Iris had done. Evidently, from the words that had come out of her mouth, her mind was taking her in that direction, though. Strangely, the idea didn't seem as far-fetched as it had a few weeks ago.

Bridget was still thinking about that when he started the engine and drove toward town. She gazed out at the countryside, which was so very different from Ireland. The land was flat where Ireland had rolling hills and cliffs to explore. Here in Texas there were cows instead of sheep. She wondered if she'd ever get used to the accent, or for that matter, used to people asking her where she was from. One thing that was the same, though, was the sky, and looking at it brought a great deal of comfort. Sometimes it was a beautiful shade of blue; sometimes a heavy gray. Always, always, though, the sunsets were absolutely stunning, even more so than the ones in Ireland.

Could the answer to her turmoil be right up above her? She looked up at the sky. Was it telling her that if she stayed, she could expect gray times and bright times, but when she came to her sunset years, that her life would still be beautiful?

She was surprised that they'd already made it to town when he nosed the truck into a parking place at the store, and asked, "Do you mind if we make a quick stop for some hot chocolate? And maybe we can also get one little bottle of chocolate milk, since our girl didn't get to play in the snow a second time? If that's too much sugar we could mix it half and half with her formula."

"Tell her no and then reward her? You are going to be a pushover daddy," Bridget told him.

"Going to be?" Maverick wiggled his eyebrows.

"Let's bring some for Granny and Wanda too," Bridget suggested, eager to change the subject.

"Sure, darlin'. Be right back."

He was only gone a couple of minutes and returned with a cardboard cup holder with four hot chocolates and a small brown sack with a bottle of chocolate milk. After he'd settled everything on the floor of the backseat, he handed Bridget a tiny bag of chocolate kisses and a wooden rose.

"What's this for?" She was surprised that it smelled like a real rose, and touched that he thought to bring her a present.

"The kisses are self-explanatory. The rose isn't real. It's made of wood and will last forever, like the way I feel about you," he said.

She loved chocolate. But it was the beautiful rose, made with layers of shaved wood, and his sweet words that melted her heart.

"It's beautiful."

"You're beautiful, and it's beauty from the heart so that makes you even more gorgeous than the women who are just shells."

"Shells?" she asked.

"That means all the beauty is on the outside. You think of others, like suggesting that we take hot chocolate to Granny and Wanda." He buried his face into her hair.

"Thank you. It seems like I just keep saying that, but I mean it. This is so sweet of you, Maverick." She leaned across the console and kissed him on the cheek.

Iris wasn't in the waiting room when they got to the rehab center. She was sitting in her chair in her room, and she reached for the baby the moment they walked in. "How's my sweet baby girl today? Have they been treating you good? Did they let you play in the snow?"

Laela snuggled down into Iris's arms like she was about to go to sleep, but then she began to wiggle. "Time for her to explore. By the time I get out of this joint, she'll have the whole room cased out."

"Here, Iris, we brought you some hot chocolate." Bridget took one of the cups from Maverick and gave it to Iris.

"Why, how sweet. That's a lovely treat for this cold day."

"Bridget thought you and Wanda might like some," Maverick chimed in.

Bridget pulled a chair up close to Iris's side and pulled out her phone. "I want to show you our pictures from playing in the snow today."

Iris had something to say about every single shot and made Bridget go through them a second time. "What I want for Christmas from you two"—she pointed at Maverick and Bridget—"is one of those collage frames that has lots of openings. I want it filled up with pictures of just the three of you, and I want the one of the snow angels to be the one in the middle. That's your first family picture together, but I also want one of the three of you all dressed up for church on Sunday morning to be in there too."

"But then you'll know what you're getting," Maverick objected as he noticed Laela crawling toward the hallway. He brought her back into the room and got out her bowl and spoon from the diaper bag. Then he filled the bowl with a few of her toys.

"Old people don't care if they're surprised or not." Iris sipped at the hot chocolate. "But I got to admit, I am enjoying this surprise." She raised her cup. "Now, close the door and pull those two chairs over there around to face me and sit down. I've made a decision and you need to hear me out."

"A decision about what?" Maverick set up the chairs and waited for Bridget to take a seat before he did.

"My future and yours," Iris said. "The ranch has gotten to be too much for me to handle, and I'm tired, Mav. I'm going to spit it out rather than try to explain. I'm going to the assisted living center where Wanda lives."

"Granny!" Maverick gasped. "You don't have to do that. I'll take care of the place and you too. Callahan Ranch is your home."

Bridget's heart did a nosedive right to the floor. Iris was leaving the ranch, and that meant she no longer had a job. She hadn't saved nearly enough money to be independent when she got back to Ireland.

"Yes, I can do that, and I already have. The lady from the assisted living place came today and we got the paperwork started. I'll have my apartment right next door to Wanda's. The care center is in Amarillo, and y'all can come and see me whenever you like. I can even leave and spend a weekend on the ranch every now and then. That way, I can see all my church friends on Sunday. But I've made up my mind," Iris said.

Maverick opened his mouth to say something, but Iris held up a palm.

"There's no amount of arguing that will make me change my mind. I put the ranch over in yours and Paxton's names five years ago. I knew this day would come eventually, but I didn't want you to come back to a raggedy-ass ranch out of obligation. I wanted it to be because you *wanted* to live here, not because you *had* to. I can see that you're ready now. Paxton can come home when he's ready. Until he's living on the place and pulling his weight, it's yours. When he comes home and starts to put in the sweat and long hours that you do, then y'all will share the profits." She stopped and took another sip of her hot chocolate.

Bridget blinked back tears. She wished that Iris would stay at the ranch until she passed away, but that was being selfish. If Iris really wanted to live in an assisted place then it was her decision. She wasn't ready to leave Texas, not after Maverick's little declaration about the wooden rose. Just the thought of waving goodbye to him at the airport made her about half nauseated.

Maverick took a deep breath and let it out very slowly. "I'm ready to take over the ranch, and I'm pretty sure Paxton will come home as soon as he can. But..."

Iris shook her head and narrowed her eyes at him. "There are no buts. Your grandpa said we were building something for your father, and we did. But he's gone now, so it goes to his sons. Take it and make it look like it did when Thomas was alive. Bring it back to something we can be proud of."

"We can do that." Maverick's voice was hoarse with emotion.

"And now for the rest. Bridget, I'm giving Ducky to you, and Dolly is Laela's. If you go back to Ireland, and I'm telling you right now, I sure hope you don't, you have to figure out a way to take them with you," Iris said.

"Why would I stay?" Bridget asked. "I was hired to take care of you, and you won't even be there."

"But the house will be, and Mav is going to need help with that part of the business. You need a home. He needs a housekeeper, a cook, and maybe even a secretary to get all those books in order, so you have a job for as long as you want it." Iris shook her finger at Bridget. "But remember, if you leave, a cat and a dog go with you."

Bridget's mind was reeling. There was no way she could take two animals plus a baby with her on a plane, and yet, she could never disappoint Iris by leaving them behind. "I've already agreed to stay a while longer, maybe until spring, so if that'd be all right—"

"Thank you." Maverick butted in and turned to face Bridget. "It'll take me a while to settle all this in my mind. Knowing that you'll be here to help me means a lot. I'll talk to Paxton. I think he'll want to stay in Sunset until fall, but it's up to him. This is going to take some getting used to, Granny."

"Just say that you'll do your best to make your grandpa proud," Iris said. "Now, Bridget, you can go get Wanda. We don't want her chocolate to get cold."

Bridget was still stunned as she walked down the hall toward Wanda's room. Maverick owned a ranch. She snapped her fingers. Just like that. He and his brother had something that was their very own. It might be in poor repair at the moment, but it was theirs. How did that affect the way Maverick felt about her? With land and a home in his possession, women would be coming out from under what few trees there were in that part of the world to flirt with him. But right now, she truly believed there was something strong and solid between them. Now she had to decide what she wanted to do, or some other woman would step right up and take her place. Like Maverick said a while back, she couldn't ride two horses with one arse. The bottom line was that she had to decide which horse she wanted to ride for the rest of her life.

*That would be whichever one rides next to the one Maverick is riding*, she thought. *Or maybe we could just ride double.*

# Chapter Twenty

Maverick awoke before daylight on Thursday morning to find Bridget's back pressed against his chest. He buried his face in her hair and inhaled. She still smelled like winter, and he loved the delicious vanilla scent of her shampoo. It was the same scent he'd fallen in love with the year before. Why was it that a woman's hair smelled so different in the winter than it did in the summer? He propped up on an elbow and tried to stare his fill of her but realized that wasn't possible. When she was ninety and her gorgeous red hair had turned silver, he'd still be trying to drink in all of her sleeping beauty every morning.

In the twinkling of an eye, things had changed drastically. Now he had a home to call his own, plus land and cattle. He had something to offer her, and it was time for him to tell her how much she meant to him—time to ask her to stay in Texas with him forever.

She opened her eyes slowly and stretched. "Good morning."

"Good mornin'," he whispered in her ear. "Sleep well?"

"Yes, I did, but we still need to talk about everything that has happened." Her eyes widened and she sat up in bed. "Laela? Did she wake up during the night?"

"She was fussing in her sleep about two thirty, so I made her a bottle and rocked her until she went back to sleep," he answered.

"You should've wakened me," she told him.

"I couldn't sleep for thinking about what all I need to do on this place, and where to start and how much I'm still in shock." He slid off the bed and pulled the drapes open. Then he hurried across the floor and slipped back under the covers. Pulling her close again, he kissed her on the forehead. "We can watch our first Texas sunrise together right out that window."

"We've watched sunrises before." She snuggled down so close that he could feel her heartbeat.

"But not in Texas. We've shared sunsets a few times, but this is a first one from a ranch that I now own with my brother, and it's going to be a beautiful one," he said.

"How do you know that?"

"Because I'm with you," he answered. "Everything is beautiful when you're in my arms."

Laela started jabbering from across the hall.

"I think she wants to watch the sunrise with us," he said as he got out of bed again, pulled on a pair of pajama pants, and padded barefoot on the cold hardwood floor to get her. He returned in a few seconds with her in his arms. Her eyes lit up, and she flashed a bright smile when she saw Bridget.

"And there's the magic of Christmas right there," he said.

"Where?" Bridget asked. "In the sunrise or in her smile?"

"Both, but I was looking at your eyes. It's a magical day

for sure. This is the good life. Family all cuddled up together in bed watching the sun come up." He gave her a sweet kiss and set the baby down between them.

"Thank you," she muttered.

"What for?" He raised an eyebrow.

"For letting me sleep and taking care of Laela. And for all that you do to make us feel special—like a family," she answered.

"No thanks necessary." Maverick leaned over the baby and kissed Bridget on the cheek. This was what it could be like forever, but he couldn't rush her. She had to tell him she was ready to stay in Texas forever before he could get down on one knee. If he tried to hurry things, she might have regrets about staying.

"We should have a celebration this morning. This is your first day to work on your ranch," Bridget said.

"But, darlin', the baby is awake." Maverick winked.

She slapped his arm. "I'm talking about food, not sex. What's your favorite breakfast ever? Tell me, and I'll make it for you."

"Cold pizza is number one, but a big stack of pancakes with butter and syrup melted together comes in a real close second," he replied.

"Laela loves pancakes too, so that's what I will make. Now let's talk about this thing with me staying. You said once that you didn't have anything to offer a woman, but now you do. Are you sure you want me to stay until spring?"

"I want you to stay forever." He opened his mouth to tell her that he loved her and he wanted her to be in his life permanently, but the words wouldn't come. He pushed a strand of hair out of her eyes and kissed her. "But I realize it's a big decision, so take your time."

"Thank you for not rushing me to make it," she said.

"I'm a patient man." He pointed at the window. "We're going to have sunshine today. Maybe it will even melt some of the snow."

"Not our snowman. We still need someone to take a picture of the three of us with it so we can put it in Iris's Christmas frame." She pushed back the covers and wrapped the sheet around her like a toga. "I'll bring it back later, but it doesn't seem right to even carry a baby across the hall when I'm naked."

"I'll go make coffee and get the skillet out for pancakes." He slid off the bed. "We're settling in to this family thing really good, aren't we?"

"I think we just might be." She picked up Laela and carried her across the hall.

Maverick was busy getting things out of the cabinet when she walked into the kitchen. She set the baby in her high chair and started making the pancake batter.

"I'm going to call Alana and set up a shopping date," she said. "Laela's outgrowing her clothes. I need to shop for a dress to wear to her New Year's party, and I haven't bought a single Christmas present. What's the first thing on your agenda for this place?"

"I'm a little overwhelmed," Maverick admitted. "I'll get the feeding done this morning, and since the weather is preventing me from doing anything else, I guess I'll begin sorting the paperwork in Mam's room. I'm thinking maybe we could move the desk to the living room. Want to help me?"

"Of course," she said without hesitation. "I used to help the owner of the pub keep books. I'm sure orders of whiskey and Guinness aren't the same as feed and hay, but it shouldn't be all that different. We'll start getting things organized soon as you get back in the house." She began to pour perfect circles of batter into the skillet.

"You are amazing," he said.

She did a cute little curtsey and then flipped the pancakes. "Keep tellin' yourself that, and we'll get along just fine, darlin'."

"Spoken like a true Texan, but I did hear a little Irish sprinkled on the top," he teased.

"That will never completely change," she said. "After more than fifty years in this place, Iris still has a little Irish in her speech."

Maverick handed Laela a spoon when she started trying to get out of her high chair. She used it to pound out a tune on the tray.

"I don't recognize that song." Bridget laughed. "It doesn't sound Irish."

"It's a country music tune called 'My Baby Don't Need to Change,'" Maverick teased.

"Is there really a song called that?" Bridget stacked pancakes onto a platter and poured four more into the skillet.

"No, but if there was, I'd buy the first copy that was for sale," he told her.

"And I'd buy the second," she said.

After they'd eaten and Maverick had his third cup of coffee, he finally pushed back his chair. "I should only be gone about an hour. I'd like to take Laela with me, but it's too cold. Come spring, she can go take care of feeding chores with me in the mornings."

* * *

"She would probably love that." Bridget suddenly got a glimpse of what it would truly mean to live on the ranch permanently, and it didn't terrify her at all. As a matter of fact, she smiled at the picture of Maverick taking Laela out with him to feed the cows.

"Yep, I do." Maverick settled his hat on his head and gave Bridget a sweet kiss. "See you in a little while."

She stopped herself a split second before she told Laela to tell Daddy goodbye.

Maverick closed the door, but not before Dolly ran inside. Laela immediately fussed to get out of her high chair, so Bridget washed the baby's hands and face and set her on the floor. She and the cat met halfway across the room. Dolly rubbed around the baby's shoulders until Laela sat up, and then the cat curled up in her lap.

"That animal is almost as big as you." Bridget laughed. "You play with her while I call Iris."

The phone only rang twice before Iris answered, "Hello, darlin'. What's on your mind?"

"How did you know that something was bothering me?" Bridget put the phone on speaker and cleaned off the table while she talked.

"I was like you at one time, remember, and I know you are struggling with the same decisions I did at your age," Iris said.

"How did you ever do this? How did you leave your home country? Did you ever regret it?" The words came out so fast that Bridget wondered if Iris even understood her.

"I never regretted my decision to leave Ireland, but I'll have to be honest, I got so homesick to hear someone speak Irish that first year that I went in the bathroom and talked to myself in the mirror." Iris laughed. "You know you don't have to make a decision based on a man. You're an independent woman, and you should give this some thought."

"I can't decide. I'm in love with Maverick," Bridget

blurted out. "But he's got all these possibilities now that he has something to offer a woman. That's what has held him back from settling down, you know."

"I believe he's in love with you too, but he just hasn't figured out a way to say it. Have you told him how you feel yet?" Iris asked.

"No, I guess I'm waiting for the right time." Bridget sighed.

"I love my grandson, but this is your life, girl," Iris said. "Leaving my friends, and especially your grandmother, was tough, but I had a husband I adored. And, honey, when I cried at night because of homesickness, that man held me in his arms. He thanked me a million times in our years together for loving him enough to marry him and leave everything I knew behind."

"Really?" Bridget had no doubt that Maverick would be like his grandfather in that respect, but was she strong enough to take that big leap over an ocean?

"I had three miscarriages in the first three years I was in Texas, and I began to think that it was punishment for leaving Ireland," Iris went on. "Thomas held me when I lost those babies and cried right along with me. I remember the first time I thought of Texas as home. I'd given birth to Maverick's father, Barton, and we were on the way home from the hospital. I can still see the proud look on my Thomas's face when he helped me into that old truck we had back then. He asked me if we needed to pick up anything from town on the way to the ranch, and I said, 'Honey, I just want to go home. I missed you so much while I was in the hospital.' He didn't even realize that it was the first time I'd called Texas home. But I'll remember it forever."

"I said that word, *home*, the other day."

"Did you tell Sean about that?" Iris asked.

"I haven't told him much of anything in several days." Bridget told her about their conversations, and how disappointed she was in him.

"Honey, we live and we die with the choices we make. George Jones sang a song that said something like that years and years ago. Sean will have to live with the choices he's making. But you have to live with yours too, so don't be too hasty. If you're patient, you'll find peace when you make your decision," Iris said. "And now I have a therapy session, so 'bye for now."

"'Bye and thank you," Bridget said and ended the call.

Laela and Dolly were both sitting at her feet. She picked the baby up and hugged her tightly. "I'm glad you're too little to ever remember the trip that brought us here."

The baby squirmed until Bridget finally let her down to crawl around again. "You're not a bit of help. You'd probably cry all the way back to Ireland if you had to leave Maverick behind."

Bridget was on her way back to Iris's bedroom to see if there was anything at all she could do to start organizing paperwork when her phone pinged. She saw that she'd missed two messages from Sean: Can we talk?

She fired one back to him: Call me.

She made sure Laela had toys and that Dolly was nearby, and then she sat down on the sofa to wait for Sean's call. "If this phone doesn't ring in five minutes, I'm going to refuse to answer it," she said.

It rang in three minutes and she answered on the first ring. "Hello, what's going on?"

"You sound like you're out of breath. Were you having sex with the cowboy?" Sean teased.

"I was moving furniture, and what I do with the cowboy is none of your business," she told him. "What's up?"

"Kelly threw another jealous fit about all my women friends on Facebook. She's gone for good, so don't get in a hurry about your things. They're just fine where they are until you want me to do something with them, or until you come home," he said. "I just wanted you to know that. You were right all along, so you can say 'I told you so.'"

"Oh, Sean, I'm sorry. This was one time I didn't really want to be right. But it's better to know this now and be done with her."

"You're absolutely right, luv. As always. But I saved the best until last." He gave a dramatic pause. "I'm buying the bakery. I have enough from my savings for a down payment and our boss is carrying the rest of the note. You'll sure enough have a job if you come home."

"Sean, that's wonderful news. Congratulations!" She took a deep breath and made a decision. "I'm extending my stay in Texas, so you might as well ship those boxes here. I'll send you the money for whatever it costs."

"Just give me an address. I think I've always known that you wouldn't be coming back," Sean said.

"It's not necessarily forever," she told him softly. "I'll text you the info."

Two horses with one arse came to her mind again. She'd decided to ride with Maverick if everything continued to work out, and the decision not only put a smile on her face but also brought peace, like Iris had mentioned, into her heart.

She picked up Laela and carried her to Iris's bedroom. The baby began to explore, and Bridget just stood, staring at the piles of papers on the desk for a good five minutes. Doing her best to keep them in the stacks they were in, she moved them all to the bed. Then she found a tape measure in one of the drawers and measured the desk.

"I think it will fit between the windows on the west wall of the living room," she muttered as she hurried out of the room. It only took a minute for her to determine that she'd been right, but when she returned to the bedroom, she couldn't find Laela. She called the baby's name twice before she heard giggling. Following the sound, she found her in Iris's bathroom. She had pulled up to the edge of the toilet and tossed her toy giraffe into the water, and was now trying to get it out.

"You little scamp," she said as she picked the baby up and held her over the vanity sink to wash her hands. "Now your favorite toy will have to be washed and dried before you can play with it again." When she'd dried Laela's hands, she put her back on the floor and fished the toy from the toilet, tossed it in the sink, and washed her own hands—twice with soap both times.

Laela didn't even respond with a look but kept crawling across the floor.

"All right, you are going into your crib for about ten minutes." Bridget picked her up and took her across the hall. She made sure Laela had toys and then went back to the desk.

She pushed up her sleeves. "If I can move this desk, I can do anything. Nana and I moved a buffet once that was bigger than this. I'm trying to remember how we did it."

The memory came back when she noticed the throw rugs on each side of Iris's bed. She and her grandmother had used two similar rugs to move the buffet. They had flipped the rugs over so the soft side was against the wood floor, and the buffet was sitting on the rubberized backside. It took all her strength to lift the corner of the heavy desk and kick the rug under it. The other end didn't seem as tough, but then, it wasn't the one with three drawers in it.

With the rugs in place, Bridget simply put her shoulder into it and slid the desk all the way to the living room. Hopefully, Maverick wouldn't be upset that she'd taken it upon herself not only to figure out where to put it but also to move it.

She'd just finished taking the papers from the bed and putting them back on the desk when Laela began to really fuss and Bridget's mobile rang. She freed Laela from her crib, took her to the living room, and set her down beside Dolly, who was sleeping next to the Christmas tree.

She shoved the phone into her hip pocket, gathered up the last stack of papers, and went back to the living room. A rattling noise caused her to head for the front door. It was a little early for Maverick to be home, but it sounded like keys. It could be Ducky scratching at the door, but she thought that he'd gone in the truck with Maverick. Then it hit her that it was probably the UPS man bringing more boxes to go in the back bedroom for Iris. That woman had bought an awful lot of Christmas.

Sure enough there were two boxes on the porch. She put them away, and when she got back to the living room, she found Laela unloading her purse in front of the sofa—tossing makeup, wallet, and everything else over to one side. In her free hand, she held Bridget's keys and was swinging them like a Christmas bell.

"You are a stinker today," Bridget said as she gathered up everything and put it back in her purse. She picked up the keys and remembered that Sean had given her the ring they were on for her birthday several years before. He had said that she was a true Libra and told her all the traits a person had when they were born under that sign. "You are indecisive and you are independent. You put everything on the scale and weigh the pros and cons before you make a decision, but when you do, your mind is made up. You are

loving and kind and you want to fix everything for everyone, often to the tune of wearing yourself out."

"He's so right," she muttered. She dropped the keys into
her purse and set it up on the bookcase, high enough that
Laela couldn't reach it.

# Chapter Twenty-one

Like always, when he finished his morning chores, Maverick came in the back door. The aroma of hot bread baking wafted out to him as he removed his coveralls and hat. "Hello," he called out. "Where are my girls hiding?"

"In the living room," Bridget yelled.

He stopped in the doorway and stared. She met him halfway across the room with open arms and a kiss. Even in jeans and a faded T-shirt, she took his breath away. When he heard Laela jabbering over by the Christmas tree, he turned his attention that way. From her tone and the way she was glaring at Dolly, he'd guess that the cat had done something she shouldn't have done. Coming home to kisses was so much better than hitting a honky-tonk once a week for a little excitement and then having nothing waiting in the house through the days and long nights.

"Look what I did." Bridget pointed toward the desk.

"How did you do that?"

"Rugs and elbow grease." She grinned.

"Well, remind me to give you a raise." He gave her a Hollywood kiss—one of those where he bent her backward and they were both breathless when it ended.

When he raised her up again, she hung on to him. "One more of those, and I'll be too weak-kneed to pick up the baby."

"I love you." He chuckled.

Had he really said those words out loud? Would it spook her? He checked her face to see if she was shocked, amused, or aggravated by his words. She was smiling as she tiptoed and cupped his face in her hands. She moistened her lips with the tip of her tongue and brought his face to hers for another kiss.

"Oh, Maverick, you saying that is the best Christmas ever," she said softly when the kiss ended.

She hadn't run for the hills, but she hadn't said the words back to him, either. Strangely, he wasn't disappointed. He would rather wait until she was ready than for her to say the words just because *he* had said them.

"Well, thank you, ma'am." He tucked her hand in his and led her to the sofa, where he pulled her down beside him. With her that close, he felt as if the whole world belonged to them—together.

"Want to start on those papers before or after we eat?" She snuggled down into his arms.

"After." He sniffed the air. "I smell homemade bread."

"It's cooling on the counter," she responded. "I made a pot of baked potato soup with ham in it for dinner."

Laela crawled over to Maverick, got a hold of his leg, and tried to stand but kept plopping down on her bottom. He picked her up and held her in his lap with one arm and kept the other one around Bridget's shoulders.

"Do you think Iris will be upset at us for changing things around, like moving her desk?" Bridget asked. "Or for sleeping together in her house?"

"We are consenting adults, and besides, if the walls of this house could talk, I can tell you right now that the stories would put a permanent blush on me and Paxton both." He chuckled.

"Oh, really?" She pulled away from him and drew her eyes down in a fake frown. "Want to tell me a few of those stories?"

He shook his head. "What you women talk about in the kitchen stays in the kitchen. What those guys used to do before they found the love of their lives, stays in the walls or at the Wild Cowboy Saloon. But, honey, I kind of lost my appetite for that kind of life. I rather like rocking the baby to sleep and then holding you." He drew her back to his side. "How about you? Do you miss the pub life?"

"Sometimes, but then Laela does something cute, and I realize that this is the good life," she answered.

Someone knocked on the door and Bridget hurried out to open it. "It's just the UPS man bringing more boxes," she yelled. "I'll put them in the back room."

Christmas! Holy hell, he'd been so tied up in knots with trying to show Bridget that she should stay in Texas that he'd forgotten about presents. He always got pretty much the same things for his brother, grandmother, and the folks that he was close to, but Bridget was another story. What on earth did he buy for her? He only had six days to figure it out.

Bridget returned to the living room and sat down beside him again. "Iris is going to have a lot of wrapping to do back there. Does she buy for everyone in the whole state?"

"I have no idea," Maverick answered. "She always has

three presents for me and three for Paxton. She says that the reason for that is that baby Jesus had three gifts brought to him."

"Then Paxton comes home for Christmas?" she asked.

"If he wants to live to see another year, he does." Maverick chuckled. "Seriously, no matter where we are, we always come to Granny's for Christmas. We arrive on Christmas Eve, and we're here through Christmas Day, at the very least. If possible, we come a little earlier and stay a little longer. Granny expects"—he paused—"no, not expects. Granny demands that much out of us, but she also deserves it."

"Sounds a lot like my nana," Bridget said.

"You mentioned that you needed to do some Christmas shopping. Want to go up to Amarillo to the mall and get it done this afternoon?" he asked.

Her eyes went to the desk. "I haven't bought anything at all, but we've got so much to do if we're going to get things organized to input into the laptop in a couple of weeks."

"It can wait until tomorrow. Let's go spend a day in the mall and have some presents under the tree when Granny and Wanda get here." Maverick stood up with Laela in his arms and carried her down the hall. "I just need to change my shirt and boots. We can even eat in the food court and save the soup and bread for supper."

* * *

Bridget followed him to the bedroom and made a mental list of all the folks she needed to purchase gifts for, and then she thought about how much money she could spend. She should be fine, she thought, to buy seven presents and maybe even splurge on a new dress for Alana's party.

Maverick got changed quicker than she did and came

straight to her bedroom. Without even asking, he started repacking the diaper bag while she finished getting Laela ready. They were already acting like a young married couple, except at night—then they acted like two love-starved teenagers who'd just discovered sex.

She was eager to see a real American mall, so she hurried through changing into a fresh pair of pants and a nice sweater. She shook her long, red hair down from her ponytail and ran a brush through it.

"Gorgeous, as always." Maverick put the baby's coat on her.

"Would you be talking to me or Laela?" she asked.

"You, darlin'," he said. "Are we ready to go, then?"

"I sure am. I've heard so much about your malls that I can't wait to get there," she told him as she headed to the foyer to get her coat.

With the baby in his arms, he followed Bridget down the hall. Bridget made a fast trip through the kitchen to fill a couple of Laela's bottles, and put the pot of potato soup in the refrigerator. Then they left the house together with him in the lead so he could get Laela into her car seat. The frozen grass crunched beneath her boots as she followed the trail they'd made when they'd rolled up snow for the snowman. It was cold but the wind wasn't blowing as hard as it had been in days past. When Maverick opened the door for her, she hopped up into the seat and fastened her seat belt.

"How far is it from here to there, and how many stores are in the mall?" she asked as he fastened his seat belt and adjusted the rear view mirror.

"It's about fifty miles up there, and if the roads are all clear, we should be there in an hour," he answered. "And there's about a hundred stores in the mall. Is that about what you have in an Irish mall?"

"Most of the malls are on the opposite coast from where

we live. There's one a little closer that we get to—maybe every two or three years. Most of the time, we shop in our own village. I can't even imagine going to a place with a hundred stores, but I sure am excited about it." She couldn't wait to take pictures of everything and send them to Sean.

Maverick got in behind the wheel and started the engine. "Would you happen to have a piece of paper in your purse? I didn't make a list, and I always do better if I have one."

"I sure do." She brought out a small notepad and a pen.

"Bridget, Laela, Granny, Wanda." He drove out of the yard and down the lane. "The following will be family presents. Emily and Justin. Retta and Cade. Levi and Claire. Tag and Nikki. Mavis and Skip. And I'll probably have them shipped from the store. They should be there on time."

"Are all these people going to be at the ranch for Christmas?" Just thinking of that many new faces and people was pretty bloody scary.

"No, but they've been good to me, so I want to send them something—maybe a box of candy or cookies." He turned on to the road leading to Daisy. "Got all that?"

"Yes, I do." She started to put the pad away.

"Not yet," he said. "Hudson, Paxton, Benjy, and something to send over to Alana's place. Granny usually makes a pumpkin bundt cake for them, since that is Alana's favorite dessert, but…"

"I can make that for you to give to her. I have Nana's recipe right up here." She tapped her forehead.

"That would be great. Thank you." He turned to her and flashed one of those sexy smiles that melted her insides. "Reckon you could make two? The second one can be my Christmas present from you."

"If you promise *not* to buy Laela a pony, I'll think about it." She smiled back at him.

"Can I buy her a stuffed one?" he asked.

"That's fine," she replied. "Just not a real one. She'll throw a fit to bring it in the house with Ducky and Dolly, and you know how hard it is for you to tell her no."

"Then it's a deal." He turned onto the major highway leading north to Amarillo.

The sky that morning was pale blue. The ever-present wind moved fluffy, white clouds from one side of it to the other. A couple of jet planes left long streaks in the sky, but they soon disappeared. Was that a symbol of her life in Ireland? If she never went back, would Sean and her other acquaintances soon forget her? More importantly, would she forget her life there and become a Texan like Iris had done?

"What are you thinkin' about so hard?" Maverick asked.

"Life and decisions," she said.

"Can't help you with that, darlin'. I got too many of those things already on my plate," he said.

"Don't we all," she said as they passed a sign welcoming them to Happy, Texas. Deidre would have told her that was an omen, for sure. Deidre read her horoscope the first thing every morning, even before her first cup of tea. She believed in signs too and was always saying that in another life she had been a psychic.

Her heart knew exactly what it should do, but she'd been arguing with it. Sean had most likely already sent her stuff to Texas. *Home is where you hang your hat and your heart.* Nana had said that often through the years. In one of those boxes was Nana's favorite old felt hat. Bridget imagined hanging it on one of the hooks on the hall tree back at the ranch and then giving her heart to Maverick. That brought a deep inner peace that she hadn't felt in a very long time.

The first thing she noticed when Maverick pulled into the

mall parking lot wasn't the enormous building housing the one hundred stores, but the acres and acres of vehicles of all kinds. Some were already parked. Some were circling in search of an empty slot.

"Does everyone in this state come here to Christmas shop?" she asked.

"No, but a lot of the folks from the panhandle do, and it's only six days until Christmas, so everyone is out getting last-minute stuff done." Maverick drove up and down several lanes, and then snagged a spot not far from the main entrance.

"The stroller." She groaned. "We should have brought it."

"They have them right inside the door for rental. We can get one of those. Laela will love it because it'll be something new," Maverick said.

"Did you date a woman with a child or something?" she asked.

"No, darlin', but remember Retta? The lady that you thought had my baby? Well, I've been in shopping malls with her a couple of times, and I've also seen mothers pushing their kids in rental strollers," he explained as he got out of the truck.

He'd gotten pretty good at putting Laela into her seat and getting her out, so by the time Bridget was out of the vehicle, he had the baby in his arms. "I need to visit the western wear store on the other end of the mall from right here. If it's all right with you, I'll take the baby with me. That'll give you time to look around at whatever you want. When I start back, I'll call you to see what store you're in." He bent toward Laela to protect her from the fierce north wind.

When they were inside the noisy mall and had a stroller rented, he waved at Bridget and disappeared into the crowd.

Suddenly, she was totally bewildered. Where did she start, and what did she buy?

She passed a kiosk selling soft throws and stopped to look at them. They'd be perfect for Wanda and Iris, since they were going to be going to the assisted living place. She was about to pay for two when she noticed one with a longhorn steer printed on it. She added it for Maverick and paid the bill. That was three of the seven, all done in five minutes. That gave her a little more confidence. At the next kiosk, she found a key chain with a Texas fob on it for Sean. It wouldn't get there before Christmas at this late date, but he'd be tickled with it when it did arrive.

She looked around at all the beautiful decorations in the store and listened to the Christmas music. She watched the people scurrying around hunting for that perfect gift for someone special in their lives, and thought about how sweet it was for Maverick to take the baby with him. The holiday spirit wrapped itself around her like a warm blanket.

"Speaking of which." She decided to give the longhorn blanket to Paxton and find something more personal for Maverick.

She almost passed right by the western wear store, but a belt buckle in the window caught her eye. She went inside and asked to see it and the saleslady brought it to her from the window.

"It's one of a kind. We have a silversmith who makes our buckles and he never makes two just alike," she explained.

That was even better, because in Bridget's eyes, Maverick was one of a kind. A longhorn bull was engraved in the middle of the buckle. The word TEXAS was above it and COWBOY below it.

"Can you do writing on the back of it?" she asked.

"Yes, ma'am. You just write down what you want to say,

and we can have it done in about five minutes." The lady slid a pad and pen across the counter.

Bridget thought about it for a few seconds, and then wrote: *Merry Christmas to my own Texas cowboy. Love, Bridget.*

"That's sweet." The woman took the buckle and the note to the back room and handed it off to a man. "Can I interest you in anything else while we wait?" she asked when she'd returned.

"No, ma'am. Just the buckle is enough," Bridget said.

"Would you like for us to gift wrap it for you? We offer that for free."

Bridget nodded. "That would be wonderful."

"Where are you from? England?" The woman got out a lovely bright red bow and a piece of gold wrapping paper.

"Ireland," Bridget answered.

"Well, I do love that accent. It's soothing."

They visited a while about exactly where in Ireland Bridget was from while she paid for the buckle. The lady deftly wrapped the present and handed it to her, told her to have a merry Christmas, and Bridget shoved the buckle down into the bottom of the bag with the throws. She was in the toy store and had picked up three gifts for Laela when her phone rang with a call from Maverick.

"Hello," she said. "Where are you?"

"Right outside the toy store. Where are you?" he asked.

"I'm in the toy store." She laughed. "Wait for me. I'll be out there in a minute."

"We'll sit on the bench until you get your shopping done. Then, will you come out here and sit with her a few minutes and let me do some lookin' in there?" Maverick asked.

"I'm in line to check out now, and I'm starving," she said. "Can we eat right after you get through in this store?"

She leaned around the woman in front of her and saw
Maverick sitting out there with the baby still in the stroller.

"We sure can." He waved at her.

She waved back and then put the toys she had selected
on the counter to be checked out. She stole sideways
glances at Maverick. He was downright sexy in his cowboy
hat and boots, but what appealed to her even more was the
way he was pointing at the huge Christmas tree in the middle of the mall. No doubt he was telling Laela all about the
oversize ornaments and the pretty lights.

Bridget paid and toted her bags out to the bench where
Maverick waited. Several large sacks with different logos on
the fronts were stacked up around the stroller. How on earth
he'd managed all those plus the baby was a mystery.

"Your turn," she said. "Just for your information, I
checked, and there are no ponies in the store."

"Oh, yeah." He wiggled his dark brows. "I'll just have to
check out every corner for myself. You might have missed
one." He brushed a sweet kiss across her lips, right there in
public, and disappeared into the store.

"Well, lassie, what do you think of this mall?" Bridget
propped her elbows on her knees. "It's the biggest place I
have ever been in, for sure."

Laela's little eyes kept shifting from the huge Christmas
tree not far away to the decorations at all the stores. Wreaths,
garlands, lights, and ornaments were everywhere. Christmas
music was being broadcast through a sound system. There
was an area just down the way a bit where Santa and the
elves were set up. There was a sign that said she could buy
a picture of her child for only two dollars. The line didn't
look very long, and she really did want a picture of Laela on
Santa's knee.

Bridget took her mobile from her purse and called

Maverick. When he answered she said, "I'm going to take Laela for her first picture with Santa Claus. I didn't want you to be worried when you came out of the store."

"I'm checking out in about two minutes. Wait for me, please. I want to see her reaction," Maverick said. "Don't tell her, but I did find a pony. It's not real, but if you go back to Ireland, you'll have to buy another suitcase just for this big feller."

"We'll talk about that later." She ended the call.

Deidre would say that his buying a toy that big and thinking of getting her a real pony later was a sign that she should marry the man, even if she had to chase him down and drag him to the church. He came out in a few minutes toting a huge bag. If her new pony was that big, she would think she had a real one, even if it didn't actually eat hay and breathe.

"Why don't I take all these bags out to the truck and shove them in the backseat?" Maverick suggested. "I can be back by the time you get to the front of the Santa Claus line. If you're finished shopping, we could go find a better place to eat than a food court."

"I'm done," she said. "What have you got in mind?"

"There's a great steak house not far from here." He loaded both arms with sacks.

"That sounds good." She stood up and pushed the stroller toward the Santa line. She was third in line when Maverick joined them.

"Y'all are such a lovely little family. The baby looks exactly like her daddy," the tall blonde said from behind them. "Isn't that just the way it goes? We go through swollen ankles, cravings, pure old bitchiness, and then labor and delivery, and the baby comes out looking like the father."

"Happens that way, ma'am." Maverick tipped his hat toward her. "Good-lookin' boy you got there, no matter who he looks like."

"And your daughter is precious," she said.

"We're hopin' for a red-haired boy next time around." Maverick grinned.

Bridget looped her arm in his. "That's what he wants. I want twin boys who look and act just like him, so he can pay for his raising."

"Where are you from?" the woman asked. "It sure ain't Texas."

"Ireland," Bridget answered and looked up at Maverick. "It's our turn, darling. You want to put her on Santa's lap or shall I?"

"Twin boys?" he asked out of the side of his mouth as they made their way to Santa. "Just remember, you'll have to help me raise them."

"That's not fair." She took Laela out of the stroller and set her on Santa's knee. "I shouldn't have to pay for your raising."

"If we should have another daughter, I'll have to pay for yours with both Laela and the new baby, so it seems pretty fair to me." Maverick stepped back and took a dozen shots of Laela pulling Santa's beard and coming close to removing his wire-rimmed glasses. She cried when she had to give up her spot on Santa's lap to let the lady behind them bring her son forward.

"It's all right, baby girl," Maverick crooned. "We'll buy you a little stuffed Santa to play with if you like him that much."

"We can't leave," Bridget gasped. "We didn't get Iris's picture frame, and we didn't get any pictures done for it."

"I found the perfect frame in one of those kiosks," Maverick said. "I thought we'd pick out the pictures together, and then I'd get prints made."

"I didn't get a dress, either." She moaned.

"We've got plenty of time to come back. Alana's party isn't until New Year's Eve," he told her. "Let's go eat, and then if you still want to shop for a dress, you can call Alana and ask about the best store to shop for that."

"Let's just eat and go home," she said, and that time, saying the word *home* felt even more right than ever before.

\* \* \*

Laela was fighting sleep on the way to the ranch that afternoon. She finally gave in to the droopy eyes and the whiny attitude and was limp as a noodle when Maverick got her out of the seat. He carried her into the house and took her straight to her crib. He removed her shoes, hat, and coat and tucked a teddy bear next to her.

"Poor little thing is exhausted," he said. "Shopping wears out a big old cowboy and babies about the same." He tiptoed out of the room and met Bridget coming out of the room at the end of the hall.

"I took some of the shopping bags in there. The rest are in the foyer," she said.

"Want to curl up with me for a nap before we go to the church to work on the decorations for Sunday?" he asked.

"No, I want a warm bath. The tub is big enough for both of us. Want to go skinny-dipping in it with me?" She took him by the hand and led him to the bathroom.

"Are you serious?" He grinned.

"I bet I can get my clothes all off before you can." She had already taken her coat off and was working on her boots.

"What's the stakes?" he asked.

"Whoever loses has to get up with the baby tonight," she said.

If he hadn't been going commando, he would have lost for sure, but he won the bet when he kicked his jeans over into the pile with her things and laughed. "I hope that when we're old and gray, we're still making bets like this."

"You win." She tossed her bra into the pile. "But guys don't have to wear bras, so you had less to take off."

Maverick started the bathwater and took her into his arms. "We've never danced naked."

Her arms snaked up around his neck, and she pressed her bare flesh to his. "What song is in your head?"

"Have you heard 'Speechless' by Dan and Shay?"

She nodded.

"That's the one that I'm hearing, especially those lines that say that you are my weakness." He swayed with her in the bathroom while their bath ran.

*Nothing could possibly go wrong, now that she'd made her decision to stay in Texas*, she thought.

# Chapter Twenty-two

Bridget had been wrapping gifts and putting them under the tree all morning. She was rushing to the kitchen to get dinner ready when she noticed Maverick standing under the mistletoe hanging above the door into the dining room. Laela made a beeline in that direction, crawling as fast as she could across the kitchen floor. Bridget walked up behind him, slipped her arms around his waist, and laid her cheek on his broad back.

"I never did pay my debt with a kiss under the mistletoe, did I?" She noticed that Laela had stopped in the middle of the floor, paused a few seconds, her little dark brows drawn down, and then she flipped around and crawled away as fast as she could.

"Did you what?" Maverick asked as he came through the back door.

Bridget looked around the man she was hugged up to, gasped, and jumped. The man turned around—definitely not Maverick—with a big smile on his face. "You must be Bridget. I'm Paxton."

"I hope that hug was meant for me." Maverick grinned as he began to peel out of his coveralls.

"I believe Bridget owes you a kiss under the mistletoe." Paxton chuckled.

The two brothers looked enough alike to be twins. Paxton was a tiny bit taller and a few pounds heavier, but they had the same dark hair. Maverick's green eyes were a little lighter than his brother's, and his face a little more rugged. Bridget should have known the moment she put her arms around Paxton that something wasn't right. Not one single steamy jolt of heat rushed through her body when she splayed her hands out on his chest. It all happened so fast, that she hadn't had time to even think about it.

Bridget was so flustered that her words came out in a rush. "Why didn't you tell me your brother was coming today? Does Iris know?"

Maverick pulled her to him for a sideways hug. "I didn't know until he called ten minutes ago and showed up at the barn. We got to talkin', and I realized it was time to come in for dinner, and he beat me to the house. Sorry about that."

"Granny knows," Paxton said. "I called her last night. She told me to put all the boxes that are in my room over in her bedroom, and that she'd see me tomorrow in church, and that I'm not to go to the Wild Cowboy Saloon tonight."

Laela peeked around the end of the bar and crawled over to Maverick. He picked her up and said, "Meet my brother Paxton. This is Laela."

Paxton's eyes widened. "Are you sure that…"

"Very sure," Bridget declared. "While I get over being so embarrassed, you two can wash up. Dinner will be on the table in five minutes."

"No need to be embarrassed." Paxton smiled. "I thought it was a very nice welcome-home gesture."

Bridget felt another blush flushing her cheeks. "Get on with the both of you before I feed the meat loaf to Ducky and make you eat peanut butter sandwiches."

She was putting the food on the table when her phone rang with a call from Iris. She answered with, "I just made a fool out of myself," and went on to tell Iris what had happened.

"That's priceless." Iris giggled. "I really thought I'd talk to you before he arrived, but my therapy session went a little longer than usual. Has he got those boxes out of his room?"

Bridget poured three glasses of sweet tea. "Where's Wanda going to sleep?"

"She's not coming after all. One of her friends at Oak Grove—that's the assisted living center where I'm going—anyway, one of her friends isn't doing well. Seems the little old guy buried his son, and he's depressed. So she's going back there this evening so she can be with him for Christmas," Iris told her.

"We've bought gifts for her." Bridget put the butter, salt, and pepper on the table.

"You can take them to her when you take me up there in the afternoon on Christmas," Iris said.

Bridget sat down in her chair at the table. "Are you sure about going to that place? You didn't even go look at it."

"I've been there several times to visit friends. It's very nice, and I'll be happy with people my age around me all the time. I'm looking forward to it," Iris said. "Now it's time for me to go to the dining room. I'll have all of my stuff packed up and ready to move out of here when Paxton picks me up for church in the morning. I'll see you and Maverick and the baby there. Bye, now."

"Is that Granny I'm hearin'?" Paxton asked as he came into the kitchen.

"It was." Bridget nodded. "You're to pick her up for church tomorrow morning."

Paxton chuckled. "I've already got my orders, right down to the minutes."

"And I've got mine." Maverick brought Laela in and put her in her high chair. "This all sure looks good. I love meat loaf."

"Me too." Paxton pulled out the chair right across the table from Bridget and sat down. "I'll pay you double what Mav is giving you if you'll come back to Canyon Creek Ranch and cook for me and Hudson."

"Hey, now!" Maverick scolded.

Laela bowed her head and closed her little eyes.

"That's my cue," Maverick said as he did the same and said a short prayer.

"Wow!" Paxton said when grace was finished. "How old is this little girl? She can't be more than four or five months old. Annie is bigger than her and she's six months. They say grace at every meal and she doesn't do that."

"Laela is seven months old, but both her parents were small. Her mother was barely five feet tall and her father was only a couple of inches taller than me," Bridget explained.

"That's still pretty smart for a baby." Paxton helped himself to the meat loaf and passed it over to Bridget.

"She'll be riding a pony next year at this time." Maverick beamed.

Bridget wondered what she'd be doing this time next year.

\* \* \*

When they had finished eating, the guys went back out to the barn to talk about what all needed to be done on the ranch. Bridget got Laela down for her nap and had all her work done. She started sorting through the papers on the desk, organizing them by date.

She was still smiling when the phone rang. Figuring it was Maverick, she answered with, "I guess we'll be sleeping in our own bedrooms tonight."

"Oh, really now? Where have you been sleeping?" Sean chuckled.

"I thought you were someone else." She blushed.

"Maverick?" he asked.

"That's right. His brother came, and..." She told him what she'd done.

She got the same reaction out of him that she'd gotten from Iris. A belly laugh and then he said, "I called to tell you that your things are on the way."

"Thank you so much, Sean," she said.

"Like I told you before, I don't want to die without having known real love. We never know just how long or how short our time is on this green Earth, but we do know that the future is fickle. I'll find the right woman someday," Sean said. "I'm going to work at the bakery and let fate bring me the right woman. Fate didn't do too bad a job when she brought Maverick to you."

"So when did Sean Cleary become a philosopher?" she asked.

"When I figured out that you needed one." He laughed.

"I love Maverick." She put the phone on speaker and leaned her head back on the sofa.

"Have you told him?" Sean asked.

"No, but I will when the time is right."

"Better not wait too long," Sean warned her.

"Thank you." She ended the call, and Alana yelled hello as she came through the front door.

"In the living room." Bridget raised her voice.

Alana dropped her coat on a rocking chair and plopped down on the sofa. "I talked to Iris this morning. She says she's determined to go to the assisted care center. I tried to talk her out of it. And she said Paxton is here? Is that permanent or just for the holiday?"

Bridget put up both palms. "I have no idea." Once again she told the story about thinking Paxton was Maverick.

"That is priceless!" Alana almost snorted.

"I'm a whole lot still embarrassed," Bridget said.

Alana winked at her. "Honey, we all have our arguments. And the make-up sex is the best in the world."

"Oh, really? And have you had make-up sex with Paxton?" Bridget cocked her head to one side and raised an eyebrow.

"Nope, but I intend to one of these days." Alana laughed. "I ran by to pick up a box of decorations. Iris said they're in her closet with CHURCH STUFF written all in capital letters on the side. We need them to finish up the props tonight."

"Follow me and we'll find them. I could have brought them with me." Bridget said. "Whoa!" She stopped in the foyer. The light finally came on! "You thought you might get to see Paxton, didn't you?"

Alana shrugged. "A girl can hope."

"Why don't you just go out there in the barn and tell him hello?" Bridget started down the hall.

"That might give him the impression I care," Alana said. "He tends to run like a scalded hound dog when a woman shows the least bit of interest in him. I'll see him tonight. Iris said that she told him he has to come to the church to help us."

Bridget wondered if that was why Maverick had pursued her. If she'd fallen all over him from the beginning, would he be running like a scared pup?

* * *

The tires on Maverick's truck slipped several times on the frozen ground as they drove around the entire ranch, checking the fence lines. Maverick drove. Paxton made notes about what places were in such bad repair that they had to be fixed soon, and which ones could wait a while longer.

"I should just come on home," Paxton said. "But I don't feel right leaving Hud and Tag right now."

"I understand," Maverick said. "I'd feel the same way if things had happened that you were the one who was here. I can hang in until you get here, but once you are, we'll have to put in some long hours, brother."

"I'll be ready for that," Pax said. "I'd like to stick around until the spring planting is done. I'll be here permanently the first week in May." Paxton grinned. "Besides, you and Bridget need a little time in the house alone for a honeymoon."

"Slow down, brother," Maverick said. "As far as that honeymoon business, you better pull back on those reins. She's just now decided to stay in Texas. I can't rush her."

"There's a difference in rushing and dragging your feet, brother. Don't wait too long. She's the right woman for you." Paxton nodded toward a length of fence that needed repairing and made notes.

"Why do you think that?" Maverick asked.

Paxton shrugged. "It's the way you look and act around her. And it's the same with her. You're happier than I've ever seen you since"—he paused—"like ever. I remember Grandpa looking at Granny when we were kids. Grandpa told me once that theirs was one of those matches made in heaven. Those don't come along too often, so don't mess it up."

"I'm doing my best not to do just that," Maverick said.

"By the way, did Granny tell you that Alana and her dad are helping with the Christmas stuff at the church?"

"No, she did not!" Paxton dropped his notebook on the floor of the truck and then bumped his head when he tried to retrieve it. "Dammit! I get all tongue-tied around Alana."

"Maybe she's the one for you," Maverick teased.

"Not that woman," Paxton said. "She can out-ride, out-rope, out-drink, out-*everything* any man in the whole state of Texas. I want someone who thinks I'm the king of the mountain."

Maverick patted him on the shoulder. "I hear they've got a few women left in Ireland."

"I'd be willing to go over there if I could find one who would light up my eyes like Bridget does yours. Now, let's finish up this job and then take a look at what cattle we've got to work with," Paxton said.

Maverick found himself wondering when it would be the right time to propose to Bridget. Should he get her an engagement ring for Christmas? He only had five days to make that decision.

Paxton pointed at a small herd under a grove of pecan trees. "There's about a dozen head. How many is Granny running now?"

"I think about seventy-five, but she hasn't kept her books in months, so I'm not sure what's going on. We'll have to cull them out come spring," Maverick said.

"Are we going to have to go to the bank for a loan to get us through this first year?" Pax asked.

"No, she told me the checkbook was on the desk. I took a look and almost fainted like a girl. She's been hoarding money for all these years, and there's plenty to keep us afloat. We won't be running in the red for a long time," he answered.

# Chapter Twenty-three

Maverick figured that finishing the last-minute decorations at the church would only take an hour at the most. For the most part, things were in place and ready.

"You've been awfully quiet this evening," Bridget said as they got into the truck. "Does it bother you that Paxton isn't coming back until May? I'm willing to do what I can to help with ranch work. The house and cooking sure doesn't keep me busy all day long."

"I didn't really expect him until summer, and thanks for the offer. If you'll get some kind of computer program for the business up and running, that would a big help. I might just take you up on that offer to drive when I need supplies from town. We'll just take it a day and a week at a time." He didn't say a word about what Paxton had said about the honeymoon business.

"I'm here when you need me. Why didn't Paxton come with us?" she asked.

"He decided that he was going to see Granny. She's called him several times about this new arrangement with the ranch, but he wanted to talk to her face-to-face," Maverick said.

"And he's avoiding Alana, isn't he?" She smiled and then chuckled.

"Oh, yeah." Maverick kept both hands on the steering wheel, and his eyes straight ahead. Deer were out feeding at this time of the evening, and he sure didn't want to hit one.

"Don't they realize that there's a spark between them?" Bridget asked.

"Yep, but they've been fighting it for so long that I'm not sure they can do anything else." Maverick pointed to the right and slowed down. "Look at the deer herd over there."

Bridget unfastened her seat belt so she could get her phone from her pocket. She snapped several photos before the buck realized they were there and led his herd toward a copse of scrub oak trees.

"With the snow still lying on the ground and the stars beginning to pop out, these pictures would make lovely Christmas cards," she said as she flipped through them.

"I was thinking more of a card with us on it next year," he said.

Bridget laid her phone on the console between them and turned to face him. "Why, Maverick Callahan, are you proposing to me?"

"You deserve a better proposal than one sitting on the side of the road in a pickup truck. But when I do propose, what kind of ring do you have in mind?" He was surprised that he could talk about such a big step without beads of sweat popping out on his forehead.

"Just a simple gold band, like Nana had," she said.

"No big diamonds? Or maybe even an emerald for the

Irish green?" He put the truck in gear and pulled back onto the highway.

"A big diamond would be for Texas, since everything is bigger in Texas. An emerald would be for Ireland. A band just says that I'm eternally yours, no matter where we go or live," she said.

"I like that." He turned onto the highway leading into Daisy. Now, he had to think about finding the perfect place to propose to her. His hands got clammy just thinking about what he'd do if she changed her mind between now and when he actually got down on one knee and popped the question.

"You missed the turn," she said.

"Guess I did." He made the next right. "The truck must've thought it was going to the rehab center instead of the church." He made another right and pulled into the church parking lot.

Matt was waiting on the small back porch and came right out to the truck to open the door for Bridget. "I just got here and saw y'all coming so I waited for you. Want me to carry in the diaper bag? I've already set the stuff from Iris's house inside the door."

"Sure and thank you." Bridget nodded. "Where's Alana? I thought she was bringing the box of decorations."

"She ran out on us tonight." Matt grinned. "She said to tell you there's a picture of the decorations from last year in the box. If you want to do things a little different this year that's fine, but she'd planned to use the picture for a guide-line."

Maverick finished getting Laela out of her car seat. "Poor baby, she's been getting in and out of this thing a lot lately."

"You're a lucky dog." Matt held the door for them and

then set the diaper bag on top of the box and carried it into the sanctuary. "I sure miss the days when Alana was a little kid."

"Is Alana still out Christmas shopping?" Bridget asked.

"Nope, she decided to go see Iris. She said that Iris probably needs some company, since it's her last night in rehab. Truth is, I think she's avoiding Paxton and she knew he was going to be here tonight." Matt handed the picture to Bridget.

Maverick chuckled and then laughed, and then he guffawed. Bridget got tickled right along with him. Laela giggled with them, as if she knew what was going on, but poor old Matt just stood there and stared at them like they had lost their minds.

Finally, Maverick wiped his eyes, hiccupped a few times, and explained, "Paxton made an excuse to go see Granny tonight so he wouldn't have to come here."

Matt bypassed the first stages of laughter and went right to the guffaw stage. Laela giggled right along with him again. When he got control, he snatched several tissues from the box at the end of the pew and wiped his eyes. "It's good enough for the both of them."

"All right, let's get this thing started," Maverick said, glancing at the photograph Alana had provided. He put Laela on the floor to explore the church and got a second string of lights from the box. This summer should be a hoot, he thought, with Paxton and Alana living so close together for the first time since they had graduated from high school. Hopefully, by the end of summer, he and Bridget would at least be properly engaged. He didn't dare hope for anything more than that, since he didn't intend to rush her into anything.

* * *

Bridget didn't have a bit of trouble getting Laela to sleep that night. Poor little lassie was so tired from crawling among the church pews that she barely even drank a third of her bottle before she was ready to be put in her crib. Maverick was reading something on his phone when she went from the bedroom to the living room. When he looked up and saw her, he grinned.

"What? Do I have something on my face?" she asked.

"I just got a text from Paxton. He's on his way to the Wild Cowboy Saloon, that honky-tonk I told you about. Seems like he needs a drink after having to sit in the same room with Alana for an hour," Maverick answered. "Looks like we got the house all to ourselves for the evening."

Bridget sat down in his lap and nibbled on his ear. "What do you think we should do?"

"I was thinking one of those skinny-dippin' baths might be right nice, and then maybe afterward, I'd give you a massage. After that, you can..."

She cupped his face in her hands. "How about we just skip the bath and massage and go straight to bed. You never know when Alana might show up at that honky-tonk because she needs a drink too. Then Paxton will come running back home."

"Are you telling me that we can't sleep together with him in the house?" Maverick leaned forward and kissed her with so much passion and heat that she could hardly breathe.

"It would just be too awkward," she said.

He cupped his hands under her butt and stood up. She wrapped her legs around his waist and her arms around his neck. He carried her back to his bedroom, and shut the door with the heel of his boot. "Then we'd better make the best of this time, hadn't we?"

"That's what I was thinking," she said.

Maverick chuckled. "Great minds think alike, darlin'."

* * *

Maverick awoke the next morning and reached for Bridget, but she wasn't there. He already hated waking up without her by his side. He grumbled on the way to the bathroom and the whole time he got dressed, then remembered that it was Sunday. That meant getting chores done in time to take a quick shower and get ready for church.

He heard voices in the kitchen when he reached the foyer. Laela was crawling toward him, so he scooped her up into his arms. "Good morning, princess. Are you hungry?"

She reached up and touched his cheek with one of her tiny hands, and immediately, he felt better. To get to have Bridget and this child in his life forever would be worth a few nights of sleeping alone.

Paxton was sitting at the table with a cup of coffee in his hands. "I was wonderin' if you were goin' to sleep all day, brother."

Maverick put Laela in her high chair and poured himself a cup of coffee. He stopped long enough to kiss Bridget on the forehead and then went to the table and sat down. "The sun isn't up yet. I'd be willin' to bet that you haven't even been to bed. You probably closed down the Wild Cowboy Saloon and then went home with some bar bunny. Am I right?"

"I was home and in bed before eleven," Paxton said.

"Are you sick?" Maverick asked.

"Nope." Paxton shook his head. "I was dancin' with this pretty little brunette, and damned if Alana didn't show up. As soon as the song ended, I started out the door and she stepped in front of me. I ran right into her. I mean, as in a physical crash that just about sent us both to the floor."

"What did you do?" Bridget set a platter of pancakes on the table.

"I apologized like the gentleman I am and slipped on out the door. Started to go on up to the Round Up Club in Amarillo, but she goes there too sometimes," Paxton told her. "Looks like Laela wants us to grace this food so she can eat."

As soon as Maverick said "Amen," Bridget asked, "How are you ever going to live here permanently?"

"I been thinkin' about that." Paxton passed the platter over to Bridget to serve herself first. "I've got until May to figure it out."

"Tell me why you're avoiding her." Bridget stacked three pancakes onto her plate, covered them with warm maple syrup, and fed Laela the first bite.

"She scares the bejesus out of me, and yet there's something between us," Paxton answered. "I just can't imagine being in a relationship with her. Didn't you ever feel like that, Mav?"

"Yep, I still feel a little like that," he admitted.

"With me?" Bridget gasped.

"Oh, yeah," Maverick answered, honestly. "You could do so much better than an old rough cowboy with so little to his name."

"Yeah, you could marry anyone in this part of Texas," Paxton teased, "or me. I'm better lookin' than Mav, and I'm a helluva lot more romantic."

"Hey, now!" Maverick shook his fist at Paxton. "That's no way to treat your brother."

Bridget thought of all the times she'd bantered like that with Deidre and was suddenly homesick. It wasn't so much for Ireland as for the friendship that would never be the same, not with Deidre gone. Maybe if she had a sibling, things would be different, but she didn't. Maybe she would have a brother-in-law someday and a sister-in-law if Paxton ever quit running from a serious relationship—and if Maverick didn't change his mind about buying her that plain gold band.

\* \* \*

Maverick couldn't have been happier than he was that Sunday morning as he took his place on the pew between his grandmother and Bridget. Paxton was sitting right on the other side of Iris, and Laela was in his lap. Talk about a Christmas miracle—it was right there in the little white church in Daisy that morning. A year ago, he and Paxton were still working on the Rocking B for the Bakers, and he had thought he'd never see Bridget again. He hated that Granny was going to an assisted living center, but he was looking forward to making the ranch into the place it used to be. Then there was the fact that Bridget had agreed to stay in Texas. Life was good, and he was a happy cowboy to have his family and, hopefully, his future family with him that morning.

The preacher took the pulpit and motioned toward the three curtains lined up across the stage. "This morning we'll be presenting our annual Christmas program and then there will be a potluck in the fellowship hall. We're glad y'all are all here this morning, and we're grateful to everyone who had a hand in getting things ready for this year's program. Now I'm going to turn this over to our choir director. Sit back and enjoy the love and joy of Christmas."

Matt and the lady who led the singing went forward from the front pew together. She went straight to the piano, and Matt pulled the first curtain back to reveal a huge Santa Claus cutout and a row of colored bells lined up in front of it. The little kids from age three to five came down the center aisle singing "We Wish You a Merry Christmas." Maverick thought they were adorable, all dressed up in their Sunday best and singing, some off-key and two words ahead of the other kids. In a couple of years, Laela would be right in there with them. He could already envision her in a red velvet dress and a big red bow in her hair.

They picked up their bells as they lined up on the stage, and their teacher held up the color they were supposed to shake so that they played "Jingle Bells." Laela's little head bobbed to the tune. Bridget leaned over and whispered, "When she gets old enough to do that, she'll want to ring her bell all the time, not just when it's her turn."

"Yep, I can see that happening," Maverick said out of the side of his mouth.

When the children had finished, they returned their bells to where they had picked them up except for the last little boy in the bunch. He held his close to his chest and cried so hard that his mama had to go forward and rescue him, but by golly, he kept his little yellow bell.

Then Bridget and Maverick's group marched up to the stage just like they'd practiced at dress rehearsal and sang "Santa Claus Is Coming to Town," as the middle set of curtains opened in the center of the stage. It looked pretty fine with the new touch-up paint job on it. Bridget nudged Maverick and whispered, "They're doing wonderful. I'm so proud of them."

They finished their three songs and the scuffling of feet could be heard all over the church as they marched up to the choir loft and took their places. Randy, bless his heart, didn't put his finger to his nose one time, but then Lily Rose was sitting right beside him, so he probably knew better.

The older kids came down the aisle singing "Silent Night" and took their places on the stage in front of a

Christmas tree. It looked a lot better with lights and all the decorations. Without those, it had been kind of pitiful, but with a pretty star on the top and all lit up, the part facing the congregation was downright gorgeous. One of the kids did a reading from the scripture about Mary finding out that she was going to have a child.

Maverick glanced over at Bridget. What would their child look like? Would he really get a little red-haired boy? They hadn't discussed kids, but he really wanted a big family. What if she didn't want to have children? What if raising Laela was all she intended to do? A cold chill shot down his back. He promised himself that he would discuss it with Bridget the very first chance he got.

That group ended their part of the program with "O Come All Ye Faithful," and again, Matt pulled the middle curtain and opened the one on the right to reveal a manger scene, complete with wise men, shepherds, and a real lamb. There was another reading and a group of young married folks gathered together on the stage to sing, "Mary, Did You Know?"

Bridget leaned over and whispered, "Will we be singing with them next year?"

"I hope so," Maverick said and kissed her on the cheek.

After a couple more songs, the service ended with the congregation singing "Away in a Manger." The preacher said a final prayer and everyone stood up to go to the fellowship hall.

"That was the best one ever," Iris said as she got a firm grip on her cane. "The tree was lovely."

"I'm glad you couldn't see the backside of it. It was bare," Bridget said. "We figured that the front was what was important."

"Good thinkin'," Iris agreed. "Let's go have some lunch,

and then y'all can take me to the ranch so I can get my afternoon nap."

Paxton helped her get from the sanctuary to the fellowship hall while Maverick and Bridget gathered up all the toys Laela had strewn about. Maverick hung back until he and Bridget were pretty much alone in that part of the church.

"What was your favorite part of the program?"

"The little bitty lads and lassies," she answered, "and after that our class of kids. They did so good, even Randy. I've always been sad that I was an only child. I would never want to raise Laela all alone. I guess we should discuss that seriously before we make any commitments, shouldn't we?"

"I was thinkin' that I'd like four kids." He smiled.

"I was thinkin' six." She tiptoed and kissed him on the cheek.

"Maybe we'll compromise with five?" he said.

"Or maybe I'll talk you into six," she teased.

"Honey, you could talk me into a dozen. It's harder for me to say no to you than it is for me to refuse Laela." He held the baby in one arm and draped the other one around Bridget's shoulders, and together they made their way to the fellowship hall.

# Chapter Twenty-four

A hard wind rattling the windows woke Bridget on Christmas Eve morning. The red numbers on the clock beside her bed told her that it was five thirty. Surely the smell of tea filling her bedroom was a figment of her imagination. The other side of the bed looked and felt empty, even though she and Maverick had never spent the night together in that bedroom—not with a baby in a crib not three feet away. She sighed and got another whiff of strong breakfast tea.

She threw off the covers and got dressed. On the way to the kitchen she combed her hair with her fingers and secured her hair in a ponytail with a holder she had in the pocket of her pants. Light flowed from the kitchen doorway out into the foyer, and she could hear Iris whispering to Ducky and Dolly.

"Good morning," she called out as she entered the room.

"Mornin' to you. Scones right out of the oven. It sure feels good to be able to get around and do a few things." Iris motioned toward the table. "Breakfast tea in the pot. Sit and talk to me until it's time to get bacon and eggs ready for the boys."

Bridget poured a cup of tea, inhaled its aroma before she took the first sip, and sighed. "Where did you get this?"

"Your nana sent me a big box of good Irish tea every year at Christmas. I kept it in the freezer so it wouldn't go stale. This is the last of last year's stash. Fitting, don't you think, that I should be sharing my last pot with you on Christmas Eve morning?" Iris asked.

"I bet you're the one who sent her American chocolates, aren't you?" Bridget sipped her tea slowly.

Iris nodded. "It was our little tradition. I've got some things to say to you that is just between us girls. Have a scone while they're still hot. I've already eaten two."

Iris did not beat around the bush about anything, and she was sharing the very last of her imported tea with Bridget. That meant she was serious about what she was about to say. Bridget's hands shook a little as she smeared strawberry jam on a warm scone.

"First thing is that I'll need some help packing this evening. I've visited friends at this place, so I know exactly what my little apartment will look like, and much of my stuff will have to stay here. It shouldn't take long."

"Of course I'll help you pack," Bridget said.

"But what we need to talk about most of all is you and Maverick," Iris said. "You two belong together, and I have every faith that someday you will be the granddaughter I never had. This is going to be your house, so move whatever you want. I already like what you did with the desk. I'd also like to see my bedroom made into a nursery for Laela. She needs a place that she can call her own from now until she grows up and leaves."

"But, Iris, you'll be coming home to visit, and..." Bridget grabbed a napkin from the dispenser in the middle of the table and wiped a tear.

"Yes, I am, and when I do, I'll stay in the guest room, which is the bedroom you're using now. I need to cut ties from the ranch and this house. It will make me happy to see Laela in that room rather than guests." Iris laid a hand on Bridget's arm.

"Why would you want to cut the ties?" Bridget sniffled.

"I'm bossy." Iris smiled. "It's just the way I am. These boys need to stand on their own two feet and run this place. They'll make good decisions, but they'll also make mistakes. If I was right here every day, it will never be their ranch. It will always be mine. Since my Thomas died, I've been lonely. I'm glad to be close to Wanda and my other friends from this area who are already at the retirement center. I'll get to spend more time with them, and I won't be spending nights wondering what to do with myself."

Bridget finished off her scone and picked up another one. "Then I'm happy for you, but please know that you are welcome here anytime you want to come home, and for as long as you want."

"Thank you, darlin'," Iris said.

Bridget almost pinched herself to see if she was dreaming. Iris gently squeezed her arm. "I can't think of a better woman to take up the reins of Callahan Ranch. It takes a special kind of lady to live on a ranch and keep her man happy. I learned that when I married Thomas Callahan. It's a wonderful life, but a busy one, and I think your nana would be happy with you making it your life. Maverick would never be happy without you, now that he's figured things out. He's just waiting for the right time to pop the question. Men are like that. They have to do things in their own time."

Iris removed her hand. "I hear them coming down the hall." She cocked her head to the side. "And Maverick is bringing Laela with him."

"How do you know that?" Bridget asked.

"He's talkin' to her," Iris replied. "My body is tired and old, but I've still got good hearing."

Paxton was the first one to come through the door. "Do I get a hug this mornin', Bridget?" he teased.

Bridget blushed. "No, but Iris has the coffee already made so you can have a cup of that while I make breakfast."

"I thought for sure I'd get a hug since it's Christmas Eve." He grinned.

"If you want a hug, I'll call Alana," Bridget shot back at him.

He laid a hand over his heart. "Ouch!"

"Looks like you done met your match, brother." Maverick brought Laela into the room and went straight to Bridget. They shared a three-way hug and then he kissed Bridget on the cheek.

"Don't dish it out if you can't take it in." Iris laughed and reached for the baby. "I'll take my morning hugs from this sweet little girl still in her pajamas."

Maverick handed her to his grandmother. "All changed, and I would have gotten her dressed, but I didn't know what Bridget wanted her to wear."

"Oven omelet and toast for breakfast?" Bridget asked.

"Sounds great!" Maverick poured two cups of coffee and handed one to Paxton.

"I'm going to ride along this morning while y'all do chores," Iris said.

"No need for you to do that, Granny." Paxton pulled out a chair and sat down beside her. "It's cold out there. You can stay in where it's warm. Don't you have packages to wrap?"

"I got that done last night, and I do have packing to do, but that can be done this afternoon. This morning, I'm going with y'all, so don't argue with me," Iris said, sternly.

"Yes, Mam," Maverick agreed.

Bridget smiled and started half a pound of sausage to frying in a cast iron skillet. Someday she hoped to be every bit as bossy with her children as Iris was with "the boys," and she also wanted to know when it was time to step down and retire. She could visualize sitting on the front porch swing with Maverick right beside her, the two of them watching their grandchildren build a snowman. She made a mental note not to lose that old hat and the scarf on the snowman still in the front yard. When the Callahan grandchildren built their snowmen, she'd bring both items for them to use again.

\* \* \*

Maverick started to help Iris up into the passenger seat of his truck, but she shook her head. "I'll sit in the back, and I learned how to do this by myself at rehab. Open the door for me, and I'll show you."

He didn't argue but did what she said. "I just use my cane and the handhold at the top edge of the door, like this." Without even a wince she lifted herself up and settled into her seat and was pulling the belt around her body.

"You going to hoist bags of feed this morning too?" Paxton asked as he got into the truck.

"I could if I wanted to, but that's y'all's job now," she told them. "I'm here to boss you around one last time."

"Are you dyin'?" Maverick asked. "That's the only time you'll ever stop bossin'."

"Not that I know of, but after tomorrow, this ranch is

y'all's, not only by deed but by me handing it over to you. What you do with it will be your legacy," she said. "And there's a few things you need to know. I've already given Bridget her talkin' to this mornin' before y'all even got out of bed." She told them briefly what she'd said about the house.

"But I haven't even proposed to her." Maverick hoped to hell that Bridget hadn't found his grandmother totally overwhelming.

"Then it's time for you to start thinking along those lines. This is for you when you quit dragging your feet." She passed a small velvet box over the seat.

Maverick took it from her and brought the truck to a complete stop. "If this is what I think it is, then I can't take it. I should pick out a ring myself, and besides, she said she didn't even want an engagement ring. She just wants a plain gold band."

"That's good to hear, but that ring is special, and you should give it to her when you propose. A woman needs something to show the world that she's taken. That is the ring that your great-grandfather Callahan gave to your great-grandmother when they got engaged. It was passed down to Thomas and he gave it to me. Your father refused to give it to your mother, which is a damn good thing, since she would have probably thrown it away when he died. It's always gone to the oldest son to give to his bride-to-be. Open the box," she said.

Maverick flipped it open to find a gold Claddagh ring with a brilliant diamond in the middle of the heart. It would match the bracelet he had found for her at the mall perfectly. He'd only bought two charms: a Claddagh and one shaped like Texas. He'd written a note and put it inside the box saying that it was to remind her of her past and her future.

"I never saw you wear this." Maverick couldn't take his eyes off the ring.

"I wore it all the time with this little gold band." She held up her left hand. "But when your father refused it, I put it away for the right time to give to my first grandson. This is the right time."

"Thank you," he whispered, hoarsely.

"I promised I wouldn't cry like a baby." Paxton brought out his handkerchief and wiped his eyes. "I couldn't believe you were giving us the ranch, and now this. I expected this to be an emotional day, but lord . . . cowboys aren't supposed to cry."

Tears streamed down Maverick's cheeks, and he took a red bandanna from his hip pocket to wipe them away. "I don't even know what to say. I figured someday you'd sell the place and use the money to buy something smaller in town. Neither of us ever thought about you just handing it over to us, *plus* all the money to run it."

"It's your inheritance, and I've put back plenty of money to keep me comfortable in the assisted living place. Build it up into something you'll be proud to give to your sons one day so the Callahan Ranch can go on and on. I knew this would be emotional. That's why I didn't want to say and do all this in front of Bridget. I love her and want her to be my granddaughter, but this is between me and my boys." Iris reached over the seat and took Paxton's handkerchief from him to wipe her own eyes. "And, Paxton, you are not being left out. I have a dinner ring that your grandfather had made for me when we were married fifty years. When you get ready to settle down, I want you to take the diamonds from that ring and have them made into an engagement ring for your lady."

"Alana will love that," Maverick teased to lighten the mood.

Paxton punched him on the arm. "That's not funny. Make him stop, Granny."

"He hit me," Maverick said. "Make him ride in the back of the truck for being mean."

"He started it," Paxton whined like a little boy.

"That's my boys, always making me either want to pinch their heads off or laugh at them. Never a dull moment." Iris grinned. "Now, start up this truck, and let's talk about fences and cattle. This is the last day I intend to put my two cents into this ranchin' business. That doesn't mean I won't still be bossy. I'm tellin' you right now, you will both come see me each week at the center, except for the weekends when I come to visit the ranch. I won't be coming back for the first month, though. Maverick needs to get things under control and propose to Bridget."

"Granny!" Maverick gasped.

"Don't you use that tone on me." Iris shook her finger at him. "Drive around the fences first and let me see the cattle. Then we're going to talk about how many to take to the sale next spring, and how much you need to spend on a new bull."

"And you weren't going to be bossy?" Paxton chuckled.

"Enjoy it, today," Iris told them.

"Does that mean we can't come to you for advice?" Maverick started to drive through the snow still piled up next to the fence row.

"Of course you can," Iris said. "But you ain't getting it without askin'. You've worked on the biggest ranch in the panhandle, and you've been foremen of that spread out there in Sunset. You've had the best education in the whole state. It's time to use it."

"We'll do our damnedest to make you proud," Paxton said.

"I don't have a doubt in the world that you'll do just that." Iris pointed toward an Angus bull standing under a pecan tree. "That old guy should be sold. He's been a good bull, but he's getting too old to throw good calves."

Maverick nodded in agreement. Emotions aside, getting the ranch in order was going to be an undertaking, but it was actually in better shape than the one he'd been helping the Baker brothers with back to the east in north central Texas. Even if Callahan Ranch didn't have the prime cattle Tag and Hud got to start with, the Callahan house was bigger, and there was a helluva lot less mesquite to clear off the land.

Then there was the fact that he also had Bridget to help him. He patted his pocket where he'd tucked the little ring box away.

# Chapter Twenty-five

Maverick was sitting on the edge of Bridget's bed when she awoke the next morning. For a few minutes, she wondered why he wasn't lying beside her and then she remembered that he'd kissed her good night at her bedroom door the night before. Until Paxton left and they got Iris moved into her new home, they wouldn't be sleeping together.

"Merry Christmas, darlin'," he whispered.

"It is Christmas." She smiled. "I get to spend Christmas with my cowboy. That's the best present ever."

"We'll see if you still think that when we open presents. Paxton and I are going outside to do morning chores before breakfast. Granny is already in the kitchen and barking orders," he said.

"Why didn't you wake me earlier?" Bridget was out of bed so fast that she was barely a blur. She grabbed a pair of pants from the back of a rocking chair and was pulling them up over her hips when Maverick reached out and put his hands around her waist.

"She will appreciate your help, I'm sure," he said. "But she needs to do this herself, darlin'. It's kind of like closure for her. She gave us our orders on the morning rounds yesterday, and I guess you got yours while y'all were having tea and scones."

Bridget nodded and picked up her little Christmas tree earring from the dresser. "And reinforcement of them while we packed. She told me to take the bed out of her room and store it, and to paint the walls pale pink so that Laela would have something feminine in her life."

"She should have both worlds," Maverick agreed. "Someday she will help run this place and it's hard work, but she needs to be a girl too."

"But she's..." Bridget held the earring up to her ear.

Maverick put his finger over her lips before she could finish. "She will be our firstborn, even though not a drop of our blood is in her veins. I want to adopt her and make her a Callahan when the time is right. Wait right here," Maverick said. "Don't move, not even your hand."

He ran across the hall and got the match to the earring and brought it back in his closed hand. "I found this tangled up in my shirt after I left your apartment that morning. I've kept it to prove that I wasn't dreaming about that night." He opened his hand. "I guess it belongs with its mate, like we belong together."

"You really are quite the romantic." She grinned as she put the earrings on. "I'm glad to have them back together. Nana bought them for me when I was a teenager and I always wore them on Christmas Day."

"I'm glad that *we* are back together," he said and turned around when he heard Laela jabbering. "Our baby girl is already awake. She's probably excited to see what Santa brought her."

"She's too young to even know what today is, but please tell me that you didn't let Paxton or Iris get her a real pony." Bridget pulled her nightshirt over her head and put on a bra and T-shirt. "She needs to be old enough to be responsible for animals before she has one of her own."

Maverick caught Bridget as she passed and pulled her onto his lap. "I figure she needs to be walking before she has a pony, and, honey, she will learn responsibility soon enough on this ranch. Until then, she can be satisfied with Dolly and Ducky." He kissed her one more time, set her back on the floor, and went to the crib. He picked the baby up and carried her to the window. "Look out there, Laela. This is your home now, and you get to spend your first Christmas in Texas."

"Da-da-da-da," Laela said.

"Did you hear that?" Maverick spun around to look at Bridget. "She said it again. She called me Daddy for the second time."

"I heard," Bridget said. "But I'm not sure she knows what she's saying or what it means."

"It's my Christmas present from her, Bridget, and it's a sign. I want more than to just live with you. I want to marry you and adopt this child, but I'm going to leave it up to you as to when you're ready to say yes," he said.

She finished buttoning her jeans, and then tiptoed and kissed him. "Thank you for that. But right now, I can't wait to open presents, so go get your morning chores done."

"Yes, ma'am." His lips met hers in a steamy hot kiss full of promise for the future. When it ended, he handed the baby to her and blew her another kiss as he left.

Bridget hummed "Let It Snow, Let It Snow" as she

dressed Laela for the day. She put a cute little red corduroy jumper on her, put her back in the crib with some of her toys, and was brushing her own hair when her phone rang. She picked it up from the nightstand and answered it on the fifth ring.

"Merry Christmas, Sean," she said.

"Merry Christmas. Did I interrupt morning sex? Are you opening presents yet?" He chuckled.

"No, but I was just about to go help Iris finish making cinnamon rolls for breakfast, and then we're having presents. Yours will be late, but you have one on the way," she told him. "And, Sean, my mind is made up. I'm definitely staying in Texas."

"I went out to the cemetery this afternoon and put a few flowers on my grandma's grave. Since you aren't here, I laid a rose on your nana's and one between Deidre's and Jimmy's. I told them Merry Christmas from you and Laela," he said.

"Thank you." Her eyes welled up with tears.

"Don't worry, luv. I'm still your friend," he said.

"And I'll come visit when I can," Bridget promised.

"I'll be here. And now I'm going to the pub for one little nip of Jameson to toast my grandpa. He never was one much for roses." Sean chuckled. "Go have a Merry Christmas with your cowboy."

"I will," she said and they ended the call.

"I'll Be Home for Christmas" had just started playing on a CD player sitting on the counter when she made it to the kitchen.

"Good morning," Bridget said. "I would have been in here helping earlier if you had told me you were getting up early."

"Honey, let me have this one last hoorah." Iris crossed

the room and hugged her and the baby at the same time. "I get to do this one last Christmas with my boys, and who knows what will happen between now and next year."

"If you come to visit us for the holidays, you can do breakfast on Christmas anytime you want," Bridget said.

"That's why I love you. You remind me so much of Virgie, your nana. I love this song." Iris nodded toward the CD player sitting on the countertop. "I had the same one on cassette tape before CDs took their place. I really like my old vinyl records better, but I can't get this one on vinyl anymore. I play it every year and think of my Thomas. I dream of the day I can join him in eternity."

"Iris!" Bridget fussed. "You aren't sick, are you?"

"Hell, no!" Iris laughed out loud. "And I'm not in a big hurry, but I do dream of that day. He hasn't gone on into heaven yet, but he's waiting at the door so we can go in together. He's a patient man, so I don't have to worry about him. Besides, there's no time or clocks in heaven. And, young lady"—Iris shook a spoon at her—"from this day forth, you will call me Granny, not Iris."

"All right." Bridget smiled. "Granny, it is."

\* \* \*

Maverick had thought about romantic ways to propose all morning as he and Paxton fed the cattle and chopped through the ice on the stream so they could get to water. Maybe a fancy dinner or a quiet evening in front of the fireplace with champagne—God, he hated champagne! But he'd drink it to make it a special evening for her. At least he had lots of time to plan.

When he and his brother were finished with the chores, they drove back to the house, parked the car, and like two little boys, had a footrace to see who could get to the house first. Paxton beat him by a few feet, but Maverick didn't even mind, because he was the lucky one. Bridget was waiting for him when he got inside, and poor old Pax still had to find the love of his life.

The smell of fresh hot bread and cinnamon filled the whole house. When he made it past the utility room, he found Iris spreading a thick layer of icing on the tops of the cinnamon rolls that she'd just taken out of the oven. He scanned the room, looking for Bridget, but she was nowhere in sight.

"She took the baby back to her bedroom to change her nappy, if that's who you're lookin' for," Iris said.

Maverick washed his hands and headed in that direction. Bridget had just finished the diaper-changing job, and Laela was still in the crib when he slipped his arms around her waist and drew her back to his chest. "You look amazing this morning. You could be a model."

"In jeans and an old T-shirt from Saint Patty's Day?" She giggled. "Besides, I'm not tall enough to be a model. But flattery will get you anything you want." She turned around and wrapped her arms around his neck, moistened her lips with the tip of her tongue and raised up on her tiptoes to kiss him—long, lingering, and passionately.

"Anything?" he teased.

"I keep my promises," she said.

"Whew!" He wiped his brow in a dramatic gesture. "I'll have to remember that flattery is the way to your heart."

"No, cowboy, flattery is the way to my bedroom. It takes more than that to get into my heart, but you've already managed that, so you don't have to worry." She kissed him on the cheek.

Maverick figured there couldn't be a more romantic or

better moment in the world to propose than right then on Christmas Day. He took a step back and dropped down on one knee. "Bridget O'Malley, I truly believe that you are my soul mate, and that we not only belong together but we would be miserable apart. Will you marry me? I've tried to dream up a romantic place that would be just right, but nothing fits like this room where I first saw you for the second time. I love you. Please say yes." He reached into his pocket and brought out the little velvet box Iris had given him and popped it open. "My great-grandfather proposed to my great-grandmother with this ring. My grandfather proposed to Granny with it, and now, I want you to wear it to let the world know that you are engaged to me."

"Yes," she said simply and held out her hand.

He slipped the ring on her finger and wasn't surprised one bit when it fit perfectly. She stared at it for a long time before she said, "It's Ireland and Texas all together. I love it."

"We'll get a gold band to go with it for the wedding day, but there's no rush. That day is for you to decide." He tipped up her chin and kissed her.

"Da-da-da-da." Laela called out from the crib.

"Yes, baby girl, I'm going to be your daddy. No matter how many kids we have, you'll always be my firstborn." He picked her up from the crib.

Laela laid her head on his shoulder.

Maverick flashed a grin toward Bridget. "I think this means she knows exactly what I said. Let's go tell Granny and Paxton that we're engaged?"

"I love you, Maverick Callahan," she said. "And I want us to start out our new life together as husband and wife on the new year."

"I bet that can be arranged," Maverick said.

# Chapter Twenty-six

Bridget and Maverick stood before the preacher in their little church on New Year's Eve. Surrounded by loving family and neighbors, Bridget's only wish was that Nana and Deidre would know somehow that she and Laela were happy and had a good life ahead of them—and that she wouldn't forget her vows.

She wore a form-fitting white velvet dress that skimmed her knees. Instead of a veil, Alana had woven white baby roses and shamrocks in her hair, and she carried a bouquet of the same. Alana served as her maid of honor, and Paxton was Maverick's best man.

"Bridget Virginia O'Malley"—Maverick took her hands in his—"I loved you from the moment I laid eyes on you in the Shamrock Pub in Ireland. I didn't recognize it as love, because I'd never felt that before. I loved you the next time I saw you on the Callahan Ranch, here in Daisy, Texas. I recognized it and I fought against it. I love you today and forever. I give you my heart. That's not enough for all the happiness you've brought into my life. It's not enough, but I hand it over to you today, until death parts us," he said.

"Maverick Thomas Callahan"—she blinked back tears—"those were the most romantic, sweetest words I've ever heard spoken. And this is the man who couldn't find words to even talk to me?"

The congregation chuckled.

She went on, "I will protect and cherish your heart, and I give you mine. When I came to Texas it was broken and hurting. Today it's whole and happy, and it's yours from now through eternity. Death can't part us, my love. What we have is strong enough to last through all eternity."

The preacher wiped his eyes with a hanky. "Those are beautiful vows. I think all I need to do is to say, I now pronounce you man and wife. Maverick, you may kiss your bride."

Maverick bent her backward in a true Hollywood kiss that brought about applause from a packed church.

"And now, I present to you Mr. and Mrs. Maverick Callahan," the preacher said. "Alana and Matt Cleary would like to extend an invitation to everyone here to come on out to the Cleary Ranch for a combination wedding reception and New Year's Eve ranch party."

Bridget looked out at the congregation—Nana would be so glad that she'd found a church family. With Laela in her lap, Granny smiled up at her—Deidre would be happy that Laela not only had parents but also a lovely great-grandmother. The little Sunday school class was standing up, clapping their hands—Randy's finger started toward his nose and Lily Rose slapped it away.

Alana handed her bouquet back to her. Maverick took her by the hand, and together they walked down the aisle to a brand-new year ahead of them and a forever future.

* * *

The first thing Alana wanted them to do at the reception was cut the four-layered cake so that it could be served all throughout the evening. Bridget set the top layer aside to be frozen for the first anniversary celebration, and then cut a small slice. She fed a bite to Maverick, and then he did the same, but he got a small bit of icing on her lower lip. She picked up a napkin to wipe it off, but he reached out and closed his big hand around hers.

"I'll take care of that." He grinned as he leaned down and kissed away the icing.

. Everyone who'd gathered around gave them another round of applause.

"A toast"—Paxton raised his voice and his glass— "seems fitting this day to have an old Irish wedding blessing. Here's to you both, a beautiful pair: on the birthday of your love affair. Here's to the husband and here's to the wife; may yourselves be lovers for the rest of your life."

"Hear, hear!" Hud raised his glass.

After the applause died down, Paxton raised his glass to his brother, but he was looking straight at Bridget. "And here's to my brother, who is one lucky son of a gun. And may his wife always check to be sure who's standing under the mistletoe. Welcome to the Callahan family to both Bridget and Laela!"

Bridget pointed a finger at him. "Thank you for the toast and for the advice!"

Paxton grinned and took a drink of his champagne. "Seriously, we're glad to have you in the family."

She smiled and took a drink from her tall fluted glass. Alana touched her on the arm, and she expected another toast, but when she turned to see what her maid of honor might say, there was a red-haired woman standing be-side her.

"I want to introduce you to my good friend, Rose O'Malley. She stopped by to visit with me on her way over to Bowie, Texas. She and I are distant cousins, and it's been years since we've seen each other," Alana said. "And this is Bridget."

"I kind of crashed your wedding and this party." Rose smiled. "It was lovely."

Rose had gorgeous thick red hair that she'd braided over one shoulder. She was taller than Bridget but not nearly as tall as Alana. She had crystal-clear blue eyes that smiled when she talked, and a perfect complexion—peaches and cream, as Nana used to say—with only a few freckles sprin-kle across her nose.

"Thank you," Bridget said. "It started out as a courthouse wedding, but it kind of grew into this amazing event. It's a pleasure to meet you."

"Likewise," Rose said.

Hud took a step back and bumped into Bridget. "So sorry." He turned to apologize and his eyes widened. "Cactus Rose O'Malley?"

"Hello, Hud," she smiled.

"Y'all know each other?" Alana asked.

"We went to school together a year in Tulia after Daddy moved us from Daisy, and it's just Rose now," she said. "I never did like my first name."

"O'Malley?" Alana asked. "Are you related to Bridget? Her last name is O'Malley."

"Probably not," Bridget said. "O'Malley is as common in Ireland as Smith is in the U.S."

Hud was one of those six-foot cowboys with a swagger—not as much as his twin brother, Tag—but enough to make the women at the party practically drool.

He had dark hair and light green eyes, and a square face. Every bit of him screamed masculinity, but right then he looked like a little boy who'd just found a toy he'd lost.

"Where have you been all these years?" he asked.

"Here and there, but now I'm on my way to Bowie. My great-aunt owns a bed-and-breakfast and needs my help," she said. "I hear you're living in that area. Small world."

"Yes, ma'am, it is," he said.

Maverick touched Bridget on the shoulder. "It's time for our first dance as a married couple."

Violin music filled the house and then Shania Twain began to sing "From This Moment." Maverick waltzed Bridget around the small dance area. "I thought we were dancing to something different," he whispered.

"Surprise." She smiled up at him. "This is my song to you. It's always been a favorite of mine."

"It's perfect." He kissed her on the forehead. "And I love surprises."

When the song ended, Paxton brought out a microphone. "It's this time when the father of the bride would dance with his daughter. Bridget lost her dad when she was sixteen, but I know in my heart he would've loved to be here this day, so if she will allow me, there's a few of us who would like to step in for her dad." He laid the microphone on the table and held out his hand as the music started and Bob Carlisle sang "Butterfly Kisses."

With tears in her eyes, Bridget put her hand in his. "Daddy would have liked this. Thank you, Pax."

"We want today to be special," Paxton said.

After a few times around the floor, Tag tapped him on the shoulder and stepped into his place. "Mav is more than a friend. He's like a brother to me. If either of you ever need anything, I'm here for you both."

Bridget had given up even caring if the tears were washing away her makeup. "Thank you," she said. How did these guys know that her father had asked for a butterfly kiss every night when he was home and could tuck her in at night? Just as the lyrics said something about his little girl being sixteen and trying her wings out in a great big world, Hud took Tag's place in the dance.

"This song couldn't be more right," she whispered and looked up into his face. "What was that between you and Rose?"

"She was my first love, but that was a long time ago. We were just kids in junior high school," he answered.

Maverick tapped him on the shoulder, and Hud took a step back. Bridget looked up at her new husband, who had Laela in his arms. She melted into his free arm and they ended the song as a family just as the lyrics said that he must've done something right. "I love you, Mrs. Callahan."

"I love you," she said.

Alana picked up the microphone. "And now it's time to throw the garter and the bouquet. If we could have all the single guys on this side of the room and the single ladies over there." She pointed. "Maverick, can I hold the baby while you remove the garter?"

He handed Laela over to her and pulled out a chair for Bridget to sit in. While Kenny Chesney sang, "She Thinks My Tractor's Sexy," he danced all around her. She giggled as he inched the garter down a little at a time, then went back to dancing. Just before the last verse, Maverick slipped it off all the way, stood up, and pulled the elastic back with his thumb. Like popping a rubber band, he let it fly, and it landed right in Hud's hands.

Paxton patted him on the back. "Thank God, you're next and not me."

"That's not necessarily true." Hud slipped it on his upper arm and several people shot a picture of him and Maverick together.

"And now for the ladies," Alana said. "Bridget picked this song out special for this event."

"Whoa!" Granny and Wanda both yelled at the same time as they slowly made their way over to the group of single women. "Ain't neither one of us married, so y'all young women better get ready to fight experienced women for that bouquet."

"Now you can start the music," Iris said.

"And we thought you weren't going to be bossy anymore." Maverick laughed.

"Can't teach an old dog new tricks, or make them unlearn what they know," she shot back at him.

"I've Had the Time of My Life" started playing, and Bridget gave Maverick a dose of his own medicine. She'd watched *Dirty Dancing* a hundred times so she knew all the moves to the song and was shocked when Maverick did a fairly good job of keeping up. So her cowboy had a few surprises of his own. When the part came where he looked into her eyes and ran the back of his hand down her cheek, she said, "I really have had the time of my life and it's just beginning."

"Amen," he said as he swung her out. She picked up her bouquet and slung it over her shoulder. It landed in Rose's hands, and Bridget threw back her head and giggled. "Let's see what Mama Fate has in store for those two."

"I thought for sure Alana would fight for the bouquet," Maverick said.

"Can't fight fate," Bridget said. "We're proof."

"Thank God." He wrapped his arms around her and kissed her one more time.

PREORDER THE NEXT BOOK
IN THE LONGHORN CANYON SERIES,

**Cowboy Courage,**

COMING IN JANUARY 2020.

# *About the Author*

Carolyn Brown is a *New York Times* and *USA Today* bestselling romance author and RITA® Finalist who has sold more than three million books. She presently writes both women's fiction and cowboy romance. She has also written historical single title, historical series, contemporary single title, and contemporary series. She lives in southern Oklahoma with her husband, a former English teacher, who is not allowed to read her books until they are published. They have three children and enough grandchildren to keep them young.

For more information you can visit:
CarolynBrownBooks.com
Facebook.com/CarolynBrownBooks
Instagram.com/CarolynBrownBooks
Twitter @TheCarolynBrown

# *Rocky Mountain Cowboy Christmas*

## Sara Richardson

When bullfighter Tucker McGrath's mom suffers a minor heart attack just before Christmas, he agrees to take her place in the town's annual Christmas pageant. But wrangling a bull sure is easier than directing a bunch of kiddos! There's also the temptation of his former high school heartthrob, Kenna Hart, who just so happens to be the pageant's music director. Kenna's still reeling from a devastating divorce, and she knows Tucker "No-Strings-Attached" McGrath is not worth falling for, but the more time she spends with him, the more she realizes how he's changed. And now he might just be the cowboy who can make all of her Christmas wishes come true.

Keep reading for a bonus novella
by Sara Richardson!

**FOREVER**

New York   Boston

# Chapter One

"Jingle bells, Batman smells, Robin laid an—"

"I'm not sure that's the best song to sing right before we get ready to tell the Christmas story." Kenna Hart pulled up in front of the old Episcopal church that now served as the town hall and winked at her boys in the rearview mirror. "We need to be on our best behavior for the rehearsal."

"Okay." Benny and Jake looked at each other with a shrug before breaking out into song again. "Grandma got run over by a reindeer..."

Shaking her head, Kenna took her time parallel parking the Jeep along the snowy curb.

Outside the car's frosted windows, the sights and sounds of Christmas gave the town that magical snow-globe ambiance. Farther down Main Street, garlands were strung above the road, anchored to wrought-iron lampposts adorned with red velvet bows. Since it was nearly dusk, the lights displayed on the storefront windows were just starting to come on, with some twinkling in different colors while others gave off a more traditional white-light welcome.

She tried to take a minute to appreciate it—to let that cheer all around her soak in and lift her spirits, but the decorations weren't enough to nudge the burdens of the last year off her shoulders.

"Come on, Mom!" Her oldest son Jake released his seat belt. "We've gotta get our costumes on and get in there!"

"Yeah!" four-year-old Benny added. "What if they start without us?"

Her son's enthusiasm warmed her heart. He'd been looking forward to being part of this pageant for over a month now. Her youngest had always been so shy, but with everything that had gone on over the last several months, he had grown even more timid, almost like he didn't want to connect with anyone because he feared they wouldn't stick around. But now it finally seemed he was starting to come out of his shell, and she had to do everything she could to fuel his excitement about getting up on that stage.

"They can't start without us." Not when she was volunteering to help with the music. Birdie McGrath had run the pageant for decades, and as the local music teacher, Kenna had always loved helping out. But that was before.

Before her husband had committed eight counts of felony insurance fraud, cheating people in town out of their hard-earned money. Before his conviction. Before the divorce. Before the financial troubles that had plagued her since. Before her life had fallen apart, Kenna had lived for the holidays—for the family time and the festivities and the charming small-town celebration that seemed to give Christmas even more meaning. But this year, all she wanted to do was hide from the pitying looks and the whispers and those overly empathetic expressions people gave her when they asked if she was doing "okay."

She didn't even know what *okay* meant anymore.

"Mooooommmm." Jake squeezed through the space between the two front seats and tumbled into the passenger's seat. "Can we please, please, please hurry?" Instead of puppy-dog eyes, his were more like a fawn's—big and bright and always overly emphatic. "I've been waiting my whole life to be a wise guy."

"You were born a wise guy," she teased, ruffling his blond hair. Which had turned out to be a blessing. Somehow, through the darkness that had descended over the last year, her boys' humor and laughter had lit her way. They had been resilient and patient and strong, and even if she wasn't feeling Christmas, she still had to make this the greatest one they'd ever had because they deserved her best. So she got out of the car. "All right, you two." She helped them climb down onto the icy sidewalk and then located the bag that held their costumes. They were both simple—a white robe and halo for Benny, who would be part of the angel choir, and a shimmery satin cape and crown for her little wise guy.

"There." She finished tying the knot on Benny's robe and stood back to admire her children. "It's really not fair to the other actors," she said, frowning.

Jake's eyes looked worried. "What's not fair?" As the oldest, he was the fair police.

"How cute you two are," she fussed, even wrinkling her nose as she lightly pinched his cheek. The inevitable groans came at her.

"Mom, I'm seven," Jake grumbled. "You can't call me cute anymore. Especially not in front of anyone else."

"Yeah," Benny agreed, crossing his arms over his chest in a harrumph, but his smile still beamed.

Before she could snap a picture, both boys bounded straight for the doors, right across the knee-deep snow that covered the hall's front lawn. "You're not wearing your boots," she reminded them, but even the snow couldn't slow them down. Within seconds, they had disappeared into the building.

Kenna, however, took her time navigating the icy walkway. As she approached the door, it flew open and Carly Lammers marched out. Just her luck. Kenna had had Carly's daughter Violet in music class last year and the woman was seemingly perfect in every way—from her sleek black always perfectly styled hair to her $500 thigh-length Frye boots. Her husband happened to be a pediatrician in Vail, and she was always showing off the new necklace or bracelet or earrings he'd brought her from one of the high-end shops that catered to tourists in the famous ski town.

"Kenna!" No matter what was going on, Carly always greeted Kenna with a worried expression, like she feared Kenna might break down in tears any second. "How *are* you?" The woman rested a hand on her shoulder, her silvery manicured nails shimmering from the light of the streetlamp a few feet away. She didn't wait for an answer. "It's so good to see you here. I know this has to be such a difficult time of year for you."

She didn't know. How could she know? Carly would spend Christmas with her husband and kids. She wasn't struggling to buy the presents her kids had been writing letters to Santa about for the better part of three months. "Well, actually—"

"It must be *so* hard being a single mom over the holidays," Carly went on. "I can't imagine! With all the events and parties and errands. How awful to have to go to everything *alone*."

Kenna didn't bother telling her she didn't plan to go to any of the events and parties this year. Not because she'd be alone but because of conversations exactly like this one. She'd been doing the *poor Kenna* song and dance routine far too long and she was tired of it.

The woman reached out and squeezed Kenna's hand. "You be sure to let me know if there's anything I can do for you, okay? Anything at all. I'm happy to help."

"Thank you." She put on a worn-out smile. "We're okay right now, but I'll definitely let you know if I need anything." She wouldn't. Carly wasn't exactly a good friend.

"You do that!" Carly swept past her, wiggling her fingers in a wave. "Toodles!"

Still holding her smile intact, Kenna gave her a silent wave and let go of her misplaced anger. It wasn't that she didn't appreciate people's concern. After the shock of Mike's deception, people in town had done their best to be supportive. But instead of dwelling on all of the horrible things that happened—instead of making *her* dwell on it— she wished everyone would start giving her high fives rather than looking at her and talking to her like she was a wounded puppy.

She tried to picture Carly giving her a high five and telling her what she needed to hear instead of what she didn't want to remember. *That last year really must've sucked, but you made it through! You owned that difficult time—way to go! Look how strong you are! After getting through that, you can get through anything!*

A real smile broke out as she let herself into the town hall. At least she'd know what to do next time one of her friends went through hell.

Warmth engulfed her the second she stepped into the foyer. Kids crowded the cramped entryway, giggling and screeching and basically bouncing off the walls the same way they had at school lately. Benny and Jake were right in there with the rest of them, competing for the loudest voice award.

"Kenna!" Birdie McGrath ambled over. From her dangling jingle bell earrings to her tinsel-accented sweater to the shiny red tennis shoes on her feet, the woman had enough spirit to fill the entire room with Christmas cheer. She could've easily passed for Mrs. Claus, too, with her comfortably round build, pink cheeks, and nest of white hair.

"Hi, Birdie." Kenna returned the woman's hug, hoping her shortage of passion didn't show. With her own mother so far away, she lingered an extra second in the embrace, somehow feeling a bit stronger.

The woman pulled back and looked her over. "You're looking positively lovely today. Have you done something different with your hair?"

"I have, actually. I had it cut and highlighted last week." Originally, she'd hoped to cut off some of the lingering sadness along with her hair, but it hadn't quite worked out that way. Still, it felt good to embrace a new style, to focus on the future instead of the past.

"Well I love it." The woman fluffed the ends of Kenna's hair, completely ignoring the chaos around them as though Birdie knew how important it was to take a few minutes to connect with her. "That gorgeous color really brings out your eyes. I'm telling you what, you'd best watch out. Next thing you know, you're going to be fending off all the eligible bachelors in town."

While she appreciated the sentiment, Kenna didn't think she'd have to worry about that. Not one eligible bachelor had looked in her direction in a very long time. She didn't blame them. They likely saw her the same way Carly did—as damaged goods. Still, it was sweet of Birdie to say. And she was a woman who obviously understood heartbreak. Her own husband had walked out on the family a good fifteen years ago, leaving Birdie to raise her teenaged son and daughter on her own. Kenna had been in high school then, so she didn't know exactly what had happened, but folks in town said Mr. McGrath had taken off right after his wife had been diagnosed with lupus.

"Speaking of eligible bachelors, there's my Tucker." Birdie's hand fluttered toward the doors, waving happily. "Over here!" she called.

Tucker McGrath sauntered across the room, a large presence in such a confined space. Kenna had known of him in school—he'd been a few years ahead of her—but they'd run in completely different circles, though she couldn't deny she'd noticed him. All the girls had.

He'd always been kind of an enigma in her mind—popular with women but quiet about it, good-looking but at the same time seemingly unconcerned with his appearance. Most of the girls in high school had agreed that his eyes were his best feature—grayish blue and nothing short of magnetic. All of him happened to be magnetic, actually, despite Kenna's best efforts not to notice. He had one of those smoldering faces, tanned skin, and a sharp-angled jaw complete with cowboy scruff. Tonight he'd traded in his Stetson for a stocking cap, which somehow made him look more approachable than he usually did. Not that she would be approaching him about anything.

"Who unleashed the lunatics?" he asked, glancing around at the kids with an amused glint lighting those eyes.

Kenna had never noticed how rich his voice sounded—deep and slow, full of a straightforward confidence.

"Oh, they're just excited." Birdie brushed away the kids' raucous volume with a wave of her hand. "It's almost Christmas after all! And they can't wait to see the new set you're going to build for the pageant." She patted Tucker's cheek like she would a little boy.

Ah, so that's why he'd come. As far as she'd heard, Tucker didn't love Christmas nearly as much as his mom did. Rumor had it, he'd once vandalized the town's Christmas display, taking all of the reindeer and sticking them into Porta-Potties at construction sites all over town. Of course, that was back in high school, so she couldn't judge him for it now.

"Tucker, you remember Kenna, I'm sure." Birdie's eyes held the same glimmer as her son's. "Didn't you two go to high school together?"

The cowboy's eyes met hers, revealing nothing other than a vague recollection. "Sure. Yeah. You were a few years behind me, right?"

Two years. She'd been two years behind him, and it had been a sad day for every girl at Topaz Falls High when he'd graduated. She played down the memory with a shrug. "Think so. Sounds about right."

"Oh perfect! Then you two can catch up while I get organized." Birdie made a quick scan of the room, grimacing in the direction of two boys who were playing football with the baby Jesus. "Max and Luke—you two stop that right now!" She backed away with an apologetic look at Kenna. "I'll just go open up the sanctuary. Hopefully we'll be ready to get started in a few minutes."

"Sure," Kenna said, though she'd rather get started right now than stand here with Tucker McGrath. God only knew what he'd heard about her situation.

"You were the girl who took around that petition,"

Tucker said as if it had just come back to him. "The petition about that football player who'd assaulted his girlfriend and was still allowed to play in the game that weekend."

So he did remember her. He'd remembered something she'd almost forgotten. "Yeah. That was me." The assault had happened her sophomore year, when he'd been a senior. It had caused quite the controversy at Topaz Falls High, with some of the kids threatening her for ruining their hopes of a winning season.

"That was pretty badass." He gave her a nod of respect. "I signed it. I remember. You marched up to me and basically didn't give me a choice."

"I was pretty passionate about it." Looking back, it was almost hard to believe she'd ever been that brave. To approach a senior—Tucker McGrath, no less—and demand he sign her petition. She couldn't help but laugh. "You could've refused. I couldn't have done much about it." Even back then, he'd been tall and muscular. Her gaze momentarily fell to his broad chest. He'd hardly changed at all.

A thoughtful look gave the corners of his eyes a slight crinkle. "I didn't want to refuse. I was impressed. Not everyone has that kind of grit. Seems to me it's served you well."

Maybe he hadn't meant it as an insinuation about the last year of her life, but something in his eyes hinted that it might be. He didn't give her that look she'd come to hate—the one that said all he could see were the terrible things that had happened to her. Instead, his face projected more of an impressed smirk, like he still saw that brave girl standing in front of him, even though Kenna had forgotten all about her.

# Chapter Two

This was the point in a conversation where Tucker would usually ask a woman out.

He and Kenna Hart had been reminiscing about their high school days for well over a half hour while his mom had herded the kids into their groups and led them into the town hall's sanctuary, where she sat them in neat rows. They'd both offered their help, but she had a system, and no one could mess with Birdie's sense of order. Well, that and he suspected his sweet mama didn't think it was such a bad idea for him to be chatting up Kenna Hart.

If it hadn't been for what Kenna had gone through in the last year, he might agree with his mom, but he couldn't ask the woman out. (A) She likely wouldn't be interested in going anyway, given the hell her ex-husband had recently put her through. And (B) she didn't exactly fit his criteria for the casual, no-strings arrangement he typically preferred.

He couldn't deny that Kenna was a real stunner—with

shoulder-length hair the color of mahogany and delicate skin that made her green eyes stand out, but the two of them lived in different worlds—she was fully immersed in the young suburbia family scene while he maintained a detached freedom on the small ranch he'd purchased near the Cortez place, where he worked as manager.

"I guess I'd better head over to the piano so I can get organized too." Kenna's smile landed somewhere between shy and cautious. "It was nice talking to you."

Surprisingly, it had been nice. To hear everyone in town talk, Kenna was barely hanging on after the divorce, but that wasn't how it seemed to him. She'd held up her end of the conversation and had even smiled and laughed some. Tucker gave her a nod. "I'm sure we'll be seeing more of each other, working on the pageant and all." Which would be tricky given the way he could tell his mom's hopes were growing bigger and bigger every time she looked in their direction.

Not gonna happen.

"See you around, then." Kenna ducked away and headed for the right side of the stage, where they'd set up the baby grand piano earlier.

His mom now stood on the center of the stage, addressing the kids, so Tucker headed for the vestibule where he'd stashed the tools and wood scraps he'd need to build the new set. Thankfully, that would keep him too busy to spend much more time getting any fancy ideas about Kenna. His mom wanted him to build a stable from scratch, complete with a bright star fashioned out of twinkling Christmas lights. He'd already drawn up some plans, but he'd have to measure the stage to see exactly how this would work.

In the hallway, he dug through one of his tool chests until he found a measuring tape and then headed back to the sanctuary. He stepped through the doors right as the music started. Kenna sat at the piano, her shoulders straight and tall, eyes focused on sheet music in front of her while her hands moved effortlessly over the keys.

Damn, she really was a beautiful woman. And off-limits, he reminded himself with a grunt. She taught music at an elementary school. She had a couple of kids. A mortgage. A woman like her would likely want a guarantee once she was ready to think about a relationship again. And he sure as hell wasn't a guarantee.

"She's very talented, isn't she?" his mom whispered. She must've snuck up behind him when he'd had his eyes on the forbidden fruit.

"She can play, that's for sure." He glanced sideways at his mom's face, trying to get a read on how long she'd been watching him watch Kenna.

"And she's such a sweet girl," his mom prompted. "Single too now, you know."

And nice. Too nice for him. He turned to the stage, blocking out his mom's not-so-subtle hints. "Do you want the stable to cover the whole stage? I thought we could put the risers for the angel choir over there." He pointed to the side opposite the piano.

Disappointment pinched the corners of her mouth, but she seemed to let it go. "Whatever you think is fine, son. You're the expert. I'd better get up there and direct these kids. They're not even singing in the right key." She took a step away from him but seemed to wobble, and then stopped suddenly.

He reached out to steady her. "You okay?"

"Of course." She shook her head and smiled like she did every time she thought he was being ridiculous. "I'm fine. My knee's been acting up lately."

He narrowed his gaze, looking for anything that would dispute that statement. "You sure that's all it is?"

"I'm sure." She patted his arm. "Goodness, you really shouldn't worry so much. It's not good for you, you know."

Tucker studied his mom. Did her face look pale? She hadn't had a bad lupus flare-up for nearly two years, but it wasn't outside the realm of possibility. "Maybe you should sit down." He took her arm, but she wriggled away.

"Sit down?" she huffed. "We only have three weeks of rehearsals. I'm *fine*." She marched up the stage steps with purpose as though she wanted to prove it. "All right, kids." She clapped her hands and Kenna stopped playing. "That sounded good, but I think we can make it even better."

Tucker kept his eyes on her while she conducted the kids in an off-key rendition of "Go Tell It on the Mountain." No more wobbling, so that was a good sign. Still, he'd have to make her set up an appointment with her doctor in the next few days. He couldn't remember the last time she'd been in for a checkup, and those flare-ups could come without warning.

His mom caught him watching her and shooed him away. Right. He'd better get going on that stable. Tucker whipped the measuring tape out of his back pocket and sauntered over to the stage, doing his best to stay on the outskirts so he didn't become a distraction. He quickly took the measurements he needed and retreated to the storage room where he'd stashed more of his supplies.

The cramped room was filled with random crap—props and fake plants and signs for just about every festival Topaz Falls celebrated throughout the year. Then there was the wood he'd laid out earlier. He'd need a couple more 4x4s to build the stable's posts, and—

"Whatcha doin'?"

The tiny voice came from the doorway. Tucker turned around and watched a little boy with blond hair walk in. Kenna's youngest son if he wasn't mistaken. He'd seen them at the Farm Café a few times. Cute kid. "I'm getting ready to build a new stable for the play," he said, walking over. "What're you doing?"

The kid quickly looked down at the floor like he knew he wasn't currently doing what he should be. "I saw you by the stage," he nearly whispered. "With that measure thing. I wanted to know what it was."

"It's my measuring tape." Tucker took a knee next to him and pulled it out of his back pocket. "See? That's how I know how big to build the new stable. All these numbers show me." He offered it to the boy.

"Wow." He took it from Tucker's hand and carefully pulled out the tape a few times before handing it back. "I'm Benny," he said, his voice seeming to gain confidence.

"Benny, huh?" Tucker stuck the measuring tape back in his pocket and stood. "I thought you were an angel."

"My mom calls me angel sometimes." Benny's mouth perked into a shy grin. "I'm not an angel all the time, though."

Could've fooled him with that grin and curly blond hair. "Well I'll bet you're real good at singing," Tucker said. "In fact, why don't we go back to the stage so I can hear you sing?" Before his mom realized he was gone and got all worried.

"Okay," Benny agreed, holding out his hand like he wanted Tucker to take it. That was a first. He didn't know if it was his height or his gruffness that held kids off, but they usually didn't warm up to him so quickly. Tucker's hand seemed to swallow up Benny's when he took it. So small and fragile. He looked down at the kid, struck with a sudden instinct to protect him.

"I can't wait to see what you build," Benny said as they walked back down the hallway side by side. "This is gonna be the best pageant ever. I didn't get to be in it last year. We had to go to California for Christmas." He looked up at Tucker and made a face. "There wasn't even any snow there."

"No snow?" Tucker shook his head. "What kind of Christmas is that?"

"I know!" The kid stopped before they reached the doors to the sanctuary. "But this year, we get to be home. And we get to do all the Christmassy stuff. Even the pageant. It's the most important thing."

That was surprising. Didn't every kid think Santa was the most important part of Christmas? "Why is the pageant so important?" Tucker couldn't quit smiling at the enthusiasm that seemed to light the boy up from the inside.

"Because it's been kind of lonely." Benny's voice quieted. "With my daddy gone. But at the pageant, we get to be with all our friends and so many people and everyone is happy. That's the best part about Christmas. Everyone being together."

The words inflicted a niggling pain that slipped beneath Tucker's ribs. He remembered that after his dad left. The loneliness. But instead of seeking out connections with people like Benny seemed to being doing, he'd shut down that part of himself.

"So what's your favorite Christmas song to sing?" Benny tugged on his hand and started toward the doors.

"Oh. Uh…" Tucker couldn't remember the last time he'd sung a Christmas song. "Well, I guess it would have to be 'Santa Claus Is Comin' to Town.'" At least that's what it had been when he was a kid.

Benny's eyes got even bigger. "That's mine too!" He

broke out into song, hitting all the right notes, while Tucker led him into the sanctuary.

Instead of music and singing, the room was complete pandemonium. All of the kids were gathered around the stage, and some of them were crying.

What the—

"Find Tucker!" Kenna yelled from where she crouched on her knees in the center of the stage.

As a couple of kids dashed to follow her instruction, he saw his mom lying on the floor next to Kenna.

It took him a second to move, to let go of Benny's hand and sprint down the aisle. He stumbled up the steps to where his mom lay and knelt across from Kenna, but his throat burned too hot to speak.

"She collapsed," Kenna said, her voice shaky. "I've called an ambulance. They're on their way." She held his mom's hand in both of hers. "I feel a pulse. It's weak, but I still feel it."

Tucker nodded, everything blurred and slow and surreal. He touched his mom's forehead. "Mom. Wake up." He should've known she wasn't okay. He should've made her sit down. Or better yet, he should've taken her right to the hospital.

Sirens whined in the distance, but he couldn't do anything while they waited. He couldn't help her, couldn't fix anything when he didn't know what was wrong.

"Kids..." Kenna looked up at the crowd surrounding them. "I need you to give us some space. Okay? The paramedics will be here in a minute and we need space. Please go sit in your seats. Everything will be fine."

Tucker latched on to those words as the kids slowly scattered. Everything would be fine. His mom would be fine.

"Hold on, Mom," he murmured over her. She had to hold on.

# Chapter Three

Snow blew against the car, nearly covering Kenna's windshield before the wiper blades could clear it again. Even with the four-wheel-drive on in her Jeep, the tires skidded and fishtailed on the icy road, but she was determined to make it to the hospital.

Somehow she'd managed to pull herself together enough to get the kids through the last half hour of rehearsal until their parents showed up. They were all traumatized after witnessing Birdie collapse, so Kenna had invited them to gather in a circle and they'd each shared what they liked best about Ms. McGrath. The kids had gone on and on about her singing voice and her hugs and happy smile. They'd talked about her love for Christmas and about how she always gave them special presents the night of the pageant.

When little Sam had asked if she was going to die, Kenna had told them not to worry, that the doctors were taking care of Birdie and everything would be okay.

But she didn't know that for sure. She'd tried to call the hospital but no one would tell her anything because she wasn't family.

Oh this damn snow. It was taking her twice as long to get to the hospital as it should. She pushed the gas pedal just a smidge harder since Jake and Benny weren't in the car with her.

When the parents had started to stream in to pick up their kids, Kenna had called her dear friends Mateo and Everly Torres and asked if they could pick up the boys and take them to their house for a while. She didn't know what she'd find at the hospital, but she didn't want Jake and Benny any more upset than they already were.

A round of hot, stinging tears only added to the terrible visibility outside the windshield. She couldn't stop thinking about Tucker, about how brittle his voice had sounded as they were loading his mom onto the stretcher, how hollow his eyes had looked when he'd followed her down the aisle. He'd gone from big strong cowboy to lost little boy in the matter of a few seconds.

Kenna swallowed back the tears. Birdie had to be okay. She couldn't quite imagine Topaz Falls—*Christmas* in Topaz Falls—without her.

Finally the hospital came into view on the right. She slowed way down to turn into the parking lot, which was mostly deserted considering the terrible weather. Without bothering to pull on her hat and gloves, she grabbed the keys from the ignition and climbed out of the car, shielding her face from the pelting snowflakes. Trudging through shin-deep snow, she blazed a path to the emergency room entrance and rushed through the doors.

Only a couple of people sat in the waiting room, and she suddenly wasn't sure what to do. It wasn't like she was family. Maybe Tucker wouldn't even want her here. Still, she had to do something, so she approached the reception desk, which was decorated with festive garlands and peppermint candies. Just as she was about to ask the receptionist for an update on Birdie, Tucker strode by, heading for the doors that led back to the exam rooms.

"Wait!" She called, chasing him down. Her hair was wet from the snow, sticking to her forehead, and her makeup was probably running, too, but that didn't matter. "Tucker! How's your mom?"

It seemed to take a minute for him to recognize her. He blinked a few times. "Oh. You came."

"Of course I came. Birdie is—" Well what could she say without bursting into tears? His mom was an inspiration to her, walking proof that there was life after betrayal. Not just life, but happiness too. "Birdie means a lot to me. And to the kids. I wanted to check on her. Is she going to be okay?"

He didn't answer right away. Instead he darted a quick look at his phone before slipping it into his pocket. "She has myocarditis. Inflammation of the heart muscle brought on by a lupus flare."

Oh God. That sounded bad. He sounded bad. Tired and crushed.

"She also had a minor heart attack," he went on. "But she's stable now." That didn't appear to give him much comfort, though.

A group of loud talkers passed by them, so Kenna tugged him to a quiet corner. "What's the prognosis?" she asked, barely holding her voice together.

He slumped against the wall. "She needs to rest. They'll keep her here while they try some new therapies for the inflammation and the lupus. But she can't do anything, even after she gets out. She'll have to take it easy for at least a month."

Okay. The tightness in her chest loosened some. It still sounded serious, but Birdie was going to make it. "She's not going to want to take it easy. Especially with the pageant three weeks away." If they weren't careful, Birdie would sneak out of the hospital so she could be at the next rehearsal. "We'll have to cancel. That way she won't be tempted to rush her recovery."

Tucker's expression grew even more pained. "We're not canceling. She made me promise to direct the pageant. In the ambulance when she came to. I couldn't tell her no." He brought a hand to his head like he was trying to knead away a headache. "But I have no idea what the hell I'm doing. I can't direct a play. With singing. And acting. And thirty wild kids..." He stared at the blank wall across from them as though he were watching a horror film.

She almost laughed. Yes, managing the pageant could definitely be overwhelming, but he wouldn't have to do it alone. "Maybe you can't do it, but we could. Together."

He suddenly angled his head to stare at her. "Together?"

For some reason he made that sound like a bad thing. "Sure. If you want my help, that is." It wouldn't be any picnic for her either, working side by side with a cowboy who'd once starred in a few of her racier teenaged dreams, but what could it hurt? It's not like Tucker would ever be interested in someone like her anyway. If memory served, he'd gravitated toward the younger, freer female demographic as opposed to mommies over thirty. Actually, that's what made it so perfect. There would be no expectations on either side. "What do you think?" she asked. "Are we partners?"

"Yeah." Something about the way Tucker's gaze slowly drifted over her made her wish she'd actually changed her clothes and brushed her hair after her wild day work. "I guess we are."

\*     \*     \*

The second Tucker showed up outside his mom's hospital room, the guilt closed in, lodging itself right above his gut. He'd almost lost her last night. Seeing her lifeless on the floor had triggered something in him. Enough screwing around. He'd wasted years avoiding her favorite holiday when he could've been making memories with her. That would stop now. He plowed through the door, driven by the need to fix things so he could shed the regrets.

"Tucker!" His mom set down her knitting and cleared a space for him on the bed next to her. "What're you doing here so early?" she asked, tipping her bifocals to the edge of her nose like she wanted to get a better look at him. For having had a cardiac episode last night, she sure looked healthy. Her eyes were bright and her hair had even been combed. That made sense considering she had half of her house here in the hospital room with her. Even while the doctors were still evaluating her in the ER, she'd written Tucker a neat list of everything she wanted him to bring her from home. After she was stable, he'd made two trips and he still hadn't gotten everything.

"You look like you hardly slept, son." Birdie leaned forward, her eyes channeling concern.

"Of course I didn't sleep." He sat on the bed beside her. "I'm worried about you." He would've stayed right by her bedside all night if she hadn't kicked him out at midnight for being "too tense."

"There's absolutely nothing to worry about," she assured him, picking up her yarn and needles again. "I'm really feeling much better this morning. After some antibiotics and a few more treatments, I'll be good as new. Hopefully in time for Christmas."

Not hopefully...he would make sure. "Christmas is exactly what I wanted to talk to you about."

"Christmas?" Her hands lowered to her lap, taking the needles and yarn with them. "Oh. Right. I know you'll be busy, dear." She made a valiant effort to seem upbeat, but he didn't miss how much her smile wobbled. "That's okay. I love helping out at the assisted living place. They don't get nearly enough volunteers there on Christmas, so I can spend the whole day serving food and visiting with the residents like I did last year. It really was such fun."

Yet again, she was letting him off the hook for Christmas. He'd always made it a point to volunteer at the Cortez Ranch on Christmas. It had seemed better to keep busy than to dwell on the fun memories his dad had left him with, but this year he'd step up. "You're not volunteering, Mom." He waited until her eyes met his. "Because we're going to celebrate Christmas together." He was going to make up for all those years he'd blown off her favorite holiday.

"What do you mean celebrate?" He recognized the skepticism in her voice. After fifteen years of not sitting down to one Christmas dinner with her, she obviously didn't have high hopes. "How would we celebrate?"

He had no damn clue how, but this wasn't the first time he'd had to pull answers out of his ass. "Well...we'll have a dinner. I'll cook. Turkey, mashed potatoes, that green bean stuff you like. The whole shebang." Not that he had any clue how to make that stuff. He'd have to enlist help from Everly Torres. "And we'll get presents," he went on, prodded by her growing smile. "Lots of presents." One for every Christmas he'd missed.

"Tucker." She took his hand, her eyes glistening. "I don't care about the presents. Just the fact that we'll be spending the day together this year is enough."

That blade of guilt still lodged under his ribs twisted. "I should've been home every year. I'm sorry I wasn't."

"Forget it," she said, abandoning her knitting so she could squeeze both of his hands. "It's this year that matters. Oh, we'll have such fun!" She let out a gasp. "Maybe we should invite Kenna and her boys! I don't know that they have anywhere to go for the holiday."

"Oh." No. Inviting Kenna to share Christmas with them was a bad idea. "I'm sure they already have plans. She has friends." And he would already be spending enough time pretending the woman didn't affect his heart rate now that they were co-directing the play. When she'd shown up at the hospital last night, he'd felt that spark, the one that had pinged back and forth between them when they'd chatted at the rehearsal. Only difference was it had gotten stronger. Granted, he'd been kind of a wreck, so maybe that was why it had hit him so hard. He'd been mighty tempted to decline her offer to help with the pageant but he couldn't pull off something of that magnitude by himself. "I'm sure Kenna won't want to come to Christmas dinner."

"And why is that?" His mother eyed him, but he looked away. "You said she offered to help you with the pageant."

"Yeah, but she's real busy. With the kids and everything." He racked his brain to come up with additional excuses.

"That's even more reason to invite them," his mom insisted. "She deserves to have someone make her a nice meal. And think of the joy those boys would bring into my house."

Tucker thought about Benny, about how open and curious he was, about how he'd reached out and grabbed Tucker's hand without a thought. "I don't know if it's a good idea." Benny had already kind of latched on to him at the rehearsal. Not that he'd minded, but he didn't want to disappoint the kid. He wasn't exactly qualified to become someone's hero. "It'd probably be best if it was just us."

His mom's mouth pursed in blatant disagreement. "Best for you, maybe." Her fierce gaze gave him nowhere to hide. "Why won't you let yourself get close to anyone, Tucker?"

What would be the point? Right now, he had what he needed without opening himself up for more disappointment. He didn't rely on anyone else and no one relied on him. Life was less complicated that way. But he wasn't prepared to discuss any of that with his mom.

His silence didn't seem to deter her. "I know your father hurt you, but he wasn't all bad. In fact, you remind me of him in so many ways."

That was the last thing he wanted to hear right now.

"Really, son. Don't you remember? He could be such fun. He always made us laugh. Never took things too seriously."

"Yeah, and he walked out." Tucker stood. He couldn't sit here and reminisce about a man he wanted nothing do with. And he sure as hell didn't want to hear about their similarities.

Determination steeled his mom's eyes. "What is it going to take for you to forgive him, son?"

"I don't know," he said honestly.

She accepted the avoidance with a nod. "Then I think maybe it's time for you to figure that out."

# Chapter Four

By the time Kenna pulled up in front of town hall, Tucker had already unloaded the rest of the supplies they'd need to finish building the set—paint, lumber, tools. He'd stacked everything on a rolling cart and was pushing it up the sidewalk.

"Sorry I'm late," she called, climbing out of the Jeep. She almost gave him an explanation but thought better of revealing that she'd changed her clothes three times before she'd left the house. Hopefully the jeans and sweater she'd settled on didn't scream *I'm trying too hard*. It's not like she was nervous to be working alone with him, exactly. More like...aware. It was high time for her to start projecting a new image of herself. Instead of Poor Kenna, she wanted to be seen as Capable Kenna. If their conversation at the hospital had been any indication, Tucker wasn't thrilled about the prospect of working with her, probably because he assumed she was still the weak, sad, charity case everyone made her out to be. So tonight she'd show him that simply wasn't true.

"You're not that late." Instead of looking at her, Tucker paused to organize the paint cans on the cart into neat rows, and then started toward the building again.

Yeah, he definitely didn't look happy to see her, but she'd prove that she could be an asset in this partnership. She might not have stellar construction skills, but she could learn. "Wait up." She followed behind him, and then awkwardly bumped past him and accidentally stepped on his toe in her haste to open the door.

Okay, *asset* might be too strong a word…

"Thanks." His gaze hardly grazed hers and he maneuvered the cart inside. Without a glance back, he continued on down the hall.

After being so chatty the other night before his mom collapsed, he'd sure clammed up all of a sudden. Kenna had heard Birdie was doing well these last couple of days, but maybe Tucker was still worried.

Once they'd made it into the auditorium, he bent to unload the items from the cart onto the floor. The flannel shirt he wore crept up his back, revealing a peek of tanned, hard flesh—cowboy muscle all tawny and knotted. The very tips of her cheeks blazed with a sudden heated rush that reached the tops of her ears.

What was wrong with her? It was only his back. It had simply been too long since she'd allowed herself the luxury of looking at a man, appreciating a man's body. And Tucker had plenty to appreciate.

"So what's the plan?" She peeled off her coat and tossed it onto a nearby pew, hoping that would cool her off.

"Well, I was thinking we could build the new risers over there." Tucker pointed out the left wing of the stage. "And the wooden stable structure can go in the middle." He rummaged through the pile of supplies until he lifted a box that was overflowing with white globe lights.

"What are those for?"

"Mom thought they'd add something to the set." He jogged up the stage steps. "She wants us to string them along the frame of the stable to add more light."

Seeing an opening for more friendly conversation, she walked up to the steps to join him. "How is your mom anyway?"

"She's better." He leaned over and set the box on the floor, flashing that muscular part of his lower back again. "Still on antibiotics, and there's still some inflammation, but the doctors are happy with her progress." He wouldn't look at Kenna directly.

Did she really annoy him that much?

"That's great." Kenna tried to shake off the awkwardness crowding the air between them. She was likeable, damn it. Why wouldn't he look at her like he'd looked at her when he brought up the whole petition thing the night Birdie had reintroduced them? "So this should be fun," she said, trying again. "Working on the set. Hammering stuff, and..." Well, she didn't know exactly what else it took to build a stable.

Tucker finally turned to face her fully. "Look, I can handle the set by myself. It's fine. Really. I don't need help if you have somewhere else to be."

Ha. Didn't he know what she'd been through over the last year? "Somewhere else?"

"Yeah." He knelt and started to organize the lumber by size. "It's two weeks before Christmas. I'm sure things must be pretty busy for you right now. There are a million holiday parties in town."

Kenna studied him. "Are you saying I should have something better to do on a Friday night?" So he really did think she was pathetic.

"I didn't mean it like that."

"Why aren't *you* at the parties?" she asked, crossing her arms for good measure. He had a lot of friends in town. Surely he was invited to the same parties she was.

It seemed Tucker McGrath had nothing to say to that.

"Come on." She moved to stand where he had to look at her. "You know my dirty little secret. How my husband screwed over me and a whole lot of other people. Why not make me feel better about myself and tell me why you're avoiding all of the festive fun?"

Tucker seemed to size her up. For some reason she couldn't hold his gaze without her heart twirling.

"I'm not big on Christmas." He stood. "That's no secret. I'm sure you've heard people call me Scrooge. I've done my best to avoid the holiday for a long time." His mouth pulled into a focused frown, but sadness hid underneath it.

That glimpse of emotion drew her in. Maybe because she could relate. "Why have you avoided it for so long?" It was none of her business but she wanted to understand, to see past the Scrooge people believed him to be.

Tucker slipped past her, marched down the steps, and retrieved a shopping bag full of nails. "My dad walked out right before Christmas," he said matter-of-factly. "When I was seventeen. Haven't celebrated since."

"Oh." She hadn't realized Mr. McGrath had left during the holidays. Wow. So he hadn't celebrated Christmas for fifteen years? "But your mom loves Christmas."

"I said *I* haven't celebrated. She always has." He stuck a pencil behind his ear. "She usually volunteers somewhere. But I've always made sure I had plenty of work so I could avoid the holiday altogether."

Two years ago, she might not have understood that, but this year... well if it weren't for Jake and Benny, she'd definitely be avoiding Christmas. "It's hard to celebrate when it feels like someone is missing." When your family looked a certain way but suddenly everything was different.

Tucker stopped moving and looked at her. For the first time that evening, he gazed directly into her eyes. An awareness flickered across his face, something that looked suspiciously similar to interest. But if that's what it was, why was he being so distant?

"Is that how it feels for you?" he asked. "Like someone's missing?"

Was he asking if she still loved her ex-husband? She supposed the question made sense. But over the last year, she'd been able to let go of her feelings for Mike. She didn't love him anymore, but somehow that hadn't made her life easier. "It's more like a dream is gone. I don't miss Mike, but I miss the feeling of having my family complete." Afraid she'd shared too much, Kenna tried to smile. "What about you? Do you still miss your dad?"

"No." That distant expression took over his face again. "I figure I'm better off without him."

Kenna watched him lug a two-by-four to the stage. If that were true, why had he avoided Christmas for so long? The question made her more desperate than ever to save this Christmas for her own children. Would that be their story someday? Would they simply close themselves off to feeling anything? *My dad went to prison the year I turned six. Haven't celebrated since.*

They needed to celebrate. Even if she didn't feel like it. Even if she didn't have the money. They needed something to believe in. Even when she was grasping to find hope. "Why did your dad walk out?" she asked quietly.

"Mom got diagnosed with lupus." Tucker hauled more lumber to the edge of the stage. Was it just her or had his movements grown tense? "He couldn't deal. Funny, I never realized how much he sucked at dealing with things until then. He never wanted to face up to anything real or hard. He wanted easy. Laughs. A good time all the time." A cold bitterness made the words sound strained.

"That must've been so hard for your family." For Birdie and his younger sister. Jade had been a few years behind Kenna in school. "I heard your sister moved away a while back." Kenna tried to get a look at his face but he kept dodging her.

"She took off for Nashville. She's hoping to make a name for herself on the music scene."

Watching him work, Kenna caught another glimpse of emotion beneath his gruff exterior. "So your dad left, and your sister left, but you stayed for your mom."

"I belong here," he said simply. "I love my job and I've got good friends."

She smiled and waited for him to finish. There was more to his story. More behind why he'd stayed in Topaz Falls.

"Don't look at me like that," he grumbled. "Like I'm some hero. There are plenty of other things I could tell you that aren't so heroic."

Be that as it may, as a mother of two young boys, she couldn't help but admire him for staying to look after his mom. "So you and your mom never do anything for Christmas?"

"Not until this year." Even when he wore a grimace, the man's face still had that classic handsome charm. "After what she's been through, I figured it was time to stop avoiding it, so I promised to bring back all of our traditions, and I'll take care of everything. Hopefully then she'll get the rest she needs."

So he was definitely still worried about his mom, and she couldn't blame him. Seeing Birdie collapse had been one of the scariest moments of Kenna's life. She couldn't imagine what it had done to *him*. "We could always work on the set another time. If you'd rather be with Birdie at the hospital."

"I was just there. She told me I was driving her crazy. Said she needed some peace and quiet." He slung a tool belt around his waist. "So what about you? Why aren't you going to the parties?"

"Are you kidding? No one wants me to come." Well, that wasn't exactly true. Her book club friends had planned a party for Sunday and they'd told her she didn't have a choice but to come. "And the boys are out Christmas shopping with Mateo and Everly. Sometimes I think they'd love to move in with those two if I'd let them." Not that it bothered her. It actually meant a lot that they had somewhere to go. More people who loved them. That's what had gotten her through the last year. "So I literally have nothing but this to do tonight."

Something in his expression changed...softened maybe? He actually looked at her for more than a quick second. "Then I guess we'd better get to work," he said, walking over to hand her a hammer.

She held the wooden handle tight, looking forward to pounding in a few nails. "Sounds good to me."

The minutes rushed by as Kenna helped him cut particleboard and nail two-by-fours together—mainly holding this piece here and that piece there. While they worked, Tucker seemed to relax. They chatted about his travels with the Cortez brothers on the circuit and about how crazy the kids in her classes got this time of year as the excitement for Christmas built. It was all so normal—the chatting, the focused work. It almost felt like the most normal thing she'd done since her life had imploded. It very well might have been the easiest conversation she'd had with anyone besides her book club friends.

By the time they'd finished building the frame for the stable, it felt like hardly any time had passed at all.

"Wow." Kenna stood back to admire their work. Well, Tucker's work really. She'd been more of an assistant, but it had felt good to contribute something. And her hammering skills had come a long way. "That looks amazing." Instead of a stable painted on plywood, they had a real structure. "The kids are going to love this. Especially with the lights." Birdie was right—that would totally brighten everything up.

"Let's go ahead and hang them." Tucker went back to the box of lights and wound the string around his arm. "I'll go grab the ladder." He disappeared and came back carrying a stepladder, which he positioned near one of the stable's posts. "Why don't you go up and I'll hand you the lights and the staple gun?"

"Me?" Tucker had quite the sense of humor. "You may not know this, but I'm quite the klutz." The last time she'd climbed a ladder to change a lightbulb, she'd accidentally missed a rung and ended up with a sprained wrist.

"You can handle it." He held the base of the ladder with both hands. "I'll keep it steady for you."

The words held a challenge, and she was done backing down. "Okay, fine." She could do this. How hard could it be to stand on a ladder and staple in a string of lights?

The first few steps up the ladder were unsteady in her heeled boots, but then she found her balance and climbed a little higher.

"Here's the first string of lights." He passed it up to her, keeping the ladder stable with his other hand. "Let me know when you're ready for the staple gun."

"Give me a minute." She really had to take her other hand off the ladder too? Her knees weren't exactly holding steady with this man watching her so closely.

"Easy. Just move slow." He held up the staple gun with a grin that did nothing to reinforce her balance.

Slowly, she pulled her hand away from the ladder, tightened every muscle in her legs, and took the staple gun out of his hand.

"Careful. Just hold the wire against the wood and staple it into place," he instructed.

Easy for him to say, standing on the ground. Wobbling, she raised her hand to press the wire against the wood and popped a staple into place. "I did it! I—"

When she whirled to look triumphantly at Tucker, her balance failed and she pitched backward, dropping the gun and flailing to grab on to the ladder again. She couldn't get a good grip before it swayed sideways.

Everything seemed to slow when she fell. Her hands grasped at the ladder but it tipped one way and she tipped the other. Just as it crashed to the floor, she thudded against Tucker's solid body and he caught her in his arms.

He seemed nearly as stunned as she was. "You okay?"

"I think so," she managed, but her heart felt like it was going to beat out of her chest. And not just from the fall, either. His arms were strong around her and the collar of his shirt smelled like cedar.

"You sure?" Tucker gently eased her feet to the ground and stood her upright, holding her a second longer.

Whoa. Her knees teetered like she was still standing on the ladder.

"I mean, you *look* fine." His eyes trailed down her body again. "Good. You look really good."

"I'm just surprised." Nothing surprised her more than

Tucker McGrath, than the sudden softness smoothing out his normally gruff voice, than the intensity heating his eyes.

"Me too." Instead of stepping back, he eased even closer, his gaze intent on her lips.

A silent *yes* resounded through her, pinging in her pulse points and settling deep in her chest.

He took his time getting there, easing into her as though giving her space to refuse him. She couldn't. The anticipation boiled up and she found it hard to be still, to wait. A kiss. Oh God, a kiss. It had been a long, lonely year and somehow even the promise of a kiss rekindled a yearning for a connection, for a physical touch. She hadn't realized how much she needed it until right now. She needed to know it was possible to still feel something.

Tucker slipped his hand around her lower back, watching her eyes while he pulled her to him. She didn't even try to disguise her impatience. *Don't wait. Don't stop. Don't think.*

Seeming to get the message, Tucker lowered his lips to hers. His mouth tasted minty. He pulled her in closer, teasing her mouth open wider with his lips and then his tongue. Desire rushed in hot and fast, spreading into every dark, cold crevice of her heart. She angled her head to get closer to him, to fully kiss him back, and Tucker scooped his hands under her butt, bringing her up against his body. She kissed him harder, cupping his jaw, making sure he stayed there, that he kept kissing her because it was like waking up, like sunshine streaming right into her, everything warm and hopeful. "I didn't think you liked me much," she gasped when he pulled back.

"That's not it," he uttered in a tortured growl. "The problem is I like you too much."

"What—"

Somewhere a door banged open.

"Mommy!"

"Oh God!" She broke out of Tucker's arms just as Benny burst into the auditorium. He stopped cold, and for a second she was sure he somehow knew what she and Tucker had been doing, but when she blinked everything into a clear focus, she realized he was staring at the new stable.

Jake came bounding in next and had the same reaction. "Wow! What *is* that? Where did you get it?"

"We built it," Tucker said, offering no hint that his heart raced the same way hers still did. "But it's not done," he told the boys. "We still have to hang the lights. Want to help?"

"Yes! We want to help!" they shouted, racing down the aisle. Tucker gave her a small private grin—because they'd kissed! And it was a hot kiss. A *Let's get rid of these clothes* kiss. A kiss that had completely stolen her ability to move or think clearly. A kiss that had made her forget she'd told Everly to drop the boys off at the town hall after they were done shopping.

"Man those boys are fast!" Everly hurried into the room but slowed when she caught sight of Kenna's face. She immediately looked over to where Tucker stood showing the boys the strings of lights. "Um. Did we interrupt something?"

Something, yes. But Kenna had no idea what. What the hell had just happened? She cleared her throat. "Everly, can you help me find some of the props in the storage room?" she asked loud enough for Tucker and the boys to hear. Without waiting for an answer, she linked their arms together and dragged Everly out of the auditorium and all the way down the hall, not saying one word until they were safely closed into the tiny room. "Tucker kissed me," she blurted.

"Yeah, baby." Everly pulled over a kid-sized stool and plopped down. "Give me details. I want to hear everything."

"I fell off the ladder and he caught me." Kenna paced, trying to make sure she hadn't dreamt it up. "And then when our eyes met, there was this moment." She hadn't imagined it, had she? How Tucker's face had changed when he looked at her?

"And?" her friend pestered, tugging on her sweater.

"Then he kissed me." In the most slow, surrendering way. "And I told him I thought he didn't like me, and he said..." She paused, trying to get the words right. " 'The problem is I like you too much.' What do you think that means?"

"Who cares what it means?" Everly leaned forward and took Kenna's shoulders in her hands. "Tucker McGrath kissed you. He's obviously attracted to you. Did you kiss him back? Did you like it?"

"It was..." Scorching...powerful...breathtaking...For some reason she couldn't describe it. "It's ridiculous. I'm a mom. I have two kids." Which also meant she had responsibilities, things she needed to focus on, especially with Christmas right around the corner.

"So?" Everly cast her a stern glare. "Does that mean you can't have a little fun? It's not like Tucker's going to want to get serious."

Everyone in town knew Tucker wasn't the settling down type. For some reason, that bothered her more than it should. "Of course I'm not opposed to fun. I'm fun. Well, I *used* to be fun..."

"Then what's the problem?" her friend demanded. "Just because you're a mom doesn't mean you're exempt from having a little fun. You're also a single woman. Which means you and Tucker can do some kissing. And maybe some other stuff. You can hang out with him. Have a good time. A secret Christmas fling would be great for you. It's like taking a baby step to opening yourself back up, to enjoy life again."

The speech struck a chord that had already been humming back to life deep inside of her. "You know what? You're right. It would be good for me." A Christmas fling sounded like the perfect way to take back her life.

# Chapter Five

There had been a time when the last day of the fall semester had Kenna humming Christmas carols and making lists of last-minute gifts to buy along with items she'd need at the grocery store for baking Christmas cookies and their special Christmas morning brunch. Instead, she sat at her desk in her music room flipping through a pile of bills she'd been avoiding for far too long.

There was the bill for the boys' last visit to the dentist. Looking at that, she had no idea why she even bothered with insurance. They seemed to cover less and less. Then there was the heating bill—also astronomically high due to the early start to winter. If those two weren't bad enough, she'd also forgotten the car insurance was due along with the balance for the urgent care visit when Jake had come down with a severe case of strep throat—on a weekend, of course. She didn't have to total everything up to know there wasn't enough in any of her accounts to cover it all.

Sighing, she opened her laptop to search for a good Realtor in the area. It was time for her to stop delaying the inevitable. She and the boys would have to move. *Embrace the future,* she reminded herself, but it did little to lift her spirits. So far her plan to break free from her past wasn't exactly taking shape quite the way she'd pictured. In fact, she hadn't even seen Tucker since he'd kissed her nearly a week ago. He'd texted her that he wasn't able to come to the rehearsal on Sunday night because Birdie was having a procedure done, but Kenna couldn't help wondering if he was avoiding her. Maybe he regretted the kiss. Maybe—

"Mommy! Mommy!" Jake and Benny bounded into the room, weighed down by their backpacks and coats.

She quickly shut her laptop and shoved the stack of bills back into her bag.

"School's out!" they chanted, jumping up and down in front of her desk. "You know what that means." Jake's eyes widened.

"No homework for the whole two-and-a-half-week break?" she guessed.

"Nooooo, Mom." His face scrunched up with an irritable disappointment. "It means we get to go pick out our Christmas tree today. Remember? That's what we *always* used to do on the last day of school. Well, except for last year when we were at Aunt Darcy's house. But this year we're home, so we can get our tree!"

"Right. Of course." Last year, with the end of her marriage so fresh, she'd taken the boys to California to visit her sister for Christmas. As a guest in someone else's house, she hadn't had to do anything, but this year clearly she would have to step up and handle all of the traditions alone.

Her empty stomach clenched.

Benny wandered forward. "We're still going to get the

tree, right, Mommy?" he asked in his sweet, shy tenor. "Even though Daddy's gone we still get a tree, don't we?" Fear hid in his baby blue eyes, and that was all Kenna ever needed to see to snap out of her own grief.

"Of course we're still getting a tree." She hopped up and quickly packed her things. "We'll leave right now. Zip up your coats. And put on your mittens and hats." She pulled on her own coat. "We'll have hot chocolate and maybe we can even buy a treat from the store."

"Yes!"

"Woohoo!"

The boys wrestled up their zippers and pulled on their identical knitted beanies, their faces lit with excitement.

Kenna did her best to match their enthusiasm as they traipsed down the hall, waving to the other teachers and students who were still clearing out of the building. It felt good walking out. She needed a break. Time with the boys. Time for fun. And there was Tucker again, taking over her thoughts. That kiss had definitely been fun, not to mention hot enough to melt all this snow...

"Come on, Mommy!" Benny clasped her hand and pulled her out the doors.

Right. Now was not the time to think of Tucker. It was probably better that he avoid her anyway. She'd never had a fling before, and she had no idea what the rules were. Or if there even were rules. Probably not. Didn't rules take away the fun? She decided not to obsess over it.

Cold air bathed her face while sunlight poured down onto the pristine blanket of snow that had fallen yesterday.

"We're gonna get the biggest tree they have!" Jake bounced around her. "Ten times taller than me!"

Kenna smiled. "We have to make sure it fits in our house, sweetie." Speaking of, she had no idea how she'd carry the thing inside by herself. Or how to set it up, for that matter. That was all stuff Mike had taken care of, but this was a new day and she'd have to figure it out on her own. She *would* figure it out.

After they'd piled into the car, she cranked up some Christmas carols and the three of them sang loudly and off key all the way out to the tree farm. It seemed a lot of people had the same idea they had. The parking lot was nearly full. She parked next to a big pickup truck. Much like the one Mike had driven. Jake looked up at it.

"Mom? How're we gonna get our tree home?"

"Um…" She cut the engine and looked around the interior of her Jeep Grand Cherokee. "Well…I guess we'll tie it to the top of the car." People did that all the time, right? She didn't need a truck. They would simply improvise.

"Come on, you two." She zipped her wallet into her coat pocket. "Let's get you guys some hot chocolate."

The boys bounded ahead of her, singing "O Christmas Tree" all the way to the entrance.

"Hi there!" a young female employee greeted them warmly. "I'll bet you two would like some hot chocolate."

"Yes, please!" Jake said in his favorite volume: loud. Benny simply nodded.

"Here you go." The girl filled two small cups from the cart and stuck lids on them. "Can I get you anything?" she asked Kenna.

"No thanks." She quickly pulled out her wallet and paid for the drinks, and then hurried after the boys before they got lost somewhere in the maze of trees. She found them standing in the shadows of a beautiful twelve-foot blue spruce, stately and elegant with perfectly symmetrical silvery branches. Even she was powerless to overlook it.

"This is amazing!" Benny brushed his hand over the needles. "Smell it, Mama! It smells so good!"

Kenna walked closer and inhaled deeply. That scent was Christmas. Crisp and piney and woodsy. "It's beautiful," she agreed, admiring the shape. She glanced at the price. *One hundred twenty-five dollars?* For a tree they'd have to turn into mulch in a few short weeks? "It's a really big tree." And way too expensive. She glanced around. "Hey, what about this one?" She led them over to a smaller fir. "This one's nice."

"That's the one I had my eye on."

That deep matter-of-fact drawl gave her heart a good kick. Kenna started to look for him, but the boys got to him first.

"Tucker!" They sprinted over to the cowboy full speed, skidding to a stop just before they knocked into him.

Kenna, however, couldn't move. He had on a heavy sheepskin-lined jean jacket and his cowboy hat. He looked every bit as good as he had the night he'd kissed her...and as he'd looked in her dreams since. Solid and in control.

"We found the perfect tree," Jake squealed.

"It's so big!" Benny added, not shying away like he usually did. "Come on!" He yanked on Tucker's hand, and Kenna's mouth fell open. Benny never reached out like that. Especially not to someone he hardly knew. While it was a sweet sight to see the cowboy holding her son's hand, she couldn't ward off a nagging concern. What would it mean for her boys to get attached to Tucker? It wasn't like she could stop it. They'd see him at the rehearsals. She would just have to be careful to keep her own attachment to the man hidden so they didn't get any ideas about the two of them being together.

"Do you want to see the tree?" her son asked.

"Sure." Tucker shot her a quick smile from underneath the brim of his hat.

Now that she knew what amazing things those lips could do, even that small quirk of his mouth was enough to turn her limbs wobbly, but she'd never let him know it. She'd show him she could keep her distance just as well as he could. "What're you doing here?" she asked, aiming for a tone of casual surprise.

"I'm looking for a tree. For my mom."

*Aw.* Okay. It looked like he was serious about giving Birdie the best Christmas ever.

"Is Miss Birdie gonna be okay?" Jake cast a worried gaze up at Tucker.

"You know what, buddy? I think she is." The cowboy ruffled his hair. "Thanks for asking. She has to stay in the hospital a little longer. But I'm hoping she can come home for Christmas."

"No one should be sick for Christmas," Benny whispered sadly.

"Exactly," Tucker agreed. "That's why I have to find the best tree. Maybe it'll help her get all better."

Judging from the catch in his voice, he'd do anything and everything in his power to make her better. "What's the latest update on her condition?" Kenna asked.

That smile of his couldn't hide a grim expression. "They're still battling the inflammation in her heart. It's kind of a waiting game right now."

God, the worry in his eyes. "I'm sorry." No one should have to deal with hospitals and sickness over the holidays. Especially not someone who loved this time of year as much as Birdie.

"That's why I'm here." He looked around at the trees. "I figured I should probably start looking for a tree so they're not all gone by the time she gets out of the hospital."

Jake gasped the way he always did when a lightbulb went

on over his head. "Let's all look for our trees together! Can we, Mom?"

If she said no, Tucker would likely guess why. He would know she felt awkward about their kiss. Well, not so much because of their kiss, more because of the radio silence following the kiss. But she wasn't broken-hearted Kenna anymore. So she shrugged and smiled like it was no big deal. "Sure." She turned to him. "Although I should warn you. We might be here another six hours. Every tree we come across is sure to be better than the last one."

He chuckled. "I can relate. I've already been here a half hour and I can't seem to make a decision myself." He stooped to the boys' level. "I'll tell you what. If you help me pick out the perfect tree for my house, I'll help you guys out too."

"Deal." Benny stuck out a hand to shake on it.

That was all she needed to see to bring the worry bubbling back up. They clearly looked up to the man, but she couldn't hide them away just because she was attracted to him. Somehow she'd have to downplay her feelings for Tucker and keep a friendly distance between them.

"So what kind of tree are you looking for?" she asked. She could do this. She could keep things light and conversational.

Tucker walked alongside her. "I think I like the firs. They're a little more understated."

Which seemed like a perfect fit for him. Incredibly good-looking but not flashy.

"We like that one!" Jake pointed out the spruce, which towered over all the others in the vicinity.

Tucker whistled low. "That's a beauty."

"An expensive beauty," Kenna muttered so the boys wouldn't hear.

Tucker leaned forward to glance at the price tag. "Ouch."

Yeah, tell her about it. She'd never relied on a credit card, but it looked like this month she'd have to start.

"I don't know." Tucker walked around the tree, looking it over thoughtfully. "It's almost too perfect."

Benny and Jake followed him as though trying to see what he saw. "It is?" Jake asked, twisting his mouth with confusion.

"Yeah." The cowboy stood back and frowned. "I mean, it's not unique. It has no personality."

Kenna hid her smile behind her mitten. He was totally talking them out of the most expensive tree on the lot so she wouldn't have to disappoint them.

"Look at this one, for example." He led the boys over to a much smaller fir tree nearby. "It leans a little to the left. And some of the branches are bushy but others aren't." He brushed snow off the needles. "I'll bet you this is the only tree that has this exact shape in the whole world. And it's the only tree that's missing this branch near the top." Tucker shook his head like he couldn't believe they'd found such a treasure. "This tree is one of a kind. There's not another one like it anywhere."

Her boys seemed to look at the tree with a new appreciation.

Tucker frowned. "I think I might take this one."

"Aww." Jake reached his hand to one of the branches. "I kinda wanted it."

"Me too," Benny echoed.

The cowboy winked at Kenna. "Well, since I like you guys so much, I'll let you have it."

"You will?" the boys asked at the exact same time.

"Sure. Come to think of it, I might wait to buy my mom one anyway. I took some pictures of other trees on my phone. I can show her and she can help me pick one of those instead. So the tree is yours. As long as it's okay with your mom."

Jake and Benny snapped their heads to look at her, their eyes wide and silently pleading.

Oh, that man. He was good. "Of course it's okay. I think it's the perfect tree." She let herself look deeply into Tucker's eyes for a minute, only a minute, in a silent thanks. Instead of the $125, this one was an affordable $45, which wouldn't put quite as big a dent in her credit card.

"Did I hear that someone picked out their tree?" A farm employee walked over, carrying a large bow saw.

"This one!" Jake all but hugged the tree. "It's one of a kind!"

"It sure is. Y'all ready to cut it down?" The man went to hand the saw to Tucker.

"But our dad always did that." Jake looked at Kenna with worry clouding his eyes. There had been so many looks exactly like that over the last year. The silent panic when one of her boys wondered, *What're we going to do?* Before Kenna could answer, Tucker took the saw from the man and held it out to her.

"Well, this time I think your mom should do the honors."

"Me? Really?" She'd never actually cut down the tree before.

"Sure." The cowboy's expression turned playful. "Any woman who can string up Christmas lights can cut down a tree."

Ha. Was he just setting her up to fall into his arms again? "The lights might've been a disaster if I hadn't had some backup," she reminded him.

"I'm more than happy to provide backup." His eyes were intent on hers, as penetrating as they'd been right before he'd kissed her.

For some reason when he looked at her like that, her confidence grew. It made her feel strong. She had so much to prove. To herself, to her boys, to Tucker. She wasn't fragile and dependent. She could be bold and desirable. "I'd love to do the honors." Kenna took the saw from Tucker with a smile.

"Just let me know when you've got her down," the farm employee said. "We'll come and load it into your car for you."

"Wow, Mom," Benny said after the man walked away. "Are you sure you know how to use that thing?"

"Of course I know how to use it." And even if she didn't, she'd figure it out to prove a point. She got on her knees and crawled under the branches while Tucker stood back and assumed a supervisory position.

She tried to remember how her butt looked in these jeans. It'd been a while since she'd cared.

"You boys can get down and help her," Tucker said. He did seem to be checking her out. "There's room for all of you to hold the saw together."

"Yes! We get to help!" Both Benny and Jake scooted in beside her and gripped the handle of the saw next to her hands.

"Now just bring it back and forth," Tucker instructed, taking a knee next to them.

Kenna strained to maneuver the blade and find a rhythm. It took more muscle than she would've thought, and within a few minutes, she'd broken a sweat.

"It's working! Look, Mom." Jake pointed out the small wedge they'd cut into the tree trunk.

"It sure is." Slowly but surely. She peeked back over her shoulder at Tucker with a wry grin. "You sure you don't want to take a turn?"

"I think you're doing a fine job."

Ha. At this rate, it might take them an hour. Her jeans were soaked—freezing her legs—but she shifted back to the trunk and started sawing away again. By the time they got the trunk cut all the way through, her forearms were cramping and the skin on her knees was raw and numb, but the tree fell over and she and the boys all jumped up whooping and high-fiving.

"We did it! We cut that tree down all by ourselves!" Jake launched himself over to hug Benny.

"Of course you did. You three can do anything." Tucker reached out a hand to help her up, and she felt herself melt for him all over again.

# Chapter Six

Well, it seemed his work was done here.

Tucker tightened the last knot on the ropes that held the tree to Kenna's Jeep roof and stood back. "Should be secure enough." But just in case it wasn't, he might have to follow her home. Being the gentleman that he was, it had been hard to stand back and watch while she cut down the tree, but that was her moment with her boys. A family moment that he had no right intruding on. He hadn't wanted Jake to feel like he was trying to step in for their dad.

That was the exact reason he'd been avoiding Kenna, why he didn't show up at the last rehearsal. He didn't trust himself around her, not after that kiss. It had been a long time since he'd lost control, but within five seconds of his lips on hers, everything had spiraled. He wanted her with a hunger that drove down deep, but what did he know about meeting the needs of a woman like Kenna? What did he know about being a family man? His mom had called him out that day they'd talked in the hospital. *Why won't you let yourself get close to anyone?* It hadn't taken him long to figure out the answer. It had hit him right after he'd kissed Kenna. He'd never wanted to hurt anyone the way his father had hurt his mother. But he especially didn't want to hurt Kenna. Like Birdie had said, he had more of his dad in him than he cared to admit. That's why he preferred to be up front about things, but he hadn't exactly had time to define anything with her before that kiss.

"Thanks for your help." It was a cruel joke that she looked even lovelier now—after the exertion of cutting down the tree, with the brisk air and the soft fading light of evening all around her.

"You're welcome." He quickly turned to the boys before she or anyone else could decipher his deepening feelings for her. "That was solid work, you two."

"Thanks again for letting us have the tree." Jake gave him a manly handshake. "If you need help picking out yours, you know who to ask."

"I sure do." He gave Benny a wink. "I think you two are the best tree hunters I've ever met."

The boy's grin nearly reached his ears. "We couldn't have found it without you. Hey!" He let out a wide-eyed gasp. "You should help us decorate it!" Benny whirled to face Kenna. "Can he? Can Tucker come over for pizza and help us put all of the ornaments on the tree?"

"Yeah!" Jake ran over to her and pulled on her hands as though trying to force her into saying yes. "Come on, Mom. He gave us *his* tree. We have to let him help!"

To say she hesitated would've been putting it mildly. Kenna's lips parted, but nothing came out, so Tucker decided to rescue her.

"Actually, thanks for the invite, guys, but I should get home. I have a lot to do."

"But what're you gonna have for dinner?" Jake asked. "You gotta eat dinner anyway. When we get our tree, we always order pizza. There'll be plenty, won't there, Mom?"

Wow, that kid had really nailed the pleading puppy-dog face.

Much as he hated to disappointment them, he really shouldn't accept the invitation. Mainly for all of those reasons he'd outlined in his head just a few minutes ago. "Thanks for the invite, but—"

"It's fine." Kenna gave him a very soft, very tempting smile. "Of course there'll be plenty of pizza. You're more than welcome. We'd love it if you'd come."

He should turn her down. But it did something to him that she seemed to want him to come. He would've hated to disappoint the boys, for sure, but for reasons he was pretty sure he didn't want to understand, he simply wasn't capable of disappointing Kenna. "If you're sure I'm not intruding."

"Not at all." She opened the car doors and helped the boys climb in, checking their seat belts while they chanted, "Tucker's coming to dinner!"

When she backed out of the Jeep and shut the door, he inched closer to her. "Are you sure about this? Because I can make up an excuse and go on home." He stood almost as close as he had when he'd kissed her, but Kenna didn't withdraw. "I'm sure." Her gaze rested firmly on his. "We would all love to have you. Me included."

"Then I'll come." He couldn't seem to look away from her. Not until she broke their stare and climbed into the driver's seat. "You can follow me."

Unease gurgled in his stomach as he climbed into the truck and pulled out of the parking spot to follow her. Nerves like he hadn't felt since Reckoning II—one of the Cortez's bulls—had charged straight at him. It was a feeling he'd never gotten because of a woman.

He followed Kenna through town and out to the eastern edge—small-town suburbia, he liked to call it. Cookie-cutter houses lined the symmetrical streets, positioned in the centers of squared lots that likely had perfectly manicured landscaping underneath all that snow. Just one more reminder that he didn't belong here with her or the boys. These were family people—husbands and wives and partners who worked nine-to-five jobs and wore clothes from high-end malls in Denver and drank fancy wines and took summer vacations to places like Hawaii. He wouldn't fit in with those people. He'd never even wanted to try. So what the hell was he doing following Kenna home?

He didn't have time to dwell on the question before Kenna made a quick left into the driveway of her house. He parked his truck on the street. The boys came running and sliding down the icy driveway to greet him.

"This is gonna be so fun!" Jake danced around him.

"Mom called to order pizza from the car," Benny added. "And she even got the cinnamon breadsticks for dessert!"

"Sounds delicious." Tucker joined Kenna at the Jeep, where they worked together to untie the tree. She insisted on helping him haul it in, and the boys called out instructions as they held open the front door.

"A little to the left," Jake said.

Benny followed closely behind them. "Watch out for the ceiling!"

"We can just set it right in here." Kenna led the way into a living room with a vaulted ceiling. "I'll go find the stand and the ornaments."

After they leaned the tree against the wall, she disappeared.

Tucker looked around. The room still depicted a happy family life. A nice but well-used couch sat along one wall and there were family pictures hanging in patterns throughout the room.

"That's our dad," Jake informed him, pointing out Mike Hart in one of the posed family shots. "He made some bad choices, so he can't live here anymore." He said it so matter-of-factly that Tucker didn't know how to respond.

He finally settled on, "I'm sorry to hear that."

"Yeah." Jake seemed to shrug it off. "But Mom said everyone makes mistakes and it doesn't mean he doesn't love us."

"And learning to forgive people for their mistakes is one of the most important things you will ever do in your whole life," Benny recited wisely.

Wasn't that the truth? It also happened to be the hardest thing to do, in his estimation.

"Did your dad make any mistakes?" Jake asked.

Tucker envied their openness. They'd shared everything with him without even blinking, yet he had a hard lump at the base of his throat just thinking about his dad. "Uh. Yeah. My dad made mistakes too."

Benny gazed up at him with a look of pure innocence. "Did you forgive him?"

"I think I'm still working on it." That wasn't exactly true. He hadn't worked on it at all. In fact, he'd completely written his father off, never taking the man's phone calls, tossing letters or cards in the trash before he opened them. Eventually the calls and letters had stopped coming.

"Maybe we could work on it together," Jake suggested.

"Work on what?" Kenna came staggering into the room under the weight of three large boxes. Instead of answering the question, Tucker lurched to help her, relieving her of the top two.

"What're you talking about?" she asked after she'd set down the box.

Tucker braced himself while he carefully set the boxes near the tree. Hopefully she'd know he wasn't the one who brought up the subject of disappointing dads.

Jake hemmed and hawed for a minute. "We were talking about Dad," the boy finally admitted warily, as if he knew that wasn't what his mom would want to hear.

"Oh, honey." She rubbed her hand up and down his back. "I'm sure Tucker doesn't want to hear about all that."

He didn't have to hear about it. He'd lived it. That disappointment, that struggle to understand how someone who was supposed to be a protector could betray him. "Actually, we were talking about my dad too. About the mistakes he made."

"Tucker said he's still working on forgiving his dad," Jake offered. Leave it to kids to tell the whole truth.

"I think that takes a while." Her gaze held Tucker's. "But let's not worry about it tonight." She suddenly beamed a bright smile. "Let's just have fun decorating the tree."

Jake and Benny took that suggestion to heart. After he and Kenna had figured out how to put the tree stand to use and then untangled the damn Christmas lights enough to wind them around the tree, the boys attacked the boxes. Every time they unwrapped an ornament, Jake and Benny oohed and aahed and told Tucker the story of when they'd gotten it or made it, and then they'd place it on the tree—all in one spot in the middle about halfway up.

Kenna didn't seem to mind the concentration of ornaments all in the same place. She let them put each one wherever they wanted and gave no instruction or correction. Instead, she smiled and chatted and teased the boys, making them giggle.

When the pizza came, they ate it on the floor—right out of the box, the boys using their shirts as napkins, taking bites in between hanging the ornaments.

Tucker found himself wrapped up in all of it—the laughter and the warmth of the room with those two boys' faces shining as bright as a Christmas star. If he'd gone on home, he would've spent a quiet evening catching up on stuff he needed to do around the house with a hockey game on in the background. He'd never thought of his life as lonely until now. Until hearing the boys laugh and tell stories. He'd been content until he'd shared these few hours with a woman who brought so much life and energy into the room. For the first time, he felt like his life was missing something. Every time Kenna looked at him and smiled, his heart stopped. His lips burned to kiss her again, but it was more than just the physical urge. She stirred something deeper.

But he couldn't shake the feeling that he didn't fit here. That no matter how much he wanted to, he couldn't be what Kenna needed. He couldn't be what these boys needed. It warred inside of him—the contentment that seemed so close he could almost grasp it against the desire to get up and leave. Walk out before things got too complicated. But that would only prove he was just like his father. So even though he felt himself withdrawing, he stayed right where he was and watched the boys hang their ornaments.

Slowly, the number of ornaments in the box dwindled until they placed the last two.

How they'd managed to fit over fifty ornaments all in one spot on the tree was beyond him. The fact that Kenna let it go made him like her even more. Not that he needed any help in that department. What he really had to start doing was keeping a list of reasons he didn't want this. Want her. He thought on it for a few minutes, but nothing came to him.

"Well I guess that's that." Kenna stood and brushed some pine needles off her jeans.

"Wait!" Benny rushed over to one of the boxes. "The

star, Mama. We almost forgot the star." He lifted it out reverently, carefully holding on to it with both hands.

"It's Benny's turn to put it on the tree this year." Jake's expression turned pained. "I did it last time." He obviously wanted to do it again, but he seemed to know the drill. They must take turns every year.

"Will you help me?" Holding the star out, Benny walked over to Tucker. "Can you lift me up?"

He hesitated. There was a weight in the air, and he didn't have to ask to know that this was something their father used to do. He glanced at Kenna, took in the sadness in her eyes.

"That's a great idea, Benny." She cleared her throat. "If Tucker doesn't mind."

He shouldn't mind, but the request rattled him. It wasn't only Kenna he worried about hurting. These boys. Especially Benny. The kid had already opened his heart to him. He could see it. *I'm not the guy you think I am,* he felt like telling them. But Benny was looking at him with those huge eyes and he couldn't refuse. "It would be an honor." He stood and lifted Benny onto his shoulders, then moved close enough to the tree that he could reach the very top. The boy stretched and reached. "I got it!" he exclaimed with triumph.

Next to Tucker, Kenna looked up at the twinkling tree. "It's perfect. This is the perfect tree."

Tucker slowly lifted Benny off his shoulders and set the boy's feet back on the ground.

"Thank you." The kid wrapped his arms around Tucker's waist.

"You're welcome, buddy." He patted the kid's back lightly, unsure of what else to do, but Benny held on even tighter.

"All right, boys. It's way past your bedtime." Kenna pried her youngest away from Tucker. "Why don't you say good-night and run upstairs? I'll be up to tuck you in in a minute."

"Bye, Tucker. I'm real glad you came." A hug from Jake hit him straight in the gut. "Next year it'll be my turn to put the star on the tree. Do you think you could lift me up?"

"Oh." He raised his eyes to Kenna.

"Next year's a long time away," she said quickly. "And who knows...the way you're growing, you might be able to reach the top all by yourself."

"I bet I will!" Jake agreed. "I mean, I *will* be eight, so I probably won't need help."

"Probably not." Tucker forced a smile to cover the sudden rise of panic. He shouldn't have come. He couldn't keep spending time with them, couldn't let them get their hopes up only to be disappointed.

Benny looked once more at the tree. "I think this is the bestest Christmas tree we've ever had."

"It's definitely the most amazing tree I've ever seen." Kenna glanced at Tucker with a soft smile that tempted him to forget all of the reasons he shouldn't be standing here with her.

"Now march, you two." She pointed toward the stairs, and both boys reluctantly headed that direction.

"Goodnight!" they called as they disappeared.

"Goodnight." Tucker was already in the entryway where he'd left his coat. "I should go too." Before he got any ideas about kissing Kenna again. He hastily pulled on his coat. "Thanks for the invite." He barely let his gaze cross hers. That chemistry between them was too intense. He could already feel it pulling at him. "It's been a long time since I've decorated a tree," he said to steer his attention away from her lips.

"Well technically, we didn't get to decorate anything." Kenna laughed and opened the front door. He followed her out onto the porch where the crisp scent of wood smoke hung in the air.

*Walk away.* Damn it, he could not kiss her again. Things between them were already tangled enough.

"Guess I'll see you around." He turned to leave but Kenna's hand caught his shoulder.

"What's wrong, Tucker?"

He turned back to her. "What'd you mean?"

"You've hardly said anything for the last hour. And you have this grim look on your face. I thought we all had a good time tonight. I know I did."

Instead of the sadness he expected to see in her eyes, he saw compassion, like she really wanted to know what was bothering him. "I just don't want to complicate things too much. For you and the boys."

"For me and the boys or for yourself?" Her head tilted and she continued to gaze at him like she could see right through him.

Damn it. This was why he avoided relationships. He wasn't good at this. At talking about the things he didn't want to face. "After everything you've been through—"

"Don't." She raised her hand between them. "Don't tell me how I should or shouldn't feel because of everything I've been through. No one knows better than me what I've been through." Her posture grew rigid. "Why did you kiss me?"

"Because I'm attracted to you." It's not like he could keep that a secret. "But I don't do relationships and you need—"

"Fun," she interrupted, stepping into his space. "I need fun. Escapism. I need people to stop treating me like I'm breakable. I'm not. I went through hell last year, but I'm not broken." She rested her hands on his shoulders, moving in so close he could see every fleck of gold in her emerald eyes. "And I'm not some needy woman who's going to get all attached if a man kisses her. Maybe all I want is a fling. Did you ever think of that?"

No. That definitely hadn't occurred to him. A yawning hunger for her opened up again, sending currents of electricity zipping around his lower body. "Are you sure that's what you want?"

"I'm sure. So what do you say?" Her eyebrows rose in a devious proposition. "Are you interested in having a little fun with me?"

She really had to ask? "Hell yes."

Kenna moved in, fitting her curves tightly against his body. "Then kiss me again, Tucker McGrath. And this time don't be shy."

# Chapter Seven

"Why are you staring at Ms. Hart?" Little Violet marched up to Tucker and stood toe-to-toe with him. "You're supposed to be teaching us the songs, but you've been staring at Ms. Hart for like ten minutes."

More like an hour. He'd done his best to periodically pull his gaze away from where Kenna stood on the stage directing the actors, but it seemed his willpower was no match for her. Not after that smokin' hot kiss on her porch last night. It had lasted all of thirty seconds before she'd backed away saying she needed to go tend to the boys, but thirty seconds had been enough to fuel plenty of fantasies. Now he was counting the milliseconds until he could get her alone again.

"You *like* her, don't you?" Violet accused. "You have a *crush* on her! Tucker has a cru-ush," she started singing.

"It's not a crush." It was a fling. But he couldn't tell Violet that. Instead, he opened up the songbook and held it out to her. "Since you're such a great singer, why don't you lead us in 'Hark the Herald Angels Sing'?"

"Really?" the girl squealed. "Me?"

Distraction accomplished. "Yes, you. Everyone, why don't you open up your books and follow along? Take it away, Violet."

The girl belted out a flat version of the song that would've made his mom cover her ears, but Tucker gave her a double thumbs-up. That ought to keep her busy for a while. Too busy to notice his obvious appreciation for a certain schoolteacher. Where'd Kenna go, anyway?

"So Violet has officially taken over the show, huh?" Kenna asked from behind him.

"Uh, yeah." He turned and kept a healthy distance between them in case her boys were watching. While she might be up for a fling, he didn't want Benny and Jake getting ideas about the two of them being together. "Violet's always talking about how good she is at singing. I thought I'd give her the chance to prove it."

Kenna slanted her head, calling him out with a sexy little smirk. "Did you make her sing so you don't have to?"

He did his best to look appalled by the suggestion, but in the end he could only stare at her lips with what was probably a greedy expression. "Of course not."

"Levi Cortez told me you used to sing." Kenna swayed her hips a step closer, obviously doing her best to torment him. "In fact, he said you were a pretty good singer back in high school. And you played the guitar too?"

Oh no she didn't. He could read the brilliant idea on her face. "Levi doesn't know what he's talking about." It had been years since he'd played. Another thing he'd given up when his father had walked out. And he definitely wasn't going to break out the guitar for the Christmas pageant.

Kenna inched even closer, her gaze lowering to his chest. "I think it would really help if the kids heard you sing." She brought her fingers to the collar of his shirt, straightening it. When her skin grazed his neck, his knees threatened to buckle. *Aw hell.* This wasn't fair.

"Nothing could be worse than Violet singing," she murmured.

He gave a gruff laugh. "I'm not sure about that." It had been years. "Besides"—he glanced at the clock behind her—"it's about time for pickup anyway."

"Come on, Tucker." Her teasing tone was driving him wild. "Won't you play the guitar? For me?"

"That depends." He couldn't help but tease her back. "On whether or not I get to see you alone soo—"

"Hi there!" A woman came out of nowhere and traipsed between them.

"Hi, Carly." Kenna's smile noticeably faded. "Have you met Birdie's son? Tucker McGrath?" Kenna asked the woman.

"Not officially." She reached out her hand and shook his. "But it's nice to meet you. I'm Violet's mom. Carly Lammers."

Ah. That made sense. Tucker looked back and forth between Violet and her mom. They seemed to have the same intense personality.

"So you two are running the pageant together this year, huh?" Carly's smile showed off her overly white teeth.

"Yes." Kenna's jaw seemed to have tensed right along with her shoulders. "With his mom in the hospital, we volunteered to take over so she can focus on getting better."

"Oh, I'm so glad, Kenna," Carly gushed, patting Kenna's shoulder. "I'm sure it's nice for you to have something to focus on during this difficult time. At least you won't be sitting at home all alone."

Well now he got why Kenna had made that speech on the porch last night. No wonder she was sick of everyone treating her like she was broken. "She definitely won't be sitting at home all alone," Tucker agreed, sliding his gaze to Kenna to make sure she caught his drift. He'd make sure she didn't sit home alone at all.

If the reappearance of Kenna's smile was any indication, she knew exactly what he meant. "Okay, well, I guess rehearsal is over for tonight." A full blush engulfed her cheeks. "Violet! Come on over here, sweetie! Your mom is here!"

Other parents streamed in behind Carly, and as usual things got chaotic. A couple of the kids couldn't find their coats while others kept Tucker busy helping them search for a lost mitten. Finally, the last of the kids followed their parents out. Well, everyone except for Benny and Jake. They stood with Kenna, pulling on coats over their costumes. Tucker was about to go tell them goodnight when Everly Brooks rushed in. "Hi! Sorry I'm late." She shook the snow off her coat.

"Mrs. Everly!" Jake opened his coat. "Look at my wise man costume! Isn't it cool?"

"It sure is." She reached down to straighten his crown. "And, Benny, that's quite the halo you're wearing."

The boy grinned—looking every bit as innocent as an angel, if you asked Tucker.

Everly turned to Kenna. "Does it still work for us to take the boys overnight tonight?"

Hold on. Overnight? Tucker eased in a few steps closer so he could hear better.

"Oh God." Kenna dropped to her knees so she could help Jake zip his coat back up. "I forgot all about that. I've had so much going on. I didn't even pack their stuff."

"That's okay." Everly gathered Jake and Benny to her side. "Mateo's waiting in the truck. We can swing by and grab whatever they need. Is the key still under the flowerpot on the porch?"

"Yes." Kenna followed the three of them to the door while Tucker hung back. "I have some cleanup to do here, so don't wait for me to come home." She bent to kiss each of the boys. "You two be good. Listen to Everly and Mateo."

"We always do," Jake assured her.

Everly smiled. "It's true. These two are an absolute joy to have around."

Tucker couldn't agree more. Though he had to admit, he wouldn't mind having Kenna all to himself for a while. Her fling proposition had inspired some late night thoughts about what kind of fun they could have.

The boys waved goodbye to him, too, before they left with Everly. After the door slammed shut, he didn't waste any time. "So it sounds like you're free tonight," he said, helping Kenna pull the front pews back into an orderly row. "Do you feel like having a little fun?"

"That depends." The smile she'd tortured him with last night slowly rose to her lips. "What did you have in mind?"

A lot. He had a lot in mind. "I can't tell you. It would ruin the surprise."

"I like surprises." She walked around the pew and came to stand across from him. "Do I need to bring anything special for the surprise?"

"No." He couldn't resist touching her. Settling his hands on her hips, he drew her in closer. "Just you and me and a whole night alone. That's all we need."

\*        \*        \*

Of all the places Kenna thought Tucker might take her, she definitely hadn't expected to wind up in the barn on his ranch.

As far as barns went, this one wasn't half bad—at least it had electricity. And who was she kidding anyway? At the moment, she honestly didn't care where they were. She was with Tucker. Alone. Which meant there would be no interruptions. No one would walk in on them. They wouldn't have to hide their feelings from anyone or pretend they didn't desire each other with an intensity that was getting harder to control. At least for her it was. On the drive over, Tucker had simply rested his hand on her thigh and her body had been simmering ever since.

Tucker finished rummaging through a bin of supplies on a shelf and came to stand behind her, threading his arms around her waist. "Close your eyes and let me lead you somewhere," he whispered in her ear. "Once I get you settled, keep them closed until I tell you to open them."

All Kenna could manage in response was a weak. "Mmm-hmmm." He smelled so good—like fresh-cut wood melded with something citrusy. He felt good, too, holding her from behind, his chest a solid wall against her back. It had been so long since a man had engaged all of her senses.

She turned into him, bringing his face in line with hers. "Are you leading me somewhere fun?" That last word hit a low, sultry note. "Because that's what you promised. Fun." Not to be impatient, but she'd gotten some ideas about what that fun might include...

"I always keep my promises." Tucker leaned in and kissed her, chasing the chill off her cheeks with his insistent heat. "We can have as much fun as you want," he murmured before taking the kiss deeper and grazing his tongue against hers.

"That was fun," she uttered when he pulled back.

"There will definitely be more of that later." Tucker's smile grew. "Now close your eyes." He slipped his glove-clad hand into hers and guided her forward.

She squeezed them nearly shut but kept one eye open a slit so she could see.

"All the way," Tucker said, his face very close.

"Fine." She'd meant to sound ornery, but her voice always went breathless when Tucker got close.

Slowly, he led her onward, their footsteps clunking on the old wooden planks. Somewhere nearby, a horse whinnied. He stopped abruptly, causing her to bump into him. "Okay, I'm going to pick you up. Just hold on."

"I'm sorry, wha—" Before she could finish, Tucker swept her up into his arms and climbed a few stairs. Whatever he was standing on creaked and wriggled as he lowered her to sit on something cushy.

"Don't open your eyes," he reminded her. "Not yet." There was more movement, and he tucked what felt like a thick woolen blanket around her. "I'll be right back."

Doing her best to grasp at patience, Kenna strained her ears to listen. There was more creaking—maybe a metal gate? And a horse or two snorting. Then the clomp of horseshoes came closer and closer until she was sure the animals had to be standing right in front of her.

"This'll only take a minute." Tucker's words sounded strained, and she could hear him huff out a breath. What on earth was he doing? There were more clomps and snorts. Wood creaked, and the bench she sat on shuddered. It seemed to go on and on before Tucker finally climbed up next to her.

"Okay," he murmured, his mouth close to her neck. "You can open your eyes."

It took a second for her vision to adjust in the dim light,

but when everything finally materialized, she gasped. They were sitting in a sleigh. A genuine red snow sleigh that looked like it had come straight from the North Pole. Two beautiful white horses were hitched to the sleigh, pawing at the ground impatiently like they couldn't wait to take off.

Kenna gaped at him. She couldn't help it. "Is this yours?"

"It was my grandpa's." Tucker clicked his tongue and jostled the reins, and the horses strained forward. At some point, he must've opened the double-wide doors at the back of the barn, and the sleigh's metal runners glided easily over the wooden floor and then out onto a snow-packed road that took them deeper into the cold night.

"I can't believe you own a sleigh." She admired the little bench they sat on, which had been finished with a luxurious red-velvet material. Tucker McGrath, the man who didn't exactly love Christmas, had Santa's sleigh hidden away in his horse barn.

"My grandpa built it." He settled back against the cushion and steered the team toward the woods up ahead as though it was second nature.

With the gentle snowflakes falling all around them and the full moon's light beaming down and the gentle whooshing of the sleigh's runners through the soft, powdery snow, Kenna felt a space deep inside her open up. Almost as though he truly were carrying her away from the financial stress, from the pressure of delivering a perfect Christmas for her children when she simply wasn't feeling it. Almost without meaning to, she let go of a sigh and settled in against him, warm and content.

"We used to take it out every Christmas Eve," he said. "We'd all crowd in here and take a midnight ride through town before going to my grandparents' house to get some sleep and wait for Santa."

Hearing that reminded her that there was so much about Tucker she didn't know. Given that he didn't seem to talk much about his past, the words felt like a gift. "That sounds like the perfect Christmas," she murmured dreamily. Like something you'd read about in a heartwarming Christmas story.

"I looked forward to it every year." He slowed the horses as they disappeared into the trees.

Kenna inhaled the crisp, cold air. Moonlight slanted through the evergreens, casting a dim glow on the snow-laden branches. It looked like another world, like they were inside a snow globe. "When's the last time you took it out?" she asked, mesmerized by the reverent quietness around them. "The sleigh, I mean."

"It hasn't been used since the last Christmas my old man was around. When I was seventeen."

"Seventeen?" She sat up straighter, inspecting the upholstery and the fine detail on the carved wood. "It's in great shape for not getting any use all those years."

"Yeah, I've kept it up." He jerked the reins, steering the horses left and up a hill. The animals moved slower through the deeper snow, chugging out breaths while they climbed the steady incline. "Over the last few years I worked on refinishing the whole thing."

"But you never wanted to use it?" She couldn't believe he'd spent all that time working on something he never used.

"I couldn't bring myself to." His lazy drawl had tightened. "Memories and all that. I've never wanted much to do with reliving the past."

It wasn't likely something he shared with just anyone, and Kenna suddenly realized they were walking a fine line with their whole fling agreement. But maybe he'd chosen to tell her because he knew she could relate. "It's painful." Reliving all of those moments when life had been the way it should be, full of happiness instead of fear and uncertainty and pain. Somehow, betrayal tarnished every single memory, even the good ones. She knew that for a fact.

But the more the sleigh glided, the more her own memories felt further and further away, lost in the dusting of powder behind them. "I guess that's why you have to make new memories." Like her and the boys cutting down that tree themselves. Though it hadn't seemed like a big deal at the time, it had been a pivotal moment for all of them. A way to bond and to forge their future together. They'd been so happy and proud. "The day-to-day struggle of living in survival mode makes it easy to ignore the fact that you have a future waiting for you," she admitted. It felt so open-ended and scary, especially when the past still haunted you.

"I wish I'd realized that a long time ago." Tucker clicked his tongue at the horses, steering the reins to the left around a thick stand of trees. "That the future matters more than the past. If my mom wouldn't have made it, I would've had all these regrets. Because I couldn't let go of the past. Because the holiday didn't mean anything to me anymore. I haven't gotten her a Christmas gift in fifteen years."

Kenna searched his face and found his eyes empty and dark.

"Then this seems like the perfect Christmas to find her the perfect gift," she said, easing her arm around his waist. "The perfect Christmas for you both to move forward." For her too. "We should make a pact not to look back this year. At least not until after the holidays."

Tucker tugged the horses to a stop and turned to face her. "You think it'll be that easy?"

"Sure," she bluffed. "Anytime you start to think about the

past, do something that makes you focus on the future instead."

"Something like this?" He dropped the reins and palmed
the back of her head, bringing her lips to his.

*Yes. Exactly this.* Kenna let herself go, edging up against
the hard muscle of him and fisting his coat in her mitten-
clad hands. His lips were cold, but when he opened his
mouth to her, a charge of warmth enveloped her entire
body and made every part of her simmer. Tucker took his
time with the kiss, keeping it slow and sensual, like he had
all night to explore how she liked to be kissed. Her heart
melted. They did have all night. *All. Night.*

Tucker kissed her until the fire burning in her lungs
spread all through her, but then he pulled back. "You
haven't even noticed the view yet."

"View?" What good was a view when he had a mouth
like that? To humor him, she followed his gaze, fully prepared to go right back to kissing him, but wow. That really
was some view. "You can see the whole town from up here."
Lights twinkled in the valley below, festive and colorful and
welcoming.

"My dad showed me this spot," he said quietly. "When I
was a kid. It's cool in the summer, but in the winter—around
Christmas—it's—"

"Magical," she whispered. Everything about this night
was magical. The sleigh and the snow and the horses. The
lights far off in the distance. Kenna turned back to Tucker,
feeling the magic reach deep inside of her. "You really
know how to show a woman a good time." Her tone teased
him, but in reality Tucker was the one teasing her. Every
time he touched her, every time he kissed her, her body responded with tingles and flutters and a growing desire to
feel more...everything he could give her.

He leaned in to kiss her, then traced his lips along her jaw all the way to her ear. "You haven't seen anything yet," he whispered.

"I need to see." Taking his jaw in her hands, she brought his lips back to hers. This time the kiss escalated so fast it drove the breath out of her lungs. Beneath the blanket, Tucker moved his hands slowly up her thighs and over her hips. He grabbed her butt, urging her to wriggle into his lap. Even through the bulk of their clothes, she could feel the hard bulge at his crotch grind against her.

A moan escaped her lips. "Take me back to your place." She couldn't wait any longer.

# Chapter Eight

The second Tucker steered the sleigh into the barn and pulled the horses to a stop, Kenna ripped off the blanket and tossed it onto the bench behind them. "That was quick." Thank God. After that little make-out session in the woods, her body quivered with impatience.

Tucker hopped down from the bench with a grin. "Yeah, those horses were in a hurry." He walked around the other side of the sleigh and slid his hands onto her waist, prompting her to jump down to the ground and land up against his body.

She fastened her hands behind his neck and pressed her hips against his. "I'm sure it was all the horses."

"Actually, it was all me," he rasped, kissing her again. The scruff on his jaw tickled her cheek, only adding to the sensations building inside of her. "I don't think you understand how much I want you, Kenna Hart." He pulled back and lowered his gaze down her body, and then swore under his breath. "I have to get the horses settled."

"Right." She let go of him and tried to breathe normally again, but Tucker had everything taken care of before her lungs could calm. He clasped her hand in his and pulled her out the door.

The wind had picked up, blowing the snow in swirls around them. Tucker pulled Kenna close against his side, ducking their heads together as they stomped through a layer of new snow up to his house. Nerves fluttered in her stomach, and it wasn't the typical butterflies. It was wild anticipation and desire and also fear all swarming together. How long had it been since she'd gone home with a man? So long she couldn't remember. What if she said the wrong thing? What if she completely chickened out?

Tucker didn't give her enough time to dwell on the *what ifs* before he urged her up the steps that led to his front door. She couldn't see much of the outside, but his place had a nice rambling front porch that had been decorated with colorful lights.

Once they were safely inside, a cozy warmth seeped into her. She shed her coat and mittens before stooping to remove her boots while Tucker did the same. Her hands trembled, making it hard to work the laces. "You have a nice place," she said to distract herself from the nerves. The house wasn't big, but it was nice and well kept. Beyond the small entryway, the space opened up into a living room with a stone fireplace. The uncluttered kitchen tucked into the far corner looked like it had recently been redone with gray cabinets, pristine white countertops, and a subway tile backsplash. Dark oak floors gleamed, and it seemed nothing in the whole house was out of place. She finally pulled off her boots and lined them up neatly next to his.

"You sound surprised." Tucker stood upright and took her hand to help her up.

"Well, I guess this is a generalization, but cowboys don't strike me as great housekeepers. Or decorators."

"Yeah, Mom helped me out." He led her into the living room, his hand at the small of her back. "But I'm pretty neat on my own. Don't like things in a mess."

"Clearly." She wandered away from him, admiring the fireplace mantel, which had been adorned with pine branches and sprigs of holly and twinkling white lights. In the corner next to the hearth stood a modest but beautiful Christmas fir, covered with colorful ornaments, some that appeared to be antiques. "You picked out a tree."

He came to stand next to her. "I showed my mom some pictures at the hospital. She wanted this one."

"It's perfect." Simple but thoughtful. Kind of like him, actually. Kenna glanced up at his face. There was that fluttering in her stomach again. If someone would've told her she was in danger of falling for Tucker McGrath, she would've told them they had another think coming. But that's exactly what was happening. It made her want to run and fall into his arms at the same time. But what would falling for Tucker mean? What would it mean for her? For the boys? Especially when he'd already told her he didn't fall for anyone?

The risk suddenly seemed too great. She simply wouldn't let herself fall for him. She would let loose and have some fun with him tonight, and then she would have to back off before her heart got involved.

"Why don't you sit?" He led her to the couch. "I'll get a fire going."

Caught up somewhere between hope and doubt, Kenna sank into the soft leather and watched Tucker work. He positioned some kindling around a crumpled newspaper and lit the edges. Once the flames caught, he wedged a couple of logs on top.

The fire gave the room a mesmerizing glow that seemed to seep into her very soul. Peace trickled through her, catching her by surprise. She hadn't gone home with a man in years, yet he made it so easy for her. Easy to talk, to be heard, to let emotions come. For once, she shoved aside the doubts. Doubts about herself, about whether she could love someone again. Doubts about whether he could love her. Like Everly had said, the answers to those questions didn't matter. She wasn't here to find love. She was here to have fun.

"Are you hungry?" From his spot on the floor, Tucker turned to face her. "I have leftover minestrone soup in the refrigerator."

She dragged her gaze up his body and looked into his eyes. "You cook too?" As if she needed more incentive to find him attractive.

"Hell no." He stood and walked to the couch. "It's Everly's soup. I buy a whole container of it every week in the winter." A smirk lit his eyes. "But if you wanted me to cook for you, I'd sure try."

His heated gaze made her feel sexy and alive, which made it that much easier to push away those nagging doubts. "I'm not hungry," she murmured, the ache of desire starting in her throat. Every part of her seemed to tighten in anticipation.

Tucker must've heard the eager notes in her voice. That same awareness flashed in his eyes when he sat down next to her. He eased his arm around her, gathering her in closer. "Tell me about Christmas when you were a kid."

Kenna rested her head on his shoulder. "It was simple, but so magical. My parents didn't have much money, but they always managed to surprise us with the most amazing gifts. Not expensive ones, but thoughtful ones. Like one time they got me this cheap plastic microphone that sounded all crackly and staticky, but they knew how much I loved to sing." It was the best gift she'd ever gotten because it was the most thoughtful.

"That sounds like my childhood Christmases." He massaged her shoulder, and she leaned into his caresses.

"We never had that much either, but it didn't matter. We were happy. Before my dad left. Before my mom got sick. We didn't need much because we were happy."

She had been too. Once. "I think I've forgotten all about that. How simple it can be. How complicated I've made it in the past with all of the running around and the pressure to make everything perfect."

"It's easy to complicate things."

She turned fully to him. "You don't seem like a very complicated man." He was straightforward and confident, and she needed more of that right now.

"I know what I want," he said, running his hand up her thigh.

Kenna inhaled with the exhilaration of that simple touch. Forget everything else. Forget what might happen tomorrow. Tonight she needed his touch, needed him to remind her how good she could feel. "I'm glad. Because my life has been far too complicated lately, and it feels good to escape. To step away from it all." She looked deeply into his eyes. "It feels good to be here. With you." Her heart was doing things she'd been sure it would never do again.

"It feels real good," Tucker agreed, leaning in to kiss her. This time there was more purpose behind it, more deliberation. His movements were swift and sure. "Tell me what you want."

"I want new memories." She unbuttoned his shirt, her fingers grazing the skin all the way down his chest. "I want to feel something again." Her hands got shaky as she slid the shirt off his shoulders to reveal the muscled torso beneath. There was so much power in him. So much strength.

Tucker eased back against the cushions, and she moved to straddle his hips. "What do *you* want, Tucker?"

"That's easy." He propped himself up on his elbows and grabbed the hem of her sweater in his fist and pulled her down to him. "You," he murmured in her ear. "I just want you." His lips grazed her neck on their way back to her mouth. He peeled off her sweater and pulled it up and over her head and Kenna reached around to unclasp her bra. Tucker watched, his eyes growing darker and darker.

Slowly, she inched the straps down her shoulders and tossed it aside.

Tucker sat up, too, bringing his mouth level with her breasts. He kissed and licked and sucked, until her head fell back and she was reduced to gasps. It had been so long since she'd been touched.

"You sure about this?" Tucker asked, peering into her eyes. "Because if you're not, now would be a good time to stop."

Stop? Oh no. They were not stopping. There was no stopping that drumming in her heart, the burn of desire swirling low in her belly. "I'm sure." Her voice sounded as sultry as the heat from the fire across from them. "I'm very sure." She unclasped his belt. "I want this." The rush, the intimacy, the euphoria.

With a grin, Tucker lowered his mouth back to her breasts. Somehow, he shifted and stood up, still holding her, still kissing her, before he gently set her feet on the floor. The waist of his jeans gapped where she'd undone his belt, displaying hard muscle stretched between his hip bones.

She got a little shaky just looking at him.

"Has anyone ever told you how damn sexy you are?" His

eyes worked their way over her, seeming to take in every inch.

"I don't think so." Mike used to call her cute, sometimes adorable. But then he'd never had as much intensity as the man standing in front of her.

"Well you are." He dropped his hands to the button on her jeans, ripping it open. "You're so sexy I can't think." His hands worked her jeans down over her hips, then moved to cup her butt. "So sexy you've got me aching."

"I'm aching too," she assured him. Every part of her ached with need. She wriggled until her jeans slid down to the floor; then she stepped out of them.

The fire's flickering light made Tucker's eyes look even darker when his gaze drifted down her body before slowly coming back to hers. "I was wrong. You're not sexy. You're hotter than sin."

"The same could be said about you." She moved closer to touch him—running her hands lightly down his abdomen to where his jeans splayed open. Her fingers fumbled with the rest of the buttons, inching them down, down, before slipping into his boxer briefs. That seemed to make him extra impatient. He shoved his jeans and underwear off and stepped out of them in one motion, and whatever strength she'd had left in her knees completely dissolved.

Tucker didn't give her much time to admire him. He stepped up to her, sliding one arm around her waist to pull her up against his body. The feel of him hard against her amplified every sensation until her entire body shook with anticipation. Breathless, she stood on her tiptoes to kiss him.

A rough and manly moan escaped his mouth as she slid her tongue against his. His hands slid lower to her hips and then nudged her legs apart. When his fingers grazed her hot wetness, she dug her fingertips into his shoulders to keep her balance.

Tucker secured his other arm around her waist while his fingers teased, sliding in deep and then back out, all the way to graze her most sensitive spot before doing it again. "You're ready for me, aren't you?" he asked in a low growl.

"Yes," she gasped. "Oh God, yes." She'd been ready for him since he'd kissed her in the sleigh. Hot and wet and desperate.

Tucker located his wallet and pulled out a condom. After he had it on, he lifted her against his body again, securing his hand under her butt and kissing her neck while he walked them over to the dining room table. He set her on the very edge and moved in between her legs, guiding her hips up to meet his as he pushed into her.

"Aw, hell." Tucker's breathing had gone ragged. "You feel so good, Kenna." He palmed the back of her head and brought her into another kiss, slow and deep, rocking his hips to match the rhythm.

Kenna braced her hands on the table behind her to hold herself up while she arched to meet his thrusts.

"That's it, baby." He rocked faster. "Let yourself go."

For the first time in so long, she could. She could give herself over to him, over to passion, over to the deepest physical connection possible. "My God, you're good at this," she panted.

Tucker laughed. "We're good together." He dipped his finger between her legs, rubbing at that spot again to completely shatter her control.

"Tuck—" She couldn't even get his name out before her body clenched around him, drawing him in as deep as he could go. His arms pulled her in tighter while his hips pumped harder, triggering aftershocks one after another until his body convulsed, emptying into her. Somehow they ended up leaning into each other, arms tangled, Tucker's forehead on Kenna's shoulder. When her breathing recovered enough that she could speak, she raised her head. "That was the most fun I've had in a really long time."

He smoothed her hair away from her face and kissed her lips before lifting her into his arms. "We're just getting started."

# Chapter Nine

In one night, Tucker had pretty much broken every rule in the casual hookups handbook.

He'd told Kenna things about his dad. Things he'd never told anyone else. Like how they used to play the guitar together and how he still couldn't hear a John Denver song without thinking about his father. Then he'd gone and asked her to stay all night, which was how they'd ended up here, all snuggled up together on the couch.

She still slept soundly in the fire's dull glow. He'd been awake for well over a half hour, noticing things he'd never bothered to notice about a woman—like the way her chest felt as it rose and fell against his, the way she looked like she was smiling even though she still slept so soundly, the way her soft hair spilled over his shoulder.

At some point last night after they'd been too exhausted to keep their eyes open any longer, he'd pulled a soft fleece blanket over them. It still covered most of them, but one of Kenna's legs—the one that was draped over his leg—stuck out, giving him the perfect view of that creamy skin. So soft. He was tempted to run his hand up her thigh, but he didn't know what would happen if he woke her. This was all foreign territory to him. It hadn't necessarily occurred to him in the moment because he'd been seriously distracted, but sex with Kenna had been different somehow. Still hot and heady, but more intimate because of the time they'd spent talking in between. Over the hours he'd seen her heart open to him, but touching her and pleasing her had allowed him to ignore the undercurrents of panic running through him.

Now, though, the panic had returned.

What the hell had he done? There was no playbook for this. For what to do when he'd let things go too deep. He'd never found himself here before.

Before he could figure something out, Kenna started to move against him. First one leg, then the other. "Mmmm." She yawned and opened her eyes.

Damn she was gorgeous. Even more so with her hair all wild and her eyes still sleepy. A strange sense of content gripped him, and he realized he didn't want her to go. Didn't want last night to be over. That meant something, right? It meant maybe he shouldn't run this time. Maybe he shouldn't have the *talk* about how he really wasn't looking for a commitment. Maybe for once he didn't need a next move. Maybe he just needed to let this ride.

Maybe that was a hell of a lot of maybes...

"What time is it?" Kenna asked, arching into an adorable stretch.

"Almost eight." Tucker started to trace his fingers down her arm, but she sat bolt upright, eyes as wide as if she'd just woken from a nightmare.

"Eight? Seriously?" She wrestled herself out of the blanket and flailed to get off the couch.

Whoa. It definitely didn't seem like he'd have to give her *the talk*, even if he'd wanted to. Suddenly Kenna didn't seem to want to talk at all.

She rushed around collecting various articles of clothing off the floor and clumsily putting them back on.

He guessed that was his cue to get moving too. After locating his boxers on the center of the coffee table, he rose to put them on. "I thought Everly wasn't expecting you to pick up the boys at the café until nine." In his estimation they could get in another round and still be on time.

"But I have to go home!" She pulled on her shirt without bothering to clasp her bra. "I have to change! And take a shower! Oh my God. I shouldn't have stayed here all night."

Um...what was he supposed to say to that? Usually he was the one rushing off in the morning, not the other way around. "Why not?"

"Because! My car was parked at the town hall all night. That's right in the middle of town! Do you know how many people probably drove by and saw it there? They're going to know. *Everyone's* going to know."

"Know what? They can't possibly know you were here with me." And so what if they did?

Instead of answering the question, Kenna tossed him the rest of his clothes. "Get dressed. I have to go. Last night was fun, but I have to get back to reality."

*Back to reality.* Tucker pulled on his jeans and shirt. He got it. Her reality and his were worlds apart. She didn't even want her friends to know they'd spent the night together. Waking up with her in his arms had brought a rush of thoughts and feelings that temporarily tricked him into thinking this thing between them might have potential to turn into more than a fling, but she'd set him straight real quick. Well, good. That meant she was willing to keep things in the fling territory exactly like he wanted. Yep. That's what he wanted. Something simple and clean.

Except it didn't seem to sit right with him this time. Rather than unpack why, he stuffed his wallet into his back pocket and grabbed his keys. "Come on, I'll take you to your car."

They both pulled on their boots and winter gear before wading through the layer of new snow that had fallen overnight. He opened the passenger door of his truck and helped her climb in. Once he settled in beside her, he started the engine and blasted the heat.

She remained as quiet as he did on the drive back to town. Tucker glanced at her a few times in between turns and stoplights, but he couldn't tell what she was thinking.

"Where's my Jeep?"

He'd been so busy trying to figure her out, he hadn't realized they'd already reached the town hall. But she was right. Her Jeep wasn't parked where it had been when they left last night. There was, however, a rectangular bare space next to the curb with snow piled up around it.

"Where's my car?" she asked again, sitting straight and tall, gaping out the window.

"I don't know." Tucker pulled over behind the bare space and let the truck idle.

Kenna tore off her seat belt and bolted out of the truck. "Where could it be?"

He got out too. She'd parked it there. He saw it himself when they left last night. It had been right there ...

"Do you think someone stole it?" She whirled to him, her face gripped by genuine panic.

"No. There's no way." Not in Topaz Falls. Though it

might have been better if it had been stolen. He had a bad feeling. She might not want her friends to know she'd spent the night with him, but the way things went in Topaz Falls, he was afraid they'd all find out. "I need to call Dev. See if he knows anything." He pulled out his phone and dialed the deputy's number but it went right to voice mail. "He's not answering. I'll bet he's at the café." Tucker headed for the driver's seat, but Kenna hung back.

"I can't show up at the café with you! The boys are there!" Now instead of panicked, she looked downright horrified. "This was supposed to be a fun fling, but now the whole town will be talking and speculating and reading into things!"

He didn't argue with her. Hell, last night had *him* reading into things. "You can wait in the truck." He tried to speak calmly. Someone had to stay calm. "I'll go in and find Dev."

They endured a silent five-minute ride to the café. He didn't think it wise to share his speculations before they were confirmed, and Kenna seemed to be in no mood to hear them anyway.

Doing his best to keep their cover intact, he parked at the far end of the café's lot and left the truck running while he ran in. Kenna had been right. The place was packed. There wasn't even a spare table. Luckily, Dev was at his usual table and the seat across from him was empty. "Hey," Tucker said as he sat across from Dev.

"Hi?" Dev might as well have asked why the hell he was sitting down. It wasn't like they'd ever shared breakfast.

He decided to get right to it. "Do you know what happened to Kenna Hart's car?"

The deputy mopped his mouth with a napkin before tossing it on his plate. "Sure," he said, all laid back. "Hank had it towed."

*Shit.* That's what he'd been afraid of. "Why?"

"Because it was parked in front of the town hall past ten," Hank yelled over from the other side of the room.

Tucker should've known. The mayor of Topaz Falls was always listening.

"It says nice and clear on the sign *no parking between ten p.m. and six a.m.* I checked at five this morning and her car was still there."

That was all it took to draw interested stares from the other patrons.

That bad feeling gouged a good-sized hole in Tucker's gut. *Uh-oh.*

"I tried to call her a few times after Hank called me," Dev said. "But it went straight to voice mail. To be honest, I got worried and drove by her house, but she didn't answer the door."

"Well, are we sure she's all right?" Betty Osterman, aka the town gossip, asked from a nearby booth. "Maybe she's in trouble. Maybe she's been abducted as a sex slave!"

Tucker gripped his forehead and squeezed.

"Nah." Dev waved off the worry. "When Kenna didn't answer the door, I called up Everly since they're close, and she told me she thought Kenna might be on a date."

"A date? *All night?*" Betty demanded.

Murmurs went around the room.

If Tucker could've slipped out unnoticed, he would have. What was he supposed to do here? Things were getting way out of hand. Kenna obviously didn't want anyone to know about their fling, but now the whole town would definitely hear by noon.

"Tucker!" Everly hurried over to their table. "I'm surprised to see you here." Her wide eyes probed him for information. After glancing around, she leaned closer. "I thought Kenna was with you," she whispered.

Dev did a double take. "She was on a date with *you* all night?"

Tucker gave them both a look meant to shut them up. "Kenna's fine," he said evenly. "There's nothing to worry about." Well, nothing for them to worry about. He had plenty to worry about. All those people staring, still trying to eavesdrop, for example. "So where's her car?" He slid out of the booth, ready to make a fast exit.

"County impound lot." At least the deputy had the decency to look remorseful. "If I'd known she was with you, I would've called your cell."

"Keep. It. Down." He didn't know why he said it. It was too late. Everyone had already heard. It was too late for damage control now.

"Did you guys have fun?" Everly whispered with a smile.

Like he was going to share that with twenty of his closest neighbors. "Where are the boys?" he asked instead.

"They're out feeding the goats and chickens with Mateo."

"Can they hang out here a little longer?"

"Of course." Her eyebrows bounced teasingly. "They can stay as long as you guys need them to."

He ignored the innuendo and started for the door. "She'll be back to pick them up in a couple of hours," he muttered to Everly. Under the watchful eyes of everyone in the room, he booked it back outside.

"Well? Did he know where my car was?" Kenna asked the second he climbed back into the truck.

"Yeah." He clicked in his seat belt and opted not to look at her directly. "Apparently Hank noticed your car this morning and had it towed."

"Oh Lord." Her hands went straight to her face. "Now

everyone'll find out! Everyone will know we spent a night together."

A night? So that was it? One night with Kenna and it was over? The unease that had sat with him all morning turned rock solid in his gut. "You sure didn't seem worried about that last night," he said, staring straight ahead. In fact, she hadn't worried about anything last night. She'd been open and relaxed and happy. Or so he'd thought.

"No. I wasn't worried. Because no one knew. But what are people going to think now? I'm a mom, Tucker. I have two little boys. Responsibilities. Commitments. And you're—" She stopped suddenly.

"I'm what?" His throat had gotten raw. Something told him he didn't want to hear the end of that sentence.

"Well, you know."

No, actually, he didn't. Not anymore. Last week he would've said he was happy with his life the way it was, but Kenna had gotten to him. Somehow she'd made him feel like he needed more.

He let her sit in the uncomfortable silence, waiting to hear her give him any indication that she felt as conflicted as he did about their arrangement.

She sighed. "You're a great guy, but it's not like this can go anywhere."

And there was his answer.

# Chapter Ten

Tucker was rarely late anywhere. In fact, he usually preferred to be at least ten minutes early anywhere he went, but tonight he was taking his sweet time to get to the rehearsal. He pulled into the hospital parking lot figuring a few more minutes wouldn't matter.

Kenna could handle things at the rehearsal until he got there, and if he was being honest, he wasn't sure he could handle seeing her. The last few days had been fine because he hadn't seen her, hadn't heard from her, had done his damnedest to not think about her. But he already knew it hadn't been long enough for the sting of her rejection to wear off, and once he saw her it wouldn't be so easy to ignore. So instead of going to face her, here he was at the hospital. He'd been by earlier that morning but his mom had asked him to go take care of some things at her house, which had inevitably turned into taking care of a whole lot of things at her house, which was how he'd lost track of time.

He climbed out of his truck and followed the familiar path through the main entrance and up the elevator. A couple of the nurses waved at him as he strode down the hall, and he stopped to thank them for all they'd done for his mom. With any luck she'd be released in a few days. The nurses had been so good to Birdie, and he wanted them to know it hadn't gone unnoticed.

And here he was procrastinating again. Tucker bid the nurses goodbye and glanced at his watch. At this point, he was more than a little late for the rehearsal, so he'd have to make the visit with his mom quick. He rushed down the hall without stopping to chat with anyone else and pushed open the door. "Hey, Mo—"

The words died in his throat.

Why the hell was his father sitting in a chair next to the bed?

The years had added more lines to the man's face and more gray to his hair, but other than that he looked about the same—complete with the full beard he'd worn for as long as Tucker could remember.

A fiery anger swelled through him, burning up everything in its path—even the shock that had silenced him. Tucker didn't walk into the room. He couldn't walk. Couldn't breathe. He could only stand there and stare at the man who had left them behind.

His father stood slowly and removed his Stetson, holding it nervously in both hands in front of his waist. His faded brown eyes locked on Tucker with a wary apprehension. "Hey there, son."

Son? No. He'd lost the right to call him that a long time ago. "Get out." Tucker held his ground just outside the door. "Get the hell out of here. You have no right to be here."

His father said nothing, but his mother swung her legs

over the side of the bed and eased herself to her feet. That got him moving. Tucker hurried to her side before she lost her balance and fell. She was still too weak to take this kind of stress. "Come on, Mom. Get back in bed."

"No." She wrenched away from him. "*No.* I won't let you do this anymore, Tucker. I called him and asked him to come. He's not leaving. Not until you two make amends."

He would rather stand in front of one of the Cortez brothers' prize-winning bulls than spend one more minute in his father's presence, but he didn't say so. He simply helped his mom back into the hospital bed.

"Dinner." His dad finally spoke. "We could go have dinner. Something quick. So we can catch up."

"Catch up." Tucker turned to him, anger pumping through him. "Sure, Dad. Let's catch up. Let me tell you all about the last fifteen years. I'd love to reminisce about all the doctor appointments you weren't there for. The hospital stays just like this one. The holidays you missed, the birthdays." The hundreds of thousands of moments his father could've been with his family. Yes, his father tried calling a few times. He'd sent a few letters, but that didn't change the fact that he'd walked out on them. He'd turned his back, so Tucker had done the same.

"I'm sorry." His father sank back into the chair and stared down at his boots.

The sight of the man's obvious remorse didn't make Tucker feel any better. It didn't numb the pain that pulsed in his chest, didn't calm the rush of blood in his ears. Nothing could. Not a dinner with his father, not yelling at the man and putting him in his place. Nothing could fill the hole his dad had left. Nothing could heal him. His father had taught him to bail out on any significant relationship before the other person could. And now Tucker always left first so no one else could leave him. Until Kenna. She made him want to stay, but now he wasn't worthy of her or her boys.

Benny's wise words came back to haunt him. *Learning to forgive people for their mistakes is one of the most important things you will ever do in your whole life.* But Tucker didn't know how. He didn't know how to sit across the table from the man he'd spent years resenting. He didn't know how to lay down the shield that had protected him from the pain.

Emotion built into a painful lump that lodged in his throat. "I have to go." Before it all came out. Anger was one thing but the pain of knowing he wasn't worth sticking around for could stay buried down deep where it belonged. "Love you, Mom. I'll swing by tomorrow." He managed to make it to the door without looking at his father.

"Tucker." Birdie's weepy voice stopped him cold. "Please don't go. Do this for me."

She'd never asked him for much. She'd never shamed him for holding a grudge. She'd never forced his hand in anything except for this. There was no way he could tell her no. And what about Benny? And Kenna? If he did this, if he faced the source of his own fears, maybe things could be different. Maybe he could find a way to fight for her...for *them.*

"Tomorrow," he muttered. "Dinner at the Tumble Inn." That should give him plenty of time to prepare.

\*       \*       \*

Kenna's fingers clumsily pounded the piano keys, hitting flats where there should've been sharps and slowing down the tempo of their fifth attempt at "Go Tell It on the Mountain." Yet again she played the wrong chord, silencing the kids' adorable singing.

Violet, her lead soloist, stood on the stage with her hands planted on her hips. "You messed up again, Miss Hart! Now we have to start all over."

"I know. I'm sorry." Unfortunately, her brain simply couldn't seem to connect with her hands today. There was simply too much going on in there. There had been too much going on in there since she'd spent the night with Tucker.

"Okay." She sat straighter, inhaled enough oxygen to fill a balloon, and started the song over again. "Take it from the top," she instructed.

The chorus of young voices rose again, keeping an impressive harmony considering most of them hadn't had any formal training. She fought to focus on the kids, on the song, but they only made it a few bars in before her mind drifted again.

Taking her eyes off the sheet music, she glanced toward the door like she had been for the last hour. Tucker hadn't shown up to rehearsal tonight. She hadn't seen him or heard from him in four days. Not since he'd dropped her off at her car at the impound lot. And it was all her fault.

She'd told him she wanted a Christmas fling, but she hadn't known she would wake up completely and totally content in his arms. For those few seconds, her body had hummed and her heart had nearly burst with a feeling of fullness, like she could stretch that second out forever and be happy.

It had been her first fling and she'd screwed it up by completely falling for the man. That's why she'd had to get away from him. She'd opened herself up without meaning to, and the realization had left her feeling vulnerable and exposed and foolish. So she'd given him an out, telling him she didn't expect it to go anywhere, and he'd obviously taken it, not even bothering to show up for the rehearsal tonight.

"Miss Hart! That wasn't right!" Violet stomped over to the edge of the stage while the other voices awkwardly wound down. "How are we ever going to get it if you don't play the song right?"

"Actually, I think you've all got it." And she clearly would not get the song right tonight. Kenna stood and collected the sheet music she hadn't been able to focus on. "So what'd you say we take a little break? I brought some cookies to celebrate our last rehearsal." Sugar cookies and some gingersnaps, which Tucker mentioned were his favorites.

But he wasn't here.

The kids all cheered—even Violet who was usually a stickler about finishing a song—and Kenna walked around handing out the cookies along with a festive napkin. The kids clumped in groups, sitting on the risers and stage while they chatted and enjoyed their cookies, content to eat and joke around, which gave her another opportunity to check her phone. No calls. No texts. Disappointment seared into her heart.

That night she and Tucker had spent together had been magical—the snow, the sleigh, and yes, the sex, but also things he'd shared with her, the pain of his father's abandonment, and how much he loved and respected his mom. Seeing that different side of him had tugged at the barriers she'd put up around her heart, pulling harder and harder until at last he'd torn them away and she'd allowed herself to connect with him on more than a physical level.

And all she could think when her senses came back to her after she woke up was that she'd set herself up to get her heart broken all over again. Who was she kidding? She wasn't bold or brave or—

A scream from the back of the stage sliced through the thought. Right as Kenna spun to see what had happened, a whole ensemble of screams broke out and kids flooded the steps, running toward her. She looked past them and let out a squeal herself when she saw the water spraying from the ceiling and gushing out through the light fixtures. A pipe must've burst...

"It's flooding! The building is flooding!" Violet yelped, bumping past her.

"Everyone stay calm!" Kenna hurried to the edge of the stage to herd the last of the kids down the steps and toward the doors. Sparks flashed behind her, making the lights buzz and flicker. "Get on your coats!" she yelled over the panicked screeches. "Everything will be fine, but we need to evacuate the building." Kneeling down to help the younger kids with their zippers, Kenna somehow managed to hit the emergency call button on her cell phone and braced it between her ear and her shoulder. She quickly told the dispatcher the situation and then hurried over to comfort Benny, who'd started to cry.

"It's okay, buddy." She took his hand in hers, searching for Jake. He was already near the front of the group, his eyes sparkling with excitement. The kid always loved a dramatic scene.

"Come on, everyone!" Kenna squeezed Benny's hand. "Let's line up and go outside." As the kids got themselves organized, she did a quick head count to make sure they were all accounted for. "Get on your mittens and hats and coats." It would be cold, but the fire department should be there shortly and maybe they could let the kids sit in the truck to keep them warm.

It wasn't exactly orderly, but the kids streamed out the doors and onto the sidewalks in front of the building.

"Mama!" Benny tugged on her hand. "What about the pageant? What's gonna happen to the pageant now?"

Kenna looked back at the building, which had gone dark. "I don't know, sweetie," she murmured, kneeling down to gather him into a hug.

Her sweet son broke out into a round of heartbreaking sobs. "Christmas is ruined."

## Chapter Eleven

Ah, the optimism of kids.

Kenna listened to Benny and Jake talk in the backseat of the Jeep. In their minds, last night had simply been an exciting adventure—especially the half hour they'd sat in the fire truck while they waited for all of the other kids' parents to come and pick them up—and now they were sure they'd be able to walk into the town hall and get right back on that stage. They'd even talked Kenna into driving them over there to check things out.

"I bet the firemen took care of everything and it's all better and we can still have the pageant," Benny told his brother with a rock-solid confidence.

Kenna wasn't so sure, but she didn't want to ruin that hope for them. What was life without hope anyway? Dull, gray, and barren. Hope added the color, the energy, the purpose. So she wouldn't take it away. They might find themselves disappointed, but that could easily be dealt with.

Above everything else, she wanted them to learn to hold
on to hope, even through the disappointment—*especially*
through the disappointment. Kind of like she was trying to
do right now.

Well, she wasn't exactly holding on…more like grasping at hope that maybe she hadn't damaged things beyond
repair with Tucker.

"Mommy, why is all the furniture on the sidewalk?" Jake
had plastered his face and both hands to his window.

Kenna glanced down the street, and sure enough, it
looked like the town hall building had been completely
emptied. Pews and cabinets and chairs and desks and even
the piano sat on the front walk.

Kenna parked on the other side of the street and glanced
at the mess, knowing what was coming but suddenly unsure
of how to prepare the boys. Her gaze stopped on a ladder.
*The* ladder. The one she'd fallen off of right before Tucker
had kissed her.

"Come on, Mom! Let's go see what's going on!" The
boys wrestled out of their booster seats and they all
climbed out of the Jeep. Kenna held their hands as they
crossed the street and walked down the sidewalk to meet
Hank Green. The mayor's grim expression seemed to
make the boys clam up.

"Hello, Mayor Green," she said, trying to keep her voice
bright. "We wanted to come by and see about the pageant."

"There isn't gonna be a pageant," Hank grumbled in his
crotchety manner. "A main pipe burst. The whole building
flooded. The restoration will take months."

Benny squeezed her hand tighter. She peeked at his face,
noting the strained expression that meant he was holding
back tears. "But surely there's someplace else we could
have it."

"Everything was destroyed." Hank indicated a large Dumpster near the main entrance. "Had to throw out the set. Don't even think we'll be able to save the piano."

"It's gone?" Benny whispered. "Everything's gone?"

"Even the new stable?" Jake asked sadly.

"I'm afraid so." The mayor's firm frown seemed to budge just a little as he looked down at her boys. "Where's Tucker anyway? Isn't he supposed to be in charge with his mom in the hospital? I thought I would've seen him by now."

Kenna's gaze wandered back to the ladder again. "I'm not sure. I haven't seen him in a few days."

"Well, then, you'd best go on over to the hospital and break the news about the pageant to Birdie."

"Right. I can do that. The boys and I will stop over there on our way home." Maybe Tucker would be there. She could at least apologize for what she'd said to him. She'd basically implied she didn't like him well enough to see a possible future, and that was a flat-out lie. She needed to be honest with him. She'd been so determined to take back her life, to move forward and embrace the future, but then she'd spooked at the first sign of feeling something for someone again.

Kenna said goodbye to Mayor Green and led the boys back to the Jeep. They sniffled the whole way.

"Now I'll never get to be a wise guy." Jake climbed into his booster seat and hung his head.

Kenna leaned in and kissed his nose. "Don't talk like that. There's always next year."

"But the stable's gone," Benny whimpered. "And it was so amazing. Tucker just built it."

"And I'll bet you he can build it again." Kenna gave each of their knees a squeeze before closing the back door and climbing into the driver's seat. "I know you're both disappointed, but we don't want to make this harder for Miss Birdie, right?" She turned around to look at them. "So when we tell her, we need to put on smiles and tell her even if we can't do the pageant this year, we'll make it ten times better next year." Though she doubted that would help. The woman lived for the pageant.

Jake and Benny seemed to consider that. "Miss Birdie's gonna be so sad," her oldest murmured. "She loves the pageant more than anyone."

"Maybe we could cheer her up," her littlest blond cherub suggested.

"Yeah!" Jake gasped. "Come on, Mom, you always tell us the best thing to do when you're sad is to make someone else happy and then you'll feel happy too."

Did she say that? She'd kind of forgotten about that philosophy. Kids never seemed to forget anything, though.

"We could go buy her one of those tiny Christmas trees at the farm," Benny said.

"And we could make ornaments at home real quick," Jake added.

"We'll make stars and reindeer and angels." Benny clapped his hands. "She'll love a Christmas tree! Everyone loves Christmas trees. It'll make her feel all better!"

How could she say no to that? "All right." Kenna took a quick right so she could get onto the highway.

The boys perked up on the drive out to the farm. When they arrived, they found the last miniature tree on the lot—a sad little Charlie Brown number that was missing more than a few branches.

"It's perfect," Jake declared as they loaded it in the back of the Jeep.

"It's even uniquer than ours," Benny agreed.

Their excitement brought tears to Kenna's eyes. They

had such tender hearts. "All right, you two," she said with a sniffle. "We'd better hurry up and make those ornaments before it gets too late."

On the drive home, Jake and Benny serenaded her with their favorite carols, and once she pulled into the garage, the boys were off.

She caught up to them at the craft cabinet where they pulled out enough construction paper and glue to wallpaper the entire house. "How about you each make ten ornaments," she suggested, glancing at her watch. "We don't want to interrupt Miss Birdie's dinner."

"Okay! We'll be quick," they promised, already engrossed in cutting out shapes.

She gave them a half hour and then corralled them back into the Jeep.

"Remember," Kenna said as she pulled into a parking spot at the front of the hospital. "This is a quick trip. We're going to drop off the tree and then be on our way."

"Yes, ma'am!" Jake saluted her and the two boys giggled as they climbed out of the car. Benny claimed the box of ornaments and Jake wanted to carry the tree "all by himself." They received plenty of looks walking in.

"Merry Christmas," Jake said to an elderly couple near the doors.

"Merry Christmas." The woman and her husband shared a smile. Kenna smiled too. Leave it to her kids to remind her what Christmas was really about. Not the perfect presents or the perfect tree or even having the perfect family all put together. It was about this. Love. Pure and simple.

If only to remind her they were human and not angels, the boys had a little scuffle over who would push the elevator button, but Benny beat out his older brother. All the way up, the boys hummed "Jingle Bells" along with the elevator music. Once they'd made it to the general care hallway, Jake and Benny made a beeline for the nurse's station. "Where's Miss Birdie?" they demanded. "We brought her a Christmas tree."

"He means could you please tell us where to find Miss McGrath," Kenna corrected.

The amused nurse sent them down the hall to room 302. This time, Kenna didn't let them run on ahead. "You let me knock first."

The boys both stuck out pouty lips, but they obeyed.

Even though the door stood partially open, Kenna knocked lightly.

"Come in!" Birdie sang.

The boys bounded past Kenna with their faces full of Christmas cheer.

"Hi, Miss Birdie!" Jake called. "We brought you a tree!"

"With ornaments and everything!" Benny added.

Kenna rushed to the bed to explain. "I'm so sorry to just show up like this, Birdie."

"Don't be sorry! This is a wonderful surprise." The woman planted her hands into the mattress and shimmied herself up to a sitting position. She looked as bright and happy as she usually did. "Come and sit." She patted a chair that had been pulled up next to the bed.

Kenna scooted into it and decided not to delay the inevitable. "I'm afraid we have some bad news."

"There was a flood last night!" Jake blurted. "During the rehearsal! Water was shooting out everywhere!"

Birdie's jovial smile fell. "What?"

"A pipe burst," Kenna explained. "We stopped by this morning, and Hank said there's no way we can do the pageant. The set was ruined, and the auditorium won't be open again for a couple of months."

Instead of the sadness Kenna had expected to see, determination narrowed the woman's eyes. "That's ridiculous. No pageant. Ha! We'll see about that. We simply can't have Christmas in Topaz Falls without a pageant."

"Don't worry, Miss Birdie." Jake approached the bed. "We're here to cheer you up. That's why we brought the tree."

"And look at that tree." Birdie reached out to touch a few of the branches. "What a fine Christmas tree."

Both boys puffed out their chests like little roosters.

"You can go ahead and set up that beautiful tree right there." She pointed to the corner near the bed.

"You got it!" Jake dragged it over and the boys got to work decorating it with their ornaments.

"What is that?" Ms. McGrath leaned closer to look at one. "A star? Oh and what a lovely angel!"

"We made them." Jake hung the angel on the tree.

"All by ourselves." Benny held out the box so she could see.

"Well, they're beautiful. They're just beautiful. And you boys sure have the right idea with Christmas spirit." When Birdie turned her attention back to Kenna, her smile had doubled in size. "Speaking of Christmas spirit, let's chat about this pageant. What did Tucker say?"

The question likely hadn't been intended to make her squirm but she did anyhow. "Oh. Uh. Actually, I'm not sure he knows about the flood."

Birdie folded her hands on the blanket that had been pulled up to her waist. "And why not?"

*Because I botched our fling and now he's avoiding me.* "I haven't seen him for a few days. And he didn't come to rehearsal last night." Kenna checked on the boys, who were still completely engrossed in covering the tree with colorful scraps of construction paper. "I'm afraid I may have upset him."

"I highly doubt that," Birdie murmured through a sigh. "It's me who upset him. That's why he didn't come to the rehearsal last night. I asked his father to come back to town to make things right with Tucker."

His father. Kenna remembered the raw pain she'd heard in his voice when he'd talked about the man. "His father came back?"

"He did." Birdie paused to collect herself. "He wanted to. He agreed it was time. I won't be around forever, and I can't stand to see my boy so closed off. He needs to make peace with the grief he never let himself feel."

So that was why Tucker didn't show up last night. Not because he was angry with her or trying to avoid her, but because he'd seen his father. God, what had that done to him? "Did they talk? Did everything go okay?" She should've called him last night...

"Tucker was shocked to see him." Worry clouded Birdie's face. "But I asked him to talk to his dad, to do it for me. So they're having dinner tonight. I know one dinner won't fix everything, but I'm hoping it will be a start."

Kenna hoped so, too, but she also knew how painful it must be for Tucker to face the man who'd wounded him so deeply.

"We're done!" Jake and Benny stood back from the tree, admiring their work.

"Wow." Birdie sat there taking it in for a long while. Tears misted her eyes. "That is the loveliest tree I've ever had. Ever."

Benny walked over to the bed and patted her hand. "Maybe it'll make you feel all better so you can go home for Christmas."

"You know, I think I'm starting to feel better already." She snatched a Kleenex off the bedside table and dabbed at her eyes. "And now I have something for you boys."

"Really?" Jake and Benny shared a look of utter anticipation. They loved surprises.

"There's a platter of the best sugar cookies you'll ever taste down at the nurse's station," Birdie said. "Why don't you boys go get yourselves one?"

"Are you sure?" Kenna held them back a minute. "I don't want them bothering the nurses." And she really should be going. She should call Tucker. If only to leave a message and let him know she was thinking about him.

"Let them have a cookie," Birdie said kindly. "Those nurses love it when kids come to visit. And they've been trying to pawn those cookies off on everyone who walks in." She shooed them away. "Go ahead, you two. It's just down the hall."

"Come right back," Kenna called behind them.

As soon as they'd cleared the doorway, Birdie leaned close. "Tucker told me about how the four of you decorated the tree at your house. He cares about you. I can see it when he talks about you. Something changes in him." She said the words quickly, like she wanted to get them out before the boys came back.

The revelation did nothing to dislodge the sadness Kenna had been carrying around for the past few days. "He cares about you too," she said, redirecting the conversation. She couldn't tell Birdie everything that had happened between them. She couldn't admit she'd knowingly pushed him away. "You should see the Christmas decorations he put up all over his house, just in case you were able to come home."

"He decorated his house?" The woman's eyes got watery again.

"He went all out. Lights and a tree. Garlands everywhere. There were even stockings hanging over the fireplace." Oh, that fireplace. It was seared into her memory. That beautiful soft glow lighting the room while they'd made love. She tried to suppress the craving that rose up but could no longer keep the truth to herself. "I'm afraid I ruined everything with him. I got scared. And I told him we couldn't have a future together."

The confession didn't seem to shock Birdie. She simply rested a comforting hand on Kenna's forearm. "After what you've been through, I know how hard it is to trust. Believe me. But even if you're not sure you can trust someone else yet, trust yourself. You're so strong, Kenna. And you've made it through some of the worst things anyone could deal with. What is your heart telling you now?"

"To go for it." The feelings she had for Tucker were raw and real and deep. That's why she'd been so scared. But Tucker had reminded her to be brave. He'd helped her out of the empty shell she'd been living in. He'd reminded her what it felt like to smile, to flirt, to *feel*. She'd feared the intensity between them, but now she was far more afraid of missing out on something beautiful because she was scared to take a risk. "I don't want to be afraid anymore. But I need your help, Birdie. I don't know how to show him I didn't mean what I said."

"Well first things first, my dear. If we find a way to make the pageant happen, you and Tucker will have to work together again." She tapped a finger against her chin a few times before letting out a gasp. "Oh! I just got the best idea. There's a live band playing at the Tumble Inn tonight, which means everyone will be there. You have to make an announcement to the entire town. Tell everyone we need their help to pull off the pageant."

"I can't make an announcement in front of everyone." She couldn't stand in the spotlight after keeping herself in the shadows for a year.

"Why ever not?"

Birdie seriously didn't know? "You've seen the way they still look at me. The whole town thinks I'm a charity case. No one will listen to me."

"Did Tucker look at you like that?" Birdie asked gently.

"No." He looked at her like the brave girl who'd taken on the high school football program. He looked at her with respect. And with enough fire to singe her eyelashes...

"Then simply think of Tucker when you get on that stage." Birdie squeezed Kenna's hands. "Trust me. Go to the Tumble Inn tonight. Tucker will be there having dinner with his father. Just trust your heart, Kenna dear, and everything else will fall into place."

# Chapter Twelve

Tucker hadn't realized there'd be live music at the Tumble Inn, but maybe it was for the best. Then he could sit across from his old man and listen to some country western band from Denver instead of actually being forced to talk, which might be safer for them both.

He crossed through the restaurant, sizing up the crowd. It was packed, so there'd also likely be plenty of interruptions and distractions from the anger he couldn't quite seem to get a handle on.

"Hey, Tucker." Lucas Cortez snagged him on his way past the bar. He sat with his brothers at a high-top table about as far away from the music as they could get.

"What's up?" Lance asked him.

Levi pushed out a stool. "We have a seat here. Got time for a beer?"

Tucker took a glance at his watch. He still had about fifteen minutes before his father would show up. *If* he showed up. After the exchange between them yesterday, Tucker wouldn't be surprised if the man skipped town again. It might not be a bad thing if he did.

"I definitely have time for a beer." He needed a beer. He joined the brothers at the table and signaled for a passing waiter to bring him the same IPA they were having.

"Hey, man, sorry to hear about the pageant," Lucas said. "I bet your mom is bummed."

Tucker gave his friend a blank look. "What did you hear about the pageant?" And why the hell would his mom be bummed?

"You haven't heard?" Levi demanded. "It got canceled. A main waterline into the building burst and flooded the town hall. I thought you would've been there when it happened."

The town hall had flooded? Shit. "Is everyone okay? All the kids?" And the woman he couldn't stop thinking about no matter how hard he tried?

Lance nodded. "They all got out quick from what I heard."

"The town hall is toast, though," Levi said. "They'll have to gut the place and start over. Hank said the set was destroyed."

Well, damn, his mother was going to have a fit. And he had to admit, he was disappointed too. No pageant meant he wouldn't be seeing much of Kenna or her boys anymore. Man, he should've been there. But this only proved he didn't belong with her. Instead of facing her, he'd done what he did every time things got complicated. He'd stayed away. Exactly like someone else he knew.

Tucker glanced at his watch. Five after six. The father he hadn't seen for fifteen years was officially late.

The waiter finally set down his beer in front of him, and Tucker took a long drink.

Lance looked him over from across the table. "You okay?"

Nope. He wasn't okay. But he had no idea what to do about it. "I'll be fine." For the first time in his life, he wasn't sure if that statement was true. After being with Kenna, he knew what he was missing. He knew it was possible to let his guard down.

"If it makes you feel better, Hank Green said Kenna already broke the news to your mom," Levi said. "So at least you don't have to worry about that."

"It doesn't help." In fact, it made him feel worse.

Tucker refocused on the band and nursed his beer while they finished their song. Seconds after the guitarist strummed the last notes, Gil Wilson, the bar's owner, lumbered onto the stage.

"Sorry to interrupt but we have a quick announcement." Groans and booing came from the audience, but Gil waved them off. "All right now, that's enough. It'll only take a minute and I'll extend happy hour another half hour." He stepped aside to the sound of cheers, and Kenna walked onto the stage.

Kenna? Tucker nearly dropped his beer bottle. What the hell was she doing up there? Wait. It didn't matter. She was here and his heart was racing and his hands were all sweaty with nerves and he couldn't take his eyes off of her. How could he have avoided her when she made him feel this way? Like she was the most important thing in the room?

She seemed nervous, too, as she looked out at the crowd. It couldn't be easy for her to stand up there, to put herself back out there like this when she'd hidden herself away from so long...

"Hi, everyone." Her voice was quiet but determined. "I'm sure you've all heard about what happened at the town hall and how we had to cancel the pageant." She cleared her throat. "Well, we thought we had to cancel it, but now I'm not so sure."

"What's she up to?" Lucas asked.

"I have no idea." Desperation pumped through him. Maybe he wasn't good enough for her—maybe she didn't see a future for them—but he did. He would find a way to show her he could be more. For her. For the boys. Before he even realized what was happening, he was on his feet.

"We all know that the pageant is one of the highlights of the Christmas season in Topaz Falls," Kenna went on, still sounding unsure.

A few murmurs of agreement came from nearby tables.

"It's one of the things that brings us all together over the holidays," she said, raising her head.

*That's it,* Tucker silently told her. *Don't let them make you feel small, Kenna.*

She inhaled deeply, which seemed to calm her. "I have to admit I wasn't looking forward to Christmas this year. I'm sure most of you sitting in this room know why." A smile made her whole face come alive. "But then I started working on the pageant with Birdie...and...well...with Tucker too. And everything started to change."

His friends all glared at him with varying degrees of suspicion.

"Seriously? You and Kenna?" Lucas pressed.

"We're going to talk about this later," Lance promised.

"Quiet." He didn't want to miss one word she said.

"Most of you know that Birdie got sick, so Tucker and I managed things together."

No, they should've managed things together, but he'd failed her. He hadn't been there when she needed him the most.

"The more time I spent with the kids—and with Tucker—the more hopeful I felt. Hope that maybe things could be different for my boys and me this year. That maybe this Christmas could be about moving forward and embracing the future."

*Yes.* He closed his eyes, holding that memory of their night together close. *Yes.* Moving forward. He needed to move forward because he needed her in his life. He needed Jake and Benny. And he would do whatever it took to figure out how to let go of the past so he could be there for them. So they could build a future...

"When the flood happened, my boys were devastated," Kenna went on, gaining momentum. "Actually, all the kids were. They've worked so hard this year, and they were so excited to share it with you all. And I... well... I don't want them to give up hope. *I* don't want to give up hope."

Then Tucker wouldn't either.

Kenna shielded her eyes from the stage's lights. "I think maybe if we all work together, we can still find a way to make the pageant happen. We can save Christmas for these kids, and for Birdie McGrath, and maybe for ourselves too."

A few people clapped, and she leaned into the mic again. "We need a venue and donations and volunteers and... well... everything really. But I know we can make this happen. So if you're willing to help, please come and find me." She grinned. "And now back to the music."

Kenna quickly exited the stage and disappeared into the crowd that had already gathered. Tucker started after her, but Lance caught his shoulder. "So what the hell happened between you two?"

He shook off his friend. He didn't have time for the third degree. "I have to go talk to her."

"I guess that answers my question," Lance said with a grin.

Tucker ignored him and headed for the stage.

"Hey," Lucas called behind him. "Why don't we have the pageant at our place?"

He turned back to them. "Seriously?"

"That's a great idea," Levi said. "We can bring in some heaters for the barn, throw together some props. I'm sure we can get everyone to help spruce the place up. Tell her we'll do whatever we can to help."

"I will. Thanks." The words were barely out before he rushed off to find her. It took elbowing his way through a whole horde of people, but he finally caught her attention.

She stopped talking to someone midsentence.

He closed in the rest of the way, doing his best to block out everyone else so he could steal a moment with her. "Thank you," he said before she could speak. "For not giving up on me. For coming here." A big part of that speech had obviously been for him.

"I'm sorry, Tucker." She pressed a hand to her heart. "I never should've pushed you away. It scared me...how I felt about you. And I—"

"It's okay." She didn't have to explain. Not here. "We need to talk. Alone." So he could tell her he was done avoiding her, avoiding relationships.

"Yes, we have a lot to talk about." The woman's smile baited his. "But you should be with your dad right now. We can talk later."

He glanced at his watch again. "So far he's thirty minutes late."

"That's awful." Kenna slipped her hand onto his waist and nudged him to the back wall, away from the crowd. "God, I can't imagine how hard it must've been for you to see him."

"Yeah you could." Maybe that's why he felt such a connection to her. Because she could relate. "You had to see Mike, right? After he hurt you?"

She nodded. "The first time I brought the boys to visit him, I thought my heart would shatter into a million pieces."

"It feels something like that," Tucker agreed. It was easy to ignore the pain year after year when you didn't have to face the person, but seeing his dad...it had hurt far worse than he could've imagined. But maybe that hurt was good. Maybe it was necessary.

"My heart didn't shatter though." Kenna eased closer. "It was broken for a while, but I think it healed stronger. And it actually helped to see him. As hard as it was, it brought some closure too."

Tucker took Kenna's hands in his, running his thumbs over her knuckles. "I think closure would help. Maybe it will make me a different man."

"I don't want a different man." Tears brightened her eyes. "I was terrified that morning I woke up with you. Because I hadn't felt anything that deeply for so long. I hadn't *let* myself feel anything, but with you I didn't have a choice. It just happened. And I panicked. I thought it wasn't what you wanted. We'd agreed on harmless fun, so I thought I'd give you the easy way out."

"I don't want the easy way out," he told her, letting emotion thicken in his throat. "Not this time. That resentment I have for my dad has been taking up too much space in my life. But you make me want to let go of it. Your boys make me want to let go of it." That was all the motivation he needed. "Sometimes I'm afraid that I'm no better than my dad. That I don't know anything about sticking it out. When things get serious, I've always walked away just like he did."

Kenna brought her hand to his face and guided it closer to

hers. "That's not true. When someone's important to you, you do know how to stick it out. You know what loyalty is. You've taken care of your mom for fifteen years. You've been there for her whenever she needed you. I'd say you know more about sticking it out than most people." She moved in like she was going to kiss him, but stopped just short of his lips. "I was kind of hoping maybe I could be important to you too."

"You already are." He couldn't hold himself back anymore. He had to taste her mouth, had to feel that connection with her again—the one that made him whole. For now he settled with brushing his lips against hers, feeling that spark ignite in the very center of him. "I was panicked that morning too. But for the first time it didn't make me want to run. I wanted to stay. I wanted *you* to stay."

"That's good because I'm not going anywhere." Kenna teased him with a lingering kiss.

"But *we* could go somewhere," he murmured, savoring the feel of her body against his.

"Where?" she asked a little too innocently.

"Back to my place?"

"Yo, Tucker." Levi laid a hand on his shoulder. "Sorry to interrupt, but isn't that your dad over there?"

Somehow he pulled away from Kenna and looked in the direction his friend pointed. The man standing by the doors was haggard and dripping wet from head to toe. "Yeah. That's him."

Without saying a word, Kenna grabbed his hand and held on while they walked to meet his father.

When they approached his dad, Tucker felt a sting of sympathy. He looked awful.

"I'm sorry I'm late, son." His coat and jeans were drenched, sticking to his gaunt frame, and his hair and beard had been matted down with snow.

"What happened to you?" Tucker asked, finding it hard to summon the hostility he'd armed himself with earlier.

"I got a flat on the highway." His father visibly shivered. "I was gonna be on time. I swear it. I was gonna be ten minutes early but the dang tire popped and I couldn't get service on that good for nothin' phone of mine."

"So you walked all the way from the highway?" He didn't know why he asked. The answer was obvious. The man was probably borderline hypothermic.

"I didn't want to let you down again," his dad said gruffly. "I know it don't make up for anything. But I wanted to be here. I wanted to look you in the face and tell you I'm sorry. I was a coward. There ain't no excuse for leavin'. It was a mistake and I'll understand if you never want to see me again."

His father was right. Hiking a few miles through the snow couldn't make up for years of abandonment, but it didn't have to. Instead of going back and trying to figure out how to be a father and son, how to fix everything that had been broken between them, they'd start something new. "I still want to have dinner with you," Tucker said, laying a hand on his dad's shoulder. "We can go out to my place so you can get warm and dry. But first I want to introduce you to someone. Someone who's real important to me." He slipped his hand onto Kenna's waist and guided her to stand in front of him. "This is Kenna Hart."

The woman who'd given him something to hope for.

# Chapter Thirteen

"Look, Mom! It's like magic!" Jake knelt and plugged in the strands of Christmas lights that highlighted the new stable's simple framed structure. White bulbs twinkled merrily, and the three-dimensional star Tucker had made from sticks and lights was mounted in the center, beaming its message of hope to everyone gathered in the barn.

"It's perfect," Kenna declared. Even on Christmas Eve, so many people had turned out to help transform the Cortez's barn into the perfect venue for the pageant. Lance, Levi, and Lucas were currently setting up rows of chairs they'd borrowed from the high school. Carly Lammers and a bunch of her friends were decorating the tables that had been set up on the outskirts of the large space. Mateo and Everly, along with Kenna's other book club friends, were setting out warming dishes filled with everything the town would need to enjoy a real Christmas feast together after the show—juicy sliced turkey, stuffing, candied sweet potatoes, and farm fresh rolls.

There were also plates of every kind of Christmas cookie imaginable for dessert.

With everyone working so hard for the last few hours, you could feel the Christmas spirit floating in the air. In order to dress up the barn even more, Kenna had driven back out to the Christmas tree farm and they'd donated everything they had left to the cause. With the help from the town's volunteer fire-fighters, she'd transported the trees back and decorated them with the ornaments the kids had made while the grown-ups had been working. To capture the spirit of giving, Kenna had also spread word for everyone to bring a wrapped present when they came back for the performance that night so they could do an exchange after dinner.

"This'll be the best pageant ever!" Jake and Benny danced around in the middle of the stable, the small tool belts Tucker had found for them sagging low on their hips. "And this is the best stable anyone'll ever see in a million years!"

"It's the best one I've ever seen, that's for sure." Tucker walked out from behind the structure, and his eyes locked on hers with a look that made both her knees go slack.

"I have an idea," he whispered, moving his mouth close to her ear. "Maybe you should hang some garlands way up there." He pointed to the stable's top tier.

Kenna answered with a smirk. "Are you trying to get me up on a ladder, Tucker McGrath?"

His low laugh spoke directly to her girly parts, heating them right up.

"I was kinda hoping..."

She moved closer to him and stared up into his eyes. "You don't have to trick me into kissing you again, you know. I'd be happy to do it without the ladder. Whenever you want. Wherever, too."

"I always want—"

"Hey, Tucker!" Jake bounded toward them, his hammer and screwdriver clanging in his belt. "When're we gonna build the manger? That's the last thing we have to do and then Mom said we can change into our costumes!"

"Yeah!" Benny loped along behind his brother. "It's almost time for the show to start!"

Tucker shared a smile with Kenna, and she totally got it. Those two were too cute to resist. "I'll tell you what," Tucker said as he laid a hand on Jake's shoulder. "You two go ahead and get all that wood we set aside for the manger earlier. I'll be right there."

"Okay!" Benny led the charge to the stack of lumber piled by the double doors.

Tucker watched them go before torturing Kenna with another ravaging stare. "I guess the kiss will have to wait."

Her inner thighs quivered. "I guess it will."

"I'll be looking forward to it. All. Night." Greed darkened his eyes, sharpening her ache to be with him again.

"Me too," she nearly whimpered. He turned and walked away, taking her gaze with him. Dear Lord in heaven, those jeans...

"So it looks like your fling with Tucker is still going pretty hot and heavy." Everly sidled up next to her and leaned an elbow on Kenna's shoulder.

"Oh, it's not a fling." She still found it difficult to focus on anything except for Tucker.

"What'd you mean?" Everly's arm dropped back to her side and she moved to stand in front of her. "I thought you weren't ready for more."

Kenna shuffled sideways so she could watch Tucker while he patiently instructed Benny and Jake as they worked on their project. "I didn't think I was ready for more, but I seem to have found him anyway."

Once again her friend blocked her view, confusion etched into the lines that crinkled the corners of her eyes. "Found who?"

"The man who makes me believe." In herself, in him, in them, in the future, in love. That's what Tucker had done for her. It wasn't at all what she'd planned—and he likely hadn't planned on it either—but that's what made it so right. It had taken them both by surprise. "I'm not so sure you have to be ready. Maybe being willing is more important." Being willing to take a risk, willing to follow your heart.

"Oh my goodness. That's the best thing I've ever heard." Everly used the sleeve of her sweater to dab at her eyes. "I'm so happy for you. And for Tucker. And for all of us. This really is going to be the best Christmas."

"It really is," Kenna agreed, getting a bit misty herself. Everyone had contributed so much. "The food smells delicious, by the way. Thank you for donating everything."

As usual, her friend shrugged off the gratitude, as if donating enough food to feed nearly two hundred people was nothing. "We were happy to. Do you want to take a peek at what we've got?"

She'd like more than a peek, but she'd do her best to wait along with everyone else. "I'd love to."

Everly walked her around and showed her the different food stations. She'd thought of everything—even down to the adorable Santa Claus napkins. After her friend let her sample one Christmas cookie, Kenna hugged her tight. "This is amazing. Seriously. I can't wait to—"

"Mom!" Jake and Benny yelled for her, waving their arms across the room. It appeared they'd finished the manger project and were now all bundled up for some reason. "Tucker says he has a surprise for us! For all three of us! Outside!"

She looked at Everly.

"Go." Her friend sent her off with a pat. "But we're having coffee ASAP. We need to catch up. I need details, honey."

She nodded a promise and hurried over to where the boys stood by the door.

"Get your coat on, Mom!" Benny tried to wrap her down jacket around her. "Hurry! We can't wait to see the surprise!"

"Okay, okay." She bundled herself up while the boys impatiently tried to help by wrapping her scarf around her neck and shoving her gloves onto her hands. "Did he say what the surprise is about?"

"No." Jake tugged her out the door. "But he said we're going to love—"

A gasp swallowed up the rest of his sentence. Right outside the barn door, Tucker stood in front of his sleigh, the horses all hooked up and ready to take them away.

"Where did you get that?" Benny ran right over to him, but Jake seemed to be too busy gawking to move.

"This was my grandpa's sleigh." Tucker lifted Benny and set him in the back.

Jake finally wandered forward, slowly and reverently like he wanted to make sure he wasn't dreaming. "It's just like Santa's." He raised his hand to run it along the side.

"My grandpa told me he got it in the North Pole," Tucker said, lifting Jake to set him by Benny. "He always used to say it was one of Santa's old sleighs."

Jake looked back at Kenna and the expression of pure wonder brought hot stinging tears to her eyes.

"So what'd you say?" Tucker asked, walking toward her. "You want to go for a ride?" He held out his hand. Behind them the boys squealed their yeses, but he waited for Kenna to answer.

Her throat still burned too much to talk, so she simply placed her hand in his. Together, they walked to the sleigh and Tucker helped her climb onto the front bench seat.

Once he was settled in next to her, he looked back at the boys. "I thought maybe you guys would want to come with me to pick up my mom."

"Your mom?" A hopeful expression opened Benny's eyes wider. "Is she all better?"

"Not quite but she's close. The hospital said she can finally come home."

Kenna closed her eyes, releasing a couple of tears. "I'm so glad she'll be home for Christmas," she murmured.

"Me too." He laughed. "And she's gonna get one heck of a surprise when we show up to break her out of the hospital in this thing."

The boys giggled. "Let's go!"

Tucker clicked his tongue and prompted the horses to get moving. While they glided along, the boys chatted about every detail of the sleigh—from the soft velvety "pillows" to the glossy red color.

"I bet Santa used magic paint!" Benny said.

"I wonder if it can still fly," Jake mused.

"I didn't used to think so." Tucker scooted closer to Kenna and slipped his arm around her. "But I'm starting to believe in magic again."

*Yes.* She rested her head on his shoulder, closed her eyes, and breathed it all in. When she opened her eyes, they were floating along Main Street in the glow of all the Christmas lights. The boys continued to trade theories about Santa's sleigh, but she stayed quiet, content to listen and simply take in the moment.

As they reached the hospital, Tucker steered the horses right up to the main entrance. "You guys wait here," he said, jumping down from the bench. "Mom and I'll be right back."

After he'd gone, the boys got antsy, but they didn't have time to get into any mischief before the doors rolled open and Tucker led his mom outside.

Birdie halted. "What on earth?"

"It's a sleigh!" the boys chanted. "We came to pick you up in a sleigh from the North Pole!"

"Tucker." His mom's hand rested in the very center of her chest as she walked closer. "When did you— How—"

Kenna brushed away a few more tears. He obviously hadn't told his mom about his upgrades to the sleigh.

"What'd you think?" Taking his mom's hand, he helped her climb in and then hoisted her suitcase onto the floor between the boys.

"It's beautiful." Her voice sounded a lot like Jake's had when he'd first seen the sleigh, all awe and happiness. "Oh, Tucker, it's like a dream. All the memories we've shared in this sled. This just brings everything back."

"Those were good times," he agreed.

Kenna watched his face carefully. They hadn't had much time to talk during the day, but he told her he and his dad had spent three hours talking last night, and while it didn't mean he'd worked through everything yet, he seemed different. Lighter somehow.

"But now it's time to make new memories," Tucker said, sending a wink to Kenna. Somehow, even in the cold night air, she found herself blushing.

"You can sit between us, Miss Birdie." Benny patted the seat between him and his brother. "We're gonna take you to the pageant now. And you're going to love it! It's the bestest pageant ever!"

"Oh, I can't wait. I just can't wait." Birdie wedged herself between the boys and Tucker covered them all with the blanket.

All the way back to the Cortez Ranch, Birdie and the boys sang Christmas carols while Kenna snuggled as close to Tucker as she could get without climbing into his lap. There was so much she wanted to say to him, but she waited, simply listening to those three in the back enjoy the ride. It ended too soon for Jake and Benny, who let out disappointed sighs when Tucker steered the horses around the cars that were parked outside the barn.

Birdie hurried to climb down before Tucker could help her. "Why don't I take you boys inside and your mom and Tucker can come in soon?"

Gratitude welled up in Kenna's eyes. They wouldn't have long before they had to go in and run the pageant, but it would be a gift to steal a few minutes alone with him before everything got started.

"Okay!"

"Yes! Then we can change into our costumes!"

Benny and Jake climbed down and politely waited for Birdie to take their hands before the three of them traipsed to the door.

Kenna stayed right where she was, still in the magic sleigh, still nestled against Tucker's side. "Well, I think it's safe to say this will go down as their favorite Christmas in the history of Christmases."

Tucker dropped the reins and turned to face her. "It's pretty amazing. To see the holiday through their eyes. It really does bring back the magic." He leaned closer with that passion glowing on his face. "You bring back the magic too, Kenna. I've felt like a part of me has been missing for so long, but you and the boys helped me find it. You helped me face things I was too afraid to confront."

She held his hands, squeezing hard to feel that connection even through their bulky gloves. "You helped us too. You made me believe again. You brought back my hope." She kissed him softly, with all the surety she felt. Like she'd told the boys, this Christmas was all about new beginnings.

And she'd finally found hers.

# Acknowledgments

Special thanks to my mom, who has always embodied Birdie's same Christmas spirit. Nowadays I know how much work goes into making the holidays magical, and I treasure the memories and traditions I get to pass down to my kids.

This is my eleventh book with the talented team at Forever, and I continue to be amazed by their hard work and dedication to every project. Thank you Amy Pierpont for your diligence and especially your patience in helping me get to the heart of every story. Working with you continues to make me a better writer. To the rest of the team—Gabi, Estelle, Jodi, and my production editor Melanie Gold— thank you for your work on my behalf. You girls rock!

None of my stories would ever see the light of day without my fabulous agent, Suzie Townsend. Thank you for continued guidance and professionalism.

As always, my husband, Will, and my two precious boys, AJ and Kaleb, deserve my deepest gratitude and thanks. Living with a writer on a deadline is not easy, but they never complain and always love me well. When I go underwater, they jump right in to rescue me and give me a safe, solid place to set my feet. Thank you for making me better, stronger, braver, happier, and so hopeful.

# *About the Author*

Sara Richardson grew up chasing adventure in Colorado's rugged mountains. She's climbed to the top of a 14,000-foot peak at midnight, swum through Class IV rapids, completed her wilderness first-aid certification, and spent seven days at a time tromping through the wilderness with a thirty-pound backpack strapped to her shoulders.

Eventually Sara did the responsible thing and got an education in writing and journalism. After a brief stint in the corporate writing world, she stopped ignoring the voices in her head and started writing fiction. Now she uses her experience as a mountain adventure guide to write stories that incorporate adventure with romance. Still indulging her adventurous spirit, Sara lives and plays in Colorado with her saint of a husband and two young sons.

Learn more at:
http://www.sararichardson.net
Twitter @sarar_books
Facebook.com/sararichardsonbooks

FOR MORE OF SARA'S CHARMING AND
SEXY COWBOYS, CHECK OUT THE ROCKY
MOUNTAIN RIDERS SERIES!